# THE
# FAIRYTALE
# C⦵DE

## ANNE ANDERSON BOOK 1

**About**

**THE FAIRYTALE CODE**

*A dead girl on a cross...*
*A global cult of women...*
*An ancient code in everyone's bedtime story...*

Anne Anderson, a brilliant folklorist on the verge of a shocking discovery about the origins of fairytales, is haunted by her memories of what happened to her sister as a child: a brutal crime that is drowning her in guilt. Anne's redemption is a lifetime quest to decipher the hidden codes her sister discovered in a certain folklore story that leads to atrocious crimes to this very day.

Detective David Tale is not that different from Anne. Witnessing his mother's murder as a child left him with an unholy lust for catching killers, especially the rich and powerful who think they're above the law. However, his mental state isn't up to par, and his superiors only cover for him because of his relentless quest for truth.

When David is assigned to solve the case of a dead teenage girl hung on a cross inside Westminster Abbey, he is exposed to a web of clues left by a killer who claims that only folklorist Anne Anderson can match his brilliance. A killer raised by a cult of women who have been keeping history's darkest secret for centuries.

A secret that will shatter the world and its history... one that has been cleverly encoded in the original version of a Brothers Grimm book from centuries ago... disguised as a fairytale.

Anne's sister was right. It's her duty to uncover the shocking secret that would pull the rug from under politicians, the Vatican, the royal family, and mankind's history that has suspiciously been written by men—and never allowed women to tell their side of the story...

* *The Fairytale Code* is NOT a fantasy. It's a real-life, factual, and

fast-paced page-turner that takes place in Europe's most neglected historical 600-mile-long strip called The Fairytale Road, where the true-life stories of fairytales originated.

* The codes and revelations in the novel are based on facts that have never been exposed before. Author Cameron Jace spent two years traveling Europe to put the puzzle together. And although the book's priority is entertainment, it presents a conclusion that will leave you speechless about history, women's rights, and your very own childhood.

* While the series is a trilogy, book 1 ends with a clear resolution, and not on a cliffhanger.

Part of Thomas Crown

# FACTS

The Fairytale Code is based on a two-year journey of research in Europe. Not the Wikipedia/Google/Online type of research, but long face-to-face conversations with locals inside one-room-sized museums in small abandoned towns in the enchanting region of the Fairytale Road — a six-hundred-mile long-forgotten place in Germany where fairytale originated.

Locations, dates, and revelations are based on facts.

# The Fairytale Road

*SIMPLIFIED MAP FOR BOOK I*

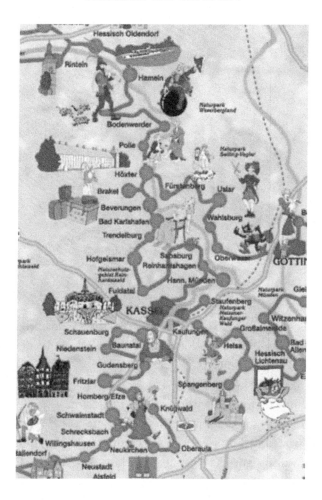

In this book we visit *Polle, Trendelburg, Hamelin, and Lohr,* starting with London in the beginning.

For detailed maps and location please visit my Pinterest Page which you can find links for in the end of the book.
It's ongoing and regularly updated.

# 1

10 A.M.

## *The British Library, London*

Anne Anderson was never late to her meetings—until today when she stopped to assist an older woman in a wheelchair, trying to enter the British Library.

"Thank you," the woman said to Anne. "That stubborn security guard wouldn't let me in without a VIP invitation."

"Don't worry about him. You're with me now," Anne replied happily, wheeling her to the VIP carpet, past the long line of eagerly awaiting guests. "It's an important day for the library, so they're a bit strict today."

"I know! That's why I'm here." The woman's eyes widened with excitement. "To see the original version of the Brothers Grimm fairytales."

"Oh, you know about it, then?" Anne's eyes shone.

In her experience, hardly anyone showed interest in fairytale origins anymore. The ones who did were mostly older, having read the physical books as children.

Anne spent her life studying these tales, her fascination beginning with her childhood copy of *The Brothers Grimm Fairytales*. Now, at thirty-three, she had a Ph.D. in folklore origins, forever solidifying her unique passion.

"I'm a fairytale buff," the woman said with pride as she looked up at Anne. "I can't wait to take a look at an authentic, two-century-old original. The two brothers devoted their lives to collecting these brilliant childhood stories. Imagine traveling from town to town to put these beloved tales together."

Anne wasn't going to argue that the Brothers Grimm neither traveled nor collected fairytales. Explaining such truth to the everyday reader almost always proved to be a fruitless task. Readers romanticized their childhood stories along with the authors who wrote them and never wanted to hear otherwise.

"My daughter was supposed to meet me here, but then she had to pick up her daughter from school," the elderly woman said as they reached the library's entrance.

"Well, don't worry, that's where I come in," Anne said, flashing her VIP invitation at the security guard.

"Folklorist Anne Anderson?" the guard said, reading her invitation with curiosity. "I've been told to let you right in. Director Jonathan Gray is waiting for you. But," he started, pointing at the woman in the wheelchair. "I can't let her in before the official opening of the ceremony."

"She's my mum," Anne said, secretly nudging the woman in the back to play along. The word *mum* had a unique taste on her tongue, as she had never met hers. "She goes wherever I go."

The guard folded his muscular arms, his brow furrowed. "How come your mum doesn't have an invitation, Professor Anderson?"

"How come your supervisor lets you smoke on the job?" Anne raised an eyebrow at the cigarette stub on the floor, then smoothly brushed ashes off his shirt.

The guard shrugged with defeat.

"I'd suggest you chew gum instead." Anne snatched back her invitation and rolled the woman past the red tape.

The woman chuckled and rubbed her hands in enthusiasm, happy the ruse worked as they entered the main hall.

Anne stopped the wheelchair in front of the stage that would host the celebration of one of the most sought-after original manuscripts of all time.

"Wait here and enjoy the show," Anne told her. "I'm late for my meeting."

The woman gratefully tapped Anne's hand and winked. "I guess my daughter wasn't late after all."

Anne felt her cheeks warm. The woman had no idea how much that meant to her.

She turned at the sound of a voice calling for her.

"Professor Anderson, what took you so long?" Jonathan Gray stood by his office door. "It's here. You won't believe your eyes."

$$\text{\textbf{i}}$$

A black limo with dark windows was parked beyond the waiting crowd outside. A man in a black, fully tailored cassock sat in the backseat. He wore a Cappello Romano hat to hide his disproportionately large head, and only if you looked closely could you tell what the hat was disguising. He sat patiently, watching Anne enter the director's office from the display screen in front of him.

The Advocate, as he was known, could've used his phone to watch her. But he preferred to keep his hands free in case he needed to reach for the gun next to him.

# 2

10:17 A.M.

### Henry VII's Lady Chapel, Westminster Abbey, London

While forensics gathered evidence at Lady Chapel's Hall, DCI—detective chief inspector—David Tale couldn't take his eyes off the dead girl who hung on the wooden cross before him.

Intricate, interlaced knots of dock line ropes bound her to the ten-foot wooden structure. It was the meticulous work of a sick mind. The staged crime was nothing short of a macabre image similar to those found in Dante's *Inferno* or *Paradise Lost*—books David had read too many times in the past, trying to solve his own mother's murder.

*Who are you staring at? What was the last thing you saw?*

David tilted his head to mirror the girl on the cross and followed her gaze.

Of all places, her dead eyes set their final gaze upon the burial vaults of Elizabeth and Mary the First, former queens of England. David's face twitched, caught between the dead from the present and the past.

Unable to develop an immediate connection between the dead

girl and the deceased queens, he let his thoughts trail off. He wondered what it felt like, knowing who killed you and unable to tell anyone.

*If God resurrected Jesus, how hard could it be to resurrect those who've been wronged to point out their killers?*

"David?" Harriet Wilde, his superintendent, interrupted, saving him from his morbid thoughts. "You still there?"

"I wish I wasn't," he spoke into his headset while his thoughts swayed like a pendulum of curiosity between the girl and the burial vault.

"Forensics sent photographs of the crime scene to my phone," Harriet said. "I've never seen anything like it. What the hell is this?"

"I'm David, Harriet, not God," he said absently.

Mary Harper, the forensics photographer, smirked next to him. "Good one. I'll have to write that down."

David's face twitched in response. His previous girlfriend had mocked him that twitching was his closest version to a smile.

"If Harriet stopped watching crimes on her phone in an air-conditioned office," he whispered to Mary, "she'd understand what it felt like down here."

"Looking darkness in the eyes," Mary agreed, nodding toward the dead girl.

"Did you say something, David?" Harriet said.

"Just a little prayer, Harriet," he said, quieting Mary and motioning to her to finish her work.

Of all his team members, he liked Mary the most. She checked all his boxes—dragon tattoos, being a history fanatic and a horror movie buff, loving morbid photography. Not to mention, everyone called her Bloody Mary, which she loved. But at twenty-two, she was too young to deal with his mess of a soul anyway.

"You don't do prayers, David," Harriet scoffed. "Just tell me what you got. I need something to take back to Her Majesty's correspondence."

The Queen of England had called Harriet an hour ago with

orders to keep the abbey's priests and clergy off limits until further notice.

David hadn't realized Her Majesty possessed such authority. Her interference suggested an inside job at hand.

"I've got nothing yet," he said. "Forensics brought in ladders and are examining her right now."

"What else?"

"We haven't identified her yet, but we've swabbed for DNA and got fingerprints. I'm waiting for the footage from the surveillance cameras and the CCTVs. One of us will question the cleaning ladies who discovered the body this morning."

"I appreciate all that, David, but I want to know what *you* think."

David squinted at the girl on the cross, honing in on the apple nailed to her left hand. "I know this isn't just about murder."

"What is it then?"

"A statement. Maybe a puzzle."

"Tell me more."

"Think about it. How long did it take the killer to get this wooden cross inside the abbey? How did he even manage to do it —and when? Or was this cross built here inside the chapel? If so, who helped him?"

"I see where you're going with this."

"Did he kill the girl outside or in here? How was the girl even murdered? I can't see a drop of blood anywhere," he said. "I doubt her ID will lead to much."

"How so?"

"Look at her. She is petite, which probably helped keep the structure erect."

"I don't follow."

"She isn't seen as human to the killer. She is just a prop to complete the image. A heavier girl would've weighed the cross down and messed up his design."

"Design?"

David sighed. "Look at the position of the cross, facing the burial vault. Why not face the hallway for the crowd to see?"

"So you're suggesting the girl is meant for the two queens' eyes," Harriet mused. "You think this is why Her Majesty called? Royal family secrets?"

"I hope not—" David's eyes caught something. "Wait. The apple."

"What about it?"

"Could you zoom in and tell me what you see?"

"Well, I see it's cut open with precision, a perfect half."

"You mean cut horizontally, right?" David approached the girl and looked up, squinting harder.

"Yes."

"You see the seeds showing at the center, right?"

"Correct."

"Part of his design, I want to believe," David said. "Rarely does anyone cut an apple horizontally by mistake. This is usually done in pagan rituals to expose the seeds and the sign they carry naturally."

"What sign?"

"Look closer, Harriet. The seeds form a shape."

Silence for a moment, and then Harriet said, "Looks like a pointed star to me."

"Not any star."

"A five-pointed star." She gasped.

"An inverted five-pointed star."

"A pentagram."

"It has many names."

"Witchcraft?"

"It has many meanings."

"But given the context, it's a clue, right?"

"A piece of the puzzle. Maybe the queen knows more about this than both of us."

"Good enough. I'll inform Her Majesty's correspondence," she said. "And David?"

"Yes?"

"I know you're in a league of your own when reading a killer's mind, but may I ask how you know about the shape in the apple?"

David didn't answer her. His mind flashed to a distant memory from his childhood, watching his mother lying dead inside a pentagram drawn in chalk on the floor. At twelve years old, waiting for the police to arrive, he tilted his head to follow her gaze, thinking:

*Who are you looking at? What's the last thing you saw?*

# 3

10:25 A.M.

### The British Library, London

Anne took off her trench coat and followed Jonathan Gray into the office.

Last year, she'd accompanied a group of professors who authenticated the original copy of Lewis Carroll's *Alice's Adventures Underground*—publicly known as *Alice in Wonderland*. She was honored to authenticate this book all by herself.

The newly discovered book of *Children's and Household Tales* (commonly known as *The Brothers Grimm Fairytales*) summoned her from the middle of the room. Jonathan had placed the tome upon a lectern with an overhead lamp stand. The light shone onto its open pages with a golden hue, reminding her of treasure findings in an Indiana Jones movie.

In Anne's mind, she heard her sister's distant voice back when they were teens in California. *You found the book, Anne, the one with all the secrets I told you about. I'm so proud of you.*

"The second most sold book of all time, after the Bible itself," Jonathan mused with fascination.

However, at first glance, the book didn't have the desired effect on Anne. In her experience, authentic finds emanated an unseen aura of a lost past and buried secrets. This one lacked it. So much that it almost looked forged.

She was about to comment, but her sister's voice stopped her: *Give it a chance, Anne. You're not always right, remember?*

Rachel, her older sister, was instrumental in Anne's obsession with folklore, ever since the first time Rachel told her the story of Snow White and Rose Red. The tale of the inseparable sisters who killed a wolf to save each other's lives. Anne's and Rachel's lives grew into a mirror image of the beloved fairytale.

"I'll leave you with this masterpiece for an hour and come back," Jonathan said. "Then we can make an official announcement to the guests outside."

"I don't need an hour, Mr. Gray." Anne put on the white gloves he'd set on the lectern and picked up the magnifier. She was ready to begin.

"Excellent!" Jonathan glanced at his Rolex that slid out from under the sleeves of his tailored Armani suit. "I didn't think you'd authenticate it this fast."

"You mean to discredit it this fast," she said.

Gray's face dimmed. Anne could tell he didn't appreciate her confidence.

"First of all"—she flipped to the first page—"this version was printed in 1812."

"Sounds about right to me."

"That's where you're wrong. The book was originally printed in 1811. Later published in 1812 due to Napoleon threatening to invade their hometown, Kassel. Therefore, the printing date should be 1811."

"You brought this up in your thesis," Jonathan commented. "Yet there's no conclusive evidence for such assumptions."

She hadn't the heart to argue her expertise with him. Jonathan barely knew enough about anything. She decided to go on a streak of objections to make her points instead.

"Also, I see this version mentions Snow White's stepmother, which isn't true—"

"I know. I know. I attended that lecture when you proved that it was Snow White's real mother who poisoned her in the early drafts."

"Exactly, and for undisclosed reasons, the Brothers Grimm later changed it to stepmother in the 1857 version."

"Probably to make it more suitable for children, Anne," Jonathan argued. "It's no big deal."

"Fairytales were never meant for children in the first place, Mr. Gray. It's a hoax invented by Disney to cash in on old stories without copyright," Anne said, knowing he was aware of this already. "The earlier versions had real names, dates, and even darker crimes. That is why folklorists dispute the origins of these tales in the first place. We want to know their meaning and why the true stories were altered."

"Anne, I am a Catholic who has a thousand questions about my religion." Jonathan sighed, rechecking his watch. "I can dispute the Bible's crazy stories all I want, but someone out there will authenticate it at the end of the day. I'm giving you a chance to be that someone here."

Anne wasn't listening, flipping through pages in frustration. "Snow White's real name was Margarette, not mentioned in this copy. Margarette's hair was blonde, not black, as in the commercial versions. In those days, blondes were considered average girls by European societal standards. Black hair was a privilege, and Snow White was a relatable story of an average-looking, pale girl who wanted to fall in love with a prince."

"Please stop—"

"And here"—she pointed at another page—"the fairytale about the five apples. The brothers never used the number five in any title. They only used one, two, three, four, six, seven, and twelve. There are twelve princesses, seven dwarves, six swans, et cetera, but never five of anything."

She knew he couldn't dispute this. After Anne discovered

authentic letters written by Wilhelm Grimm to his wife, Jonathan had witnessed the approval of that thesis with the board from Oxford University. The letters mentioned the "seven numbers," eliminating the number five from all titles. Wilhelm explained how he changed the title of a tale called "The Five Servants" to "The Six Servants" to *honor the code.*

"Anne, you're wasting an opportunity," Jonathan said. "This book will make us both a lot of money. Imagine the rights to reprints, the Disney movies that will be retold, the events we'll host here in the museum."

"I'm not in it for opportunities. May I ask who found this copy?"

"The descendants of a hundred-and-two-year-old librarian in London. They discovered it in a closet in her small apartment after she died last week."

"Her name?"

"Lady Ovitz," he said as his phone rang. He checked the number and ran his hand over his face, heaving a deep breath. "Anne, they're waiting for you outside."

"I'm not going to authenticate this one, Jonathan." Anne took off the gloves and returned the magnifier.

"Then I have no choice but to tell the press your darkest secret," he threatened, his voice low and desperate.

"What did you just say to me?" She tilted her head in disbelief.

He stepped closer, staring into her eyes.

"I'll tell the press what you did to your sister eighteen years ago, Anne."

Anne felt her face numb, astounded that he knew about her past. She'd done everything to keep it a secret. Did he know, or was he bluffing?

"You know what this information would do to your career," Jonathan smirked. "Your credibility will be scrutinized, not to mention your mental health. You'll be ruined."

The numbness ran through her body down to her arms. She was afraid her knees would buckle underneath her. Jonathan laid a check written for a quarter of a million pounds in her name right over the book.

"Authenticate it, Anne," Jonathan said. "Or one of your colleagues will."

# 4

10:47 A.M.

## *Henry VII's Lady Chapel, Westminster Abbey, London*

"What do you think she's looking at, Mary?" David contemplated, still facing the girl on the cross.

"You want *my* opinion?" Mary looked startled. "I'm just the photographer."

"That's why I'm asking you," David said. "What do you see through the lens of your camera?"

"Things, however morbid, look better through the lens, David. I don't think it'll help."

"We used your photos to zoom on the apple and found the pentagram. I know you've dabbled with the occult. Let me see with your eyes."

"I think you read too much into that apple part," she said.

"You don't think it matters?"

"I don't know. I'm surprised you overlooked the bigger picture."

"Which is?"

"The connection between the burial vault and the girl on the cross."

"I've been trying to connect the dots but haven't figured it out. You have a theory?"

"Uh-huh." She pointed at the tombs. "Here lies Queen Mary the First, aka Mary Tudor. She was infamous for burning Christian Protestants at the stake."

"You think the girl symbolizes one of her victims?"

"Can't see it any other way."

"The girl is tied to a cross, not burned at the stake," David said, then shook his head, realizing his foolishness. "Then again, I wouldn't expect the killer to actually burn a girl at the stake and ruin his masterful design. Interesting theory, Mary."

"It also explains why she is tied to the cross, not nailed."

"Because burned victims were tied to the stake—and with dock line ropes if I remember correctly. She was brutal, Mary Tudor."

"They didn't call her Bloody Mary for nothing."

David quirked an eyebrow. "I guess we shouldn't call you that anymore."

"I didn't burn anyone, swear to God." Mary raised a hand jokingly. "It's a nickname bullies gave me at school because they thought I was as ugly as the infamous queen."

David grimaced. He was about to say something when a man dressed in expensive clothes from head to toe burst into the crime scene.

"Stop gossiping and do your job!" the man roared. Then he flashed some ID in the air. "Tom John, representing Her Majesty. I want all reports sent to me right now."

David and Mary exchanged eye rolls.

"I guess the pentagram apple really bothered Her Majesty," Mary said between pressed teeth. "I'll get back to work and let you welcome your royal guest, David."

David checked his phone and saw Harriet had sent a text message about the queen sending someone.

"Tom John." Tom stretched a hand to David. "I represent Her—"

"You already said that." David pulled back his brown leather jacket and tucked his hands in his pants pockets. He wondered at Tom not mentioning a title before his name. Was he Her Majesty's henchman or what?

"You're David Tale—"

"You already know that."

"I see." Tom rubbed his chin, flashing his expensive watch. "How about you fill me in on what you've discovered so far."

"We discovered we need a historian. One who's an expert in Mary Tudor's era."

"A historian?" Tom chuckled. "Are you serious?"

"You asked. I answered. We believe the killer is trying to tell us something."

"So you think this is some Dan Brown shit?" Tom laughed, looking around at the forensics team to back him up. No one did, so he turned his gaze back to the dead girl. "This is merely the work of a bloody sick fuck, that's all."

"David!" Mary interrupted. She was kneeling by Mary Tudor's tomb and pointing at the inscription on the side. "You have to see this."

David knelt and read the Latin sentence, although he didn't know what it meant:

*Regno consores & vrna hic obdor Mimvs Elizabetha et Maria sorores in spe resvrrec tionis.*

Mary translated, *"Partners both in throne and grave, here rest we two sisters, Elizabeth and Mary, in the hope of the Resurrection."*

"Except that certain letters are circled in blood," Tom pointed out, standing over them. "And you, Detective Tale, claimed you couldn't find a single drop of blood at the crime scene, huh?"

David dismissed Tom and examined the circled letters:

*R e g n o co n sores & vr n a hic ob d or Mimvs Eliz a b e th a et Maria s or o res in spe resv r rec tio n is*

"The circled letters are e. n. n. n. d. a. e. a. s. o. r. n." David read the letters aloud. "That's what the girl is looking at. Not the tomb itself, but the message the killer left us."

"So, we do need a historian? Or someone who can explain this?" Mary asked.

"Tom," David beckoned. "Be a good boy to Her Majesty and type those letters into an online anagram generator."

Tom froze at David's insult, so Mary picked up her phone.

"Did I authorize you to do this?" Tom grunted.

"Mary?" David said.

"Too many variables. That's if the answer is an anagram."

"Stop there." Tom pointed at the screen, breathing over her shoulder. "This name."

"The anagram is a name?" David squinted. "The victim's?"

"Not the victim," Tom said. "Someone I know."

"I'm not following," David said.

"Let me spell it out to you, Detective. It seems the killer disagrees with you about needing a historian," Tom said, hands in pockets, leaning back, delighted with his discovery. "He recommends a folklorist, and her name is Anne Anderson."

# 5

11:05 A.M.

## *The British Library, London*

Although Anne's nonfiction book, *A Fairytale in Lies,* was a best-seller, she still stared at the check Jonathan offered her. But this wasn't about money. Her reputation and credibility were at stake, and she couldn't share her sister's secret with the world yet. In a momentary lapse of judgment, she reached for the check. Jonathan grinned next to her.

"Good decision, Professor," Jonathan said. "Time to greet the visitors outside and make some money."

*Don't authenticate this trash,* Rachel's voice returned. *Turn the tables on him, as I taught you.*

Anne nodded as if Rachel stood before her eyes. She took a breath and ripped the cheque into pieces.

Jonathan recoiled at her sudden change in attitude.

"My phone has been recording from the moment I entered this room," she told him. "You bribing me will soon go viral on the web if I don't interrupt the upload."

Jonathan's eyes narrowed to slits. "You're bluffing." He looked like he was about to rip her clothes and pull out the phone.

"Maybe. Maybe not," Anne said matter-of-factly. "It's a risk you can't afford. I have secrets. So do you. Let's part ways at that."

His eyes shifted toward the camera in the corner of the room, as if to ask for permission from whoever watched them. Anne didn't care. They either contained the situation or let it catch fire and burn everyone.

"I'll leave now, Jonathan." She went for her trench coat. "And I won't tell anyone about what happened. If you bribe someone to authenticate this book, I don't care. I'll find the real book eventually."

Anne opened the door and left.

The hall outside the office was crowded, so she sped up toward the main entrance and exited the building. The snow had thickened, and Christmas shoppers strolled along the sidewalks. Anne worked so hard that she kept forgetting the holidays were on their way.

She noticed the guard from earlier smoking a cigarette in the cold.

"I'm sorry, I shouldn't be smoking." He was about to kill the cigarette when she snatched it from between his lips. She took a long drag with closed eyes before exhaling in spirals.

"Didn't know you're a smoker, Professor," he said.

"I'm not," she replied and killed the cigarette on the ground.

"Me neither." The guard grinned. "It's bad for your health."

"Not as much as people." She smiled thinly.

London's chilled air felt good on Anne's face, and the smoke reminded her of Rachel. She took a deep breath and dialed her sister's number. She was eager to tell her that she had kept her promise. Rachel would be so proud.

❧

The Advocate lowered his window to watch Anne in real life.

Unlike on-screen, she looked alive and attractive as she dialed someone's number.

He could see her hands shake, though. Whoever she called didn't pick up, and it distressed her. He watched her redial as he fiddled with the gun in his hand.

"I wonder if she knows," the Advocate said to his driver. He had a thick Italian accent, which his employers compared to Don Corleone from *The Godfather*.

"After she leaves, drive me to the back entrance," he said to the driver. "I need to speak to Mr. Gray."

However, Anne didn't leave just yet.

A police car stopped by the curb. Two officers got out and approached her.

🍎

"Anne Anderson?" one of the officers asked.

"Yes?" she said, tucking her phone back in her purse.

"DCI David Tale would like to see you."

"Who?" She looked behind her, wondering if Jonathan was playing games with her.

"We need your expertise as a folklorist at a crime scene," the officer said, pulling out his phone.

"Why would a crime scene need a folklorist?" she questioned.

"We're as perplexed as you are, Professor, but I'll explain more on our way," he said, showing her a video of the girl on the cross. "Do you know this girl?"

The video attacked Anne's senses. She struggled to comprehend what she was looking at, "I don't know her. Who is she?"

"We don't know yet, but maybe you could help." He pulled up another video. "This is footage of the apparent killer."

The video showed someone in a red cloak escaping the chapel —a noticeably short someone. Anne couldn't help but wonder if this was all a cruel joke.

She looked quizzically at the officer. "A *child* killed this girl?"

# 6

11:30 A.M.

### *Somewhere in London*

The Killer entered her London flat, not bothering to remove her red cloak. She felt content. She had completed her part of the plan.

It wasn't a perfect plan by any means, but she had no choice. Lady Ovitz's death last week happened suddenly. Her legacy had to be passed on to the world or forever perish.

Turning on her phone, the Killer watched Jonathan Gray confirming the authenticity of the original Brothers Grimm book. Authenticated by a folklorist other than Anne Anderson.

"You didn't do it." The Killer smiled. "I guess Lady Ovitz was right; you may be the one."

She put the phone aside and cranked up the volume of her speakers. "The Show Must Go On" by Freddie Mercury blasted throughout her tiny apartment and shook the neighbors' walls. The same way the girl on the cross was about to shake the world at its core. The loud sound gave the Killer a chance to cry without being heard. She missed her grandmother, Lady Ovitz, so much.

Only a teenager, the Killer had no one else left in this world. No one except for the Sisterhood and their centuries-long bond. She began dancing while pulling down the books from the shelves all around her. Books that had belonged to her grandmother.

"Books!" she yelled with tears in her eyes. "Lies. Lies. Lies!"

She danced until she collapsed on the floor, but she couldn't linger. She took a quick shower, dressed, and then collected her belongings into a duffel bag. It was time to blend in again as an average college student. She was already late for the lecture on Oral History at Queen Mary's University.

But first, she dared a glance at her stunted height in the mirror on the wall.

*We're dwarves, Lily*, her grandmother used to say, *but we do the work of giants.*

Lily the Killer smiled bitterly and recited her grandmother's favorite hymn in the mirror:

**Oh, ye shepherd, dig my bones, tell my tale about thy devil's crone.**

# 7

---

11:51 A.M.

*Henry VII's Lady Chapel, Westminster Abbey, London*

Anne stared at the girl on the cross for five minutes straight. Part of her was perplexed by the imagery, and another part was encouraged by Rachel's voice to figure out why her name came up in this case.

The two sisters were no strangers to the grotesque, after all. Tales of ancient folklore were full of atrocious depictions of necrophilia, cannibalism, and even rape. Anne's was a childhood that she wished to forget as much as to remember.

"Is it safe to say that your work inspired the killer, Professor Anne?" Tom John said.

He and Mary, the photographer, stood to her left while DCI David Tale leaned against the tomb to her right. He had been silent since their introduction and now chewed on a toothpick between his rugged lips.

Mary was the chatty one. On the other hand, Tom John, Jonathan Gray's son, hammered her with unrealistic accusations.

Dealing with him and his father within an hour made her wonder if she was cursed.

"I don't see the possibility, Mr. Gray," she said, intentionally addressing him by his family name. "Nothing here resembles fairytales or folklore."

"The killer seems to think otherwise," Tom said, pointing at the inscription on the vault.

"I'm not sure about that," she said. "After all, that was *your* interpretation of the anagram."

"Don't question my intelligence, Professor," Tom snapped. "I know what I'm doing."

"Then why haven't you caught the killer yet?"

"I will," Tom countered. "How hard will it be, catching a dwarf?"

"And the victim, do you know who she is?"

"I'm glad you asked." He faked a smile and pointed at the forensics team up the ladder. "It depends on how slow my team is."

"Professor Anderson," Mary chimed in, easing up the tension. "How about the Mary Tudor references I told you about?"

"The original fairytales mentioned many kings and queens, but I've never come across Mary the First," Anne stated. "Scotland, Ireland, and Wales are rich with folklore and legends. My expertise is in the Brothers Grimm fairytales, which originated in Germany. In a specific region called the Fairytale Road."

"Do those fairytale road Nazis ever mention the royal family?" Tom said.

"They're not Nazis. They are peaceful village people whose towns are like beautiful jigsaws cut from a forgotten past—but no, they don't bring up the British royal family," Anne said. "And since you asked, could you explain to me Her Majesty's unusual interest in this murder?"

"I'm the one asking questions here," Tom scolded. "I have to say you haven't been useful far. I think—

"May I take your coat, Professor?" DCI Tale finally spoke. He approached her with an open palm as if he were about to ask her for a dance. He did so stoically, without emotion but still uncannily charming. "I think it's too hot in here." He discreetly winked in Tom's direction.

"I couldn't agree more." Anne sighed and removed her coat. "I appreciate it, Detective."

"Please call me David. I tend to bring down the Goliaths of this world."

Anne smiled with pursed lips. She found the sarcastic reference endearing. Most men she met talked about cars or muscles and hardly ever referenced mythology or history.

"A drink, maybe?" he suggested, carefully folding her coat over his forearm. "It's a chore dealing with us. The narcissistic and tense individuals in this room, that is."

"Thank you, I'm good." Anne suppressed her curious smile. David's first impression had been far from courteous. Mary stood wide-eyed and open-mouthed, staring at him from behind. She must not have seen this side of him before.

"Fantastic," David said. "Now, let's talk blood, gore, and pentagrams inside apples."

"Why not?" Anne glanced at the apple in the victim's hand. "I'm afraid that five is a number the Brothers Grimm never used."

"How so?"

She told him about Wilhelm Grimm's letter to his wife.

"Interesting," David said. "Are you telling me that fairytales never mention pentagrams?"

"Not to my knowledge."

"How about when you look at the victim? Does she resemble a fairytale character, maybe?"

"I can't recall a single fairytale about a girl on a cross."

"How about one burned at the stake?"

"Nothing comes to mind."

"How about the apple, then?" David said. "Isn't it a recurring motif in fairytales? Snow White and such?"

"Apples are also biblical. Forbidden fruits, aka Adam and Eve. Not to mention Snow White was poisoned and kept in a glass coffin, not hung on a cross."

"Good point. I'm only trying to bridge the gap between your expertise and the killer."

Anne wished Rachel's voice would guide her, but it was absent. Instead, she thought about it for a moment.

"I could propose a theory if you're open to tackling the realm of possibility," she said.

"Please do."

"If—and only if—the killer read my book, the apple could be part of a mapestry."

"Mapestry?" David's eyes widened. "I like the sound of that."

"It's an expression coined by the Brothers Grimm. Etymology-wise, it's a combination of the words *map* and *mystery*."

"Tell me about this tapestry," Tom interrupted.

"Don't scare her, Tommy," David said as he handed over Anne's coat. "Take the coat. It'll keep you calm."

"And it's mapestry, not a tapestry," Mary corrected.

Tom took the coat and speechlessly swallowed his pride.

David motioned for Anne to continue.

"Before I open a can of worms by telling you," Anne said, "I need to ask about the girl's cause of death first."

"We don't have an official cause yet."

"Could she have been poisoned?"

David looked back at the forensics woman on the ladder. "Could she?"

"Can't say without the lab analysis," the woman said.

"Even if it's cyanide?" Anne said to her.

"What do you mean?"

"I know cyanide can leave traces on the lips," Anne said. "Well, that's what I learned in my research."

"You're right about that, but the lab will still have the final say," the woman said. "Let me do a quick swab and find out. It'll take a minute."

"Why cyanide?" David asked Anne.

"It can be found in apple seeds," Anne explained. "You crush a large enough amount, and you can make yourself a potent poison."

David looked impressed. "What made you research cyanide?"

"It's a suggested cause of death in Snow White's case with the apple. Except that no one called it cyanide two centuries ago."

"You're talking about Snow White as an actual person?" David asked curiously.

"She was. Most so-called fairytale characters were. That is my quest. To reveal the true stories to the world."

"So it's *you* who the killer wants on the scene after all," Tom grunted. "See? I was right. You, Professor, are on your way to being an accessory to murder."

"Anne." David faced her and blocked Tom with his back. "I still don't understand what a mapestry is or what it has to do with the poisoning theory."

"A mapestry is a series of clues that lead to a grand reveal," she said. "The clues are more like double entendres."

"Double what?" Tom nudged David away this time.

"A double meaning," she answered Tom, and looked back to David. "It's a tactic to mislead the common person who lacks knowledge in a specific subject. All the while, the person of expertise would be able to understand the true meaning."

"Could you give me an example?" David said.

"Sure. There was a famous case when Wilhelm Grimm used to play the mapestry as a game with his brother, Jacob. He left him beans that formed the numbers 666 on the table in their house. When an outsider saw it, they thought Wilhelm was summoning the devil, when in fact he sent a perfectly sound message to Jacob."

"How so?"

"Jacob, knowing his brother and being an expert in folklore, knew about the tale of Jack and the Beanstalk, where a boy sold his cow for 666 magic beans...."

"Which meant Jacob's next clue was to go check the cow in the barn," Mary chimed in with excitement. "Hence the mapestry is a code, a map that leads to another location or object."

"It explains the lack of blood," David considered. "The pentagrams aren't witchcraft. They resemble the apple seeds, which is the killer's way to tell us that the girl was poisoned."

"The first clue in the mapestry," Anne said. "And if I'm right, the next clue will be found on the girl's lips, tongue, or whichever part of her that is affected by the poisoning."

"I told you he is a sick fuck," Tom exclaimed. "You up there! What's the verdict?"

The woman dismissed Tom and David, then nodded at Anne. "You're right. She was poisoned, Detective Anderson."

# 8

---

12:06 (P.M.)

## *The British Library, London*

Jonathan Gray watched The Advocate limp his way into his office. He used a cane, but it hardly helped with his devastating medical condition—whatever it was. Jonathan was grateful for The Advocate's long cassock, which hid any deformities he had underneath, even if it did make the man look like an evil wizard from another time.

No wonder The Advocate's employers called him The Beast behind his back.

"I brought you a drink." The Advocate pulled out a small bottle of liqueur from the pockets of his cassock.

"I hope it's not the blood of Christ," Jonathan chuckled. His lame attempt at a joke went dismissed by The Advocate.

Jonathan loosened his tie and pulled out two glasses from his desk. He carefully watched The Beast pour the drinks.

"Apple wine," The Advocate raised a glass. "Vecchia Melo! The finest in Tuscany."

"I appreciate it," Jonathan said. "The ceremony was a success."

"You still owe me two hundred thousand pounds," The Advocate said, putting down his glass. "You paid Anne's substitute only fifty."

"To each his price." Jonathan shrugged. "I intended to return the difference."

"Of course, Jonathan. You're an honest man," The Advocate said, flipping through the book's pages.

Jonathan couldn't tell whether he was condescending or sarcastic. It baffled him why The Advocate didn't like him. Sure, Jonathan was far from being honest, but The Advocate was a ruthless assassin for all he knew.

"I'm truly puzzled by Anne's behavior," The Advocate said, stopping at a specific tale in the book.

"Don't worry about her. She'd never risk exposing her sister's story to the public."

"That's not what I meant." The Advocate ran his hands over the text. "I'm puzzled why she didn't check the authenticity of this specific fairytale."

Jonathan poured himself more wine, then put on his glasses to read the tale's name: "The Singing Bone." "Come on. You don't believe in this bloody myth."

"The Singing Bone is real, Jonathan. You may not believe it, but my employers would slit a child's throat for it."

Jonathan couldn't tell if it was the wine that dizzied him or The Advocate's obscene allegory. He listened as The Advocate read a line from the tale as if he were reciting a hymn:

**Oh, ye shepherd, dig my bones, tell my tale about thy devil's crone.**

Jonathan slumped back on the couch, talking with beady eyes. "There is no shepherd, and there are no bones, man. It's all made up...."

"Don't worry about it, Jonathan," The Advocate said. "The wine you drank is made of crushed apple seeds. Poisonous seeds. You'll soon be paralyzed."

Jonathan's limbs spasmed involuntarily, and the glass of wine crashed to the floor. He jerked suddenly and stopped moving, eyes glazed over, lifeless.

"You shouldn't have taken that money, Jonathan, as I can't trust you anymore." The Advocate leaned forward, looking into his eyes as if inspecting them. "This is a slow poison, Jonathan. It kills you in about seven days after it ruthlessly tortures you. Most people, unable to tolerate their lungs and guts being shredded from inside out, kill themselves on day five. Let's see if someone comes for you, greedy man."

The Advocate ran his disfigured fingers upon Jonathan's eyes and closed them. He turned to leave and called his driver. "Any news about where the officers took Anne Anderson?"

"Westminster Abbey," the driver said. "The place is sealed. They wouldn't let anyone inside, not even the priests."

"Keep watching," The Advocate said. "Tell my employer that the book doesn't expose the Singing Bone's location. Anne doesn't seem to know about it either. I need more time to find it."

# 9

12:13 (P.M.)

## *Henry VII's Lady Chapel, Westminster Abbey, London*

David couldn't take his eyes off Anne as she discussed the next clue with forensics. She looked shocked, knowing the killer likely had used her books as motivation for a crime.

He admired her for not showing her weakness to anyone. David could relate. Unlike him, she didn't build a wall between herself and the world. She absorbed her surroundings and kept her pain to herself.

It was obvious that she suffered from a trauma in her childhood. David could spot such fellow individuals easily.

"Are you smiling, David?" Mary stood next to him, watching him watch Anne converse with the forensics.

"Why would I smile, Mary?"

"You're smiling. Admit it. When you look at Anne, you do that lopsided curve with your lips."

"I'm not smiling, Mary. That's how I look without a toothpick. Go back to work."

"And you took care of her coat?" she teased. "David, you never even asked for my phone number."

"Mary." David chewed on whatever little hints his lips gave away. "I want you to go up that ladder and film everything forensics does so we don't miss the evidence when it pops up."

He watched her do as she was told. This youngster was too smart for her own good.

While he waited for Anne, he saw Tom standing in the far corner of the hall, chatting on the phone. Whatever happened with Her Majesty behind the scenes was none of his business. David had learned long ago that the high-powered always had secret agendas. Unless they attempted to suppress the truth, he couldn't care less about their insecurities and privileged struggles. However, he worried about Harriet, who had stopped calling. Her Majesty must've ordered her to lie low while Tom took over.

"David," The forensics woman's voice echoed in the hall. "I can't find clues in the girl's lips or tongue."

"It's hard to find something when we don't know what we're looking for," he said. He approached Anne. "Suggestions, Detective Anderson?"

"Don't make fun of me," Anne said, rubbing her arms as if hugging herself to calm down.

"I'm not. You're the only one who knows how to take the next step in this mapestry."

"Well, I failed, okay?" she said. "I can't believe I inspired a killer."

"So, we only checked tongue and lips?" David overlooked her angst. He could sense she was stronger than that. "From what you taught me, the rules of the mapestry demand the next clue be found in whatever is affected by the poison—which I assume is the victim's body."

"Then we have no choice but to pull the girl's corpse down from the cross," the forensics tech stated.

"Let's give it one last shot first," David said.

"What do you have in mind?"

"I'm not an expert in cyanide, but I assume it damages the respiratory system?"

"I can look at her chest, ribcage, and throat if that's what you're asking," the woman said.

David and Anne observed as the woman slid a flexible tube with a tiny camera into the girl's throat. A small ultrasound-like monitor showed the girl's insides next to them.

"I can't think of what he would possibly have left inside her body," Anne said.

"You'd be surprised at serial killers' obsessions with stuffing objects inside their victims' throats," David said. His eyes stayed glued to the monitor.

"Serial killer?"

"Only serial killers have something to say. A one-time murderer usually has a clear motive. Premeditated puzzles like these are the work of someone in it for the long haul."

"Are you suggesting he will kill again?"

"I hope not—but hope isn't a strategy."

"Have you caught a killer like him before?"

David's face twitched at her question.

"David has solved every case in his career," Mary chimed in as usual.

"Good to know," Anne said. "I don't know how I could forgive myself if you don't catch him."

"Don't get your hopes up." David squinted at the monitor. "I caught them all, except the one who killed my mother."

He saw Anne didn't have the nerve to respond. He couldn't blame her. He shouldn't have been so transparent about his personal misery.

"What the hell is that?" David pointed at the monitor.

"God in heavens, what did he do to her sternum?" remarked the forensics tech.

"You mean her breastbone?" Anne shared David's gaze into the monitor.

"I don't know how he did it, but he carved it out?" said the tech.

"Does it mean anything to you, Anne?" David said.

"I think so." Anne stuttered out the words. "Could you pull it out?"

"Working on it," the forensics tech said. "I can't believe I'm doing this. Who is this guy? A surgeon? I have no idea how he carved it out without the rest of her ribcage collapsing on itself."

"Hurry up," Mary said, filming the procedure. "Before Tom returns and claims he discovered this."

David and Anne watched with anticipation. David had seen moths, butterflies, rings, and papers stuffed inside victims. He'd seen nothing like this.

"I can't permit you to touch it, David," the forensics woman said. "I'll have to bag it and send it to the lab."

"Not yet," David said. "If this is part of a mapestry, then it is made to be inspected on scene."

"I can't let you do that, David. I'll lose my job." She nodded in Tom's direction.

"Wait." Anne tiptoed forward. "Are these holes on the side of the breastbone?"

"Yes," the forensics tech confirmed. "The killer carved these in. Or wait, is this not *her* breastbone?"

"How many holes?" Anne's face went red. "Seven?"

The forensics tech carefully flipped the breastbone and nodded. "How did you know?"

Anne took a step back, staring at it with bulging eyes.

"Is it something you mentioned in your book?" David said.

"On the contrary," she exclaimed. "It's the one thing every folk-lorist is looking for—and I refuted, calling it a myth in my book."

"What is it?" Mary asked, lowering her camera.

Anne gazed at David and said in a fragile voice, "It's a Singing Bone."

# 10

12:32 (P.M.)

*Oral History Lecture, Queen Mary's University, London*

Lily the Killer, aka Lily Ovitz, sat in the last row of the lecture hall. Four thick volumes of books underneath her made her seem as tall as the other students. No one sat in the last row beside her. No one talked to Lily most of the time, except when she walked the halls and they made fun of her height. Comments about her being short weren't the worst. It was calling her a child that hurt the most. For heaven's sake, she was becoming a woman, and no one would look at her that way.

Whenever she talked to the Sisterhood about it, they reminded her that it didn't matter. She was going to have to sacrifice herself sooner or later for a greater cause. Lily knew this. She considered herself a nun of sorts.

If anything distracted her from her predicament, it was her passion for oral history, the forgotten art of passing stories from person to person. Her deceased grandmother had taught her that the documented history was full of lies; that actual witnesses or reliable individuals didn't write it. History was sadly made up by those who *printed* it first. Thus, oral history was the only true path to tracking back what happened in the past.

"Lily?" Her sister Lara stood with books pressed to her chest. "Can I sit?"

Lily nodded with excitement. Almost her exact height, Lara was the closest to her of all her sisters. She wore a necklace with a short Singing Bone, like all the women in the Sisterhood.

"I missed you, Lara." Lily pulled two books from underneath her and shoved them Lara's way. "I have so much to tell you."

"I know," Lara whispered, smiling at her. "The Sisterhood is pleased with what you did. You've made us proud."

"I haven't done enough yet," Lily said. "When will I be able to do more?"

"That's why I'm here," Lara said. "Are you sure you don't want me to complete your work?"

"You're three years younger than me," Lily said, gently running her fingers through Lara's hair, which was as ginger as Lily's. "You needn't do the hard work yet. Live a little."

"Then here you go, Lily." Lara slid a plane ticket toward her over the desk.

Lily stared at it for a while, fighting the fear inside her. She picked it up, eyeing it closely, "A one-way ticket, I see."

"Your final destination for you, Lily," Lara discreetly squeezed Lily's hand under the desk. "You've always been the dearest to my heart. You know that?"

Lily nodded. "So were you—after Lady Ovitz, of course."

"After your love for the Sisterhood," Lara corrected her.

"After my love for all the women who suffered in the past," Lily said.

"Exactly," Lara said. "Do you want to talk about the girl on the cross first?"

"No," Lily dismissed quickly. "God bless her in Heaven now."

"God bless her," Lara said, gripping her Singing Bone as if it were a cross. "Have you prayed today?"

"Of course," Lily said, almost offended by the implication that she didn't. She pulled out her necklace from under her shirt and showed it to her. A bone the size of a finger, complete with seven holes and letters scribbled on the side.

"Good. It's going to be a rough forty-eight hours, you know."

"Did the countdown start already?"

"Any minute now, Lily."

"Anne found the Singing Bone, didn't she?" Lily asked, almost fearfully.

Lara blinked, yes.

"She is good," Lily said.

"Looks like it. She solved the first clues of the mapestry in no time."

"Rachel taught her."

"It's sad that she doesn't know the full truth, though."

"She will, eventually. I'm only worried she is not strong enough to handle what will happen."

"May we be forgiven for the blood that will be shed," Lara said with a sigh.

"Will someone else die?" Lily asked.

"Does it matter? They'll never match the numbers of those who died in the past."

Lily wanted to argue but remembered that she had already become a killer. "Lara," she asked, "how did you know about Anne solving the mapestry?"

"Our queen sent one of us to the abbey. Pray with me that no more blood will be shed."

# 11

12:58 (P.M.)

## *Henry VII's Lady Chapel, Westminster Abbey, London*

Anne was about to inspect the Singing Bone when Tom John hung up on his call and roared across the hall, "Hands off, Professor Anderson! This long-lost property belongs to the royal family."

Anne winced at his declaration. She knew it wasn't. It was supposed to be mythical in the first place. How did Tom even know about it?

"It's part of the killer's mapestry, Tom," David objected. "It belongs to no one."

"Tell that to Her Majesty, Detective," Tom approached the forensics tech with an open palm, waiting for her to hand it over. "Clean it up, ziplock it, and give it to me."

The tech glanced at David for permission. David's hesitancy, trying to send a message to Harriet, ensured the woman followed Tom's orders. Having replaced Harriet, Tom had the upper hand now.

The tech forced herself to wipe away the slime from the girl's insides and bagged it before handing it over.

"Now get down from the ladder and leave the hall," Tom said. "An officer will take care of you."

The forensics woman climbed down, eyes darting left and right, unsure whom to trust. David watched her leave as she was escorted out by one of Tom's men who had evacuated the hall earlier. The hall was empty now; only David, Anne, Mary, and Tom stood together.

Tom gripped the Singing Bone, irritated by its smell but also looking as if he'd found a magic wand. "Whew," he said. "I didn't think it'd be that easy."

"You knew we'd find this inside the girl?" David said, having found Harriet's phone out of service suddenly.

"Don't ask questions above your pay grade, Detective." Tom lifted the bag for a second inspection under the daylight from the dome above. The tall reflection of his shadow on the floor matched his current ego. "During the phone call that I just made, I was instructed to hand over whatever objects we discover at the crime scene to Her Majesty."

"Were you also instructed to evacuate the hall?" David said with unapologetic suspicion.

"Only following orders, Detective," Tom said, flashing a fake smile.

"I'm still baffled why the queen is interested in this bone," Anne said. "Do you even know what a Singing Bone is?"

"I don't know, and I don't care. My job was to bring it back to where it belongs."

"Probably to those who don't understand the value of this flute," Anne said.

"Flute?" Tom blew out a sarcastic whistle while David looked inquisitive.

"Yes, flute." Anne stepped up to him. "It is made from the girl's breastbone, and there is a reason for that."

"A flute made from the victim's bones." Tom stared with fascination. "Ah! A Singing Bone. Didn't I say he is a sick fuck?"

"Give it back, Tom," David said. "The killer will strike again, and only Professor Anderson can solve the riddles to help find him."

"That is true," Tom said. "And that's why I was also told to bring her with me." He turned to face Anne. "Authorized by Protection Command, I order you to follow me now."

Anne looked at David, puzzled.

"The Protection Command officially protects the royal family," David explained.

"I'm not going anywhere." Anne glared at Tom. "If anyone needs protection, it's this device you're holding."

"It's a device now?" Tom rolled his eyes.

"You have no idea how many people would kill for the clues it may offer! This includes whoever sent you here to collect it."

Anne's last words resonated with Tom. He suddenly smirked, lowering his head and raising his piercing eyes upward at her. "I have an idea, Professor." He pulled out his gun and aimed it at her.

# 12

13:06 (P.M.)

## *Henry VII's Lady Chapel, Westminster Abbey, London*

"What are you doing, Tom?" David started toward him. "Are you out of your mind?"

"Stay where you are, Detective." Tom aimed at him. "I told you this is above your pay grade."

Anne saw David stop. She guessed he sensed what kind of a maniac Tom could be. Remembering Jonathan Gray's insistence that she authenticates the Brothers Grimm book this morning, Anne couldn't help but wonder if the two events coincided. But how?

"Professor Anderson," Tom said, "since you've resisted coming with me, I will now charge you with accessory to murder."

"You can't be serious," Anne scoffed. "What is this?"

"Are you really surprised that the woman who solved the killer's puzzles at the drop of a hat is considered a suspect?" he asked. "Either you taught the killer or worked with him to write your name on the inscription to get you into the abbey and cover for his crime by eluding us."

Anne didn't know what to say. She had to admit, though, that she understood how her situation could be interpreted that way.

Tom pointed at the security cameras overhead. "It's all on tape."

"So is your act of aiming a gun at me," she said.

"No, it's not." He stepped closer. "Why do you think we have these cameras all over London? It's how we control the narrative. Did you ever notice how many of these cameras are reported as dysfunctional in court or having a blind spot?"

"Stop the nonsensical James Bond's villain speech, please," David said. "She is not going anywhere until you get an official order from my superiors."

"I *am* your superior," Tom said between gritted teeth. "Or is it that you're drunk on the job again, Detective? Did you and Mary smoke a blunt in the field like a couple of weeks ago?"

Anne was surprised at David's face twitching with anger. He didn't seem the type to do such things on the job.

"You two are the perfect criminals." Tom smiled victoriously. "Each of you is an easy target, so don't do anything stupid and let me do my job."

Anne speculated that Jonathan had told his son about her past, for Tom seemed overly confident with his insane attitude.

While David readied his fist for a punch, Anne gently pulled his arm back, then faced Tom. "I'm coming with you. It's okay."

"See? We all abide by the law in the end." Tom looked relieved. "Let's go, Professor."

"No, she won't!"

The voice that spoke these words sent chills through Anne's body. Not only because of its confidence and defiance but because of the speaker's sudden and utterly unbelievable change in demeanor.

This was shaping up to be a day Anne would never forget—that was if she survived it with Mary, the photographer, pointing another gun at them all.

# 13

13:18 (P.M.)

### *Henry VII's Lady Chapel, Westminster Abbey, London*

Watching Mary Harper pointing a gun at Tom John made David realize he had never really known her. Whatever explanation she would offer wouldn't deter him from being a terrible judge of character.

Tom, too, acted unexpectedly. He wasn't afraid, nor did he buckle under his weight. Instead, his veins stuck out, and his neck stiffened defiantly yet arrogant.

Before he could speak, Mary struck the back of his head with her gun. Tom dropped to his knees, letting go of his weapon.

Mary finished him with a second blow that laid him flat on his stomach without a word.

"Mary!" David shouted, trying his best to convey his authority. "What are you doing?"

"I know what I'm doing, David," Mary said. She pointed her gun at him and Anne. "None of you knows what's going on."

If Tom's behavior had been on the edge of madness, Mary's sudden transformation was a horror movie at its climax.

"No, we don't, but I believe you know exactly what you're doing," Anne said. "Because you didn't let the Singing Bone drop."

David saw Mary had caught it before it fell to the ground. Anne was right. Mary realized its value. The only question now: who was she, really?

"The fact that we both know its value doesn't necessarily mean we're on the same side." Mary kicked Tom's gun in Anne's direction. "Pick it up and point it at Tom."

"What are you talking about, Mary?" Anne said.

"I'm Bloody Mary!" she yelled at Anne. "I will pull the trigger and kill you if you don't."

Hesitantly, Anne knelt and picked up the gun. She pointed it at Tom with shaky hands. "Satisfied?"

"Good," Mary said, looking at the security camera above and ensuring she was out of frame. "Now, put the gun back on the floor and kick it back to me."

Anne gripped the gun tighter with both hands, contemplating aiming it at Mary.

Mary smirked. "You don't know how to shoot guns, Anne. I'm not stupid. And David won't risk me shooting you if he came near it. Now, do as I say."

Anne set the gun on the floor and kicked it toward Mary. She exchanged puzzled looks with David, whose face showed his shock.

"Mary—I mean Bloody Mary," David said calmly. "What's going on?"

"Shut up," Mary said, handing the Singing Bone to Anne. "Take it and pull it out of the bag."

With no other choice, Anne did as she was told.

"No one can be trusted with this Singing Bone more than you, Professor," Mary said. "Now that you have it, please continue solving this murder and fulfill your destiny."

Even in such a dark moment, David could see Anne's sincere interest in the breastbone on her face. It was as if she'd forgotten what was going on around her.

Mary asked her to take care of the bone while threatening her, which didn't make sense. Yet, this wasn't the time to ask Anne to explain what this Singing Bone was. He'd also given up on questioning Mary's motives. He had known the young woman for three years. If she had managed to fool him this long, there was nothing he could do to make her change her mind now.

"What exactly do you want me to do now?" Anne asked Mary.

Mary pointed at one of the ends of the bone. "Solve the next clue in the mapestry."

Anne inspected the part she'd pointed at. Like any flute, the bone's core was hollow. One of its ends had a built-in metallic socket head cap shaped like a hollow five-star. It looked like it was missing another metallic part to latch into it.

"A key?" David said to Mary.

"That's right," Mary replied. "See that wooden panel where Tom stood when he made his phone call?"

David and Anne looked at it. A random piece of wood surrounded with yellow tape with a construction warning.

"There is a secret door behind it," Mary said. "It's your only way out."

David was the first to walk to the door. Curious, he ripped the yellow tape off and pulled the panel back. He then looked over his shoulder.

"Don't worry, I won't shoot you," Mary said. "You acted fast, so I guess someone told you about secret doors in the abbey before."

"I've heard stories," David said, then summoned Anne to join. "Look."

Anne came over and saw the part in the door that was supposed to latch onto the bone.

"The door's keyhole is pentagram shaped," she said.

"Just like the apple," David said. "The mapestry comes full circle, I guess."

"Come to think of it, it's meticulously done," Anne said. "A girl on the cross, whose eyes stare at the inscription that hides my name. Only for me to come and inspect it and see the five-pointed star apple in the girl's hand, which hints that she was poisoned.

Then the poison leads to her respiratory system, where we find her breastbone inside. It's a perfect mapestry."

"I'll need to know what this Singing Bone is," David said, taking it from her and using it on the door.

It was a perfect fit. All David had to do was turn the knob.

Its squeaking sound added to the creepy atmosphere. The eeriness let them both know they were about to enter a new world and leave this one behind.

A final clunk in the door's clockwork announced it open. David and Anne stared back at Mary.

"Don't waste any more time," Mary said, talking to Anne specifically. "Go! Find out who killed the girl on the cross before you end up like her."

# 14

### *Henry VII's Lady Chapel, Westminster Abbey, London*

Bloody Mary took a moment to catch her breath and remind herself of who she really was. Having faked her nerdy personality in the police force for so long, she had a hard time remembering the calling her ancestors had paved for her in life.

She checked Tom's pulse to ensure he wasn't dead. She still needed him in her plan.

Her motives were paradoxical, she knew, but what in her life wasn't?

She walked toward the girl on the cross and knelt, lacing their hands together before speaking.

"I'll see you on the other side, sister," Mary whispered. "You were small but did the work of giants."

Mary then picked up her phone and typed a message:

*Fix the video footage like you did with Lily. Delete all but the part of Anne threatening Tom. Make sure I'm not in the frame.*

. . .

Suddenly, someone entered the hall from yet another secret door. Mary quickly aimed her gun in the direction of the sound. She immediately recognized one of the abbey cleaners.

"The Sisterhood is trying to reach you, Bloody Mary," the woman said.

"I'll deal with it," Mary said. "You're allowed to leave the abbey. Don't contact anyone. You've done well."

"Are you going to be all right?" the woman asked, looking at the chapel's main door. "Soon, they'll suspect something is wrong in here and break in."

"Don't worry about me." Mary stood up. "I'm Bloody Mary. I know what I'm doing."

The cleaning lady bowed and walked back to where she came from.

Mary felt the need to stop her though. "Is that a wedding ring you are wearing?"

"Yes, I have kids." The women shrugged and brushed the ring with her finger. "He is a good man."

Mary nodded, unsure how to respond, and then let her go.

She knelt down next to Tom again, slapping him on the face. "Wake up. You've got a job to do!"

# 15

---

### *Westminster Abbey's Labyrinth of Tunnels, London*

"Why weren't you surprised about the secret door, David?" Anne asked.

She followed him down the stairs after locking the door behind them. A spiral staircase led to a dimly lit underground tunnel.

"Everyone's heard stories about the labyrinth of underground tunnels running underneath Westminster Abbey." David used his phone to light up the arched pathway. His boots occasionally splashed into small puddles of water on the floor. "Supposedly, the tunnels begin underneath 10 Downing Street, running from Parliament Square all the way to Buckingham Palace."

"I thought the London underground tunnels were a myth." Anne felt the cold bite at her bare arms, wishing she still had her coat.

"Says the folklorist specializing in debunking myths." David's boots splotched in a deeper puddle. A rat scurried away.

"I can't believe we're walking the tunnels that the monarchy built to evacuate the abbey in case of an attack," she said in astonishment. "How was this ever kept a secret?"

"The tunnels were private, so they were never documented or photographed," David said, noticing piles of wood logs against the wall on one side. "A few years back, an architect discovered one of them during the restoration of the Houses of Parliament."

"I don't even know why I'm so interested in knowing about this. I should be occupied with what happened in the abbey."

"It's a survival mechanism. The mind needs to stay occupied with unnecessary trivial thoughts. Not to think about the trauma at hand," he said, lending her a hand to step over his boot instead of in the puddle of water. "I read too much Darwin, I guess."

"I can tell, but thank you," she said, holding his rough hand as their eyes met under the phone's light.

"There is so much I don't understand myself right now," he said. "If I sought explanations, I'd want to know why Mary did what she did and how she fooled me all this time. But time isn't a luxury anymore."

"You're right about that. Whether it's Tom or Mary we should worry about, I'm sure that my footage of pointing the gun at Tom will soon surface in the media," Anne said, leading the way under her own phone's light now.

"Don't worry. I won't let them harm you. Let's focus on solving the mapestry and catching the killer."

"Killers," Anne corrected him, stopping suddenly.

David shone his light on her face. "What do you mean?"

"As you said, there is so little time to explain to you all that I know about the Singing Bone. But I promise you, this murder is the work of several people." She gently redirected his phone to another pile of logs against the wall. "That's the same wood the cross was made of, isn't it?"

David knelt. It indeed looked similar. He rummaged through it and found his answer. "Here is the rest of the docking rope he—or they—used."

"It explains how the crime scene was built."

"From inside the abbey."

"They used the tunnels and had all the time to build it."

"It's probably how the killer escaped, too," he said. "The footage of him leaving through the main door was a distraction. That way no one discovers the tunnels. You're right. This is the work of many."

"And one of them controls the security cameras. They delete whatever they want. Remember when Tom bragged about controlling the cameras? You think he's involved?"

"Tom is arrogant but I doubt he could plan all this," David said. "Has to be Mary or whoever she works for, because she made you point the gun at Tom."

"Too many puzzling questions," Anne sighed. "And we haven't even tackled the idea of the killer being a dwarf yet."

"Let's focus on the murder victim now," David suggested. "She was probably poisoned outside and dragged through these tunnels. They built the cross and set it up at night while everyone was away. It means that the night shift or the cleaning ladies of the abbey helped."

"If Mary killed the girl with help from the inside, why let us go to find the killer?"

"I know." David shook his head. "It doesn't add up. Also, since the royal family definitely knows about the tunnels, how did they not figure out the plan that was being concocted?"

"Maybe the tunnels were locked. Kept hidden behind panels and brick walls. And then only Mary's people made it available recently," Anne mused. "You said it yourself; it took an architect to accidentally discover that tunnel."

"It still doesn't make sense. If Mary and Tom, and whoever both represent, have access to the same secret information about the abbey and its tunnels, why are they on opposite sides?"

"I don't have the answer to that," Anne said. "What I do know is everyone is after this." She waved the Singing Bone.

"How long will it take you to tell me why this thing is so important?" he said, checking the time on his phone.

"Five minutes," Anne said, unfazed by the scurrying rat at her feet.

David stared at her inquisitively.

Anne shrugged. "Rats don't scare me. In case you were wondering," she said. "I was locked in a well with my sister when we were kids, and it was full of them."

"That sounds horrible. Tell me about it."

"That happens to be the day when Rachel told me about the Brothers Grimm tale number twenty-eight: 'The Singing Bone.'"

# 16

## *18 Years Ago*

Anne cried in Rachel's arms.

The well was dark but dry. It was an abandoned one amidst a California vineyard they'd snuck into earlier. They had climbed down to escape something terrible above. It was so deep that the circular light atop was nothing but a pale blue dot. Far, far away.

How they ended up here was the last thing Anne wanted to think about now. The sound of squeaking rats surrounding them in the dark wasn't the worst thing. Neither was the rat that crawled over her legs, which Rachel kicked away. At fifteen years old, Anne couldn't care less about that. The one thing that occupied her mind was the bones on the floor beside them.

At the bottom of the well were the remains of what looked like a very young girl; they looked like they'd been here for many years. The two sisters surmised she was a girl from the feminine shoes and what was left of her dress.

"Who did this to her?" Anne sobbed in Rachel's arms.

Rachel, three years older, was the one she had always relied on.

Even though boys thirsted after Rachel's radiant beauty, she always dismissed them to spend time with Anne and protected her at all costs.

Rachel was mature for her age. Calmness and rational reasoning were two of her most common traits. That, and the fact that she wanted to become a writer and was fascinated with folklore tales.

To Anne, who'd never met her mother and hardly spent any time with her father, Rachel was everything.

"Don't worry about it, Rose Red. You're safe with me now." Rachel's nickname for Anne was inspired by the first fairytale they read about the two inseparable sisters, Snow White and Rose Red.

Rachel was Snow White because she had dark hair, pale skin, and full red lips. Anne was as pale but with blonde hair and blue eyes. She resembled nothing of the Rose Red in the story but for being the younger.

"I'm worried no one will ever find this girl's killer," Anne said. "Will her parents ever know what happened to her?"

"Of course they will," Rachel assured her, courageously picking up one of the girl's bones. "See this?"

"I don't want to look," Anne cried.

"Trust me," Rachel said. "You will want to look at this beautiful bone when you hear this fairytale, one I've never told you yet."

Rachel was obsessed with fairytales. They reminded her of their mother, whom Rachel claimed she remembered. Their mother told Rachel bedtime stories when Rachel was three. And supposedly, Rachel could remember it at such a young age.

"Okay." Anne dried her tears with the back of her hand. Hearing Rachel's stories always comforted her.

"The Brothers Grimm story number twenty-eight has the greatest secret of all," Rachel began. "I think it's the key to my discoveries."

"What's it called?"

"'The Singing Bone,'" Rachel said. "It's about a girl named Fae who was killed at the Troll's Bridge."

Anne began to relax. Rachel had a soothing voice and knew

how to tell a story, both of which were good enough to make her forget their current predicament.

"Fae was murdered, and the Troll wouldn't admit he did it," Rachel said. "Then an old mysterious stranger, whom the village people called The Shepherd, arrived and offered to find Fae's killer."

"Shepherd?"

"They called him The Shepherd because he traveled from town to town with his flock of sheep. He was a mysterious person who hid his face under a red cloak. No one could tell whether he was a woman or a man, but he sounded like a man from under the cloak."

"How did he find the killer, then?"

"You see, The Shepherd dabbled with witchcraft, but the benevolent kind. He offered to find Fae's killer if they let him dig up her bones from the grave."

"Isn't that disrespectful?" Anne had always been naive. With her mother dead and having been raised in an isolated cabin behind the vineyard by a cruel father, her maturity had been stunted.

"It's more disrespectful not to catch her killer," Rachel said. "So, The Shepherd was allowed to dig out the girl's bones. All he needed was one."

"Like the one you're holding now?"

"Kinda," Rachel said. "The Shepherd needed the girl's breastbone."

"Specifically?"

"The breastbone was believed to help us breathe and speak. It was the only bone he needed to listen to the girl's voice from the other side."

"Listen to the dead Fae?"

"That was what he learned in witchcraft, to make the dead speak and expose their killers."

Anne's eyes widened in fascination. "So the bone spoke to him?"

"It sang to him," Rachel said. "The Shepherd carved seven holes into it."

"Why holes?"

"To turn it into a flute."

"Aha," Anne said. "It's called the Singing Bone. Why seven?"

"There are seven main melodic notes in the world," Rachel told her. "Well, in Western culture, there are actually twelve. And in Eastern cultures, there are many more. But seven were the main ones, common across all cultures at the time."

"Did he play the flute to awaken the girl?"

"He did," Rachel said. "Though it wasn't an easy task. You see, every one of us has our own secret melody made from the seven notes of our bones. A melody unique to our name, personality, and essence. The seven unique notes open up our souls. The Shepherd took some time to figure that out."

"But he did figure it out, right?" Anne questioned as she snatched the dead girl's bone from Rachel. She stared at it, expecting to see the seven holes. She was disappointed it hadn't been turned into a flute yet.

"He did." Rachel nuzzled her sister's nose. "He summoned Fae's voice, and she answered him."

"What did she say?"

*"Oh, ye shepherd, dig my bones,*
*tell my tale about thy devil's crone.*
*was killed by the bridge I walked upon,*
*by that troll, it was near dawn."*

"So we'll catch this girl's killer once we leave this well, Rachel?"

"We will, Anne." Rachel hugged her. "We will dig seven holes and summon her to tell us."

"Why do you think this tale is your Brothers Grimm's greatest discovery?" Anne asked as she hugged her sister.

"I believe that the Singing Bone story holds the keys to the origins of all fairytales. What they really are and why they were told. They used to have real names, specific dates, and addresses in the past. But someone changed them and turned them into children's stories to hide the truth."

"What do you think really happened, Rachel?"

"Terrible things, Anne, terrible things," Rachel said quietly. "Imagine if the Singing Bone was real and it survived centuries and exposed history's darkest lies when dug up."

# 17

## Westminster Abbey's Tunnels, London

Anne's story, though interesting, only stirred up memories of David's mother. If a Singing Bone existed in such an unforgivable world, he would have caught his mother's killer by now. It sounded too good to be true.

*What are you staring at, Mother? What was the last thing you saw?*

"Look," Anne said, pointing at a set of stairs ahead. "We've arrived."

"You think so?" David pointed at the fork in the tunnel's path. One side led up to the steps, and the other continued to the left.

"So we'll have to choose," Anne said.

"How? We need to solve the next clue in the mapestry first."

"You're right," Anne said, rolling the Singing Bone between her fingers, "though I'm not sure what to look for."

"Can I?" David focused his phone's light upon the flute while Anne continued rotating it. "Is there a chance that any of this is connected to the Pied Piper's folktale?"

"Hmm," Anne considered. "Why do you ask?"

"It's the only fairytale that interested me as a child."

"I don't see you reading 'Sleeping Beauty' or 'Beauty and the Beast' for sure."

"Why?" David asked, still inspecting the bone. "I like the Beast."

His eyes met Anne's again. He wondered if she'd say something cheesy like "and I like the Beauty," but she didn't. This woman wasn't afraid of rats, he reminded himself. She was different.

"I guess you like the Pied Piper's tale because of the mystery of the children that he kidnapped," Anne said. "Detective curiosity, I suppose."

"True." David nodded. "I only mentioned it now because you're holding a flute in a rat-infested tunnel."

"Oh." Anne smiled. "Impressive investigative thinking. I hadn't thought about it. How will that help us know where to go next?"

"You're right. It doesn't," David said. "But this could help." He pointed at the seven holes. "Are these letters of the alphabet carved next to each hole?"

Anne looked closer. She saw a thinly carved letter that was barely visible.

"Not bad, David." Anne patted him on the shoulder. "It could be our next clue."

David squinted, reading the seven letters in order from the first hole to the last, and raised an eyebrow at Anne.

Anne adjusted the flute horizontally. She pointed at the hole numbers and the letters beneath so that he could see it in perspective:

### DEADFAE

"Dead Fae," Anne said, locking eyes with him.

"I feel like I'm part of your folklore world suddenly," David said. "How can these letters help us know where to go next to find the killer?"

"I'm trying to figure it out," she said. "You should know that the seven musical melodies my sister was talking about are in the form of alphabets."

"Okay?"

"**A, b, c, d, e, f, g,**" Anne explained.

"Dead Fae is made of some of these letters. Does it translate to music?"

Anne pulled the flute up to her mouth and wiped the breathing end with her hands. David and Anne had ignored the bone's terrible smell so far. But now, breathing into it was another level of daring.

He watched her play the melody, deadfae, pressing her fingers against the holes as she breathed into the flute.

It astonished him how good she was. Even better was how clear the flute sounded, having supposedly been made from a dead girl's breastbone. It was as eerie as it was fascinating.

"Nothing happened," Anne said, lowering the flute.

"What did you expect?"

"I don't know; nearby door opening or a secret compartment in the flute opening. Something."

"From what I've seen so far, nothing is fantastical or other-worldly about these clues," David said. "Yes, its origins are rooted in the fantastical but the revelations are applicable in real life."

"What do you suggest?"

"Maybe the letters don't translate to music," David offered. "You said the mapestry has two meanings. One to elude the enemy, and one only the expert figures out."

"If so, then it has to translate to music. I'm the expert here." Anne sounded offended. "I've spent my life studying this."

David said nothing, respecting her passion for her profession.

"Is there a chance you could call Rachel and ask her?"

"I've been trying to all morning. She didn't pick up." She mopped her head, faintly sweating in the cold.

David tapped his foot, feeling unusually nervous. Anne's sweating made him think she was hiding something. Was it about her sister?

He checked the time on his phone, and his face twitched again.

"I know," Anne said, waving hands in the air. "We're late. Just let me think."

"Let's just think of them as numbers, not melodies," David insisted.

She stopped, staring at the flute again. "It could be."

"If we translate the 'deadfae' to numbers, what do we get?" David questioned.

Anne used a writing app on her phone and showed him the code:

$$1\ 2\ 3\ 4\ 5\ 6\ 7$$
$$a\ b\ c\ d\ e\ f\ g$$

"**D** is 4, **e** is 5, **a** is 1, and so on," she said.

"According to this, *deadfae* translates to 4514615," David figured quickly. "Seven numbers. Do they mean anything to you?"

"No," she said. "Maybe there's a digital pad on a door up the stairs or something."

"There are no digital pads in this forsaken tunnel. Think of something else. Do you have anything that operates with numbers? A suitcase, a password on your computer, a phone's password?"

Anne's eyes fixated on the numbers. She silently kept reciting them. "Phone number?"

"Not a bad idea."

"Wait, phone numbers in London are nine or ten digits, not seven."

"It's almost a given to add a 07 when calling from another cell-phone in London," David said.

"You mean this should read 074514615?" Anne immediately dialed the number on her phone. "It's ringing."

David stretched his arm and pressed the speaker button on her phone. "Let me talk first. Just in case you'd be in danger if they heard your voice."

"Okay, macho man." She rolled her eyes.

"Luggage Hero," a woman chirped on the other end. "How can I help you?"

"Mmm, you're who?" David asked, perplexed.

"Luggage Hero at your service. How and where would you like to pick up your luggage?"

Anne and David exchanged looks. Swiftly David googled the company's name and showed it to Anne.

"Sir?"

"I'm sorry, ma'am," David said. "I seem to have forgotten where I've left my luggage."

"Happens all the time." She sounded just as happy. "Could you provide your code, please?"

"Code?" David asked.

"4514615," Anne chimed in. She mirrored the woman's voice to sound as friendly. "I'm his wife."

"Of course," the woman said. "I'm afraid this number doesn't exist, though."

"How about 1,2,3,4,6,7, and 12?" Anne replied with the only numbers the Brothers Grimm used in their titles.

"You don't seem sure of your numbers." The woman's voice lost excitement.

"I'm sorry, ma'am," David said. "My wife keeps losing stuff."

The woman sounded impatient now. "I really have a lot to do, so please excuse me—"

"Wait!" Anne said. "I can use my name, right?"

"Depends on who submitted the luggage in the first place."

"Mary Harper?" David suggested.

"No Mary Harper here. Is that your wife's name, sir?"

"No, his ex," Anne said, realizing the woman should've called them out by now. "Please try Anne Anderson."

"Full name please?"

"Anne Christian Anderson."

"You're not a descendant of Hans Christian Andersen, are you?" the woman said while typing.

"No, I'm not." Anne giggled, leaving David puzzled. "It's rare to find someone who knows who Hans Christian Andersen is. Also his is spelled differently."

"We old folks know this stuff. Everyone thinks the Brothers Grimm wrote those tales. In fact, they stole most of them from the amazing Hans Christian Andersen, Jeanne-Marie Beaumont, the Xaver family, and God knows who else." Suddenly, the woman's friendly voice returned. "And here you are, Anne Anderson. Your luggage has been ready since six o'clock this morning."

"Oh?" Anne snatched back her phone from David.

"When do you want to pick it up?" the woman inquired.

"Right now," Anne said.

"That'll be £0.95 per hour. Please come and pick it up from The Steam Engine delivery restaurant. It's about a kilometer from Westminster Station."

"Thank you." Anne hung up and looked at David. "It worked."

"So did Mary's video," David replied grimly as he showed Anne the footage of her pointing the gun at Tom, broadcast on the BBC. "You're officially a criminal right now, and they will hunt us down."

# 18

### *Henry VII's Lady Chapel, Westminster Abbey, London*

Tom John sat cross-legged on a chair in the middle of the chapel, pressing an ice pack against the back of his neck. The frantic police officers around him were attempting to figure out how Mary escaped. Tom was well aware of her having discovered the tunnels already.

He had repeatedly asked his superiors to map out the underground tunnels, but they reasoned that they weren't a good escape route anymore. An A-class helicopter would always do a better job.

And though he could've ordered Harriet to look for secret doors nonetheless, he reckoned he didn't have the authority to expose them in the first place.

Besides, he cared less about Mary now. It was all about the Singing Bone that Anne Anderson probably took.

"So, Mary Harper knocked you down, probably helped David and Anne escape, then woke you up and told you to go catch David and Anne?" Harriet Wilde questioned. Tom had called her over, wanting to speak to her.

In her late forties, she was as overdressed as him. Had she kissed ass and done as she was told without questioning, she'd have been a candidate to join his elite circle of friends.

"I just told you," Tom grunted in pain. "She is a lunatic."

"I truly apologize, but she's never shown signs of such behavior. She is one of our best forensic photographers. I didn't think she could even shoot a gun."

"Well, she can, and you'll lose your job for this," Tom threatened. "How could you hire a killer?"

"Are you implying she helped kill the girl on the cross?"

"I don't know, and I don't want to. I only care about Anne escaping with Her Majesty's property right now."

"How do you know that Mary isn't the one who took that thing?"

"Only Anne knows the value of it, Harriet. You don't know what you're talking about."

"Could you at least explain, then, why someone deleted the security footage and only kept the part showing Anne pointing a gun at you? Had Anne been a suspect somehow, she'd have deleted that part. I strongly think it's Mary who took that thing."

Tom stood up, struggling with balance, but ignored her.

"I'm only asking because you handed the video footage to the BBC," Harriet insisted. "How do you know what happened when you were unconscious most of the time?"

Tom continued to ignore her. He hurled the ice pack away, almost hitting one of the police officers, yelling, "Someone get me a colder ice pack!"

Harriet winced at his temper.

"I, Thomas Jonathan Gray, was ordered by Her Majesty to investigate this crime and get the bloody device under any circumstances," Tom shouted. "From now on, our priority is finding Anne Anderson and that thing."

"I understand." Harriet gave up arguing. "What about David? He's probably playing along with Professor Anderson to find the killer. You don't think he is involved in anything malicious?"

"He would've answered your call by now if he weren't an

accomplice. Besides, we all know how messed up he is," Tom said icily. "Now go find me Anne Anderson without telling about the crime at hand. Try to keep the whole situation as low key as possible, especially from the press."

"But you've already sent the BBC the video," Harriet said.

Tom fisted a hand in the air and left her standing.

A few feet away, he realized in how much of a dire situation this Bloody Mary had placed him. Not only did he have to find the device and Anne Anderson at any cost, but he had to find a way to stop the public from knowing anything about what was really going on.

After all, he wasn't the one who sent the BBC the footage. His orders were to not expose any details to the world about the situation. But Mary, Bloody Mary, why the hell did she send that footage to the BBC?

Who was she? And what kind of sick, nonsensical game was she playing?

# 19

## *Westminster Train Station, London*

After climbing the spiral stairs, Anne and David used the bone's pentagram to open a similar door. It led to a dark room that smelled of detergent.

"I hope we didn't end up in the prime minister's bathroom," David whispered.

"I can use a luxurious shower myself," Anne said, realizing that she may have been influenced by David's stoic sarcasm.

Like he said, making meaningless or comedic remarks under stress might be a Darwinian thing.

Suddenly, a dusty light bulb flickered over her head.

"I didn't expect that," David said, his hands resting on the switch on the wall.

"It's a storage room, inside a train station." she realized she was too close to David in the narrow space. He smelled good, but a faint hint of alcohol lingered on his jacket.

"You can hear the sound from here?" David asked.

"I feel the rumble in the walls," she replied. "I take the train most days."

"Westminster Station?"

"It's the closest to the abbey. If the mapestry is effective, we should be close enough to walk to the Steam Engine shop. I'm still surprised by this luggage company."

"Instead of using the train station luggage service, you pay a fee and leave it at authorized cafes, tobacco, and souvenir shops."

"Someone left it for us," Anne considered. "We can find out who from the records."

"I hope so," David said, opening the door and looking out. "It's Westminster Station."

It was no surprise that none of the busy passengers in the station noticed David and Anne exit the storage room. This was London in rush hour after all; each to his own in this everyday survivalist quest to find transportation. David held Anne's hand and they hurried to the nearest exit.

"You're not my husband, you know," Anne commented.

"No, husbands hardly want to hold hands," David said, not looking at her but to the closest escalator.

"Too crowded in here," Anne said as they took the escalator. "Is that good or bad for me?"

"Because of the video, you mean?"

"Yes."

"Well, Mary, or Tom, did us a great favor by sending it to BBC," David said. "Because who watches the news on TV anymore?"

"You mean it'll take some time before it's all over the web?"

"And that's when we become Bonnie and Clyde, my dear professor."

They climbed several escalators to reach the street atop. The snow had thickened, and the Christmas vibes had taken over the streets. Anne wondered what would happen if those happy pedestrians knew about what was going on in Westminster Abbey.

David stopped holding her hand and pointed at a thrift shop nearby. A sign hung loosely from the top: *Why pay more and wear less when you can pay less and wear more?*

"We're getting dressed, wifey," David said.

"In there?" While Anne knew they were going to buy new clothes for disguise, she thought the shop was too funky for David's taste.

She then saw him kneel by a homeless man across from the shop. His face was too dirty, as if he'd deliberately painted it with makeup.

"Keith Richards," David said to the man, and Anne realized the man did indeed look just like the guitarist of The Rolling Stones, although of course it wasn't really him. "How much did you make today?"

Keith groaned and pointed at the sign next to him. It said something about being homeless with no food or ID, and having lost his job.

It shocked Anne to see David grab the man by his collar. "I'm the police, Keith. How much did you make today?"

Keith sneakily opened one eye, looked at David, and then mumbled about how sick he was.

David wiped the homeless man's makeup from his face with his rigid fingers. "You think you're playing a part in *Les Miserables* now?"

"How can I help you, Officer?" Keith's demeanor changed instantly. He spoke in clearer, pronounced words. "I'm done snitching for the police."

"You watch too many American movies," David said. "But I understand, pulling on tourists' heartstrings is easy money," David said. "Here's the deal. You hand me over the money you made today, and I'll give you one of my credit cards."

"What's the catch?" Keith asked.

"I need cash." David had already stuck his hand into the man's jacket and pulled out a hefty amount of money. He then gave him his credit card. "Here you go, under one condition."

"All ears, Officer."

"You don't use it here in the area. You hear me?" David said.

"You're not the police," the man scoffed. "You're a scumbag like me."

Anne worried David would punch him, but he let it slide and said, "Use the machine an hour walk from here."

"And how am I supposed to get there?" Keith said.

"Get an Uber," David said, standing up. "You're rich now."

Anne followed David toward the funky shop. "What was that all about?"

"We need cash to buy clothes. We could use the diversion of him using the credit card in the wrong location to buy us some time."

"I mean the homeless man. He's not homeless?"

"You'd be surprised at the legally illegal ways people make money in this city, Anne," David said, crossing the street. "Now let's go shopping."

"What should I wear then?" Anne asked.

"Anything that'd make you look less attractive."

# 20

---

## *Westminster Train Station, London*

Ten minutes later, Anne had bought herself a light blue yoga outfit with pink sneakers. She was surprised by the quality of the second-hand products she found in the shop, even though most of it was sportswear.

She also bought cheap glasses and a yoga head wrap.

Looking at herself in the mirror, she felt David would be embarrassed to walk next to her. She looked like she'd just come out of an '80s workout videotape.

But that was the point. No one was supposed to recognize she was Professor Anne Anderson. She added a last-minute puffer jacket with a hood for the cold.

"I said less attractive," David said, gritting his teeth.

Anne was going to respond when she saw him in a similar sporty outfit. He looked like a YouTube fitness trainer. Except his color was bright green with a white cap that read *Beast Mode* with a printed drawing of someone's biceps. She was impressed at how fit David was.

*Didn't Tom hint at him being an alcoholic?*

"Now we're officially a couple." She surpassed a laugh.

"Fugitive minds think alike," David said, again without a trace of humor on his face.

She began to wonder if he was aware of his dry sarcasm.

They paid for their disguises and left, heading toward the Steam Engine shop to pick up whatever luggage the mapestry had in store.

"Shouldn't we dispose of our phones?" Anne said, still walking as fast as possible. She realized her outfit wasn't warm enough.

"We should, but we need them for following the mapestry," David said. "It's a risk, and you're right, we'll soon have to get rid of them."

"Just tell me before we do, so I can try to call Rachel again."

"Better do it now. Who knows when our cover will be blown?"

"I tried while in the shop. She didn't pick up."

"Does she usually not pick up?"

"Usually, she is more into nature and leaving technology behind. I wish I could be there with her in California."

"Why live in London then?" David asked, following his phone's GPS.

"So I'd be closer to the locations of my studies."

"You mean that Fairytale Road you told us about?"

"Yes," Anne said. She tried her best to stop him from asking more about Rachel. The more he asked, the more she was going to lie. So, she sped up and led the way to the shop.

David followed her inside when they arrived.

It was more of a small cafe with a huge delivery menu. Luckily, it was mostly empty, even at this time of day.

"Hi," Anne said to the chirpy woman from the phone. "I'm Anne Anderson. I called for my luggage?"

"Ah, the girl who is not a descendant of Hans Christian Andersen. Let me check for a second," she said, looking at her computer screen. "Here it is."

Anne and David stood there, curious to know how big the luggage was—and what was inside.

"One traveling bag for you." The woman pulled up a black laptop roller bag with an extended silver handle.

Anne looked back at David, who was as clueless as she was.

"You don't need his permission, honey," the woman said. "If I were your mother, I'd remind you we're in modern times now."

Anne turned back to face her and smiled broadly. All the older women she met seemed to know how to pull her heartstrings today.

"Come closer." The woman leaned over the bar. "I have something for you."

"Oh?" Anne giggled. The child in her could never resist the charm of a potential mother figure. "A secret?"

"Yes," the woman whispered. "I was told about your affair with our handsome Rhett Butler over there."

"Really? He's not my husband?" Anne played along. "I'm having an affair with him?"

"Don't be shy," the woman said. "You're young and beautiful. Trust me, it'll help you later in life to find something to remember and look back on fondly."

"I'll take your word for it. May I ask who told you about this?"

"The lady who sent you the luggage, who else?" the woman said.

Anne saw David wanting to approach, but she signaled him away with her hand behind her back.

"Did you meet her this morning when she left me the bag?" Anne asked.

"I don't wake up that early, dear. It was my daughter here earlier. I chatted with the lady on the phone a few times. She's called almost every hour to see if you received the bag."

Anne was going to ask about a name or address, but then the older woman said, "Oh, I almost forgot. She left you instructions."

"Instructions?"

The woman pulled out an envelope and passed it to Anne, who upon opening it realized they were plane tickets. Unusual tickets, devoid of an airliner's logo or gate number. She looked up, too overwhelmed to think of checking the destination listed on the tickets.

"Two tickets sent by email an hour ago." The woman giggled again. "Private Jet, too. Mr. Handsome must be loaded."

"I'm sorry, ma'am." Anne's face dimmed as she feared the answer to her question would shock her. "I need to know the sender's name—and address if possible."

"Ah, I forgot. Comes with the white hair, darling." The woman clicked her forefinger and thumb in midair, then turned the monitor to Anne's side so she could read the name. "Here it is. She left no last name, which isn't exactly legal, but she left a hefty tip."

Anne's cheeks went numb as she read the sender's first name on the screen: *Rachel aka Snow White.*

# 21

---

### *International Flights, Heathrow Airport, London*

Lily fidgeted in her seat at the gate. The closest passenger sat two seats away from her. Like always, people hardly registered her existence.

Her sisters, Lady Ovitz's grandchildren, were used to society treating them as if they were second-class citizens. People kept away. Almost as if her kind was Mother Nature's mistake, a disease, if not a fault in mankind's genetic evolution. That's why she loved reading Charles Darwin. *Those who adapt, survive.* She learned it the hard way.

Being a dwarf wasn't as fantastical as in fairytales. The things people said they loved in movies and books were the opposite of what they loved in real life. The Ewoks of George Lucas and the dwarves in *Lord of the Rings* were all welcomed on a movie screen. But not in real life.

Only two of her seven sisters lived a relatively normal life, and that was because they had grown into normal-looking women. Most people didn't know that dwarves occasionally birthed taller children. It didn't occur often, but it happened, nonetheless. It happened to her two sisters.

It didn't matter, though. She was handed the shorter straw—pun intended. The consequences of such she had learned to deal with, although she did the work of giants like her grandmother told her.

*Soon the world will know, and those who got away with their crimes will face their sins.*

On her phone, Lily saw Anne's video surfacing on the internet. People were gossiping about what could have happened in Westminster Abbey this morning. The BBC had released footage of Professor Anne Anderson's attack on Tom John, head of the Protection Command. No further details were given, other than that she was a wanted fugitive.

No one spoke of the girl on the cross. Not yet.

Lily knew that it would take time. As usual, the royal family, the Vatican, and the elite tried their best to postpone the exposition of facts so they could buy themselves enough time to rearrange their cards—and tell more lies.

The fact that no one discussed how Anne and David escaped the abbey only showed her that no one cared. Soon enough, the secret tunnels would be exposed to the public.

Thinking of the tunnels reminded her of the three nights she spent in there. She took care of the girl on the cross while watching her being poisoned. She also supervised building the wooden cross, which was far from an easy task. None of her sisters wanted to participate in the sacrifice. She didn't blame them. It was traumatic.

She was grateful for the cleaning ladies, though. They brought her food and lent a hand erecting the cross. They helped her with the last touches of the mapestry. They also had access to the camera footage and deleted what needed to be. It mesmerized her that two of them had graduated from IT universities. So many women with great career potential wasted it on the Sisterhood.

It had taken the Sisterhood years to implant the cleaners into the abbey's system. They knew that Lady Ovitz wasn't going to live forever. They knew that the moment she died, the search for her secret would shatter the world.

Her grandmother's memory forced a smile on Lily's face.

How could she forget the great times of her childhood at the library in London? They lived in that crammed small apartment on top of it. The same one Lily had left a few hours ago, never to return.

Lady Ovitz had magically transformed her childhood into a pleasant nostalgic fairytale that kept them happy and alive. The fairytales she read to them. The way she called them "the female seven dwarves." How they joked that they'd find a handsome prince in a glass coffin and kiss him awake. That they'd all take care of him and bring him back to his beloved princess. Lady Ovitz gifted them with an enchanted childhood. A beautiful childhood of lies.

Without her childhood, Lily would be nothing. Only these innocent memories of the past gave her hope for the future.

Yet, she knew she had no future either, being thought of as a killer now. Watching the girl on the cross changed her soul. She could feel it, and could also feel that she was destined to kill again.

Her ringtone of Beethoven's Fifth Symphony interrupted her train of thought. She checked the caller's name and was stunned it was the Sisterhood's leader: Our Queen.

Not the Queen of England, but the one who had influenced women in the world for years.

They called her the Queen as a way of honoring the real women who should have been crowned as queens in past history. Those who instead were killed or denied due to the elite's trickery and control of monarchies.

The Queen was the Sisterhood's messenger, hailed as the first female prophet of all time. And like most prophets, no one ever saw her. Not even Lady Ovitz. Because of this, Lily was honored and picked up immediately.

"Yes, my Queen?" Lily bowed her head to an imaginary version of the Sisterhood's leader as she spoke.

"I'm proud of you, Lily," the Queen said. "So is your grandmother in her grave."

"It's an honor." Lily fought the tears in her eyes.

"Was it your idea to send a fake version of the Brothers Grimm to Jonathan Gray, Lily?"

"It was, my Queen. After Lady Ovitz died, I needed to distract those who were after the original version. I thought that when they read the so-called original version and realized it didn't lead to the Singing Bone, they might give up on chasing us."

"The royal family will never give up on looking for the Singing Bone, Lily, and neither will the other families," the Queen said skeptically. "It was never the Sisterhood's intention to make the world think the original book was a joke, too."

"I thought it would give us time to distract them." Lily realized she hadn't impressed the Queen. In fact, she had angered her. "After Lady Ovitz's death, I found the library in shambles. They knew she kept the secret to the Singing Bone somewhere."

"Your reckless tactic did buy us time, I must admit," the Queen said. "I guess you did what you had to do, considering that Lady Ovitz refused to tell any of us about her Singing Bone's secret."

"I wish she had trusted us," Lily said. "We're her bloodline."

"After all we've been through over the years, trust is the hardest thing to acquire in the Sisterhood," the Queen said. "Look at all that you did for us. And yet, you haven't been anointed as a True Sister."

"I'll do whatever I can to deserve anointment," Lily said.

"Good," the Queen said. "You know whom to sacrifice next and where."

Lily stared at the ticket in her hands, ready to get on the plane.

# 22

14:30 (P.M.)

**Streets of London**

David followed Anne as she stormed out of the shop. He could tell she was furious and worried about her sister.

"I have to call her," Anne insisted, while dialing Rachel's number.

"Sure," David said, gently taking the plane tickets and the bag from her. "I better give you some privacy."

He stepped away without letting her out of sight. In his mind, Rachel wasn't going to pick up. Anne's sister was in no position to talk, whether she was the orchestrator of this event or another victim. It was the tickets' destination that mattered the most now. It had to be. Why would she have sent them otherwise?

From his experience, and how things had unfolded so far, he feared the worst. Rachel had probably been kidnapped and impersonated by the killer.

Why? He had no clue.

There was a lot to process. None of it seemed to clearly answer their questions. But at least the puzzle was slowly, yet vaguely, coming together.

He watched Anne redial her sister's number. Over and over again, with no results.

He unfolded the tickets. He had to see where the mapestry was going to send them.

These so-called tickets were only luxurious, handwritten passes to a private jet.

The destination? Kassel, Germany.

David reckoned the location was most likely connected to Anne's specialization. The killer knew her too well. Even though his reasoning behind the puzzles remained unknown, the killer surely had a bigger mission for her. Bloody Mary wouldn't have helped them escape if this wasn't true.

He didn't know much about Kassel, but the flight's schedule alerted him. They were supposed to be at the airport within an hour.

"She's not picking up." Anne was hysterical, almost bumping into pedestrians. "How could she be involved in this crime? What's going on? I think something happened to her."

"I don't think so," David lied, handing her the tickets. "I have a feeling she's okay. We need to follow the mapestry's plan."

"Kassel?" Anne's voice rose in pitch when reading the tickets.

"You've been there?"

"Many times. It's the Brothers Grimm's birthplace."

"Huh," David said as he suddenly stopped two boys in hoods and headphones. He knew Anne wouldn't understand what he was going to do, but he needed to act fast without explaining himself.

"Kassel is part of that Fairytale Road I told you about where it all originated," Anne said, watching him stop and search the teenagers.

David pulled out a tiny bag of marijuana from the boys' pockets. "I thought so," David said. He turned to the older boy. "How old are you?"

"Eighteen," the boy said. "I swear the drugs aren't mine, sir."

"I don't care about the drugs," David said. "You have an Uber app?"

"What?"

"Be quick, or you'll be dead. I'm a police officer," David said to the boy, realizing how silly he looked in his sports outfit. "I'm undercover. So let me ask you again: do you have an Uber app?"

"Yes." The boy showed it to him on his phone.

"Good," David said. "Book me an Uber to the Biggin Hill Airport, in Bromley. *London.*"

"You're the police," the younger one objected. "You can't make us do that."

"Were the drugs yours, huh?" David grunted, almost childishly.

"Okay, okay," the older one said. "I'll book you a bloody ride, sir."

"David," Anne interrupted, standing between him and the boys. "What are you doing, bullying these kids like that?"

"I'm not a kid. I'm eighteen!" the boy objected.

"Shut up." David pointed a finger at him. He turned to Anne. "We have to be at the airport within the hour. We can't risk booking a ride from our phones, let alone paying with our credit card."

"Are we getting on that plane?" Anne said.

"We have no choice. It's what the killer wants. The longer we stay here, the higher the risk we're going to jail."

"It's here, sir." The older boy pointed at a black Mercedes E Class, slowing at the curb.

"You booked an Uber Deluxe?" David rolled his eyes. He hurried to the car with the laptop bag.

"Sorry, boys," Anne smiled at them apologetically. "he has a temper. Really sorry," she said again as she slid into the backseat.

"Why do girls always go for the bad boy?" one of the boys said to her as she shut the door.

Inside the Mercedes, the elderly driver's eyes squinted. He looked between his phone and David's reflection in the mirror. "Little Johnny X?"

"Excuse me?" David said.

"Your name, sir, is Little Johnny X on the app?"

Anne would've smiled if she wasn't occupied with messaging Rachel.

"You have a problem with me calling myself Little Johnny X?" David said, realizing it was the boy's name.

"No, sir," the man said politely. Still, he scoffed under his breath. "Millennials."

David opened the bag in the backseat and pulled out a laptop, a PC that looked old and worn out. There were several stickers of fairytale characters all over it. He set it on Anne's lap.

"It's for you," he said. "The next puzzle."

Anne opened the latch, a little taken aback by the desktop's wallpaper. It was a familiar image. An image of the Seven Dwarves. They were standing over a glass coffin from the 1937 Disney movie of Snow White.

"Oh my God, it must be Rachel's," Anne said.

"Because she was Snow White when you were kids," David said practically. "It still could be someone impersonating her to bait you into the next puzzle."

"I understand what you mean. This is getting more personal by the minute."

"Password?" David pointed at the flashing cursor inside the empty box in the middle of the screen. The cursor was shaped like a tiny flute.

"Am I supposed to know it?" Anne said. "Just like that?"

"Did you and Rachel ever share passwords?" David said. "Any word you think she would use?"

Anne shrugged. Again, he could sense she wasn't telling him something crucial about her sister.

"Rachel doesn't like technology," Anne explained. "She loved handwriting, embroidery, paperback books, and forests."

"If so, then this magic wand is still our only hope," David suggested as he pulled out the Singing Bone. "Maybe the puzzle is actually a melody this time."

# 23

14:35 (P.M.)

## *Uber, Streets of London*

Anne rotated the Singing Bone in her hands, looking for another cipher. Meanwhile, David pestered the driver for not using short-cuts instead of sticking to the GPS routes.

"I doubt the flute has the password, David," Anne said. "The rules of the game indicate that the new item, in our case this laptop, is the new mapestry."

David sighed impatiently as Anne flipped the keyboard around. She was looking for more notes or musical numbers on the back. The fairytale character stickers didn't promise a resolution either.

"It looks like a child's laptop," David said.

"Which fits perfectly," Anne said. "Remember I told you the mapestry has to misdirect the common person. But it will make sense to a folklorist like me."

"What about the image of the Seven Dwarves on the wallpaper?"

"They definitely match the stickers on the back. I just don't see how it gives the password away. Did you know that *Snow White* was the first animated movie Disney ever made?"

David's look made her shrug. He certainly didn't want to know about this.

She seized the chance and teased him again to calm him down. "Did you also know Disney's *Alice in Wonderland* was infused with all kinds of drug references?"

"Yeah, mushrooms, cocaine, et cetera. I know about this one," David said. "You may have heard Tom talk about my addictions in the past."

"I did." Anne admired David's openness about his setbacks and insecurities. She'd never had the courage to announce hers to the world. "I have an idea. Let's try this password for a start."

She typed "12346712." The seven numbers the Brothers Grimm used in their titles.

"You seem adamant these numbers will solve one of the riddles," David commented.

"I'm wrong again." she said as the password was rejected.

"It says we have only two more entries. Then it will lock itself." David pointed at the screen. "I still think the key to the password is hiding within wallpaper."

"Let me think. Snow White and the Seven Dwarves," she pondered. "A Disney movie made in 1937—"

"1937 is a number," David remarked.

"It is," Anne considered. "But why do we assume the password is only numbers?"

"Passwords usually aren't. It's just that this musical notes thing seems to only translate to numbers," David said. "What about the fact that the killer looked like a dwarf?"

"I see the connection. I don't know what to do with it."

David flipped the plane tickets in his hands, looking for clues. "No flight number, seats, or gate here."

"Why is that?"

"Private jets don't necessarily have them. Especially if they take off from a business aviation airport like this Biggin Hill Airport."

"You mean it's a private airport that has no commercial flights?"

"I haven't been there, but yes. It's for the considerably rich who are ready to board a flight anytime they choose. Just as fast as hopping onto a bike parked outside the house."

"So, the killer has money and connections," Anne said. "I find it scary."

"We don't have the luxury to think about that now. Let's not get distracted from the password," David said. "From what I've seen so far, the killer is precise with his riddles."

"She," Anne suggested. "I think with all the women involved in this crime, we should start to think it could be a she."

"Women? What do you mean?"

"The girl on the cross. The Tudor sisters. Her Majesty. Bloody Mary. The cleaning ladies. And now Rachel," Anne said. "You and Tom are the only men involved. And neither of you has a personal connection to the crime—at least I doubt Tom does."

"I agree. It's an interesting theory. So, I guess it takes a female folklorist to catch a female killer."

"You betcha," Anne said, eyes on the wallpaper again.

"This is a wallpaper of Snow White lying in a glass coffin, waiting for the necrophiliac prince to come and kiss her," David mumbled, thinking.

It amused her that he said it this way. In her mind, and in some studies, people had commented the same. Why would someone ever kiss a dead person unless they were morbidly unstable?

"She is surrounded by seven dwarves." David continued his train of thought.

"Seven," Anne commented. "Another number, just saying."

"Eight if you count Snow White."

"You said to focus. So think simple. It's in the killer's best interest that we solve the puzzles, it seems. I don't think complex riddles are a favorite of his."

"Simple, huh. What about the names of the dwarves?"

"Interesting." Anne clicked a thumb and forefinger together while the driver just shook his head in the mirror. He probably thought Little Johnny X and his girlfriend were still stuck in childhood.

"One of them was called Dopey," David said. "I used to call my drug dealer Dopey."

"Bashful, Doc, Dopey, Grumpy, Happy, Sleepy, and Sneezy," Anne counted on her fingers. "What if we take the first letter from each name? Seven numbers like the earlier puzzle of the bone?"

"Happy, Sneezy, and Sleepy start with an H and an S," David said. "It doesn't work."

"It does."

"Huh?"

"Nazis encountered the same issue when using these musical codes for communication orders during World War Two," Anne said.

"Nazis used codes inspired by the Brothers Grimm?"

"They were enamored with fairytales. Don't get me started about the fairytale propaganda movies they filmed with Hitler in the main role," Anne said. "Anyway, the issue the Nazis faced was: what happens if they needed to use letters other than a, b, c, d, e, f, and g in their secret messages? If that was a code by the Nazis, they would have overlooked the first letters in Happy, Sleepy, and Sneezy. Instead, they would have counted the first one that followed the code after."

"You mean they would use 'a' for Happy, 'e' for Sleepy, and also 'e' for Sneezy?"

"Exactly," Anne nodded. "The code for the seven dwarves wallpaper would be: *BDDGAEE*."

"Which would be the numbers 2447155," David figured. "Which should we use? Numbers or letters?"

Anne entered the seven numbers. If she was wrong, they still had one more entry left to try the letters.

The computer took a moment and accepted the password. It loaded and redirected them to another screen.

"Another seven dwarves? And there is a box for a second password to be entered?" David rapped his hands on his lap. "You've got to be joking."

"Except it's a black-and-white image of real dwarves." Anne's face dimmed, knowing whom she was looking at. "In the second world war."

The decades-old photo looked grainy, its sides tinted with a fading green. A scan of an original photo that probably didn't exist anymore. There was no mistake about it. The photo of the seven dwarves was taken in a concentration camp. Behind them stood Hitler's doctor, Josef Mengele. He was smiling broadly. Almost proud of the shorter crowd.

"What is this?" David said, realizing his earlier feeling about the murder was true. This wasn't just about a dead girl. This was something else he could not comprehend at all. "How did the girl on the cross's mapestry lead us back to an almost eighty-year-old photo?"

Anne sympathized with David's reaction. He looked at her for explanation, but she was just as shocked. She wasn't sure how to explain this to him—or even to herself.

"I've always suspected this, David," she began. "But I could never prove it."

"What couldn't you prove, Anne? I'm bloody confused out of my brains here. Who are these dwarves in the picture?"

"I worry you'll laugh if I tell you."

"My jaw is too tense with frustration to laugh."

"Okay, then. You're looking at what some folklorists consider the true origin of a so-called fairytale," she said, as the driver stopped at a red light. "The *real* seven dwarves."

Anne was about to explain to David when a man in the street stood staring at her while looking back his phone, then pointed a finger at her with an open mouth.

# 24

## *Outside of Westminster Abbey, London*

Hunched in the backseat, the Advocate lowered his phone and kept his eyes on Westminster Abbey. The police still gave nothing away. Even the press couldn't speculate what had happened inside yet.

He had seen the video of Anne threatening Tom John already, and was left puzzled by the whole thing.

"Maybe she knows," The Advocate said to his driver.

"I think she does," said the driver.

"But I've been watching her for so long, and she seemed oblivious," he said, tapping his cane.

"What if her refusal to authenticate Lady Ovitz's fake version of the book was just an act?" The driver said.

"Women aren't that smart," The Advocate declared bluntly. "Then again, why is she needed in the abbey? And what about that fake video of her with Tom John?"

"Fake, sir?"

"Of course it's fake. She apparently never shot a gun before in her life," The Advocate said, rewatching the video on his phone. "Not that the public would notice."

"I think you're right, sir. Her grip on the gun looks awkward."

"Also, is that a forensic ziplock bag on the floor beside her in the video?"

"It looks similar, sir."

"I think Anne was needed in a crime scene."

"You think it has to do with the death of Lady Ovitz?"

"I don't know. I'm more concerned with whatever was inside that ziplock bag."

"Evidence? Crime scene weapon?"

The Advocate zoomed in. It only took him a moment to notice someone's faint shadow on the floor. A shadow created by the light from the dome above. Whoever was behind Tom was careful enough to stay out of frame, standing instead in the camera's blind spot.

A woman, The Advocate believed. She held a gun. Was she pointing it at Anne? Or at that detective beside her?

It didn't matter because The Advocate found what he'd been looking for. To confirm his suspicions, he zoomed in at 500%. He changed the contrast and brightness of the video to dim all surrounding colors.

And there he saw it. The shadow of what looked like a short rod in the girl's hand. It was hard to confirm it being a flute. But it was just as hard to eliminate the possibility of it being the Singing Bone.

"Tom is leaving the building, sir," the driver informed him. "He looks furious. He's shouting at someone on the phone."

"But of course, he is furious." The Advocate looked out his window and proudly tapped his Italian hat. "Like a little rat, I seduced you out of your hiding, Tommy boy. I wonder if your father originally wanted to name you Jerry."

"You did that, sir?" the driver said. "How? And why is he so furious?"

"I sent him a message about his father's paralysis," The Advocate said. "And guess who was the last person caught visiting Jonathan Gray on camera?"

"Us, I assume?"

"We entered from the back door. The last one who entered from the front door was Anne Anderson." The Advocate smirked.

"Didn't Jonathan Gray hire some unreliable folklorist to authenticate the book after Anne left?" the driver said.

"He did, but she never entered the office or even read it. He just told her what to say."

"He is that corrupt, huh."

"Aren't we all?" The Advocate said. "And now that Jerry the Rat is out, I'm confident that Anne escaped earlier. Otherwise, he would have brought her out with him."

"You're a genius, sir."

"That's why you will call my employer now and tell him that my price has doubled."

"But of course, sir," the driver said. "May I ask what the plan is now?"

"That's the easy part." The Advocate smiled, watching Tom John get in his car. "We follow the rat to where the cheese is."

# 25

*Uber, London*

Anne was about to urge the elderly driver to push the gas pedal when the lights broke into yellow and he just took off.

"Close call," Anne sighed. "You think that man recognized me from the news? Are people nosy enough they stare inside Ubers?"

"Or he might have never seen an E-Class Mercedes as an Uber before," David said. "That doesn't mean people aren't nosy, though. No, tell me what you mean by the real seven dwarves." David pointed at the black-and-white photo. "Are you telling me those are the real dwarves whom the fairytale was based on?"

"I could never prove it. I stumbled upon them in my research," Anne said.

"This photo was taken in a concentration camp in World War Two, Anne. Your fairytales are centuries old. It doesn't add up."

"I know that." She waved a hand, looking nervous again. "But if there was any true resemblance to the seven dwarves, then it would be them. A family of dwarves. Keeping the princess safe. The Ovitz family."

"Are you suggesting that all these innuendos point out to them guarding the origins of the Snow White story?"

Anne looked reluctant to reply. "I'm not sure. Just saying."

"I can't imagine how this story has origins to kill for," David said. "Forget about it, then. Tell me, what did the Ovitz family do?"

"Traveling musicians. They sang and played music and performed in the war. Their act was called the Lilliput Troupe."

"Lilliput?"

"Yes. The family later only named their children and grandchildren similar names that started with an L. Lily, Lara, Lucia, and so on."

"They were Germans?"

"Romanians. They used to perform in Hungary and Czechoslovakia in the 1930s and 1940s. That is, until the Nazis brought them to Auschwitz," Anne said. "Their stunted heights denied them most jobs, which meant the Nazis had no use for them, but kept them alive for entertainment purposes."

David didn't fathom how this could possibly solve the girl's murder. Despite this, he trusted Anne and kept on listening. After all, the killer seemed to want them to investigate this part of the puzzle.

"In reality, the Ovitz family were more than seven. A big family, but they performed on the stage as seven dwarves to attract the curious crowd."

"Smart thinking. Using folktales to bring food to the table in the middle of such terrible circumstances. I like that."

"In today's words, you could say they used an IP—an intellectual property. The same way Disney did with fairytales and the movies with Marvel Comics today."

"Ahead of their time," David said. "What do you think they have to do with the girl on the cross?"

"I don't know, David. I'm trying to figure it out now." Anne still sounded stressed. "The taller relatives in the Ovitz family helped with promotion and serving backstage."

"They weren't all dwarves?"

"Contrary to popular belief, dwarves can occasionally give birth to taller people."

"I read a lot of Darwin, yet I never knew that. Go on."

"The Ovitz sang in Yiddish, Hungarian, Romanian, Russian, and German," Anne recited what she knew, hoping something would click in her mind. Something that would relate the story to the current murder. "Their matriarch, the leader, was Lady Ovitz. She may have had a real first name but they all called her Lady—oh my God!"

"Found a connection?"

"Not sure what it is, but I was invited to authenticate the original copy of the Brothers Grimm manuscript in the British Library this morning," Anne said. "I was told a librarian by the name of Lady Ovitz found it."

"Lady Ovitz is still alive? How old would she be?"

"I was told she died at one hundred and two, if I remember correctly," Anne said. "Jonathan told me her family found the book in the library or her closet after her death."

As always, David swiftly used his phone and announced, "Lady Ovitz died yesterday."

"So Lady Ovitz dies yesterday. They find her Brothers Grimm book and want me to authenticate it today. And then the death of a girl on a cross in Westminster Abbey leads me back to Lady Ovitz?" Anne said. "I feel like there is a connection. I just can't grasp it. What is going on, David?"

"I hate when people ask me this," David said. "How did the authentication meeting go this morning?"

"I refused to authenticate because it was fake."

"Fake?" David grimaced. "Are you sure?"

"Yes."

"Do you think it was fake because it was actually fake? Or because maybe Jonathan showed you a fake one and kept the real copy for himself?"

"I didn't think about that," Anne said. "Does it matter?"

"I'm trying to connect the dots," David said. "My hunch is that Lady Ovitz knew someone would come after the book after she died. So maybe her family faked one up well before she died. Jonathan Gray, being greedy, didn't care. It worked. I wonder who benefits from getting their hand on the book. Are they looking for its contents or the Singing Bone?"

"They're the same. The book contains the story. The Singing Bone supposedly unlocks the secret in the book or leads to its original version."

"Let me ask you this: if the Singing Bone supposedly exposed the killer of the bone's deceased, does that mean, and I'm really reaching here, that there are thousands of other Singing Bones?"

"A very interesting thought," Anne said. "I don't know. But if you're asking whether the Singing Bone is a metaphor for exposing a historical crime—or crimes—of the past, then yes. That's what folklorists are trying to figure out all over the world."

"I can't believe a children's book holds something so precious people would kill for it," David said.

"It's not a children's book, David!"

"Okay. Okay. My bad," David said. "Can I ask if religion has anything to do with this whole mess?"

"Religion? You mean because the girl was hung on a cross?"

"It's been a pressing question that I've been trying to avoid since I saw her," David said. "A female Jesus Christ or something?"

"It crossed my mind as well." Anne shrugged. "I think it's bigger than religion."

"I can't imagine anything bigger than religion." David cocked his head. "Nothing makes people kill and misjudge each other more than religion."

"Folklore is bigger than religion."

"Oh, come on," he said skeptically. "I know you're passionate about your profession and all that but—"

"Here is proof." She challenged him like she did with Jonathan by going over a streak of evidence. "How many Christians share Muslim traditions? How many Jews share Buddhist beliefs? Few, right?"

"Okay?"

"Now ask yourself how many people—Christians, Muslims,

Jews, Buddhists, including every other religion you've heard of—know about Snow White, Sleeping Beauty, and Little Red Riding Hood?"

David shrugged. What she said had never occurred to him before.

"Many, many more," she said. "And you know why?"

"Because every child is fed these bedtime stories all over the world." He almost mumbled the revelation to himself. "In spite of their religion or nationality."

"That's what Rachel found out." Anne began to slightly shiver. "She knew something was wrong with the world. Something that was implanted in our childhood."

"I get your point." David reached out and patted her shoulder. He was reluctant to touch her because he wanted it a little too much, and too soon. He could also have asked her to tell him more about Rachel. Yet he knew it would only aggravate her. Rachel could've been hurt by now. He needed Anne to stay strong.

"And here is another proof that this transcends religion," Anne said. "What do you think the Ovitz family practiced as religion?"

"I assumed they're Christians. Given their vague connection to a girl hung on a cross inside the abbey and a fairytale book written by two devout Christians."

"No, David. They were Jews," Anne said.

David's face twisted again. "This case is only getting more baffling by the minute. Who are we really chasing here, Anne?"

Suddenly the driver slammed the brakes. David and Anne jostled in the backseat. Trying to settle themselves after the sudden impact, they both looked out the window. Their eyes were met with two female airport security guards at the gate.

This time, it was a real situation because the guards were aiming their semiautomatics at them.

# 26

### *The British Library, London*

Tom John stood looking down at his paralyzed father on the couch. Jonathan Gray's eyes hung wide open but stiff. He seemed unable to move any of his limbs as well, and was left staring at his now-absent killer.

"He can't talk," said the emergency doctor they had called in. "But he is alive."

Tom bit on his fisted knuckles to fight back the tears. It was more about pride than pain. He felt insulted that Anne did this to him. Since he made a lavish living from following orders, 'why' wasn't a question he normally contemplated. The world was a complex place of lies and obscurities. Jonathan had taught Tom how to make a living by pleasing those who made the rules. Not that Tom liked his father for raising him this way. But he still would have to avenge him if he died.

"How is that possible?" Tom asked the doctor.

"I must examine him further. Not to mention, move him to the clinic."

"We're not moving him anywhere," Tom said. "I'm ordered to keep it discreet."

"He could suffer complications," the doctor argued.

"I have orders from Her Majesty," Tom snarled at him, burning on the inside. Her Majesty's office had specifically ordered him to keep it discreet today. They'd said that the girl on the cross was just a start. The beginning of a series of murders. And that the press shouldn't know about any of it before forty-eight hours. Little did he know his father was going to be one of the victims.

It also didn't help that Bloody Mary sent Anne's tape to the BBC. He didn't have enough leverage to ask the office for favors and save his father now.

"You say this wine did this to him?" Tom collected himself and asked as calmly possible.

"Probably," the doctor said. "We sent it to the lab to examine it."

"Anne left the wine for us." Tom knelt, looking at his father. "Why?"

"I don't know. We also found this." The doctor pointed at a half-bitten apple set upon the Brothers Grimm book.

Tom pressed his teeth. He needed to hide his anguish from the doctor and the police officers surrounding him. With hands in pockets, he approached the podium and bent over. "It's cut horizontally."

"Pardon me?" the doctor said.

"I can see the apple seeds form a pentagram." Tom couldn't take his eyes off it, but he could not bring himself to touch it.

"Really?" The doctor unconsciously gripped the cross that dangled from his neck.

"The killer left it to tell us that my father was poisoned with cyanide." Tom felt full of himself. He was remembering Anne's confidence in the abbey.

"Good grief," the doctor said, admiring Tom's brilliance. "Apple seeds do contain cyanide—but wait, it has to be a large amount to become poisonous."

"Vecchia Melo," Tom nodded at the wine bottle.

"I see," the doctor said. "No wonder the office sent you, sir. You're too good."

"I know," Tom said. "I'm the best."

"I will contact the lab right away."

"Do that, Doctor, but don't you dare talk to the press," Tom warned him. "And please give me a moment alone with my father?"

"Certainly," the doctor said. He left the room with the rest of the police officers.

Alone, Tom stared at the apple. He wondered if the killer, who probably was the same person who killed the girl on the cross, had left him a mapestry.

He slowly turned to Jonathan and bent over to touch his face. "I'm sorry, father, for I will do this to you," he whispered in his ears. "For Queen and country, you know."

Tom parted his father's mouth, about to shove to shove his fingers down his throat. That's when the unexpected happened.

# 27

15:11 (P.M.)

## *Biggin Hill Airport, Bromley, London*

"Are you sure this is the right address, Little Johnny X?" the driver asked David in the mirror. "I mean this is a high-class business aviation airport. I don't blame security for wanting to shoot us."

"You mean because we're dressed like bums?" David said nonchalantly. His eyes scanned the entrance curiously. "People in suits work for people in shorts and caps nowadays, if you haven't heard."

"But he is right, David." Anne pinched him, pointing at the two cars behind them. A Bentley and a Rolls Royce. "We don't look the part."

"It may be the Chocolate Factory"—David flashed the tickets at the soldier—"but we have the golden tickets."

He rolled down his window and handed the papers to one of the female guards at the gate. The skeptical armed security guard told them to wait and then returned to the cubicle and made a call.

"You'll have to tell me more about those World War Two seven dwarves later," David said to Anne. "Once we get on that plane."

The security woman returned with a smile. She handed the tickets back to David. "Please come in, sir," she said. "Your plane is about to take off."

David nodded without thanking her. He wasn't sure he trusted that hundred-and-eighty-degree change of heart.

"You still have time to get dressed in the guest house, though," the security woman said. "Our Heiress has set up a black suit for you, sir, and an adequate white outfit for Professor Anderson."

"Heiress?" Anne stuck her neck out.

"Madame, Heiress Jacqueline de Rais. Owner of the famous Fraternité fashion brand." The security woman nodded. "I'm sure she will be pleased you accompany her on her flight to Kassel."

🍎

The astonished driver paused to allow the Bentley and Rolls Royce to pass by before making the final stop to David and Anne's cabin inside the almost vacant airport. Anne explained to David who Jacqueline de Rais was as they hopped out.

"I don't know much about her. Only that she is one of the richest women in the world. I hear she is a philanthropist, too," Anne said as a blonde girl in a luxurious uniform ushered them silently into the cabin. "Fraternité is both a fashion and a make-up brand. It's known for its 'independent women' outfits. If that makes any sense."

"I'm not interested in that, but I can't imagine her connection to the killer. Why do you think Rachel sent you tickets to get on this woman's plane?" David spotted his black suit on the bed right away. Perfect size.

"We both know Rachel may not have sent me the tickets. I'm not naive. She could be in danger. I have no answer for your question though," Anne said. She spotted her outfit stretched on the sofa and picked it up.

A luxurious but casual business outfit of black trousers and a white blouse. Beautiful fabric, but a little too revealing at the cleavage's opening. She knew the Fraternité brand was big on women's sexual freedom, so she wasn't surprised. The classic shoes slightly glimmered in gold. They fit perfectly and complemented the style. A white card upon the outfit labeled it a "power suit."

"Do you think this Jacqueline woman helped in killing the girl on the cross—" David began.

Anne shushed him, looking at the usher girl by the door.

"You can go now," David said to her. "We may be getting on a French plane but we're not French enough to get naked in front of other people."

"David!" Anne sneered at him. She then asked the usher in French to kindly excuse herself and apologized for having no money to tip her.

"You're not of French descent, are you?" David said once the girl left.

"I'm of German descent, David. And you shouldn't say such things to people," she said. "If it matters, I happen to speak a few European languages, okay? It helps with reading ancient manuscripts, as well as talking to locals in possession of valuable information about my research. Now turn around so I can change."

"Oh," He raised an eyebrow. "I shouldn't have insulted the French earlier, I guess."

"Shut up!"

🍎

Five minutes later, the Bentley that had been behind their Uber car returned to pick them up. The female driver nodded at them. She made it clear she wasn't going to say a word.

"I have the feeling that Tom John will appear from out of nowhere and arrest us," David murmured while gripping the laptop bag in the back.

"Me, too," Anne said. "Actually, I'm worried it'd be Bloody Mary who'd come for us. I still can't believe or understand why she led us onto this journey, David. You must have seen this coming."

"I'm David, not Nostradamus," he said, focusing on the road ahead with suspicious eyes.

"I can't believe we're getting on this plane. Not even knowing why. It's part of the mapestry, I know. But I understand that we can't go back now or we'll be thrown in jail."

"What's so important about Kassel?" David said.

"I don't have the slightest idea. But the Fairytale Road runs for six hundred miles from north to south in Germany. Bremen is the first city in the North. You could say Munich is the last city in the South. Kassel, where the Brothers Grimm lived, is right in the middle."

"So maybe whatever secret this Singing Bone holds can be revealed in Kassel?"

Anne didn't have a chance to contemplate the thought, as the Bentley rolled to a stop near the private plane.

"Is that Jacqueline?" David pointed outside his window.

"Yes, in the flesh," Anne nodded, "She looks pretty young and in shape for a woman in her late fifties. I tried to interview her once because... Wait a minute."

"What?"

"See that burly man in the extravagant black-brown fur coat next to her?"

"Another rich fellow fashionista?"

"Not even close," Anne said. "Aside from being the first man we've seen in the airport, this is Franz Xaver. He's a direct descendant of the Schönwerth family."

"Pretty intense name," David said. "Why are you shocked to see him?"

"Xaver is the most prominent, and richest, folklorist of our time. His ancestors were the Grimm brothers' greatest enemy."

"So?"

"If anyone actually knows the location of the handwritten original copy of the Brothers Grimm tales, then it's him."

# 28

## Biggin Hill Airport, Bromley, London

In utter silence, Anne and David climbed up the ladder to the private plane. None of the four accompanying passengers gestured or addressed them or each other. The two female bodyguards, who looked nothing less than bodybuilders, made it clear that approaching Madame de Rais or Xaver was out of the question.

David's fight-or-flight eyes didn't escape Anne's attention. She was more curious than worried. But she didn't mind it. None of this made sense, not even in an over-the-top fairytale from her childhood.

She reasoned that they didn't have any choice but to follow the clues that led them here. And she knew that whoever sent them the tickets and the laptop had impersonated Rachel's identity to lure her in. Rachel couldn't have done this; however, Anne wouldn't let her thoughts dig up the old and darker memories.

*You know I wouldn't do this,* Rachel's voice returned. *Someone knows about us. Someone knows what happened, and is using it against you. Don't tell anyone.*

"Let's sit in the back," David whispered, entering the luxurious interior of the plane. "I prefer to have eyes on the rest of the passengers."

Anne agreed and sat by the window in the last row. David sat next to her, eyes on the aisle. It was a spacious and comfortable interior with plush seats and an open bar in the middle. The silence, however, was unsettling.

Franz Xaver and Jacqueline de Rais sat far apart from each other in the front. They didn't speak to each other and were occupied with their phones. Xaver munched on a handful of exotic nuts while Jacqueline's jewelry glimmered like a little source of sunshine. They were both using the same app, if David wasn't mistaken. It looked like a betting app of some kind.

He wished he sat nearer to know more about it. Were these rich folks betting on them? Was this all some sort of game? And were these numbers in the millions?

"So we don't need our passports to get on the plane?" Anne whispered to David.

"I don't dine with the rich like Tom John, but I can only assume as long as you travel in Europe, there is no need for it. Besides, this Jacqueline heiress woman looks powerful enough to break a few laws."

"I see. How about Tom John, should we also assume we're safe here from him?"

"I'd assume nothing and trust no one." David pointed at the two female bodyguards carrying guns under their jackets. "Why are all employees women in here?"

"Jacqueline's brand is about independent women. She is known to substitute men with women in every job title, as long as it's feasible."

"So it's only me and you, Xaver, huh." David eyed the old folklorist.

"Are you intimidated being surrounded by women, David?" Anne couldn't help but tease him. Something·about it entertained her and made her relax.

David didn't have the chance to answer, as the flight attendant arrived and offered them a drink.

"Please accept this rare *Fairy-floss* martini," she said. "A welcome drink from Madame De Rais." She spoke in a French accent.

Anne squeezed David's hand. She could see he was going to comment on the *Fairy-floss* part. She then announced her appreciation in French.

The attendant smiled at her. They exchanged a few words.

"She said she likes my books," Anne explained to him.

"Are you that famous?"

"You could say I'm known in the social book circles, but I haven't had a flight attendant approach me in a plane before," Anne said. "Then again, here we are, on the same plane with one of folklore's greatest scholars."

"Yeah, Mr. Goldfinger." David looked at Xaver's clean-shaven head.

"Goldfinger?"

"It's a reference to James Bond's most famous villain from the sixties," David said.

"What's your deal with James Bond?"

"He always catches the killer, I like that." David raised the martini glass at her. "And he drinks a lot without consequence."

"Flawed logic, but okay," she said. "Still, I don't see why you think Xaver is a villain."

"Everyone I've met today is a villain but you, Anne. Tell me more about him."

"His ancestors proposed a theory that the Brothers Grimm never collected fairytales. That they made up the stories to sell books and get famous."

"Is that true?"

"The fact they didn't travel from house to house in Europe and collect these tales is a given by now. I wrote in my book that that most famous fairytale of all is that they convinced the world they actually did that," she said. "However, it's the part about where they got the stories from that is controversial. There are so many theories."

"At least they didn't climb up a mountain and claim the guy in the clouds spoke to them, or did they?"

"No, they didn't," Anne said. "They only did strange things, like changing the stories and omitting parts in every new edition, and omitting names and dates and locations."

"Fairytales were that specific at first?"

"Supposedly, but it's not proven," Anne said. "But think of how stereotypical the characters come across. Snow White, Sleeping Beauty, the Little Mermaid. It feels odd."

"So what's Xaver's theory?"

"His theory is wild, to be honest. You see, his family were true folktale collectors. They actually traveled and asked people about olden folklore. They confirmed the authenticity of these stories by gathering them from different sources and making sure the majority of the sources matched. They went as far as closely surveilling each storyteller's behavior to determine their honesty and integrity."

"Surveilling, you said?"

"Centuries ago, when people had no means to tell whether someone lied or told the truth, they resorted to one of two things. Either the storyteller swore in front of a high priest in the house of holy, or those who collected these stories surveilled the storytellers' behavior for months to tell if they were apt to tell no lies."

"So, it's like investigating jurors' authenticity and unbiasedness in the American legal court before choosing them. But whoa. I'm surprised the Xaver family was that meticulous about it."

"The Vatican used to do this when authenticating various versions of the bible. In Islam, the collectors of Hadith, the prophet's wisdom, did the same. History was documented 'after the fact' by talking to people who allegedly were present when it occurred. There was no one running around with quill and paper documenting the event that occurred in real time in famine and war. So the storytellers may have lied, or even forgotten what happened. Sometimes, they were biased and recited events the way they wanted to look back at them."

"I bet that some were afraid to tell the truth because of the dire consequences that may have occurred to their families if they told the truth."

"So you know about that?"

"A little. My mother was an atheist who independently studied Darwinism, if there was such a thing. She never got a degree. Instead, she inherited the studies from her father. He traveled the world to collect tales to prove that many high priests in religions were atheists themselves but coveted their beliefs for power and money. It's a debatable and borderline offensive study that made her a lot of enemies. She always told me that people never told the truth because they feared for their families from the powerful in authority."

Anne was about to ask if his mother's biases had something to do with her death, but she held her breath. She didn't have the courage to spell it out.

"If Xaver thinks the Grimm brothers stole his family's stories," David asked, "how come he is so rich now?"

"Rumor has it that he owns Memoria, an oral investigative institute."

"I don't know what that is."

"I know little about it, but it tracks rich people's ancestors."

"Ah, as in genealogy and such?"

"Not, as in oral evidence," Anne said.

"That's a first for me. Could you explain?"

"Let's say you're Elon Musk and want to take back your true family's origins, Memoria finds it out for you for a lot of money. How? Not through documented evidence, but through a thorough private investigation of top specialists who orally ask people all around the world about authenticated past stories connected to your family tree."

"Smart man. No wonder he's loaded."

"It's a known science, by the way, and it's called Oral History."

"Huh," David said.

"What's on your mind?"

"Do you think that the mapestry is leading us to Memoria?" David said. "I mean a place where we can trace the origins of the girl murdered from one of England's most vicious queens?"

"I know, right?" Anne felt like David took the words out of her mouth. "I was just thinking about it, given Her Majesty's unwarranted interest in the murder."

"And given that we're on the same plane with the man who owns Memoria." David eyed Xaver, but before he could unbuckle and go confront him against the guards' orders, the plane took off.

🍎

Once the plane stabilized in the air, David and Anne's plan was to request talking to Franz Xaver, but were surprised to see Jacqueline de Rais loosing her belt and coming over. She walked elegantly toward them with a drink in her hand.

Anne admired her grace and confidence. She couldn't help but wonder if her mother was like Jacqueline. Or maybe a more friendly type like the woman she met this morning in the wheelchair? Rachel used to describe their mother having an angelic look on her face before she left without return.

"Jacqueline de Rais," she introduced herself with a diplomatic smile on her face.

"Anne Anderson," Anne said. She wondered if she was supposed to stand up and greet her. "This is David."

David raised his empty glass to salute her, but didn't look as friendly. "You know who we are."

"I do." Jacqueline sat opposite them. She set down her drink and gracefully rested her hands on the sides of the seat as if she sat upon a throne. Specifically addressing Anne, she said, "I wonder if you know who I really am?"

Anne knew who Jacqueline really was, but hadn't told David because she didn't think it mattered.

"I'm a descendant of the de Rais family," she said. "My great-great-great-grandfather was the French baron Gilles de Rais."

"Who is Gilles de Rais?" asked David, looking at both women.

Jacqueline and Anne exchanged looks then said in unison, "Baron Bluebeard."

"Blue who?"

"Known in folklore as Bluebeard," Anne explained to David while unable to take her eyes off Jacqueline. "He is said to have summoned a demon called 'Baron' and then—"

"Summoned the devil, Anne," Jacqueline insisted. "The devil."

"Okay, the devil." Anne fidgeted a little, uncomfortable now. She turned to face David to finish her thought. "In the sixteenth century, he was known to marry a lot, kill his wives, and lock them up in his medieval castle Château de Tiffauges in Vendée, France."

"And that's because?" David tilted his head, looking like he was overthinking everything.

"He was a blatant hater of women, if I may say." Jacqueline handed her empty glass to the flight attendant and then lit a cigarette. "Not to mention, he sometimes hung them on a cross." Jacqueline blew out spirals of smoke.

David tensed enough to grip the edges of his seat. He looked like he was ready to arrest the rich aristocrat here and there.

Anne waited. She had never heard of Bluebeard hanging his wives on a cross. She almost expected what Jacqueline was going to say next, but not quite sure of its effect on David.

Anne watched Jacqueline lean forward and blatantly manipulate David's psychology. "You see, Detective," she said with what looked like both vanity and regret at the same time. "My great-grandfather is thought of as a fantastically morbid fairytale character. When in reality, he is history's first ever documented serial killer."

# 29

## The British Library, London

Tom couldn't believe Bloody Mary was aiming a gun at him again.

"What the hell are you? A ghost?" He gritted his teeth, pondering whether to call the officer inside or not. Something about her made him curious. He wondered if she knew something that would help him find Anne. "How the hell did you get in the library?"

"I'm Bloody Mary. I can do anything," she said. "Besides, your daddy has a back door that is accessed from behind the desk."

Tom turned to look, feeling betrayed.

"Oh, daddy didn't share all of his secrets with you, fancy boy?"

"What do you want?"

"Well, first of all, you weren't going to find no Singing Bone in your father's throat," she said. "I made that up."

"To mess with me?"

"Now you're learning," she said. "I like games. It's boring being the one who knows too much, so I have to entertain myself."

"What is it that you know, then?"

"I know that you haven't announced the murder of the girl on the cross to the public yet," she said. "Before you tell me that you have orders, let me tell you that you're going to take orders from me from now on."

"And why would I do that?" he said. "My men will arrest you. You won't make it out of here, secret door or not. Not even if you shoot me."

"Stop the babbling and listen," she said. "Here's the deal."

"Deal?"

"The man who poisoned your father has an antidote," she explained. "Don't ask me why he tried to kill him. This man kills for the sake of it. Your father must have pissed him off. This man doesn't like the human race in its entirety. I mean it. He doesn't like the human species."

"Tell me his name and I'll torture him until he begs me to kill him."

"Shut up, ugh," Bloody Mary said. "David was right about you thinking you're a James Bond villain. You talk too much."

"Okay. I'm listening." The veins in his neck stuck out again. "What the hell is this all about?"

"I told you." She again pushed the gun against his neck. "We make a deal. I can get you the antidote to your father's condition. It's an ancient poison, almost untraceable. It's been used to poison queens, mistresses, and even recent world leaders. If you do as I say, I'll use it to save your father's life."

"And you want what in return?"

Bloody Mary smirked. "Be a man and get your ass on the BBC. Time to announce what happened in Westminster Abbey. The people need to know."

"And risk Her Majesty's trust?"

"You're not even sure you're working for her," she said. "You're reporting to an office that is full of politicians with agendas you don't know about. They will get rid of you in the blink of an eye. You think any of the elite men and women your father dined with cares about his condition now?"

Tom considered her words for a moment. He didn't want to

admit it, but he believed her, and plus he knew he would be lost without his father in his life.

"I'll add a bonus to the mix," Mary said.

"I'm listening."

"I'll tell you where Anne is right now," she whispered, teasingly. "So you get to save your father and get to catch her. I'm quite sure your superiors will forgive you for exposing the girl on the cross to the world then."

"I don't see the appeal in your bonus offer," Tom said. "My men will find Anne eventually."

Mary chuckled. "Oh, you naive boy. Anne isn't even in Britain anymore."

Tom tensed. "How is that possible?"

"Just make the announcement, and I will let you kill two birds with one stone," Mary said.

Tom took a last look at his father, and realized Mary was right about no one coming to save him.

He only had one last question for her, one that bothered him the most. "Why are you doing this? You let Anne and David escape and then keep helping me to find them? Why?"

Mary lowered her gun and stared into his eyes. "Don't ask questions above your pay grade, Thomas Jonathan Gray."

# 30

15:31 (P.M.)

### *Jacqueline de Rais's Private Jet*

"Is this what it's about?" David asked Jacqueline. "Continuing your ancestor's killing legacy?"

"Don't jump to conclusions, Detective," Jacqueline said as she took a drag from her cigarette. "But then again, you're a man. That's what you do."

"This has nothing to do with my gender," David said. "The girl on the cross needs justice."

"Justice is man-made, Detective. The very same way *his-story* was actually *her-story*," Jacqueline said.

"I'm not into word games," David said. "I don't even want to participate in this game. How about you tell me the victim's name, and why she was killed."

"You're asking *me* about her name?" Jacqueline said. "Aren't you the police?"

"Your Bloody Mary interrupted the investigation and forced us to leave. Otherwise, I would have done my job," he said.

"I don't know anyone by the name of Bloody Mary," Jacqueline said. "But do you honestly believe the authorities were going to announce the girl's name on the news?"

"Why wouldn't they?"

"Don't you find it strange that no one has mentioned her in the media so far?"

David didn't know what to say. She was right about that part.

"You'll figure it out, Detective. Give it time," Jacqueline said. "I'm not the enemy. I have only mentioned my ancestors to back up Anne's theories about fairytales being true stories that have been distorted to conceal a most terrifying revelation. I'm living proof."

"With all due respect, we're here to find the girl's killer," Anne said. "Not listen to your story."

"Are you sure that's what this is about? Catching a killer?" Jacqueline said. "Come on, Anne. You're curious. Ask me. What do you really want to know?"

Anne briefly looked at David, asking for permission. As much as she was curious about the subject she'd spent her life studying, this was about a girl's murder, not her personal interests.

David gave her a "go ahead" nod.

"Let's start with you, Madame de Rais," Anne said. "Why you never answered my emails when I requested to interview you for my book."

"Isn't it obvious why?"

"No, it isn't. I've found all the documents supporting the story of Bluebeard. He was based on Gilles de Rais, who murdered his wives in the fifteenth century. I found evidence that someone wanted to erase the first serial killer from the history books. For reasons unknown. But I needed *your* side of the story. You never gave it to me."

"Well, here is my answer: because it would have hurt my business, chérie," Jacqueline said. "Reputations are golden when you own such a big business like mine. People can't know that I've descended from darkness."

"I can relate," David said. He remembered his mother's reputation as a devout atheist. Yet he didn't tell her. "But why talk to Anne now?"

"Lady Ovitz's death is why."

"You knew her?" Anne said.

"Not personally. I knew *of* her, and that she served the Sisterhood."

"There is no Sisterhood, madame," Anne countered. "My research proved it to be a myth."

"The same way you claimed there was no Singing Bone?" Jacqueline said. "Did you notice you have a tendency to deny the things that scare you most?"

"What do you mean?"

"You don't believe in a Singing Bone because it will leave you racked with guilt for never finding out the killer of the girl you and Rachel found in the well as kids."

Anne swallowed audibly.

"You hated Rachel for telling you that justice was only a flute away, when later you failed at applying it in real life. Is that why you're searching for the origins of fairytales, Anne? To prove your sister wrong, or is it something else?" Jacqueline said. "In all cases, you're denying the Sisterhood the same way you denied the Singing Bone. Because you're afraid it's true."

"How can you accuse me of not wanting to find out something that I have been chasing all my life?" Anne's fingers clung to her clothes.

"The same way an atheist would go off the deep end to prove the nonexistence of God, only secretly wishing to be proven wrong," Jacqueline said.

David wasn't quite sure if she was talking about him, but it didn't matter. Apparently, this women knew a lot about them, so he asked about what was at hand. "What is the Sisterhood?"

"Listen and do not interfere, Detective," Jacqueline said, eyes on Anne. "Who knows, you might learn a thing or two."

David said nothing, unfazed by her insult. Had a man told him so, a fight might have ensued. But out of respect for his mother, he'd vowed never to take a woman's backfire personally. Something about resilient women interested him in ways he could never understand—or admit.

"I'll tell David about what I know later," Anne told Jacqueline. "If you're not going to tell us the murdered girl's identity, then at least tell us about her connection to Lady Ovitz."

"It doesn't take a genius to connect the dots," Jacqueline said. "Lady Ovitz earned the title of True Sister in the Sisterhood, which is the equivalent to a monastic nun in Catholicism."

"Meaning?" Anne said.

"A most devout one," Jacqueline said. "Lady Ovitz was anointed, and then given the honorable task of being the sole prayer of one of the untold Brothers Grimm stories."

"Prayer?" Anne said.

"Keeper of Sacred Stories, that is," Jacqueline said. "A True Sister is tasked with guarding one of the original stories of a so-called fairytale until she finds a way to pass it to another trusted sister before her death."

"A generational passing of a secret," David noted. "Impressive."

"Those stories include names, dates, documentations, photographs, and everything else."

"How do you know that?" Anne said.

"I'm rich."

"Excuse me?"

"Money loses its value when you can buy everything," Jacqueline said. "So I chose to pay for valuable knowledge that's extremely unattainable."

"So, the stories aren't actually in an original copy of the book?" Anne said, experiencing an epiphany. "The Sisterhood fooled those after the book and the secret of the Singing Bone by scattering the stories amongst their True Sisters."

"All over the world, my dear," Jacqueline said.

"Does this mean that Lady Ovitz passed the story she guarded to the girl on the cross before she died maybe?"

"I don't know about that," Jacqueline said. "Rumor has it that Lady Ovitz, being in undisclosed conflict with the Sisterhood itself, did the unimaginable."

"She split it among her seven granddaughters," David predicted. "That's why the mapestry keeps hinting at the seven dwarves."

"That's why the footage showed the killer to be a dwarf, too," Anne said. "Not that it explains everything, but we're getting close."

"See? I'm not the enemy," Jacqueline said. "and as proof of my good intentions; the names of Lady Ovitz's seven granddaughters: Lily, Lara, Lucia, Layla, Lisbeth, Lisa, and Lilith."

# 31

### *Age of Aquarius Hotel Room, London*

Bloody Mary sauntered naked all over the room. In the dim-lit, curtain-draped, shady hotel room, the tattoos covering her body made her almost invisible. She looked like part of the green and dusty furniture.

She smoked a cigarette with her eyes glued to her phone and headphones in her ears. Freddie Mercury's "The Show Must Go On" blocked her from her surroundings. She wished it to end though, waiting for the one after, "Another One Bites the Dust," her all-time favorite.

Watching what happened in the world right now, and then sending a few texts, she realized the BBC hadn't aired Tom John's announcement about the girl on the cross yet. She didn't worry though. Tom was going to bend over sooner or later, like all men in her life.

Well, all except David actually. She did like him, but it didn't mean she wasn't going to kill him at some point.

She stopped by the bathroom, crossed one foot over another in an X shape, and took off her headphones. The police officer she had just slept with stood proudly naked in front of the mirror. Men were weird like that, she thought to herself. Sex elated them, and they somehow needed to brag about it with their friends or stand nakedly narcissistic in the mirror, bragging about it to themselves.

She put on her seductive face and sauntered into the bathroom and hugged the burly officer from behind. He was twice her size, and much taller. This didn't mean he was stronger though.

"Like it, teddy bear?" she said, staring at him with doe eyes into the moist mirror.

"I hope you like it," he said.

She didn't answer. One could lie only so much, she thought. Instead, she tucked the cigarette into his mouth. "I like that you helped me get in and out of the British Library."

"You were good on your own though, using that secret door," he said. "I just made sure you didn't get in trouble—and occupied the other policemen outside while you had this smug Tom John by his balls."

"You're so cute, burly, burly," She tiptoed and squeezed his chin with her bare hands.

He chuckled. "How did you even know about the secret door in the library?"

"I'm Bloody Mary. I know everything," she said. "Speaking of Bloody Mary, did you ever play the game?"

"You mean the mirror game?" he asked.

"Yeah," she said, tickling him. "Let's do it. Come on. Come on."

"Now?"

"Yes. Yes. Yes," she said, sounding like a child all over again. "It'll be fun."

"Oh, I see what you're doing," he said. "It's because you call yourself Bloody Mary, and I call you three times, it'll be you who pops up out of the mirror."

"Smart little big boy," she said. She turned off the lights and whispered seductively in his ear. "Say it!"

"Bloody Mary," he said reluctantly in the dark.

"One more time."

"Bloody Mary." He chuckled uncomfortably.

"And again."

"Bloody Mar—"

The blood that gushed on her face made her close her eyes and inhale deeply, which she didn't mind. She was disappointed at the giant police officer's instant slump against the ceramic floor. When she turned the lights back on, she realized she'd managed to hit his carotid artery in the dark.

In the background, Freddie Mercury began singing: *Another one bites the dust.*

## 32

15:41 (P.M.)

### *Jacqueline de Rais's Private Jet*

"So now that the murder is connected to a lost story which Lady Ovitz once guarded and passed on to her granddaughters," David said, "am I supposed to assume that story is about a girl on the cross?"

"That is correct," Jacqueline said.

"I've spent my life scouring the earth for every single fairytale," Anne said. "And I've never come across one with a girl on the cross."

"How do you know that, Anne, when you haven't unveiled every fairytale's origin story yet?" Jacqueline said.

Anne couldn't oppose her argument.

"So let me ask you this, Madame de Rais," David said. "Are you familiar with the term 'mapestry'?"

"But of course. Xaver is a good friend of mine. He told me about it," Jacqueline said and then pointed at the laptop bag. "Besides, how do you think you ended up on my jet?"

"Tell me about that," David said, leaning forward with intent and forcing her to finally address him. "How did we end up on your plane?"

"You, Detective—I mean Professor Anderson—found the Singing Bone and from there followed the clues that led you to this point in time." Jacqueline's eyes darted briefly between the two of them, letting them know she wasn't going to deny anything. "You see, Detective, Xaver and I know a lot about this case. None of which we will tell you. But we also don't know all of it."

"I'll tell you what I know," David said, eyes on the bodyguards. "I know you are involved in the killing of the girl in Westminster Abbey, and now have us kidnapped, and will eventually be brought to justice."

"Speaking of Xaver," Jacqueline said, "did you know that someone contacted him and claimed they can prove the Grimm brothers never wrote the fairytales we have now? But they wouldn't tell who they were."

"And?"

"Xaver was asked to plant your luggage with a laptop that secret someone sent."

"Why impersonate Rachel, then?" David asked.

"Ask Anne," Jacqueline said.

"Why should I know that?" Anne said.

"Because you and I know what happened with Rachel. Though I suppose David doesn't know yet," Jacqueline said.

"Anne?" David said gently.

"She isn't going to tell you, David," Jacqueline said. "Let's just say this. The killer succeeded in winning Anne's undivided attention and devotion to this case by doing that."

David surprisingly squeezed her hand for assurance. He wasn't going to pressure her to know about Rachel. Anne's hand was a tad too cold when he did. She also failed to conceal the slight shivers in her lower jaw.

"Xaver and I don't want to catch the killer, Detective. We want the truth about our ancestors' past. Whatever the price." Jacqueline killed her cigarette and clicked her fingers for another pink drink. "Let me tell you what I know is going to happen now."

"Please do," Anne said.

"As per the killer's instructions, you won't be landing in Kassel, Germany. At least not now."

"Go on," Anne said.

"Xaver and I are attending a clandestine but historical event in Kassel. One that you haven't earned the right to attend yet," Jacqueline said. "According to the killer, we're supposed to transport you to wherever the mapestry leads."

"Okay?" Anne said.

"Once you land, I suggest you take care. There are so many parties I know who would want to get their hands on whatever the Singing Bone leads you to. Not to mention those who would kill to stop you from exposing the truth," Jacqueline said. "Then, if you survive, I'm sure we'll meet again."

"I suppose the next mapestry leads to a location on the Fairytale Road?" Anne asked.

"You suppose right, Professor," Jacqueline said. "Now start working before we fly too far from your yet unknown destination."

"I will, but I'll ask you a favor." Anne leaned forward and grabbed Jacqueline's nimble hand between hers.

Jacqueline fidgeted a little, not sure why she allowed Anne to touch her. "What do you have in mind?"

"You and I spent our lives digging into the past to get answers. I respect you having empowered women in your way through the years," Anne said. "I mean you and I, in different circumstances, may have been friends. Fighting for the same cause, Madame Jacqueline."

"Where is this going?" Jacqueline pulled away. "Why are you trying to charm me, Anne?"

"If you know, for the truth's sake, tell me who the girl on the cross was," Anne said. "I promise I won't ask anything else of you."

Jacqueline sighed. "All I know is that she was a dwarf."

David frowned. "She didn't look like a dwarf."

"Not as stunted as most. You may have noticed she was way too light and small," Jacqueline explained. "So-called dwarfism is a spectrum of many conditions. You can be born stunted. Some are taller. Some are even as tall as normal people but would still have disproportioned heads or limbs. It differs, and I'm not an expert."

"So, the girl on the cross was not a prop? Someone chosen for being light and small enough, to help erect the design?" David said.

"She wasn't a prop. God forbid." Jacqueline sounded offended. "She was a human being. A dwarf who was smaller and lighter with a bone disease. One that made her look almost like a skinny teenager. She was a sacrifice. God bless her."

"What did you just say?" Anne couldn't believe her ears.

"I won't say more. Like I said, you haven't earned such knowledge yet." Jacqueline stiffened. Her two female bodyguards approached immediately. "The best I can do is admit I know her name, and who she is. But you will have to figure the rest out on your own."

"You knew her name all along," Anne said.

"I also knew she was going to be sacrificed all along," Jacqueline said. "Do you want me to tell you her name or not? I need to leave you two to solve the mapestry and drop you wherever you need to be right now. Shall I indulge you?"

"Please do," David said.

Jacqueline snapped her fingers to calm the bodyguards down. Standing up to leave, she said, "The girl on the cross's name is Layla Ovitz."

# 33

15:44 (P.M.)

***Somewhere in Europe***

Lily's plane landed minutes ago.

She carried nothing besides her purse. That, and the heavy inheritance of her ancestors upon her shoulders. The voices of pedestrians all around her faded into thin air as she trudged on through the snowy ground. She walked for what seemed like ages before entering an old house to her left.

Using her Singing Bone, she opened the house's wooden door. A three-story building, located on a narrow cobblestone street with a flickering single overhead lamp. Hardly anyone walked by as she latched the pentagram cap into the door's clockwork until it gave in.

Inside, she picked up a torch hung on the wall to her left. It lit her way through the dusty darkness. The house was without electricity so no one would come snoop around, and the vaulted ceiling leaked. It reminded her of the underground tunnel in London where she sacrificed the girl on the cross. Now the smell of Vecchia Melo, the apple wine, attacked her nostrils everywhere.

She climbed a spiral staircase. Slow and careful. The old steps creaked, even underneath her light weight. The fragility was designed on purpose, so those who came after the Sisterhood would collapse before they could find them, as they were always of normal size.

Reaching the door on the third floor, she stopped before it. She took a deep breath and then played a melody on her flute. Beethoven's Fifth Symphony rang out, using the notes GGGE.

The door was big enough to let in dwarves and children only. She entered the room.

"Lucia!" Lily smiled with tears in her eyes. She beckoned the girl standing by the balcony overlooking the holy landmark outside.

Lucia Ovitz took Lily in her arms. She was just as short and carried a bottle of apple wine. "I missed you, Lily."

"Me too, Lucia. I miss Grandmother more."

"We all do," Lucia said, pointing at the balcony overlooking the city. "I hope you had a nice flight. Shall we?"

Lily followed Lucia to where the curtains fluttered in the breeze from outside. They saw the city's most prominent landmark from where they stood. A beautiful ancient place. Now civilized in lies.

The two girls stood over the wooden chairs and looked at the long, snowy facade before the religious landmark. Christmas meant more here than anywhere else in the world. It resembled religious sanctuary more than celebrated holidays of food and gifts in other places.

"Soon." Lucia squeezed Lily's hand.

Lily's heart raced. She touched her flute for assurance. Then recited her recurring prayer about the shepherd, the bones, and the devil's crone.

"The Queen herself called me," Lily said.

"I heard," Lucia said with wide eyes. "What does she sound like?"

"Familiar, I have to say."

"You think she is someone we know?"

"I think so, but I'm not sure," Lily said. "Her voice felt warm. She reminded me of Lady Ovitz."

"She called me, too, to inform me about your arrival," Lucia said. "She wasn't as nice to me, though. I envy you, Lily. In a good way, of course. You're almost there. Soon you will be officially anointed as a True Sister."

"I feel blessed. But also scared. It's not as easy as I thought."

"Do you want to talk about it?" Lucia said, tears forming behind her eyes. "I mean do you want to talk about her?"

"Why don't you address her by her name?" Lily said. "Layla was your sister as much as she was mine."

"I think the Girl on the Cross is a more honorable description of her, now that she is gone," Lucia said.

Lily shook her head, fighting the tears.

"You didn't kill her, you know," Lucia said. "You gave her purpose. You gave us hope. And the world, the truth."

Lily's body shuddered from neck to toe.

"Don't blame yourself, Lily." Lucia hugged her tightly and ran her fingers through her ginger hair.

"I couldn't do it," Lily sobbed in her sister's arms. "I couldn't kill Layla. I couldn't make her drink the poison and I attempted to stop her and give up on the Sisterhood altogether."

"Then how did she die?"

"Layla took the apple wine and poisoned herself, slowly dying for seven days in the tunnels, so she can fulfill my destiny."

# 34

## *Jacqueline de Rais's Private Jet*

David and Anne were instructed not to converse with Xaver or Jacqueline anymore, not until they solved the next puzzle and figured out their next destination.

Both had given up on logical reasoning and attempts of defiance at this point. David could tell Anne would stop at nothing until she found answers for her lifelong quest—including how Rachel was tied to it. He had no choice but to get to the crux of why the girl on the cross was murdered and then lock up those lunatics involved, including Bloody Mary.

The fact that a member of the Ovitz family was sacrificed scared them so much that he couldn't deny the tug he felt in his heart.

Now he and Anne needed to figure out the password for the curious picture of the seven dwarves in WWII, or they would miss landing in the right location in the mapestry.

"As much as I'm angry and baffled," David said to Anne, "I

think that there is no point in discussing the death of the girl on the cross at the moment."

"You mean Layla Ovitz," Anne said. "She has a name, David."

"You're right, we can't call her the girl on the cross anymore or we would be committing the crime of fairytales again," he said. "Gaslighting actual crimes by generalizing their victims into stereotypical princesses and queens."

"We're only an hour away from Kassel," Anne said. "Listen." She pointed at the screen showing their location inside the jet. "We're already past the city of Bremen where the Fairytale Road begins from north to south. We need the password."

David had already opened the laptop and was counting on Anne to conjure her magic.

Anne looked at the black-and-white photo of the Auschwitz concentration camp. Seven short members of the Ovitz family, including the vibrant Lady Ovitz, stood holding their musical instruments before a fence with Hitler's "death doctor" Joseph Mengele standing amongst them.

In the middle of the picture, the laptop's cursor flickered inside a rectangular white box, awaiting the next password.

"I see them holding musical instruments," David said. "A clue?"

"None of the instruments are flutes," Anne said. "A harp, percussions, and a ukulele, but no wind instruments. I don't even know what the puzzle is about, so I don't know where to start."

"How about you think out loud. Maybe I can catch something interesting," David said. "We are our worst critics when we're inside our heads."

"You sound like my psychologist," Anne said. "But okay. I will."

David fought the urge to ask her about her psychologist. On the outside, she didn't look like someone who needed one. Then again, everybody wore their own mask to face the world. What if she had looked darkness in the eyes like him?

"All right." Anne clapped her hands. "I'm looking at the Ovitz family in a black-and-white picture in 1945."

"Uh-huh."

"They made a living with their Lilliput act, which was more like a traveling carnival. All over Romania, they made children smile, watching dwarves make fun of themselves," Anne continued. "The seven dwarves were so beloved that the few taller members, whom they jokingly called 'Vecchia Melo,' had to help and work backstage."

"Vecchia Melo?"

"Bad apples in some old Italian dialect. Maybe poisoned apples, I'm not sure," Anne said. "The dwarves rather envied their taller sister and brother with them being normal."

"Noted."

"Then Hitler invaded Romania," Anne said. "Arrested them because they were Jews and sent them to a concentration camp. Hitler was generally fascinated with fairytales, and thus dwarves."

"Joseph Mengele was known to have great interest in epigenetics," David said. "Did he experiment on them, maybe?"

"That was my assumption," Anne said. "You could say it was my main reason that I didn't think the Ovitz family would help me in my research. I thought their being seven dwarves was a mere coincidence."

"I still can't buy it that Hitler loved fairytales," David said. "I know fairytales weren't originally meant for children but he couldn't have possibly known that. How could a man like that have such interest in a children's book?"

"You have no idea," Anne said. "The Nazis, being the kings of propaganda, and occult fanatics, spent hefty money on films about fairytales."

"Nazi fairytales?" David raised his glass. He was about to order another drink, but Anne stopped him, so he put it down. He reminded himself that this was how it always started. An exciting conversation over endless amounts of alcohol, ending in someone's bed in a seedy neighborhood, or on the streets, sleeping next to the homeless like Keith Richards.

"Look." She pulled out her phone and loaded up a video before showing it to him. A black-and-white propaganda movie about Little Red Riding Hood.

David watched with utter disbelief. A man resembling Hitler

himself was part of the movie. In fact, he appeared in the end and entered the house. He was the one who saved Little Red Riding Hood from the wolf. All while wearing his SS uniform.

"I can't believe this was actually filmed," David said. "Are there more movies like this?"

"A dozen. If you search the internet archives, you'll find many. This copy, I practically stole from the German archives in Bremen where Hitler burned books in the past. It's long story. The short of it is that there are even bestselling books about this subject."

"Why weren't they popular?"

"I never understood why. Maybe he lost the war before he had a chance to. Now I wonder if he discovered something about the fairytales and decided to keep quiet about it," Anne said.

David pulled out his own phone. He had an idea.

"What's this?" David asked as he pointed at it.

"It's the same photo of the seven dwarves," Anne said. "Like on this desktop. What are you thinking?"

"I'm thinking why make the puzzle a black-and-white picture of the Ovitz family that is freely available online?"

"There are tons of stories and images of the Ovitz family on the internet," Anne said. "It's just that they're never connected to the Brothers Grimm fairytales."

"That's not what I'm asking." David zoomed in. "What I'm saying is, that part of the image is hidden behind the password box on the laptop."

"Oh," Anne grabbed the phone. "let me see."

"The password box in the middle of the laptop hides Lady Ovitz's hands by her sides. She was making an inverted V sign with her hands. Is that a clue?" David said.

Anne gasped, so much so that Jacqueline and Xaver lazily craned their heads back at them.

"Are you two birdies all right?" Jacqueline said.

"We were pulling a prank on you. See if you'd look," David said without looking at her. "Sorry for interrupting your pistachio munching, Professor Goldfinger."

"It's a victory sign that Lady Ovitz shows in the picture," Anne whispered to David as Jacqueline looked away. "She probably inverted it because she was afraid of Joseph Mengele."

"So, this is the puzzle we're looking for?" David whispered back.

"It is," Anne said. "You see, the V for victory was invented in World War Two."

"Interesting. I never knew it had an origin story."

"Everything has an origin story, David," Anne said. "Anyway, the Belgians first created it as defiance to the Nazis' occupation; a gesture for the upcoming revolution against Hitler."

"So, Lady Ovitz risked flashing it in the picture to announce her beliefs?"

"She probably wanted to make a point that she didn't approve of Nazis, in case smiling in a photograph with Joseph Mengele insinuated an opposite impression," Anne said. "Had you not discovered it was hidden behind the password box on the laptop, we may not have given it much attention."

"It was intentional because the password box should've made us curious about the missing part behind it," David said. "These puzzles are a bit too random sometimes, though. What if we hadn't discovered it?"

"Don't ask me. I'm just the nerdy folklorist who didn't ask for any of this." Anne opened the laptop. "Let's type in the password."

"You've already figured it out from the victory sign?"

"Oh, sorry, I forgot to explain the relevance," Anne said. "The Allies used the V sign to contact each other during the war. The only problem was that they had to translate it to Morse Code, which was the common way of communicating back then."

"And?"

"Morse Code is generated by tapping a device in peculiar beats, which are called 'dots' and 'dashes.' I'm sure you've seen it being used in some old war movie," Anne said. "In order to write the V for victory, they tapped *dot dot dot dash*."

"So?"

"At some point they discovered that the *dot dot dot dash*, if translated to numbers, equals the letters GGGE."

"A musical code." David smiled, impressed with his newly acquired skills.

"Exactly," Anne said. "When Winston Churchill found this out, he urged the allies to use that musical code instead of Morse Code everywhere. They used it in the field, on the bus, and even on the phone to recognize each other."

"Wasn't that risky?" David said. "What if the Nazis realized the melody and caught them?"

"That was the genius part, because how could the Nazis ever suspect that Beethoven's Fifth Symphony was a code for allies?" Anne smirked. She felt so proud of herself.

"GGGE." David pulled out the Singing Bone and stared at it, then waved his hands in the air like a mad orchestra conductor. "Ta, ta, ta, ta." He whispered the famous first four notes of one of history's most popular musical intros. Beethoven's Fifth.

"You're going to expose us, aren't you?" Anne glared with her eyes darting toward Xaver and Jacqueline.

She then typed GGGE in the password box and pressed enter. The laptop chimed and opened to the next message.

"Another damn picture." David pressed his lips together. "I can't play this game anymore."

He was looking at a picture of some ancient European castle near a river, except that this one seemed like it had been taken recently with a regular phone camera.

"Don't worry, it's not a puzzle. I know where on the Fairytale Road we should go next." Anne smiled broadly and craned her neck toward Jacqueline de Rais. "We need to land near Castle Everstein in Polle, Madame."

"The Cinderella castle," Jacqueline chirped. She raised her phone to show them their own photos on the news. "It's about time because you two have a price on your heads already."

# 35

16:00 (P.M.)

## 4 P.M. Programme,
## Early Evening News, BBC Radio Four

*Representing a newly formed special branch in the Protection Command, Thomas Jonathan Gray declared the following statement a few minutes ago:*

"As of this morning, a terrible crime has occurred inside Westminster Abbey. An identified teenage girl has been murdered and hung on a wooden cross right in front of the burial vault in Lady Chapel's hall.

"American professor Anne Anderson is the Metropolitan Police's main suspect. Not only has she been recorded pointing a gun at our police officer before escaping with conspiratorial detective David Tale, but Anne has also poisoned renowned museum curator Jonathan Gray this morning. Video footage of her being the last person leaving his office will be provided as well right after the announcement.

"At the moment, we don't have a motive or clear grasp of why these murders have been committed. We only know of the deceased girl's name:

*Layla Ovitz. She was a freshman at Queen Mary's University, studying Oral History.*

*"It is important to note Detective David Tale's history of substance and alcohol abuse, as well as his violent interrogations, have put his fellow officers in great danger in the past. Superintendent Harriet Wilde has been relieved of her position for covering up for him. She will also be interrogated about the current murders. It's still unclear why David Tale escaped with the American professor at this time.*

*"As for Anne Anderson, a history of a troubled childhood with an alcoholic father is to be noted. Her career is riddled with copyright allegations and stealing documentation that belonged to other institutes before claiming it was hers.*

*"Lastly, Professor Anne Anderson also has an ongoing history of mental illness. We're contacting her former psychologist for further information."*

*Thomas Gray also mentioned the importance to inform the public of how dangerous both suspects are. They're a clear threat to national security, and evidence suggests they're not working alone. It is suspected they could be members—or leaders—of a systemic cult, trying to erase our well-known and cherished history from the popular culture.*

*When Thomas Gray was asked by a reporter about rumors of Anne Anderson and David Tale having fled the country already, he refused to reply. He assured the public that the British Metropolitan Police force promises to catch them—dead or alive.*

# 36

### *Polle, the Fairytale Road, Germany*

The folklorist and the detective watched the private jet land in an abandoned runway in the middle of the snow-covered forest near Polle. Anne was enamored by the beauty of the scene from above but didn't want to gush about it.

She had been here too many times, traveling for hours through these roads, learning about each city's traditions and forgotten past. She slept in these half-timber motels that looked like houses cut from chunks of candy from the Hansel and Gretel story. She drank the local beers and watched the girls dancing in the summer. She basically fell in love with these beautiful small towns no one knew anything about.

Whoever mapped her journey to arrive here had played on her lifelong love for this place, and she couldn't help but question the real motives for why she was chosen to take the journey.

"There shouldn't be an airport here," David said to Jacqueline, who had returned to join them after Anne told her about their next stop. "In fact, looking at Google maps, there are no airports in Polle in the first place."

"You've got to stop counting on Google telling you the truth, Detective," Jacqueline said, sharing with them the beautiful view of the Weser River from above. "Can't you enjoy the beauty of this place for a moment?"

"Where are you taking us?" David didn't fall for her attempted charm. "What is this abandoned runway in the middle of the forest?"

"An old Nazi emergency plan. Satisfied?" Jacqueline said. "You wouldn't find it on the map, of course, because you shouldn't know about it. But it will lead you to your desired destination. Trust me."

"That doesn't make sense," David said. "Google would have scanned it."

Jacqueline sighed with exasperation and looked at Anne. "Tell him to grow up and understand that those who hold the narrative can do whatever they want with it."

"It's like when Tom John told us about the CCTV cameras in London, David," Anne said. "The fact that you didn't see it on a virtual map doesn't mean it doesn't exist. I mean look at the quest we're on. Who would believe us if we told them?"

Still suspicious, David said nothing, trying to think of a nonexistent counterargument. Anne sympathized. He was a strong man and all, but his need for accurately and plausible scientific explanation was his weakest point. The Fairytale Road didn't abide by such rules.

"How far is this runway from the Everstein Castle in Polle?" Anne asked Jacqueline.

"A ten-minute walk into the forest," Jacqueline said. "Don't worry, it's a man-made road. It's like Hitler's Donkey Trail in the Spessart Forest where the real Snow White once lived—and was brutally murdered. You won't miss it."

Anne nodded. She knew David wished to know more about the Spessart Forest in southern Germany, and about the real Snow White, Margarette, but she hadn't the luxury of time to go into all that now.

"Follow the trail, and you will find yourself near the castle," Jacqueline said. "I'm sure you know your way from there."

"I do," Anne said. "But I'm surprised you do, too."

"I love the Fairytale Road," Jacqueline said. "Always have. In fact, I've sponsored a petition against Disney for stealing their designs from it."

"Stealing?" David said.

"Take a look at this, Detective." Jacqueline handed him her phone. It showed a picture of a castle with enormous turrets in the middle of the German forest. It looked impressive, even to David. In fact, he thought it was photoshopped at first. Until he zoomed in. "Familiar?"

"Definitely," David said. "Even for a guy like me who doesn't like Disneyland."

"The photo is of the Neuschwanstein Castle," Jacqueline said. "A nineteenth century, intricately designed masterpiece in the reign of King Ludwig the Second. It was built on a rugged hill above the village of Hohenschwangau near Füssen in southwest Bavaria. At some point it was used as the official retreat for Germany's utmost respected composer Wilhelm Richard Wagner."

"Then why does it look like a copy of Cinderella's Castle in Disneyland?" David's question was rhetorical.

"It's Disney's Cinderella that looks like it, David," Anne said "Walt Disney claimed the German castle inspired him. Instead, he stole the design to a T."

"That and the endless fine designs of timber houses, art, and other smaller castles on the Fairytale Road," Jacqueline added. It sounded as if she and Anne had become friends suddenly. "You know what I dislike about Germans the most? That they never sold or presented the Fairytale Road the way it should have been. They could've made fortunes."

"Not to mention the legacy and tradition of fairytales that was blatantly Americanized," Anne said. "So much so that young people think all these stories are all American in origin."

"How come the Americans got away with it? Is it legal?"

"There is a copyright law that states that all properties before the 1920s are in the public domain," Anne explained. "Meaning it's too old to track its owner and is considered without one. They reason that creations made before actual legal rules were instilled in societies all over the world were open for reuse without permission for anyone."

"The ironic things are that if you reused any of Disney's recent fairytale movies, you will be sued." Jacqueline shook her in disdain. "Because Disney copyrighted the stolen versions after 1920 and made them their own. Not to mention that they messed up the stories by turning them into damsel in distress, sappy, and downright laughable adventures."

"I guess I know why I despise fairytales now," David said. "I wonder if I'd have been interested in them had they stayed dark, authentic, and downright brutal."

"Here is some advice to keep in mind, David," Jacqueline said, addressing him by name for the first time. "In case we never meet again."

"People are usually too scared to give me advice," David said as the sign to buckle up flashed on top. "So I appreciate it."

Jacqueline buckled her seatbelt and said, "History, tradition, and whatever you call 'truth' are made by those who printed it, or filmed it, or claimed it first. Not by those who actually owned it."

🍎

Once the plane landed, Jacqueline wished them both luck and handed Anne some cash. She said that if they survived the next few hours on their own, she had a feeling they would meet again.

The female guards escorted Anne and David out of the plane and showed them the road. The sun was about to set soon, and as beautiful as the snow-covered forest appeared to be, it would soon be veiled by darkness.

David led the way and Anne followed.

Minutes later, they heard the small private jet take off.

"So, the mapestry is leading us to this castle in Polle," David said. "Then what?"

"I have no idea," Anne said. "There are no more passwords needed in the laptop, so the castle image itself is our only clue."

"Does this image of the Everstein Castle in Polle present any significance to you?"

"Of course it does. I didn't have time to explain it before, but Polle is where Cinderella's story originated."

Anne stepped ahead and sped up. Reaching the end of the road was going to take some time. Yet, she could already see the Everstein Castle peeking above from the between the scattered canopy of trees.

"Not quite the castle like Neuschwanstein," David commented. "I was expecting something as epic."

"The Neuschwanstein is in the South," Anne said. "Bavaria is, and has always been, rich. Polle isn't as wealthy. Besides, these are the *remains* of the Everstein Castle. It was almost destroyed in the Thirty Years' War."

"Thirty Years' War?"

"The most destructive war in European history. Lasting from 1618 and 1648," Anne said, parting a bush with her bare hands. "It started as a battle among the Catholic and Protestant states that formed the Holy Roman Empire."

"Wait," David said, and stopped. "Did you just say Catholic and Protestant? A three-decade war?"

"Yes," Anne said. "What caught you off guard?"

"I was thinking about Bloody Mary's theory. The one about the girl on the cross staring at the burial vault of Mary Tudor the First," David said. "Could it be that she was hinting at something about Polle?"

"She seemed adamant on talking about it with me when I first arrived at the abbey, but I don't know."

"She lectured me about it before you arrived, too," David said. "In fact, that was my first impression of the crime scene."

"That it had to do with Mary Tudor having burned so many men and women on the stake for being Protestants?" Anne considered. "I'm not going to lie to you. Thinking of the image of the girl on the cross does make it a possible connection."

"The real puzzle is, what does it have to do with Lady Ovitz and fairytales?"

"That's why the connection is also farfetched," Anne said. "The Ovitz family were Jewish. They guarded a book that was written by devoted Christians, and the girl on the cross was placed in front of Mary Tudor's tomb. Hmm."

"And here we are." David pointed at the castle. "Following the breadcrumbs to a place destroyed by that war."

"Well, Mary Tudor died 1558. This war started around 1618, so I guess this ends our argument," Anne said. "But look at you, using the phrase 'following the breadcrumbs.'" Anne smiled. "You're slowly tuning into your childhood again, David. Good for you."

Anne watched David suppress a grin. It was as if she had touched something beautiful about his dark childhood, but he wouldn't admit it.

"Oh, I forgot," Anne said. "You don't know how to smile."

She continued to lead the walk then.

"Why did you say that to me?" David followed her eagerly.

"Say what?"

"Why did you claim I can't smile?" He sounded offended for the first time since she met him. "I can smile."

"No, you can't, David. I mean maybe you want to, but you look as if someone would chop off your head if you did," she said, hurrying up before dark arrived. "You twitch. There is a difference. Why do you ask? Did I strike a chord?"

"Nah."

She knew he was lying.

He changed the subject again when they stood at the threshold of Polle's main road, now seeing the castle in full. "So that's the castle where Cinderella attended the prince's ball?"

"Hermann Everstein the Third was his name, as far as I know," Anne said. "He wasn't a prince. He was a count."

The small town looked family friendly and far from dangerous. "What was Cinderella's name, then?"

"I'll tell you all about it, but later," Anne said. "Because I figured out what we're supposed to look for to find our next clue."

# 37

16:51(P.M.)

## *Heathrow Airport, London*

Tom John waited impatiently to get on the plane to Germany. He sat amidst the crowd, trying to blend in like any other passenger. Her Majesty's office had instructed him to keep Anne and David's new location from the public. He had done enough damage by broadcasting about the girl on the cross in the abbey. Social media was on fire already, speculating and theorizing about it.

He felt he did the right thing, though. The best he could do to save his father. Tapping his foot, he couldn't fathom who this Bloody Mary was, or why she played that game of hers.

It also puzzled him why she had insisted he wait outside the office while she cured his father. He assumed she didn't want him to know how she did it, but what followed was stranger than fiction.

He tried the surveillance cameras while she was inside, but Mary had them covered with something. Eavesdropping, Tom thought he heard her play a flute inside. Was she resurrecting his father with music?

Breaking in was out of the question, as he couldn't risk his father's mortality.

A few minutes later, when she allowed him entry, Jonathan Gray sat grinning on the couch. He looked drunk.

"It won't last long," Bloody Mary said. "The antidote does have a few side effects. He won't be able to talk for a few minutes."

Jonathan Gray confirmed he felt better by nodding at his son.

"He won't die?" Tom asked Mary.

"From greed, maybe, but not from the poison," Bloody Mary said.

"How do you know so much about this poison?"

"As if I'm going to tell you," she said. "Your father might also remember things he thought he didn't know about in the past, by the way."

"What is that supposed to mean?" Tom said.

"You'll know when it happens. I wouldn't worry about it now," she said. "When will they air your announcement on the BBC?"

"Soon, don't worry. Bureaucracy is still a thing."

"Thank for keeping your word, Tommy boy."

"Honor among thieves." He tried his best to match her cunning. She made him feel like he was hanging out with the cool kids, which had never happened when he was a child, and had to find a way to impress them. It was odd to feel that way, and odder still that he admired her resilience. Her freedom to do whatever the hell she wanted. That she feared no consequences. "Why didn't you send footage of the girl on the cross to the BBC earlier, instead of making me do it?"

"You don't get it, do you?" she said. "Ordinary citizens like me have no say in things. No one listens to us. Had I sent such footage, no one would have announced it, at least not before asking permission from the above."

"But you sent them Anne's footage."

"Because she attacked an officer of law," she scoffed. "That's the kind of footage the BBC will show the world instantly. Honorable police officers being attacked, that's news. Sending a grim and morbid image of a girl on the cross wouldn't have worked for me. It had to be confirmed by an authority like you."

"So, you've toyed with me. I've never had anyone treat me this way."

"Time to grow." She touched his chin with her thumb. It was as if he were under her spell. "I hit you too hard in the abbey," she said as she brushed at the swollen side of his neck.

"Is that an apology?" He grimaced.

"Far from it," she said. "It's a note to self for the future, so I go easier on people I want to knock down but not kill. Now that your father is alive, ask me."

"Ask you what?"

"That which is eating at you right now."

He hated that she read his mind. "Where are Anne and David?"

"Given that Anne is a brilliant folklorist and followed the mapestry, they should be on the Fairytale Road in Germany by now."

"Where exactly?"

"A small town in the north called Polle," Mary said. "Maybe call your superiors. Ask them to connect you with the German police, since you won't have any jurisdiction there. As for me, I'm gone—for now." She walked to the back door in the library then looked back at him. "Order your men not to come near me, or Jonathan won't get his second antidote."

"Second antidote?"

"The one I performed on him saved his life," she said. "Unless I send you the second dose, he will forever suffer from dementia."

Tom stood stiffened and angry. "Who. Are. You?"

"You ever played chess?"

He nodded, playing along.

"In terms of a chess game, you're a pawn, my friend," she said.

"And you? The queen?"

"Funny you said that, but nah. I'm the chess master. I created the game in the first place." She blew him a kiss.

Now, as the passengers were asked to get on the plane, Tom

received a message from his contact in Germany, informing him that an Inspector Martin Wolf was going to hunt Anne and David down until he arrived.

A few strides behind Tom, The Advocate sat hunched over his cane, waiting to get on the same plane. In his boredom, he was trying to entice a child to leave his mother's hand and come take a bite from one of his poisoned apples.

# 38

---

17:14 (P.M.)

## *Polle, the Fairytale Road, Germany*

David followed Anne into the picturesque small town of Polle. Not since his childhood had someone acted this youthful around him. She was naively happy and recklessly explorative as they made their way into the city. She made him tap into a long-lost feeling, back when everything was fresh and new, and the sky was the limit.

He chuckled as she guided him toward the cobblestone streets, covered with thick layers of snow and weaving in between half-timbered houses that looked so innocent it put Disney to shame. The sun was about to kiss the day goodbye, and the orange street lamps began to flicker all around, promising a night of fun and adventure. The orange flare contrasted with the white blanket of snow covering the street in a way that made him consider relaxing for a moment.

Pedestrians around them were few and far between. The city's demographic was certainly of the old. Only a few younger teens showed up here and there. The children were many, though. They gripped their grandparents' hands as they strolled together, wearing thick furry caps, double-padded jackets, and colorful unlaced shoes.

The rattle and chatter that came from the shops was the quiet type. No loudmouths and or beer drinking extravaganza here. This was a place that wasn't supposed to exist anymore in modern life. Quiet and magical, where a fairytale or a Christmas movie would take place. Jacqueline was right about despising the Germans for not monetizing the Fairytale Road. Then again, he wondered if this place would've still exuded its magic had it been commercialized.

"Come on, David." Anne pulled his hand. "Let's sit on that bank."

She guided him to a series of benches that overlooked an open space of grass, now covered in thick snow. David couldn't help but notice how the snow in this city lit its surroundings. As the sun was about to set, it was as much a source of light as the moon above and the street lamps that looked like lanterns.

"What do you think?" Anne still held his hand, sitting on the bank and facing the wide space before the castle.

"I think the castle looks like the photo on the laptop from here," he said, not sure if he was supposed to keep holding her hand. He tried his best not to press back just in case she didn't appreciate it.

"I'm not talking about the castle." She sighed, closing her eyes for a second. "Can you smell the air? Can you feel the serenity and peace?"

David's eyes moved right and left. He was trying to figure out what was going on. Did she just forget that they were being chased?

It's not like he didn't appreciate her, or this precious moment in time. He just wondered if enjoying themselves was a good idea right now. In the back of his mind, he wanted to ask her about the fact that she saw a psychologist. Was it wise to insist to know of her past?

After all, he was a pessimistic soul himself. He had no right to ask her or judge her. Or anyone else for that matter. The taste of that martini on his lips from the plane made him want to drink more. In fact, that was what he would have done had Anne not been with him now.

"But you're right." Anne opened her eyes, looking serious now. She pulled her hand away and said, "I thought we'd sit on this particular bank because whoever took the photo sat in this exact spot. You can tell from the imposed angle."

David pulled out the laptop to confirm her assumption. "Are we looking at the exact position the killer took the photo from now?"

"About as close as we can be, I think," Anne said. "He probably knelt down a few feet behind the bank to take it. It's a little off angle, as if he wanted to glorify the castle, make it look imposing."

"Like when they film a vampire's castle in movies, I get it."

"He wants us to see something about the castle from here."

"I see people who sit and watch the castle where the Cinderella story happened, that's all," David said, surpassing the need to reach for her hand again.

"Normally, locals would climb up the fort of the castle. Up there by the ruins," she pointed. "Standing on top of that tower to the right, you can see the whole city of Polle and the Weser River."

David squinted. Though old and archaic, the castle was bright with yellow illuminance in every direction. It added to its romantic appeal. The locals did a good job in turning the ruins of war into something special. He noticed that there weren't many tourists. Everyone sounded and looked local. German farmers and families, content and quietly celebrating the days before Christmas. They liked keeping to themselves.

"Part of the Weser River runs tangent to the Fairytale Road from north to south," Anne said. "Until this city where it detours away at a place called the Weser Bend."

"Where are we on the Fairytale Road exactly?"

"One-third from the North, you could say," she said, showing him the map on her phone.

"So, it starts from Bremen, then it runs toward Hamelin?" He pointed at the map.

"Yes, the city of your favorite tale about the rats and the Pied Piper," she said. "I guess it has nothing to do with our mapestry because we passed it already."

"Then here is Polle," he said. "About one-third, like you said. We're also so close to Kassel in the middle. What about this city between Polle and Kassel?" David pointed to it.

"That's Trendelburg," she said, pointing to her left at the Weser River. "It's very close from here. It can be accessed by a ferry from the river."

"There are ferries here?" He craned his neck to look to the left. The river was close by, down a snowy slope, and a very short walking distance. But with less light and more privacy at the shore. The ferry dock was busier with a spacious tangle of woods underneath.

"There is also a cycling road parallel to it," Anne said. "It's called the River Weser Cycling Road. Very famous around here."

David's eyes couldn't stop mapping his surroundings. He was thinking about which route he would take in case Tom John's men arrived. The people here weren't big on vehicles, and he wasn't going to steal someone's car with their family and kids around. He had a soft spot for families, and the river seemed like the best escape route if need be.

"Did you know that Trendelburg is where Rapunzel's story originated?" Anne said.

"Tell me about it," he said, not paying attention. He understood she was trying to get him to relax, and knowing more about the nearest city was good information. Just in case it made for a proper place to spend the night.

"It has the Trendelburg Castle, the actual castle where Rapunzel was locked up," Anne said.

"Even the girl with long hair was real, huh?"

"I told you, they all are."

"You realize that Tom John is coming for us, right?" he asked.

"I know." Her nod trailed off as she saw something at the bottom of laptop photo. "You see that?"

David pulled the laptop close enough to look again. "Someone wrote something small with black ink at the bottom. A signature?"

"It's too long for a signature." She pulled the laptop from him.

"How can we zoom in on a wallpaper image?" he said.

Anne pulled out her phone and took a photo of the screen, then zoomed in. "It's not a signature. It's a quote. Finally, the next puzzle."

David read it with her:

> *We shall not cease from exploration.*
> *And the end of all our exploring,*
> *will be to arrive where we started,*
> *and know the place for the first time.*

# 39

## Polle, Fairytale Road, Germany

"It's from a poem by T.S. Eliot," Anne said. She began looking around her, as if expecting to see the killer nearby. "He was an American-English poet."

"I thought the killer only referenced fairytales."

"T.S. Eliot researched fairytales, too. He also supported the Franz Xaver idea, that the Grimm brothers neither collected nor wrote fairytales," Anne said, looking back at David. "He wrote a poem reimagining one of the Brothers Grimm's most important tales."

"The Singing Bone?"

"Not exactly. He wrote a poem about the Juniper Tree story." Anne googled the poem and showed it to David. "Read the first sentence and you'll get the connection."

David read the first line and didn't need to read further. It said:

**_Under a juniper-tree the bones sang..._**

"It's nevertheless about the concept of the Singing Bone," David said. "What is a juniper tree?"

"It's an evergreen. A coniferous plant with scaly leaves—but that's beside the point," Anne said. "It's the rest of the tale that matters."

"Let me guess," David said. "A tale about someone who was unjustly buried, and then their bones sang the killer's name."

"You got that right."

"So, the Singing Bone is a running theme in fairytales," David said.

"True."

"T.S. Eliot was like you and Xaver, looking for answers in a centuries-old book," David said. "But why would the killer send you a quote of his to solve the next puzzle?"

"I feel it's more like a welcome note," Anne said. "I'm the one who 'never ceased exploration.' And in the end of my exploring, I've returned to the place 'for the first time.'" Anne's eyes took in her surroundings. "The Fairytale Road."

"So, he is implying that this time, you will find what you are looking for," David said. "Experiencing as if it were for the first time. I must agree with Tom John. This killer has a poetic sick mind."

Anne kept looking around, almost frantically, searching for the killer. David could tell she felt violated, as if someone knowing so much about her scared her.

"You think he's watching us?" Anne craned her neck up at the tower in the Everstein Castle.

"Let's not overthink it," David said. "And actually solve the puzzle."

"That's what we're doing, David," she said. "Why do you think I sat here?"

"To imitate the position of who took the photo of the castle, I know. But where is this leading?"

"To this." She pointed at a small crowd of women gathered

upon the snowy grass right in front of the castle. They looked like performers, preparing for a stage play.

"What am I looking at exactly?" David said.

"It's a recreation of the original Cinderella story. The locals like to watch it every now and then," Anne explained. "A show they've been performing in Polle since 1995. The locals participate in it. A handsome man plays the prince. A girl chosen by the crowd plays Cinderella. Then they circle the castle as a tour guide shows them the exact steps Cinderella took to return home before midnight."

"Okay?" David wasn't sure where this was going.

"Every third Sunday of the year, from May to September, the play takes place at two fifteen p.m.," Anne said.

"We're in December, and it's almost six in the evening," David said. "So this play shouldn't be happening, right?"

"Here is our next clue of the mapestry," Anne said. "We sat where the killer sat and saw what he wanted us to see."

"No wonder the mapestry is made for you," David said. "How was anyone else supposed to—"

"Easy with the flattery," she said. She leaned forward to wave to one of the performers.

"What are you doing? We don't need the attention," David said.

"Easy, David," Anne said. She was smiling at the girl in a blue Cinderella costume. "She contacted me first."

"How so?"

"She made an inverted V sign from far away and winked at me."

David watched the teenage dwarf advance and stand before Anne.

"I don't like your costume," she said playfully to Anne. She spoke in English but her accent sounded East European.

"May I ask why?" Anne said gently.

"Too businesslike," the girl said. "You should have dressed in a Cinderella outfit."

"I suppose I should've." Anne wiggled her nose. "I'm Anne, by the way."

"And he is David," the girl said.

David tried his best not to give in to his twitching face.

Instead of asking the girl how she knew their names, Anne leaned forward and broadened her smile. "And you are?"

The dwarf girl looked left and right, acting overly theatrical, as if joking, and whispered, "They call me Helena Weitz around here, but that's not my real name."

"I'd prefer to call people by their real names, though," Anne said.

"My name is Lisbeth."

"Beautiful name, Lisbeth."

The girl giggled and said, "Lisbeth Ovitz."

# 40

## *Polle, Fairytale Road, Germany*

Anne let Lisbeth guide her across the snowy grass. They walked toward the performers, who had finished preparing for the upcoming show. She was aware of David silently trudging along next to her, ready for foul play.

"Tell him to relax," Lisbeth told Anne. "I'm here to help you solve the mapestry."

"Wouldn't it be easier if you tell us about who killed Layla Ovitz?"

"Now it's you who needs to relax," Lisbeth said, sauntering as her dress caught snow. "This isn't about my sister Layla. This is about the Singing Bone."

"I have it, if you want it," Anne offered.

"You have my sister's bones, one of many Singing Bones. Not the one that really matters," Lisbeth said. "Keep it though. It will come in handy later."

"If you're really an Ovitz family member," David said, "why aren't you upset your sister was killed?"

Lisbeth stopped. She turned and stared with moist eyes at him. "My sister was sacrificed, not killed. And she chose to be."

"She what?" Anne said.

"Stop asking questions and smile. Not all of the performers know who I am, or who you are." Lisbeth's face suddenly changed to one filled with glee.

Anne and David watched her wave at her fellow performers. "I found two volunteers for today's performance."

The performers, some dwarves and some not, cheered with open hands at Anne and David.

A few girls ran up to Anne, excited and speaking to her in German. "You look like a Cinderella!"

Anne gave in, not sure how to respond.

"We must get you a blue Cinderella dress. Something fluffy and medieval," a girl told her. "You're German, right?"

"Not really," Anne said in English. "But my mother was."

"Your mother was. Is she dead?"

"I'm not sure," Anne said. "She left when I was a child."

"Poor Cinderella." The girls hugged Anne, who blushed, looking at David, who tensed. He didn't like any of this sticky-sweet cheese fest at all.

"You make a good prince." One of the dwarf girls pointed a finger at him, almost as if accusing him of something.

David leaned his tall frame back. He truly felt out of place. Anne laughed, unable to control herself.

"No, I don't," David said with pursed lips, trying to avoid the dwarf girl touching him.

"He is a man, girls," Lisbeth said. "So he is not in touch with his inner feminine."

"Inner what?" David said.

"Girls." Lisbeth snapped a finger. "Educate him."

"Prince Charming isn't the prince from Cinderella," one of the girls told David. "He is rich. A descendent from the Everstein family. He was muscular, but not as much as you. Why are you so muscular?"

David looked like he was about run away.

"Can you play that part?" the educating girl inquired.

Anne saw David looking back at her, as if asking her permission.

"Just say yes, David," she laughed. "You can do it."

"Okay," David said to the girls. "I'll play Prince Everstein. Just don't touch me, please."

"Count Everstein." The dwarf girl saw through his insecurity and started poking at him.

"He is handsome," they said to each other. "But stupid."

Anne burst into more laughter, not sure what to do. If Lisbeth said this was their next mapestry, then she had no choice but to wait and see where this was heading.

"Can you speak German?" one of the dwarf girls asked David. "Of course you can't. You don't look German. You're going to ruin the play."

"We can teach him how to say something like, 'you left your shoes, misses,'" Lisbeth offered in the worst imitation possible of a male's gruff voice. "Or even better, let's perform in English this time. We've never done this before."

Anne and David were dragged by the young, giggling, all-female performers into the castle.

They passed underneath a pointed arch, then instead of climbing up, they entered a basement through a spiral concrete staircase. It was lavishly wide in diameter with unusually large landings and looked like they were entering a dungeon, not a basement in a castle.

At the bottom of the stairs, they reached a reasonably lit basement. This was where the performers kept their costumes. Anne noticed the window in the basement overlooked the Weser River. Since the castle was built on a sloping hill, the basement, in comparison to the river, was only ground floor.

She even saw a ramshackle, double-gated door leading outside.

"This is where we dress up and do our makeup before the play," Lisbeth explained. She guided Anne to sit on a chair in front of the makeup mirror. "The girls will do your makeup while I find you a Cinderella outfit your size."

"I don't remember having changed into so many outfits in one day before in my life," Anne said to David, who wasn't listening.

She saw him, like usual, scanning the basement for all sorts of ambushes and threats.

"What's that?" He pointed at what looked like a large vehicle enclosed in a waterproof cover.

"It's a Schwimwagen," Lisbeth said.

David reached to uncover it. "May I?"

Lisbeth didn't mind. "It's an old vehicle that you can drive on both water and ground."

David's face gave away his fascination. He stared at the vehicle after uncovering it.

"You like it?" Lisbeth said.

"It's manufactured by Volkswagen, huh," he said. "It's literally a swimming car. I read about it."

"It was used by the Nazis in World War Two," Lisbeth elaborated.

"A four-wheel drive, amphibious vehicle." David ran his hand over it while circling it as if it were a brand-new Corvette.

"It's the most-produced amphibious car in history, too," Lisbeth said. "Type 128."

Anne saw David was impressed by Lisbeth's knowledge.

"I love old cars," Lisbeth said. "Not necessarily Nazi vehicles."

"Speaking of Nazis," David said, "what brought this precious piece of art here?"

"Nazis used old remnants and castles for secret meetings," Lisbeth said. "They liked to remind themselves of their own history and cherish it. This is the last functioning piece they left behind."

"Does it work to this day?" David almost grinned. Anne couldn't believe he was wasting precious time talking about a car.

"Not always," Lisbeth said. "But mostly. We used it in some local festivals. It's quite a scene driving a 1941 vehicle in water next to the ferries. The children love it."

The conversation was interrupted by a taller performer asking him to hand her his phone.

"Why?" David said.

"No phones allowed in the play," Lisbeth explained. "Also, didn't you notice most people don't have phones outside?"

"I didn't," Anne said. "Why?"

Lisbeth approached Anne and looked in her eyes. "This is the Fairytale Road. It's supposed to take you back in time when life was different and simple. It's part of the experience. Now hand us your phones."

Anne exchanged looks with David. He seemed okay with it now. In his eyes, she read that they had to dispose of the phones sooner or later. They had talked about it before in London. They were lucky enough no one had tracked their location so far.

"It's part of the experience." David locked his phone and handed it to Lisbeth. He looked at Anne, rolling his eyes. "Ancient castles, old vehicles, no phone, and an attractive maid who lost her shoe. I must be in Heaven."

After makeup, Anne donned the dress they found for her. She was ready to go out and perform in the play. Once the girls left, she pulled Lisbeth aside. "What clue am I looking for now?"

"The play will reveal it to you. It will lead you to the next city in the mapestry," Lisbeth said.

"Solving the mapestry will lead me to different cities now?"

"Why do you think you're back on the Fairytale Road, Anne? London was just a starting point," Lisbeth said. "Be fast, though. I have information that the German police will be coming for you soon. Unlike London, Martin Wolf won't wait for a restraining order or negotiate with you. He is known to fabricate terrorist attacks and massacres to get rid of his targets."

"Martin Wolf?"

"The head of the German Metropolitan Police. Again, we won't be able to protect you. It will only expose us."

"By we, you mean the Ovitz family?"

"I mean the Sisterhood, Anne," Lisbeth said. "The one Rachel was looking for and would have saved her had she found them earlier."

# 41

17:37 (P.M.)

## *Somewhere in Europe*

Lily Ovitz had spent the last two hours in a separate room. She was alone, asking for forgiveness in the dark. Whoever she asked, she mentioned that being the older one, she had wished it could have been her to die on the cross instead of Layla. But Layla had leukemia, and she was in her last stages. As a family they decided to honor her first. She was going to suffer in this life anyway.

*A death with purpose is better than a life without,* Layla had said.

"Grandmother would not have approved of our sacrifices in the first place," Lily had argued with her in Westminster Abbey's tunnel. "She was always against these extremities."

"Now she is gone," Layla had said. "Now all we've got is the Sisterhood, and Our Queen. We only answer to her now."

"We could escape, Layla," Lily had said. "You and me. We could go to Lucia in Italy or Lisbeth in Germany, or..."

"There is no escaping the Sisterhood, Lily," Layla shushed her. "Who will take care of us on our own?"

"We can take care of ourselves. Being dwarves doesn't mean we can't enjoy life."

"It's not about that. It's about being who we are. Our bloodline. Those who wish to bury the Singing Bone rule the world, Lily. They will kill us off one by one."

"So we kill ourselves instead?" Lily scoffed.

"We sacrifice ourselves for the cause," Layla said. "A death with purpose is better than a life without."

"Then let me die on the cross," Lily said. "Not you."

"You have to stay alive to claim an honored rank as True Sister after Grandmother, Lily," Layla said. "Lara is too young. Lucia is still learning. And I'm sick. It must be you."

"You didn't mention the last, Lisa and Lilith," Lily said angrily.

"The tall ones?" Layla joked. "They're not our sisters anymore. They live a different life. They have a chance to blend in. They don't have a purpose like us. They don't care."

"You're relatively tall as well," Lily said. "I mean you have a bone and blood deficiency and are only five foot tall, but you can still blend in."

"You make me laugh, Lily," Layla said. "I love you so much."

Lily's memory was interrupted by Lucia's knock on the door. "We're ready."

"Is it time yet?"

"The next sacrifice, Lily," Lucia said. "We're on schedule. Would you like me to execute it?"

"No!" Lily stood up and wiped her tears. "I'm coming."

Lucia was waiting for her by the balcony when she opened the door. Lily stood next to her as they both watched the sunset behind the holy landmark ahead.

"They prepared the cross," Lucia said. She would not take her eyes of the now-crowded religious location. "They're expecting you."

Lily checked her watch and took a deep breath. "We can still spend some time together, you know?"

"I'm not afraid, Lily."

"I know," Lily said. "I guess I'm the only who is worried."

"You're the one who is going to become a True Sister. You will be chosen to carry on Lady Ovitz's secret. You will have a couple of children who will birth a total of seven children. Seven grandchildren of yours who then will carry on. It's our destiny."

"A death with a purpose," Lily said.

"...instead of a life without," Lucia finished.

The two sisters held hands. Together they watched the sun go down on St. Peter's Basilica in the Vatican City.

# 42

---

## *Castle Everstein, Polle, Fairytale Road, Germany*

"Now that you have your beautiful blue dress on, here is how our ceremonial play goes," Lisbeth said. "David, you're Prince Everstein. And Cinder, that'll be you, Anne."

"Cinder?" David asked. "You mean Cinderella."

"Please explain to him, Anne. I need to organize with the girls." She shook her head impatiently.

"Cinder is rumored to be the true name of whoever was the real Cinderella in the past," Anne explained. "It's a rare Germanic translation for the word *Zünder*, meaning fire or ignite, just like in English."

"Sounds a bit made up. Don't you think?"

"In the original script, Cinderella was always covered in ashes from the stove she cleaned in her stepmother's house," Anne explained. "That's why the two ugly stepsisters called her Cinder. It derives from the German word *Zünder*, meaning 'to ignite.'"

David shook his head. He felt like he was stuck in a nightmare.

"Anything wrong with what I explained?" Anne said.

"Other than I can't believe I'm discussing evil stepmothers, ugly stepsisters, and silver slippers?" David grunted. "Nothing at all. I *Iooove* fairytales."

"Golden slippers, by the way." Anne patted him again. "Please be kind to these girls. They really, really cherish these stories. This is their culture. Their lives. It's not folklore to them. Rather a history they wish to fully restore. They will stand you up if you scoff or make fun of them. Please play kind until we figure out how this can lead us to the next clue."

"I'm a prince, lady, so I'm kind." David adjusted the necktie the girls had given him. He looked like he was suffocating. "Until someone isn't kind to me."

Anne shook her head in response. She held his hand to follow Lisbeth and her friends up the stairs to the ruins of the Everstein Castle.

On top, David could see the direction and escape routes better. It was clear that the ferry was the most appropriate escape in case of emergency. They'd run around the castle and hop on one.

"Beautiful city from here, right?" Anne engaged his arm. "So picturesque."

David didn't comment. Silent, he was eyeing the curious crowd below.

"Don't look back at them like that," Anne said. "They're friendly families with cute children. Just wondering who this year's prince and princess are."

"I liked the green sport outfit better," David grunted. "At least I could relate to being a teenage punk trying to look cool."

"Prince David Everstein," Lisbeth announced loudly, "is this year's volunteer!"

Anne hid her face with her hands, trying not to laugh at David, who looked like he wished the earth would swallow him whole.

The adult crowd below and around the castle cheered his name. They weren't many but loud with a little too much alcohol in them. A teenage girl beckoned his attention by winking. She smiled coyly and did her best to flirt, spinning a bit in her dress. David shook his head.

"Can I get a drink?" he whispered to Lisbeth, leaning toward her.

"Now?"

"I was told I function better with alcohol," David said. "I have stage fright."

"I'll get you some, then," Lisbeth said, then pointed a finger at him. "But you can't have stage fright, you understand? Don't mess up my play!"

"Just make it a double, and I'm Prince Frankenstein all you want, all night long."

"Prince Everstein!" Lisbeth gritted her teeth. "Now until I get you what you want, read this to the crowd. While you read, we show them the Cinderella memorabilia all around the castle."

David followed Lisbeth down the stairs to join the crowd. They were circling the outer walls of the castle while looking inquisitively at Anne. "What did she give me to read?"

"A summary of Cinderella's story," Anne said. She was still doing her best to keep her composure.

"I don't want to read a Cinderella story," David whined.

"I'm afraid you will have to, David," Anne said. "And loud enough they can all hear you while Lisbeth guides the people around the castle."

"I'm not going to read a story for nobody," David said. "Besides, aren't they supposed to be Germans? Why would they listen to an English narration of their story?"

"It's amusing to them because you're a foreigner," Lisbeth announced. She arrived with a glass of liquor. "I made it triple, so gulp and read while I show them around."

Anne watched David gulp it in one shot. It was as if he was pumping himself up for a fight or something. "You keep an eye out for Tom John's men if they appear," he told Anne. "I'm going to pretend this is a nightmare right now."

"It's sad that they've confiscated our phones. I would have recorded you entertaining the crowd," Anne said. "Try to be fun, David."

"Once upon a time," David began. The crowd with him walked

in a long line around the castle. It was if they were in a ritualistic ceremony.

"Louder!" someone yelled.

"Once upon a time in a village!" David rapped the papers and burped. He enjoyed that drink. "There lived a beautiful girl named Cinderella."

"Zünder!" an elderly man with a cane demanded.

"Why don't you read then, grandpa?" David sneered at him.

"I'm not as handsome as you," grandpa said. "Just read. Don't make mistakes."

"Zünder lived with her wicked stepmother and two stepsisters." David untied his necktie. "She worked hard all day, and then they all went to a ball in the palace."

Anne grabbed one of David's hands and pointed at the Everstein palace.

"The stepsisters hated Zünder. So they left her behind and she felt sad," David read. "Suddenly there was a burst of light and the fairy godmother appeared."

Anne gave him a thumbs-up as she mingled with the rest. She followed Lisbeth while she showed them around. She stopped by a caved in spot on the outer wall. It resembled Cinderella's stove from the story. She handed David a small wooden log as he continued reading.

"With a flick of her magic she turned Zünder into a beautiful princess." David waved the stick like a magic wand. "Then she gave her golden glass slippers," David said. He watched Lisbeth stop by a pair of golden glass slippers that were bolted to the ground. They were a little larger than normal shoes but not much. Although Anne and the rest liked his narration, he saw that teenage girl giving him much more attention. She was attempting to flirt with him again.

Except that he noticed she swayed her dress toward the glass slippers. Swaying with focused intent. David wasn't sure what was going on. Did she want him to get her one?

He shook his head again and looked away. He continued reading, telling the story of Zünder riding the horse carriage toward the Everstein castle under one condition—that she returned home before midnight.

This time, he was sure the flirting girl pointed at the golden shoes on the ground. He looked at Anne for explanation. Anne was occupied with her silly childish behavior, dancing and chatting with the crowd.

If his weak spot was alcohol, then hers was fairytales.

He continued reading about when Zünder arrived at the ball.

He tapped Anne on the shoulder. "This alcohol in me won't last long," he said. "I'm warning you."

"Don't worry. The story is about to end," Anne said. "Prince is enamored with Cinderella. Her stepsisters get jealous. She must leave before midnight. Forgets her one golden slipper. Prince goes to look for the owner of the slippers and finds her."

"Why couldn't I just read the synopsis like that?" David said.

"Just read on," Anne said. "We're almost done."

After a while, they had circled the whole castle, eventually returning to the starting point.

David exhaled with relief while the crowd clapped. He had to bow like a magician, expressing his gratitude.

"Now that we all know the story," Lisbeth announced, joining Anne's and David's hands, "it's time for our final dance."

"Dance?" David pulled his hand away.

"Of course, Prince Everstein." Anne took his hand back. "It's time for the Cinderella Waltz."

David wanted to tell Anne about the flirty girl. He thought he could see the girl mouth something to him. Something about returning to the starting point again. Just like in the T.S. Eliot poem. But heck, when Anne turned into a giggling child, she not only got what she wanted. She unconditionally melted his heart.

❦

A few miles away, the German Metropolitan Police drove toward Polle. Martin Wolf sat in the passenger seat of the lead vehicle.

Martin, gray hair, late thirties, with early white patches on his beard, chewed gum constantly. Not because he liked it. God knew his diabetes had him in a chokehold. Sugar was not a good friend to him. Martin chewed gum because he didn't like to talk. He didn't like being asked questions. He didn't like asking questions. He didn't even like being a policeman. Especially now.

When he was younger, he thought police work was fun. Now older, Martin's day was nothing but a troubled journey of trying to go back home again. Let people live. Let people die. Let people steal. Let people get arrested. *And let me chew my gum in silence.*

He especially didn't like to talk to people he arrested. With a license to kill, he was straightforward about the mission: Find David and Anne. Get the Singing Bone from them. Give it to the annoying Brits and cut the fluff. In other words, they preferred he cleaned things up, no loose ends. This meant he was to shoot David and Anne and claim they resisted arrest. Then announce that he couldn't find that device everyone wanted. He wanted everything to be clean and easy too. That way he could finally go home to his dog, who didn't like to talk either.

# 43

---

18:23 (P.M.)

## *Castle Everstein, Polle, Fairytale Road, Germany*

"Just follow my steps," Anne told David. She gently rested his hand on her waist and laced her other hand into his fingers. "I know how to dance."

"Do you?" David said, having sobered up now.

"Just don't look at me, so you don't trip."

"Where did you learn to dance?" David began following her steps.

"I watched the cartoon version of *Beauty and the Beast* so many times," she said.

"So you're an imposter of a folklorist, huh?"

"I know fairytales are lies, David," she said. "Even though I can't help it. Beautiful lies."

They danced with all eyes on them. He cared less that they were supposed to be reincarnating Cinderella's dance with the prince. If the next step was to find Anne's shoe, he would have complied. Because these people were crazy. They didn't live in the real world. They probably hadn't seen real darkness. Not that it was something he didn't like about them. In fact, he almost envied their naive serenity.

David only worried that he and Anne were wasting time. That following Lisbeth's festive performance wasn't going to lead to solving the next clue. Something about all this fluff seemed wrong. Still, he couldn't deny Anne these little moments of utter mirth she was experiencing.

"Rachel taught me, too. The boys would go crazy about her, but she would still leave them and dance with me," Anne said, slowing down so he wouldn't trip. "Keep it up, champ. If you lose the rhythm, I will miss the beat. Yin and yang, Detective. We don't want to upset our friends."

"What else did Rachel teach you?" David asked while they rotated and changed direction.

"Don't do this," Anne said. "I don't want to talk about her."

"Did she tell you about the T.S. Eliot poem?" David didn't know why he pushed it now. He worried this precious moment would end with both of them caught by Tom John and sent to jail.

Anne nodded but then her mouth parted with surprise once David took the lead.

He smoothly parted ways while holding her hand and then pulled her back into his arms. She circled two times on her way back to him. He did it effortlessly and so well it scared her. A man who rarely smiled but danced this well wasn't something she fully grasped.

"You bastard." She grinned. "I thought you didn't dance."

"I'm a fast learner," he said while the crowd whistled with excitement.

"No, you aren't," Anne said as he moved behind her and nudged her by the waist, just before gently pushing her away while still hanging onto her. "You know how to tango. That's why I thought you were asking me to dance in Westminster Abbey when you took my coat."

"You know why a man and woman part in tango while holding hands before joining again?"

"No, I don't. Why?"

"They're giving each other space. To each their own choice to live independently. Their return represents that they equally have chosen not to stay alone."

"That's deep, David, especially for you. Who taught you?"

"Someone I used to dance with," he said, and she could see he was starting to enjoy himself.

"Someone you used to love?" she asked.

"I loved all women I met in my life," he said. "In different ways."

"Was she good?" Anne said.

"Someone is curious."

"Someone is keeping secrets," she said as she pulled him in, taking control now.

"Men lead in tango. Not women." He pulled her back again, a little rougher this time. She almost bumped into his chest. Still, she was amazed he didn't lose the rhythm.

"So do you actually know about music more than you told me?" she asked.

"No," he replied. "I was asked to dance at someone's birthday. I had to learn to do it for that."

"Who was she?"

"I didn't say it was a 'she.'"

"Shut up, you wouldn't dance with a man, not in a million years," she laughed.

"I was eleven. She was thirteen."

"Puppy love, I suppose?" she asked, trying to gaze into his eyes while they swung left and right. The crowd behind them were going crazy.

"It was love. But it was different. Not what you have in mind," David said, noticing the flirty girl again. She was dancing on her own behind Anne while staring at him. David nudged Anne to look back at her. "What's wrong with this girl?"

"Does she remind you of the one you danced with as kids?" Anne said.

"No, really," David said. "When we were circling the building, I thought she was flirting with me. Now it seems like she is trying to tell me something."

"Like what?"

"I'm not sure if I understood. It was like she was reciting your poem in the photo," David said.

Anne stopped immediately. "You're joking."

"Keep dancing." David pulled her back into the rhythm. "We don't want to alert anyone. We don't know who this crowd really is. Who knows if they're the enemy, not our friends?"

"Did the girl recite the poem to you?"

"Not exactly," David said. "Look, I was tipsy, and I tend to enjoy it too much when liquor is in me. I assume she was pointing out something about having circled the castle and returned to where we started."

"Which is the equivalent to the poem's meaning." Anne gritted her teeth. "Let me go talk to her."

"Wait." David's grip became ruthless. "Not until you tell me what the poem really means to you."

"Let go of me, David," she said. "You're hurting me."

"Tell me why Rachel told you about the poem, Anne," David insisted. "Why did the killer send it to you? We've been wasting time. Dancing and fooling around, for what? We need to solve the puzzle."

"You're drunk, let go of me." Anne pulled away.

The music suddenly stopped. The cheery crowd went silent, watching Anne forcefully pull away. Tension saturated the air, and David felt bad for grabbing her so tightly.

Lisbeth glared at him.

David stretched out his hand. "I'm sorry, Anne..."

But he was too late. Unexpectedly, Anne collapsed under her own weight. The crowd shrieked. The performing girls went to help her while the rest taunted David for being the worst prince ever.

"Anne," David said as he knelt at her side. "What's wrong?"

His question lingered in the air. Anne fainted and her body

contorted into a fetal position. She wasn't her anymore. She was with Rachel now.

## 44

*18 years ago*

Anne hid under the bed.

Her stepfather growled all over the cottage, looking for Rachel. She shivered. Hearing his morbid voice, she wished she could press her hands against her ears and block him out of existence. But she couldn't. What if Rachel needed her help?

Rachel never needed help, though. She had tucked Anne under the bed and made her promise not to come looking for her.

"He's just drunk, Rose Red, that's all," Rachel had said. "I can handle it."

"How?" Anne had whimpered.

"Like I always do," Rachel had said. "I'll distract him until he sobers up."

"Why did Mother ever leave us?" Anne cried. "How could she leave us with him?"

"Who knows?" Rachel said softly. "Who knows?"

After a few hours of her stepfather drunkenly raging at the

world all around him, he finally collapsed under his own darkness and fell asleep.

Rachel came back a little later. She gently pulled Anne from under the bed. They hugged and clung to each other for a long time.

"I can break his bones while he is asleep," Rachel said.

Anne's eyes widened with horror.

"I saw it on TV," Rachel said. "He'd wake up limping. Or disfigured, or something. He won't be able to hurt us again. Remember that fairytale about Rose Red and Snow White? They joined forces and killed the wolf in the end. He is our wolf, Anne."

"You won't do it, Rachel," Anne said. "It's not like you. We're not bad people."

"I know, but sometimes I think about it. Who said good people can't do bad things?" Rachel said. "I think Mother wanted to kill him, too."

"You were too young," Anne said. "You couldn't possibly remember that."

"But I do." Rachel touched her sister's cheeks. "Did I tell you I remember things I don't think I have experienced in my lifetime?"

"I don't quite understand what you're saying."

"I read that it's called déjà vu."

"What is déjà vu?"

"I think it's when something happens, and it feels like it happened before," Rachel said. "That's not what I remember, though."

"Then what is it?"

"I don't know, Anne," Rachel said. "It's like someone put stories in my head. Old stories that happened long ago."

"And you remember them? I mean vividly?"

"No. But they're horrible stories. Stories of women. Many, many women, and bad, evil men," Rachel said.

"Like him." Anne pointed at her stepfather.

Rachel nodded. "Yet not all men are bad. Many are good. Also a few women in these stories are truly evil as well. I don't know what I'm saying."

Anne let Rachel cry in her arms. She felt honored she could at least give back to her elder sister by listening to her.

"I think Mother put these stories in my head," Rachel said.

"Do you hear Mother's voice? Do you see her face when you hear these stories?"

"I don't see her face, but I recognize her from a necklace she used to wear."

"Necklace?"

"It's the only one she owned. It had a wooden swan dangling from it," Rachel said. "There is one poem where her voice is unmistakable." Rachel began to recite the words. It was the part of T.S. Eliot's poem about returning to the place for the first time.

"What does it mean, Rachel?" Anne asked.

"I think it means that we sometimes take faraway journeys. Like we are looking for something, upset with where we are right now," Rachel sobbed. "When we return to the place we left in the first place, we realize it wasn't that bad. Or maybe we realize we needed the journey to look at it from a different perspective. We suddenly see it from a different angle. With our new experiences, *for the first time.*"

"I can't imagine Mother meant that," Anne said. "I mean look at this drunk man we live with. I will never see this place through better eyes."

Rachel wiped her tears and said, "I think Mother meant it about herself. I'm not sure."

"How so?"

"I think she left on her own journey to come back again. Stronger maybe. Different, I don't know. Maybe to help us out."

Anne wanted to believe that. She realized then that she would forgive her mother if she ever came back.

Rachel, being as analytical as she was, dug deep into her studies and managed to relate T.S. Eliot's poem about the bones to the Brothers Grimm. Sometimes Anne thought Rachel connected invisible dots that weren't there. Still, her observations were uncannily interesting.

That was until one night when their stepfather took his anger to another level. So much that the only way to escape him was to hide in the well in the vineyard. That's where they found the other girl's bones.

He could not climb down because of his claustrophobia. That, and he worried he'd fall when he was drunk. Sometimes Rose Red and Snow White spent hours down in the well, escaping the wolf. Staying safe until he tired or needed a drink and left. They spent hours with dead girl's bones.

One day when Rachel was away, Anne had to escape her stepfather on her own. She climbed down the well with their secret docking rope. It had a hook at its end that they pulled along and then had to climb up again using the voided brick in the inner walls. Rachel had jokingly named the rope Rapunzel's hair. As for the deliberately carved voids they used as a ladder to climb up again, it was probably designed by whoever left the dead girl in the well.

Anne spent hours alone down in the well. She could hear the wolf huff and puff up there. Claiming Anne wasn't as beautiful as Rachel, and that if he had to choose between them, he would never choose her. He was yelling obscenities, and that she better die young because she was never going to find a man.

Anne balled herself up and sobbed for hours. She hated that she was alone. Well, not quite alone. The dead girl's bones were mere feet from her. The well was much scarier without Rachel here with her to comfort her. Her eyes could not stop spilling tears and her throat thirsted for a drop of clean water. She prayed her mother would come back. She prayed that Rachel was right about her returning to the place for the first time, whatever that meant.

Rachel wouldn't return from working in the vineyard until sunset. Eventually, Anne had no more tears to cry. She knew she would have to wait for her sister before she felt safe enough to emerge from the well.

In her waiting, Anne picked up one of the dead girl's bones and used a sharp stone to carve a flute from it. Just then, she suspected something: these weren't the same bones of the girl like before.

Rummaging through the darkened bottom of the well, she

came upon the truth, finding several pairs of skeletal hands. The well was a dumpster for many other dead girls.

Anne shuddered in fear and disgust. She felt her entire perspective on life change in that moment. She realized how growing up wasn't everything she hoped it to be. Bright colors dimmed and hopes and dreams diminished as one grew up. That's when she understood the power of the poem Rachel recited to her.

Left alone in the bottom of the well, discovering it was a tomb for many dead girls, she felt her foot step over something solid. When she knelt down to pick it up, she saw what it was. She understood that her mother wasn't going to come back as Rachel suggested. Anne felt as if she had a revelation, something she felt for the very first time. She had found her mother's necklace with the wooden swan dangling from it.

Anne had returned to the well and uncovered its darkest secret, seeing it for the first time in the worst ways possible.

# 45

18:45 (P.M.)

## *Castle Everstein, Polle, Fairytale Road, Germany*

David winced at Anne's sudden awakening. Opening her eyes and jumping to her feet, she began reciting the poem's last part: *And the end of all our exploring, will be to arrive where we started, and know the place for the first time.*

"It's okay." David tried to hug her tightly.

"You don't understand." Anne pulled away. "You don't understand. You don't understand."

"I don't." David tried to calm her down. "I'm sorry for pressuring you."

"No, David, you don't understand!" She was looking for something around her like she did before. "You helped me. I remember now."

"Remember what?"

'Remember what it means," she said and grabbed Lisbeth by the shoulder. "I'm dizzy. How do I get back to the benches by the garden outside?"

"Why do you want to go back?" Lisbeth said.

Anne shouted at her, "Show me the way!"

"I'll show you." David lent her his firm hand.

"Yes, please," Anne said.

David showed her the way back. They hurried down the steps to where they had circled the castle earlier.

"They're coming for us, David." Anne ripped off the lower sides of her dress so she could run faster. "You said it. They're coming for us."

"Where are we going now?" David said, running in the snowy garden with her.

"To the bank where we sat when we first arrived," Anne said and sped up. Behind them, the performers stood speechless. Anne looked like someone who lost her mind and was talking nonsense.

"Okay," David said. "I'm with you, but what's there by the bank?"

"Do you have the laptop with you?" she said, not slowing down.

"I can go back and get it," he said.

"No, it's okay." She reached the bank where a couple sat listening to music with shared headphones. "I remember the photo."

David thought he understood what was going on, but not quite. He watched Anne yell at the couple to leave the bank and didn't interrupt her. She was angry but didn't seem crazy to him.

The couple moved, swearing at her in German. Anne walked past the bank. She then turned around and looked back at the castle, forming an imaginary camera with her thumbs and fore-fingers.

"Is that about the angle the photo on the laptop showed the castle?" David said. He wasn't that good with dimensions, but he stood beside her, trying to give it a shot. "I think if you take a step or two back and kneel down, it would be about right."

Anne took a step back but tripped on something buried in the snow and fell backwards. Before he could help, he saw what she tripped on. Another Cinderella golden shoe that was bolted to the ground and half buried in the snow.

Anne clasped a hand on her mouth, staring at the shoe. "You're right, David. The killer knows me too well."

"How so, Anne?" He knelt beside her.

David thought she understood something that he hadn't grasped yet. He remembered the flirting girl hinting at the Cinderella shoes by the castle. He reached inside this one, and to his surprise, he found something.

"Is this what you're looking for?" David said, holding a necklace with a swan dangling from it.

"Oh my God." Anne stared at it, afraid to touch it.

David immediately noticed a small, rolled up paper the size of a fortune cookie wrapped around the necklace.

"*And the end of all our exploring, will be to arrive where we started, and know the place for the first time,*" Anne repeated to herself. She pointed at the castle with that camera gesture of her thumbs and forefingers again.

David got it. He closed his eyes for being stupid earlier, and waited for Anne to confirm his suspicions.

"We weren't meant to look at the castle through the photo," Anne explained. "We were meant to know the exact position the killer left this necklace behind, right where he stood taking the photo."

"Because in a mapestry we have double meanings," David reminded himself. "To the common person the photo of the castle would get them interested in the castle. Someone like you should have looked for the opposite possibility. That's where the killer stood with the right angle taking the photo. That's where X marked the spot."

Anne unwrapped the fortune cookie and read the next puzzle.

"The killer shifted from musical notes to poems and rhymes now?" she said.

"Read it to me," David said.

Anne read:


**Once upon a time, at sixteen-oh-two,**

*in the big apple, a river bit through.*
*Children used to sing, in streets so mute,*
*deep in abyss mark, two towers tribute.*

"Mean anything to you?" David said.

"No," Anne said, feeling as frustrated as him. "I have to admit, this is getting silly."

"We can't keep solving child games this way," David said. "I'll have to ask you now, Anne, who knows this much about you other than Rachel?"

"No one," Anne said.

"Then tell me more about her," David said. "Maybe she is the killer—"

A shot broke through the benches with a loud, startling echo. They looked at one another with regret. Now they realized how much time they had wasted dancing.

# 46

---

## *Castle Everstein, Polle, Fairytale Road, Germany*

David covered Anne with his body and hugged her tightly as the next bullet hit the bank again. It was pure luck that they had knelt behind it, or they would have been hit. Anne felt him pull her closer and then force her to roll with him down the snowy slope toward the river.

It wasn't a smooth maneuver. The snow was bumpy underneath them and the cold only added to their panic. Let alone the screams of the innocent families all around.

Was the attacker shooting at everyone? Not just them?

Anne wished to unchain herself from David's protective grip, but she couldn't physically match his strength. The panic in his eyes scared her. It was as if he was looking at the past while saving them both.

David's spontaneous tactic only took them so far. They bumped into a nearby tree that stopped their path towards the river. Anne was about to look up at the screams behind her, but

David pulled her back down again. The shooting didn't stop, and neither could they locate its source.

No police force or attackers were visible. Almost as if this was an assassin's doing. Was this done by one man? But where would he hide?

"Who is shooting at us?" Anne panted. "I can't believe this is happening. If it's Tom's men, aren't they supposed to arrest us, read us our rights?"

David dragged her by the dress behind him as he crawled down on all fours, down the path closer to the river. Animal instinct at its finest. Looking down at the ground from behind him, she saw a trail of blood on the snow.

"You're shot!"

"No, I'm not," David said as they reached the edge of the river. He then pulled her behind another tree and craned his neck out a little to look. "I can't see our shooter, but people are panicking left and right."

"Poor people," Anne said. "We have to help them."

"We have to what?" David grabbed her arms and pulled her near. "Think of your survival right now. Don't give me that super-hero crap."

Anne took his words like a pebble in the face. He was right, but she didn't agree. She wished to do more to help. But she was being unrealistic as well. David reminded her so much of Rachel right now. She would have told her the same.

"How about we take the ferry, then?" she said proactively. "We can run in a beeline to it and avoid being shot."

"We can't run in this snow," David considered. "And who do you think will operate a ferry now? Look at the few families ducking there, afraid for their lives. They are paralyzed, chained by indecision."

"Then we swim," Anne said and crawled down to the river's edge.

"You know how cold the river will be?" David said, but Anne was already there. He had no choice but to crawl down after her.

At first the bullets seemed to have stopped, but then another one hit the nearby dock.

"Shit, it's a sniper." David hugged her close again. "Long-distance rifle. He must be up a hill or something."

The sounds of screaming families were all around them. They shrieked in uninterrupted panic, some trying to call the police. They spoke in German, but Anne translated to David.

"They say there is a terrorist sniper in the Everstein tower," Anne said.

"Crap," David scoffed. "A terrorist in a small fairytale town that has almost no tourists, and during Christmas? Nonsense."

"So, it's Tom John?"

"Him, the royal family, or Jacqueline de Rais, it doesn't matter," David said. "Someone wants you dead."

"Actually, I think they don't," Anne said. "They wouldn't risk losing the Singing Bone and where it leads. You still have it, right?"

"I do, but I dropped the necklace and don't remember the last puzzle."

"I remember it, don't worry." Anne realized she hadn't told him about her mother's bones yet. "So how do we get out of this?"

"Depends on if you know a place this river can take us to," David said.

"I know a lot of places, like the Rapunzel Castle in Trendel-burg," Anne said. "But we can't swim that far, or we will freeze. When I said swim, I meant hide under the dock for a while," she said with chattering teeth. "Damn it, I'm freezing. How didn't I notice?"

"Welcome to my fight-or-flight world." He held her tighter and locked eyes with her. "Do you trust me?"

"I think so." She shivered in his arms.

"Well, thank you very much." He rolled his eyes but then lost all his humor when he saw someone get shot up on the deck. "I'll get you out of here."

She was about to tell him he was suffocating her when he began ripping her dress while on top of her. It looked dangerously out of context to whoever didn't understand what was going on. As much as she trusted him, his recklessness scared her a little.

"You're worried the river is cold and want to send me into it half naked now?" she said, astonished by his hand's strength. He ripped every part of her dress in seconds.

"I'd let you rip mine, if I wore a dress that would make me float in the river," he said, locking eyes with her and looking like a madman. Her lower lip quivered from the cold now. "Take a deep breath and don't worry. It's like free-falling in love."

Anne fell with David into the river, shocked by the cold, realizing she was about to die. Her body contorted and numbed instantly, and she was about to faint again.

David turned to wrap her arms around his back, but she was partially gone. Instead, he gripped her by one leg behind him and awkwardly paddled with one hand toward the dock.

Underneath the dock, he realized the castle was a little farther away now. He stopped his mind from playing games with him and reminding him of the past. Not his dead mother, though. He'd returned home and found her that way, so he couldn't do anything to interfere. It was that thirteen-year-old girl, the one he danced with, and the one who turned his mother into an atheist, whom he remembered. The one he should've saved but couldn't.

Tangent to the snowy garden, they were lucky. Just after the ferry, closer to the castle, they were protected by half a wall of ruins. Probably erected to stop the river from seeping onto the land. David pulled Anne out of the water and held her with both arms. They had to get out of the cold. He ran toward the castle's back door by the river's side.

Anne's shivers escalated to violent spasms, and she sincerely thought she would die in his arms.

*Everyone dies in your arms, David,* his darker half taunted him, *you're so charming.*

"Rachel..." Anne's mouth barely moved. "I'm sorry."

# 47

## *Main Road, Polle, Germany*

Martin Wolf began chewing on a new piece of gum. Fantastic Mastic, his favorite new brand. This one had been prescribed to him by his Internal Affairs psychiatrist, Dr. Carter Pillar, an eccentric out-of-this-world professor who looked like he needed a psychiatrist himself.

Mr. Wolf was told that mastication was recently proved to calm anxiety and depression, so he bought a pack a day. It also helped him quit smoking cigarettes.

However, today was a special day. Martin had worn out the first pack already.

Still sitting in the back of his car, further away from Castle Everstein, he listened to his men following his instructions on the dispatch.

"We missed them," a police officer told him. "Anne and David aren't anywhere to be found."

Martin didn't reply. Again, he didn't like talking.

"And we accidentally shot a civilian," the police officer said.

"Are those two fugitives that important? Your man up the tower is a lunatic."

Martin had sent one of his men up the tower to shoot Anne and David. He wanted to make it look like a terrorist attack by a random hooligan who escaped a nearby asylum. It wasn't the best of ideas, really, and hardly plausible. But the world was a mad-fest, and whenever he watched the news, he listened to incidents of terrorism worse than the weird story he now cooked up on the fly.

Not having the capacity to deal with his superiors' bullshit, he thought it would be best to end this mess and kill everyone so he could go home to his dog. *Create a fabricated, random terrorist attack by some Christmas lunatic, and kill whoever needs to be killed.*

A real terrorist had killed his wife and kids in a bus collision into the Christmas Market years ago anyway.

"Should we still proceed, Mr. Wolf?" The officer struggled with the echoing screams around him.

Martin chewed harder on the gum. The officer took that as a yes and proceeded with the plan.

Martin then received a message from Tom John. He had arrived at the Kassel airport and was on his way to Polle. Martin didn't reply. He pulled back the passenger's seat and laid his hands behind his back and meditated on his mastic gum.

*Why couldn't the world be such a silent place?*

Mr. Wolf's doctor had diagnosed him as apathetic.

"Do apathetic people talk much?" Wolf had asked his doctor.

"Actually, no. Because in their eyes, nothing matters."

"Good," Wolf said. "Don't you dare prescribe a cure for my apathy or I will put an apathetic bullet up your skull."

Hoping his men would kill this Anne and David who had now spoiled his day, Mr. Wolf wondered if he should give his dog a Christmas present when he went back home tonight.

*Would his Siberian husky enjoy a Singing Bone?*

# 48

## *Basement, Castle Everstein, Polle, Fairytale Road, Germany*

Anne woke up in the castle's basement. She could hear David struggling with something and cursing at everyone. All she saw were Lisbeth and the performer dwarves surrounding her as if she were Snow White.

"You'll be okay," Lisbeth said. "Drink this. It will keep you warm. It's Our Queen's Fairytale Hot Chocolate Bomb."

Anne's neck hurt as she propped herself up on her elbows. She was slowly realizing they had dressed her in jeans and layered her with blankets and laid her on a table. The shooting outside still hadn't stopped.

"We've locked the basement gate from inside," Lisbeth explained. "But they'll soon break in."

"How did I get here? How long has it been?" Anne said.

"Twenty minutes or so. There is a crazed terrorist on the tower's top, killing people left and right, but we know he is looking for you. I caught the so-called police dispatcher mentioning your names."

Another performer chimed in. "Your David—or Herr Hercules here—broke into the basement through the wooden door overlooking the river. He saved your life."

Anne turned sideways and saw David trying to get the Schwimwagen working. He wasn't listening to them. She doubted that saving her insinuated anything intimate, even though he'd dropped that 'free-falling in love' line on her by the river. He was probably exercising his Darwinian theory of easing the moment by saying trivial and meaningless things.

It didn't matter. People were being killed outside because of her, or this damned mapestry. She would never forgive herself for not doing anything about it.

Rachel never ceased to taunt her for one moment: *You ungrateful little sister. After all I've taught you, you still give up on other people. Just like you did to me.*

The pain in Anne's neck jolted her wandering mind back to the present.

The police were now attempting to break in from outside.

Just then a loud rumble filled the air. David got the Schwimwagen to work. The engine caused the dwarves to erupt in cheers.

"Hurry," Lisbeth said. "I doubt the police know about the back door leading to the river yet."

The police outside gave them a one-minute ultimatum.

"Hop in," David said to Anne.

Anne did and asked Lisbeth if she and her friends wanted to get in, too.

"We're too many. Too heavy. The old vehicle will sink," Lisbeth said. "Besides, we're ready to die. We always have been."

David was ready to drive through the door out to the river, but Anne stopped him for one last second.

"Why are you doing this, Lisbeth?" Anne said. "Why can't you tell me what's going on? Why do you think you have to die?"

Lisbeth smiled and without hesitation replied, "Lady Ovitz said you're the one, let's leave it at that."

"The one? Me? What do you mean?"

Time was up. The police were breaking down the door.

David jammed down the gas pedal, and the reluctant old car propelled through the back door and roared away into the night.

"Lisbeth!" Anne yelled. Her words were swallowed by the noisy Schwimwagen splashing into the river. Her only reply was the screams of the dwarves stalling the police.

Anne rocked with the bouncing, unsteady motions but was astounded by the vehicle's resilience and power.

"Whooh!" David spat water, hand on the steering wheel. "German excellence, even if it's as old as 1941."

"I can't believe it's working," Anne said, looking back at the dwarves at the castle. She couldn't see much in the dark now. The Schwimwagen was relatively fast for a water car. Luckily, the dark prevented the German police from accurately shooting at them. The only light she saw was the sharp and short brightness caused by the bullets darting in the night.

Behind them, Lisbeth yelled at Anne.

"Trust in the Sisterhood, Anne," Lisbeth shouted with all her might. "They trust in you and they need you."

"Why does everyone insist they exist?" Anne turned around and humped over to the edge of the vehicle, yelling back at Lisbeth. "Who are they? How can I find them? Why are they doing this to me?"

"Because only you will prove that the Brothers Grimm never wrote the book," Lisbeth said. "It was she who wrote it."

"She? Who?" Anne shouted back, almost tumbling out of the vehicle and back into the river.

"Dorothea Wild," Lisbeth yelled, looking back at her friends fighting the police, then back at Anne. "Wilhelm's wife. It was her-story, not his-story."

Anne's mouth hung open, but she could no longer see Lisbeth in the dark and smoke all around the castle. David had driven far enough the two women couldn't hear each other anymore.

Anne contemplated swimming back to Lisbeth, but David pulled her back in the vehicle. Slumped back into the passenger seat, she remembered that she had always known about Dorothea

Grimm aka Dorothea Wild aka Dortchen Wild. The housewife, the mother, the one who prepared dinner and made the bed and raised the kids, she had been called by many different names. She was the one who stood by her husband as he became a famous scholar.

"Dorothea initiated the Sisterhood, but she didn't create it," Lisbeth's faint voice emanated from the dark like a ghost's. "Fairytales were not written by men. They were written by women, and there is a reason for that!"

# 49

19:35 (P.M.)

## *Saint Peter's Basilica, the Vatican*

Lily and Lucia silently walked the underground tunnel from their house all the way to St. Peter's. The Vatican tunnels were much longer than those under Westminster Abbey. In fact, they weren't a secret. Many knew about them but accessing them was almost impossible.

The tunnel had been erected to save past popes from invading forces. This underground world had witnessed so much blood due to the Catholic Church having to protect their faith by using them. They weren't only tunnels. They also acted as shelters from an inevitable apocalypse. One that the Vatican called the Fairytale Plague but never announced the meaning behind it.

"Did you know that the Vatican's biggest secret is neither the tunnels nor archives?" Lucia broke the silence. "It's a bathroom, decorated in erotic frescos, inside the papal apartment."

"Really?" Lily said, unbothered by the echoes of prayer that resonated from the basilica. It was interesting how the sounds traveling through the tunnels made a holy prayer sound like a demon's call. She most definitely wasn't interested in Lucia's ridiculous findings about the place. But she played nice, nonetheless.

Lucia's phone chimed and upon reading a message she said, "Lisbeth has been shot."

"Why? How?" Lily said, trying to mask her emotions. She wished she could express her pain, but she did not want to come across as weak in front of her sister who looked up to her.

"Tom John's men tried to kill Anne and David, but they escaped," Lucia explained. "Lisbeth helped."

"Is it bad?"

"I don't know, but the message says she will survive."

"Who sent the message?"

"A representative of Our Queen," Lucia looked proud about it.

"You seem to care about hearing from Our Queen more than your own sister."

"I know that this is how I come across, Lily, but Lisbeth and Layla are my sisters, too."

"Then what happened to you?"

"What happened is that I surrendered my soul to Our Queen. She makes me feel strong, unlike how Lady Ovitz made us feel when she was alive," Lucia said.

"How did Lady Ovitz make us feel?"

"She made me feel like a dwarf."

"We are dwarves," Lily said. "And Lady Ovitz always said we may be small, but we do the work of giants."

"Not Our Queen," Lucia insisted. "She doesn't just talk and spread unbelievable goodness. She makes me feel powerful. She makes me feel like a woman. She gives us the power to strike back and let our voices be heard, even if it means that we'll sacrifice ourselves, Lily. A death with a purpose is better than a life without."

"We haven't even met her, Lucia. Who knows what arrogant psycho she is?"

"Says the girl who is aspiring to become a True Sister under Our Queen's doctrine," Lucia said.

Lily stood tongue-tied. Lucia was right. Lily was as sinful as the rest. She only aspired to find a better way, but she was no different. All goodness was lost in the Sisterhood after Lady Ovitz died.

They resumed walking in silence until a couple of nuns emanated from the darkness and stopped them. They spoke in Italian to Lucia.

"They want you to know that they appreciate what you're doing," Lucia told Lily. "And wish you the best in your journey of becoming a True Sister."

"Tell them it's an honor," Lily said. "After all, I don't think a True Sister could ever aspire to be as respected and hailed as a nun."

"They say they admire your humbleness," Lucia translated. "And they admire this moment where Jews and Christians come together for the sake of one human race."

"Tell them Grandmother always joked that fairytales should've been the one religion that united the world," Lily said.

"They say you missed the most important part," Lucia said. "They say it still wouldn't have united the world because it would have been a women's only religion."

Lily didn't know what to say to that. She wasn't crazy about the idea, even if the Sisterhood's members were only women. She shoved the thought aside and instead made a practical request. "Ask them if they're ready."

"They are," Lucia said, "and so is the cross."

# 50

## *Weser River, Fairytale Road, Germany*

"Are you sure you know where we're heading?" David said, driving the Schwimwagen.

The night had settled, and a feeble moon helped them stay low in the shadows. It was only the Schwimwagen's noisy drone-like sound that could give them away. Luckily, the sound of traveling ferries and celebrations in a smaller town across the river balanced it out.

Both Anne and David wondered how much the event in Polle had spread out in the news. Few people in these regions watched TV or used their phones like in the cities. It was one of many reasons Anne liked the Fairytale Road.

"I don't know how much longer this machine will keep going," David said.

"And no GPS, I know," Anne said. "Don't worry. I know this road by heart. Do you think they're hurt badly back there?"

"The dwarves?" David said. "Who knows? I hope not. I really liked them."

"You didn't save them though, David."

"How many times do I have to tell you that I'm David..."

"...not God," Anne said. "I know, but we left them behind. And don't denigrate me for wanting to save the world and make everyone happy."

"I'm not denigrating you, Anne," David said. "You just turn into this naive kiddo with these fairytales around you."

"What does that mean?"

"You become a giddy child who refuses to grow up," David said. "Look back at the castle, or at what happened in Westminster Abbey. Does any of this strike you as a folktale of princesses and dwarves and dancing balls? Life is a nightmare, Anne. That's why people dream. It's a way to balance it out."

"We've met princesses and dwarves and we danced, David," Anne said. "Life is not a nightmare. Life is so close to being as good as we expect it to be. We need to work a little harder at it, that's all."

"I fixed the German car and drove into the water," David said. "I think I'm working as hard as I can."

"What about just a little harder?"

"I got shot, so I worked even more than 'just a little harder.'" He changed his position and showed her the blood dripping from the side of his arm.

"David," Anne shrieked. "You need a doctor."

"Don't worry. It's a surface-level injury. As long as the bullet didn't get in, I'm fine. I like to bleed."

"That's an odd thing to say."

"It makes me appreciate what I have, but I wouldn't impose my dark thoughts onto you now," he said. "In fact, I take it back. Maybe life is a fairytale. We're still alive, aren't we?"

She sighed. "It's like an action movie more than a fairytale, to be honest. One where one needs to suspend belief."

"Life is stranger than fiction, they say," David said.

Anne smiled involuntarily. "I mean you being shot in the shoulder is such a copout. The kind of plot they write in movies to make the audience sympathize with the hero but know he will be all right."

"Heroes don't die, Anne. I will one day," David said. "But I guess that makes you the heroine?"

"I am." She pointed proudly, yet sarcastically at herself. "This story is all about me, you know. Me. Me. Me. Pure narcissism at its finest."

"No, that's not you. In fact, you have this weakness that you want to please everyone." He shook his head. "But tell me, are you saying you'll end up with the villain being your father like in *Star Wars*? That's a plot point I laugh at, always."

"We don't know who the villain is yet, David."

"You got that right," he sighed. "But you know what heroines do in movies to heroes who have been shot, right?"

Even in the dark, Anne saw a flirty side of him she didn't think existed. She wondered if he was really flirting or simply entertaining a conversation to occupy the mind with trivial thoughts.

"I'm not going to fall for you, hero," Anne said, dead serious.

"Who said I want you to?"

"You said it yourself before we plowed into the icy river earlier," she said.

"Did I?"

"You're not going to deny it now, are you?"

"I don't remember what I said," he said. "It must have fitted the moment. We were falling into the river, so I spiced it up with a comment, probably to escape the panic."

"Okay, then," she said, not sure whether she was disappointed or not. One thing Rachel had taught her was that emotion under pressure or need was not true emotion. It wouldn't last. "I've only known you for about a day anyway. I don't know who you are. *You* could be a villain."

"I wish I was. At least I'd know what's going on all the time." He raised an eyebrow. "Besides, meeting you feels like a lifetime ago to me. I mean we changed clothes more in one day than a catwalk model."

"So, what do heroines do with heroes in movies again?"

"Nothing much," David said. "Just mend my wounds when we settle somewhere. Sit me in the chair, take off my shirt, tell me I'll be okay, and then stitch that wound."

"I can stitch that wound, for sure," Anne said. "So hard that it hurts again. How about that?"

"I thought you liked fairytales," David said. "It's the sentimental part of every story, isn't it?"

"You don't know anything about fairytales, David. Don't even try."

"I know Cinderella's stepmother got her eyes poked out by a penguin in the end of the original version." David raised an eyebrow again.

"Who told you that?"

"Lisbeth. We had a moment while you were doing your makeup before the dance." David's face dimmed. "I hope she's okay."

"Me, too," Anne said, then silence draped over them both for a few moments before she added, "All of the Ovitz family members, for that matter."

Their little flirty conversation didn't last long, crumbling under the weight of their circumstances. It didn't matter how much they tried to lighten up the mood, what happened in Polle was unjust.

"I heard Lisbeth mention the name of the woman who formed the Sisterhood." David returned to his usual investigative tone. "Tell me about that."

"I have to admit I've never believed in that part of the fairytale origins because I could never authenticate," Anne said. "So what I'm going to tell you is nothing but rumors, told orally from person to person. A legend that many believe but can't really prove."

"Like the Holy Grail, the Ark of Covenant, or the Fountain of Youth. I get it," David said. "I've seen enough today to be open to myths and legends."

"The main idea is that Dorothea Wild formed the Sisterhood and wrote the tales instead of her husband, Wilhelm," Anne said. "I guess to put it in a broader context, you could say fairytales weren't actually written by men but women."

"Her story, not his," David considered. "I'm not an expert, and

I'm by no means fond of the way media clashes men against women, but...

"But?"

"I do support the idea that these female-driven, centuries-old stories could've been written by women," David said. "Why not?"

"Wait until you hear how it supposedly happened," Anne said. "Let me tell you about Wilhelm Grimm's wife, Dorothea Wild. One of the most overlooked but important women in modern history."

"I can imagine."

"According to the legends, she formed the Sisterhood in 1801, one year after she married Wilhelm Grimm," Anne said. "But their dark practices started in 1811, a year before the Brothers Grimm published the book."

"Dark practices?"

"Uh-huh," Anne said. "The part that made me dismiss the theory in the beginning."

# 51

## *Polle, Fairytale Road, Germany*

Martin Wolf saw Tom John cursing and shouting at him because of Anne and David's escape. Coolly, he reached for the pack of gum in his back pocket. *Good*, he told himself, *I have enough to outlive this creep*.

"I can't believe they escaped in some old German vehicle that hasn't been manufactured for over thirty years," Tom John blurted, standing near the bank and looking at the castle.

The location looked like it had hosted a wild high school party where things got out of hand. Three people had been shot by the sniper, one killed, and the press was all over the place.

Martin Wolf said nothing, but his police assistant replied in a thick accent. "It's a Volkswagen, sir, and no, not all Volkswagens are Beetles," he said. "German cars are heavy duty, unlike British ones. Do you even manufacture cars, sir?"

Tom failed to register the comeback. He was occupied with pessimistic projections about his own future in the service. His

career was shambles now. How many more setbacks were his superiors going to tolerate of him?

"Did you know that Volkswagen means 'folk-wagon'?" The
policeman snickered with hands on his belt. "Considering you're
chasing a woman who is a folklorist?'

"Get out of my way," Tom snapped and addressed Martin Wolf.
"How fast is this swimming car they escaped in?"

"It's a relatively slow vehicle, but we're not going to chase it
with police boats down the river," the officer replied on Mr. Wolf's
behalf. "It's Christmas, sir. Besides, we don't want to panic our
peaceful people."

"Panic?" Tom said. "Look at the massacre behind you. The
press will turn this into a 'panic' fest within minutes. It's best to
make people panic so they want to help with catching the
fugitives."

"A terrorist in a tower isn't a recurring incident, sir," the officer
said. "It's shocking and will spoil Christmas celebrations, but in no
way does anyone in the region think it will happen again. Besides,
even the one man who supposedly died from the shot ended up
just being injured. So practically no one died."

"In what world do you live in? People hear 'terrorist' and they
run for their lives everywhere," Tom said.

"Well, let me be blunt, sir," the officer said. "He isn't quite a
terrorist. The story we fabricated of an escaped asylum lunatic
doesn't happen every day. Also"—the officer took a step forward
and whispered in Tom's ear—"he is neither Middle Eastern,
African, nor Asian, or the stereotype people in this region think of
as terrorists. I'm not being racist, sir, but I also am being racist,
sir."

The officer's words troubled John. For a moment, he couldn't
assess who was worse. Him, his father, the officer, or the shooter.
How did he end up surrounded by corruption and filth in every
direction? So much that the worst he did was not as bad as he
thought it would be?

"Look. We have an agreement. We won't discuss why Anne and
David are dangerous. All we must do is catch them—or if neces-

sary, terminate them—for the lack of a better word," Tom said, a little calmer. "So you and your silent Mr. Bean inspector here track them down and hand their device to me. Understood?"

The officer turned for permission from Martin Wolf but realized his superior had walked away.

Tom was about to scream in frustration when he saw Martin Wolf. He was standing by the golden shoe in the snow behind the bank with a tiny piece of paper in his hand.

The officer took the slip of paper and handed it to Tom John. "Does it look like it belongs to the fugitives, sir?"

"Looks like it, and it sounds like a puzzle," Tom said, reading it. "And witnesses reported Anne and David running back to this spot."

"What is it, sir?" the officer said.

"Part of a mapestry," Tom John said. "I think that is what it's called."

"What's a mapestry, sir?"

"Some bloody game of Clue which Anne is solving for some bloody reason that doesn't bloody make any bloody sense," Tom said.

"Bloody *scheisse*, sir." The officer nodded.

"Bloody what?"

"*Scheisse*, sir," the officer said. "*Scheisse* is shit in German, sir."

"Ask your inspector how he found it," Tom said. "He couldn't have possibly just stumbled upon it."

The officer asked Mr. Wolf, who finally answered in a low voice Tom couldn't hear.

The officer said, "He says a teenage girl in a pink dress handed it to him and then ran off."

# 52

20:11 (P.M.)

### *Weser River, Fairytale Road, Germany*

"Europe was under attack," Anne began. "Napoleon Bonaparte invaded every city possible. His troops headed to Germany, awaiting instructions. The German citizens of Kassel lived in perpetual panic since.

"Years before, Wilhelm and Jacob Grimm had planned to collect German folklore. Now, they were in dire need to finish the job before Napoleon invaded and erased everything about their history.

"Napoleon was known for his ruthlessness. He burned cities and rid them of their culture and traditions. His troops didn't just invade places. They terminated them. They brought down monuments and burned books in their native languages. German tradition and folklore were bound to go extinct.

"I don't want to get into the Grimm brothers' interesting upbringing because it's a rather long story. But you should know that they came from extreme poverty. They weren't originally born and raised in Kassel, but a much smaller town up north. Their nights were cold, the food was scarce, and jobs were few. Their father died at a young age, and they never knew him. In fact, where they were born, coupled with that time of history, people rarely knew their fathers.

"Traveling men, soldiers, or whoever passed about these towns with a sack of beans, wheat, or the most precious salt in their time, slept with the poor town's women in exchange for goodies and left.

"It's what the world was like then. Harsh and unforgiving. It makes me wonder why people complain these days.

"Anyway, Jacob and Wilhelm are said to be the illegitimate sons of a salt trader. Someone they were never going to meet. Even if they had met him, he would have never recognized them.

"Records differ about who their mother was, same with the names of their dead brothers and sisters."

"Dead?"

"People hardly survived in these small towns after the age of thirteen," Anne said. "There is a German quote about 'thirteen and thirty' that I don't recall exactly, but it simply says that if you survived thirteen, you hardly survived the age of thirty at that time."

"Bloody bleak."

"Jacob, Wilhelm, and their youngest sister, Lotte, were the only survivors of the Grimm family. Jacob was born into sickness. The famous incident of him selling their only cow to a man in a black cassock and black hat hiding a disproportioned head in exchange for magic beans really happened.

"Funny enough, it's made into a fairytale now called Jack and the Beanstalk, originally called Jacob and the Beanstalk. Since 'Jacob' was a Biblical name, and those who rewrote fairytales liked to generalize ideas, they used names like Jack that worked for most cultures without religious implications or specifics.

"Anyway, Jacob was dreamy. Wilhelm, the older, was tough and serious. Jacob loved Lotte because they spent time listening to folktales. So, when that stranger convinced Jacob to give up their only cow for beans, Jacob believed him. He believed that he had saved the family with magic beans."

"You say 'listen' to folktales?" David asked.

"Neither Jacob nor Lotte had learned to read then," Anne said. "Wilhelm taught himself because, like I said, he was the rational one. He saw only one way to save himself and his two siblings: by moving to Kassel, where he would study and they would find work. Kassel was an important German city then, still is."

"I see."

"Fairytales, in their infancy, weren't told in the written word, not for centuries. They were remembered by heart and told in a traveling circus and nights by the fire. That's why folklorists are frustrated with older tales like the Pied Piper of Hamelin that happened in 1284. It's impossible to trace the origins of a story that happened so many centuries ago but was only first documented in the 1400s. What happened in the years before? Was it changed? Did they tell the truth? No one knows."

"I'd like to hear more about that," David said. "Just briefly and return to the Sisterhood story."

"For instance, the single piece of true evidence of the Pied Piper of Hamelin is a glass plaque that was inspired by an older wooden one they found. The wooden plaque was made right after the incident in 1284. When the plaque was discovered centuries later, the new glass one was made. It hung in Hamelin's most prestigious store in town.

"But when war hit the city, even the new glass piece was lost. All that is left of it are paintings of it inside the store. I just want you to understand how hard it was to pass a true story along for future generations."

"I get it," David said. "People were poor. It was a mess. Mothers raised fatherless children. Salt was king. Hardly anyone survived beyond thirty. And kids lived on stories of magic and wonder told by one another, just like all the young adult and children's books in our time."

"Wilhelm beat his little brother, Jacob, for being a dreamer. Then years later, he took his brother and sister and left for Kassel. Jacob grew up there, still fascinated by fairytales, and persuaded Wilhelm to study folklore. Wilhelm hadn't realized people studied such things. Yet when his mentor, who is sometimes referred to as one of Franz Xaver's ancestors, taught him, the two brothers finally made a decent living."

"How about Lotte?"

"Lotte wasn't sure what she wanted to do. She resorted to staying at home in Kassel. She observed her brothers studying these tales and contributed what she learned from her childhood. Wilhelm's and Jacob's studies weren't exclusive to folklore. They contributed to a lot of theories and mathematics, and especially paper printing. This was a new invention that had only recently been perfected and made available to the masses.

"That's when Wilhelm thought of giving back to their country. As well as honoring their childhood by collecting these German folktales in a printed medium.

"It was an ambitious idea. Finally, there was a way to pass along these stories and document them forever."

"Imagine how it felt to live in a time where printing paper, which is going extinct now, was the new technology."

"But the Brothers Grimm learned that folktales differed all over Germany. That these stories were actually true in their origins and were actually never made for children in the first place."

"How so?"

"These stories had been brought to German towns by the salt, wheat, and goodies travelers. They told stories about other cities in Germany, and Europe in general. Of things they'd heard, seen, and sometimes witnessed with their own eyes.

"They learned that the blood, gore, rape, and killings in the stories existed. These stories resonated because again, blood, gore, killing, and rape were things that happened every day around the Grimm brothers as children. In that time of history, no one cared if a child was exposed to such grim—pun intended—visuals or imagery.

"Who cared? Children were already traumatized, and only wished to live as long as possible and have food on the table by the end of the day."

"So where did the fairy grandmother, the sexy prince, and all this sticky sweet optimism and fantasy come from?"

"Did you ever play a game of telephone, David?" Anne said. "Did the final sentence ever match the one in the beginning?"

"I understand." David nodded. "Stories were told orally from one to another and ended up something different."

"Sometimes the stories ended up being slightly different, and sometimes a completely new beast," Anne said. "So, in order for Wilhelm and Jacob to collect these stories, they realized they had to travel all over Germany. They needed to ask people about their sources, and if they heard different versions. Then they would have to go to different people in other cities and ask them again to confirm these stories."

"And of course, they didn't," David said. "Because who would?"

"In all honesty, some people did. Like the Xaver family, but they did it as a hobby without the burden of writing an authentic book.

"Wilhelm and Jacob were frustrated, knowing their desired project was bound to fail. I must note that they were sincere about their intentions. They really were fascinated with 'print' being commercially available. Fascinated they could use it to sum up the common man's folktales into one volume that would teach the coming generations about their ancestors' traditions and life."

"I'm sure they were."

"And though they almost gave up, Napoleon's awaited attack on Kassel elevated their need to do so. The time to collect these fairy-tales was now, in 1811, right before Kassel would be attacked by the French."

"You've basically built a solid case of how it is impossible that the Grimm brothers actually collected these tales," David said. "They had no access to the source material, and they were out of time. If so, then what made the Sisterhood any different?"

"It started with Lotte, the brothers' youngest sister," Anne said. "Right after she was invited to the creepy house across the street where the Sisterhood was formed, and dark practices took place."

# 53

20:11 (P.M.)

## Polle, Fairytale Road, Germany

The Advocate waited atop the tower next to his driver where the sniper stood earlier. He watched Tom John and Martin Wolf and then lowered his binoculars to look at the girl in pink. She was hiding by the castle's ruins beneath the tower. He could tell she was smoking a cigarette in the cold, and dialing a phone number.

"Can you hear what she is saying from up here?" the driver asked The Advocate.

"I look like a wizard in this black cassock but I'm not," The Advocate said in his thick Italian accent. "Why don't you climb down and find out who she is talking to?"

🍎

Down below, the girl in pink waited for someone to pick up the phone. Once they did, she killed the cigarette on the snowy ground, out of fear and respect. "It's Nicoletta, My Queen, from Polle."

"Ah, the girl in pink," the Queen said. "You made sure David and Anne read the next puzzle?"

"I did, Our Queen," Nicoletta said, wishing to please her. "I also gave the same riddle to the inspector, so he knows what they're up to next."

"We don't know what they're up to next," the Queen said. "That's up to Anne, but you did well. How is Lisbeth doing? I heard she's been shot."

"Yes, she is in the hospital now," Nicoletta said.

"Go there and see if she will survive gracefully," the Queen said. "But if she looks like she will live the rest of her life in pain and misery, even more than being stunted and overlooked, kill her."

The girl in pink wished to oppose the idea but then she reminded herself of the mysterious Queen's recent title. The Sisterhood now called her "She Who Must Be Obeyed."

$$\bullet$$

Atop the tower again, and while waiting for his driver's return, The Advocate tried to entice a looming crow with the apple in his hand.

"Come here, boy," he said. "Aren't you hungry?"

The black crow's pupils widened, as if he understood the words of The Advocate, but wouldn't advance.

"It's a dirty apple full of worms," The Advocate hissed. "I know you like to eat trash and the scum of the earth. Come here, I won't hurt you."

The crow stiffened its neck, looking like it feared the man in the black cassock and black hat with such disproportioned limbs.

"Ah," The Advocate said, "I think I know what you want." He reached for something inside the pockets of his cassock. "Normally you'd prefer a dead prey's flesh," he continued, "but I have something that's even better. I have magic. People, and animals, fall for magic."

Just like a magician, The Advocate laid a hefty amount of black beans and worms on the edge of the tower's wall for the crow, who, like Jacob Grimm centuries ago, couldn't resist the magic beans.

# 54

### *Weser River, Fairytale Road, Germany*

"Not to interrupt you, Anne, but we're getting closer," David said, squinting in the darkness while driving. "At some point we will have to abandon the Schwimwagen to distract whoever is after us. We then must take the rest of our journey on land whichever way. I'm just saying, get to the point: how did Dorothea create the Sisterhood?"

"After marrying Wilhelm Grimm, Dorothea and Lotte discovered the creepy house across the street," Anne said. "But then they became friends with its charming owner, Dorothea Viehmann. A lot of myths and secrets surround that house. It's still a renowned tourist attraction in Kassel this very day.

"Viehmann was an established storyteller. Meaning, people in Kassel booked appointments and paid money to listen to her. And her house was called Märchenhaus, meaning House of Stories. The same place where the Six Swans, aka the Sisterhood, gathered."

"Six Swans?"

"Viehmann liked Dortchen and Lotte. She made them join her

in the daily late night gatherings to share stories. She then added three more women to the mix; the Hassenpflug sisters, Jeanette and Amalie. And a sixth one who remained undocumented," Anne said.

"So, Dorothea Viehmann, the storyteller, Dorothea Wild, Wilhelm's wife, Lotte Grimm, their sister, and two other sisters, the Hassenpflugs," David counted. "And one more who remains anonymous. Just reminding myself, as I think I will need to in the future."

"The Six Swans' friendship was based on their love for folktales," Anne said. "The real attraction and bonding emanated from the fact that Viehmann accidentally created a sort of a shrine where people came to her and confirmed or denied stories. She accidentally, yet brilliantly, solved the problem that the Xaver family faced. No longer did the Six Swans need to travel the country. Due to their reputation, people came to them and told them what needed be told."

"Why didn't the Grimm brothers collaborate with the Six Swans then?"

"Here is where it gets messy." Anne took a deep breath. "The Sisterhood never got along with the Brothers Grimm.

"It started with Viehmann calling them imposters. Men who didn't care much for the cause they proposed but wanted to gain financially from collecting the tales. Even Lotte and Dortchen couldn't convince her otherwise.

"Then one day, a peasant girl visited the Sisterhood and told them about a peculiar story that would change the history of folktales forever.

"It was about a poor girl who married a rich aristocrat in exchange for her family keeping the land they lost in debt. It seemed like a bland story. Neither was the girl in the story the fairest of them all or an ugly duckling. There was no good-looking prince who'd save a damsel in distress, and no evil goblins or wolves at hand. It simply didn't relate to any of the 'type stories.'"

"Type stories?"

"The Sisterhood had dissected all folktales into 'types,'" Anne said. "Rags to Riches stories, for example. Quest Stories. Reluctant Hero. Orphaned Prince or Princess, and so on.

"They built an intricate system that was later organized by Aarne-Thompson into types we use in our academic studies. For example, 'The Singing Bone' is story type 780: Murderer Exposed."

"Those people put their heart and soul into this," David said. "So did the Sisterhood reject the peasant's 'out of type' story?"

"At first, but the peasant returned a few days later," Anne said. "She said that she remembered a traveler telling her more about this specific story. She said that when the poor girl's family went to visit their daughter, the rich husband claimed she left and never came back.

"This got the Sisterhood interested. The story had drama and mystery to it now, so they asked the peasant storyteller if she knew what happened next."

"My mother told me that the secret to successful storytelling is to make the listener ask that specific question," David said. "I'm hooked; what happened next?"

"The peasant storyteller said that upon investigating the aristocrat husband, they discovered their daughter wasn't the first to vanish. That he remarried a lot using his influence and money to help poor families with younger daughters pay their debt. And that they all disappeared.

"Still, the Sisterhood needed more, so the peasant storyteller returned a few days later. Guess what she told them?"

"That the aristocrat man killed all his previous wives," David said. "That he wanted each wife not to open a certain door in the mansion. But out of curiosity, one of them did and found the corpses of his previous wives dead and hung on a cross."

Anne stared at him with an open mouth. "You're getting good at this."

"It's the story that Jacqueline de Rais told us," David said. "I guess what happened next was that the Sisterhood still didn't think the story was worth their collection, so the peasant girl had to finally give in and tell them that the story wasn't a folktale, but a true one."

"And I worried it was going to take me forever to explain it to you."

"I'm practical, Anne, and like I said, you have a passion for this. You just take a little too long to get to the point," David said. "I don't blame you. You're enamored by the tales. Deep inside, you actually wish they were only fairytales, even if you spent your life trying to prove otherwise. I'm just a detective, looking for a killer, so I'm unbiased."

Anne didn't comment or entertain the thought. She preferred to continue the story, "So the Sisterhood were shocked when the peasant girl gave away the name of Baron Gilles de Rais and the date of the killings, which was from February 1429 to November 1435. She also provided the name of the castle where it happened, which was Château de Tiffauges, now known as Château de Barbe-Bleue."

"So it happened three centuries earlier," David said. "And yet no one figured it out?"

"No one," Anne said. "There had been rumors about Gilles de Rais, who ended up exiled and killed—but for summoning the devil, not killing his wives."

"How did this peasant girl know about it then?"

"A stroke of moral luck, you could say," Anne said. "Her great-grandmother's sister worked in the castle. She passed on the story, which the family thought of as personal heritage and kept passing it on."

"I assume they feared the consequences of publishing the story," David said. "That's why they kept it in the family."

"That was part of it," Anne said. "But also, who cared? Who was going to believe such a thing happened so long ago? Who was going to go the length and correct history?"

"No one usually does," David said. "So Viehmann and her Swans found themselves in a peculiar position they hadn't asked for."

"Avenging the poor women who got killed centuries ago but having to find a way to tell the world about it," Anne said. "Imagine what kind of burden that was."

"So why did you call the House of Stories a creepy house in the beginning?"

"I'm glad you still remember because I thought I'd have to postpone it for later. Just don't laugh at me when I tell you," Anne said.

"I can't smile, remember?" David said.

"After the incident of the peasant girl, there were rumors about a seance session being held in Viehmann's house," Anne said. "Lotte and Dortchen hardly came home while it was going on. Strange-looking people entered the house. Sound of hymns and prayers emanated from the house each night, right after the peasant girl joined them."

"That's quite a turn of events," David said.

"Locals reported seeing blood on the walls. The members of the Sisterhood got skinnier and shabbier. Lotte was seen walking alone at dawn and talking to herself, reciting words that weren't words. The Hassenpflug sisters turned out to be dabblers of the occult and witchcraft. Even Dortchen was caught by her husband strapping herself to a cord hung from the ceiling to stay awake all night, repeating words about a shepherd, bones, and the devil's crone.

"One day, Jacob found Lotte writing in her blood on animal skin then burning it the next day in the field. Women came into the house and were locked into rooms, talking to themselves all night. Rumors of darker things spread all over Kassel. The only reason no one acted upon it was that Napoleon was at the borders. No one had the time to deal with six women going insane."

"Are you sure none of these incidents are a folktale in and of themselves?" David said. "All of this is beginning to sound utterly supernatural, which can't be the case."

"I know," Anne said, as an arriving ferry suddenly flashed their lights at them. "But you're missing the point of the whole story about the Sisterhood."

"What do you mean?" David shielded his eyes from the direct light and had to stop the Schwimwagen. "I've listened carefully to every word you said."

"Maybe I've rambled on too much, to put you in the picture," Anne said, now seeing the passengers on the coming ferry pointing at the Schwimwagen. She couldn't tell whether they had figured them out, if they had been reported as escaping in one earlier, or if it was just some enthusiastic crowd that hadn't seen a swimming car before. Either way they had to stop and deal with it.

"Since we're going to have to deal with the ferry," David said, "why don't you summarize the crux of the story to me in a single sentence."

"If Lisbeth is right about the Sisterhood, and the Brothers Grimm fairytales were written by women," Anne said, "then I've been looking for the wrong answer for my whole life."

"How so?"

"I was looking for the origins of fairytales," Anne said, "when I now have to find out why did women write those dark and disturbing tales?"

# 55

### *Saint Peters Basilica's tunnels, the Vatican*

Lily, Lucia, and the two nuns stood over the cross laid on the floor in a spot right beneath the basilica's night ceremony. Lily watched Lucia and the nuns, awaiting their signal to proceed.

"Father Firelle upstairs will give us a sign when they empty the basilica for cleaning," one of the nuns said. "We should get started."

"I'm ready," Lucia said.

"I'm not," Lily followed.

"We're going to be late," Lucia argued.

"I don't think this is the right thing to do," Lily countered. "Can't we call Our Queen and ask her for another way to do this?"

"There are many ways to do this, but how will you become a True Sister without executing this? You did it once in Westminster Abbey, and you can do it again," one of the nuns argued.

"What if I don't want to become a True Sister?" Lily said.

"Someone has to replace Lady Ovitz and guard the story," the nun said. "Our Queen insisted it be you, Lily."

"Our Queen has always been an extremist," Lily dared say finally. "When Lady Ovitz was alive, she couldn't do any of this."

The nuns and Lucia exchanged long, tired glances for an uncomfortable moment. Lily wondered if they had come to their senses and were considering her objection.

She was wrong.

Lucia, without warning, pulled out a Vecchia Melo bottle and uncorked it in an instant. Lily stood shocked. She was too late to save her sister, who had already gulped the poison.

Upstairs, at the open-air St. Peter's Square, Bloody Mary enjoyed her new nun's disguise.

She had watched the German news announcing the events at Polle. They reported the lunatic sniper being caught by the silent Martin Wolf, who was going to send him to trial.

There was no mention of David and Anne's escape, though. No matter how she pushed the media to talk about the events, they always managed to tone it down so that the world wouldn't connect the dots.

Mary spat on the floor with disgust. An old woman beside her looked offended by her vulgar manners and walked away.

"What?" Mary snickered after her. "I just saw the devil's shadow on the floor and spat on him."

Spewing her maniacal tendencies at the woman wasn't helping. She was angered at the enemy repeatedly lying to the media. It was important that Anne and David's escape be broadcast to the world. It was important to get everyone's attention. Yet, the enemy's forces were stubborn enough to keep lying.

Unlike what she did to Tom in London to coerce him into announcing the truth, she had no means to make this happen this time. Unless she called him and threatened to deprive his father of the second dose of antidote.

There wasn't a second dose of the antidote anyway, but that

wasn't what stopped her. She had an important task to finish in the Vatican first, so calling Tom had to be postponed.

She wondered why Lily and Lucia were taking so long down in the tunnels. She wished that it wasn't like last time in Westminster Abbey where she still had to take matters into her own hands. Lily had a soft soul, and if Layla hadn't drunk the poison, their plan would've been sabotaged.

The second sacrifice had to be executed in a timely manner; one dead girl on the cross in Westminster Abbey, and one dead girl on the cross in the Vatican.

It seemed she had to take matters into her own hands again. Bloody Mary cracked her knuckles and neck and then walked toward the basilica. She had to make sure Lucia sacrificed herself tonight. That way, she would go finalize her masterpiece of a plan after.

# 56

### *Trendelburg, Fairytale Road, Germany*

Anne, considering David's tendency to use force, took matters into her own hands. She waved back at the ferry crowd, who turned out never to have seen a Schwimwagen before, and pretended she was German. Given her flawless accent that Rachel had taught her, along with her relatively European looks, it worked.

First, she picked the most family-friendly-looking passengers and waved at them. She cooked up a story about her British husband, David, having been fooled by a German tourist company that made him rent the Schwimwagen. But they realized that they would be too late for picking up their children, who were visiting the Rapunzel castle in Trendelburg. And now the Schwimwagen had broken down.

Surprised at herself being a genuinely good liar, she added icing on the cake: that she and her husband were worried for their children in Trendelburg. Especially after what happened in Polle today.

It turned out that the families on the ferry hadn't yet heard about that. They had been on the ferry for two hours, and the parents had denied their children phones on the trip. The younger folks protested now and demanded their phones back so they could begin googling the incident.

David nudged Anne in the back. He was worried their faces would show up in the news somehow. Even though Jacqueline de Rais's words still stuck with him, and he understood that higher powers were trying to always prevent the true events from being published, they couldn't risk it.

Anne told a third lie, that she was a professor of technology and that phones were dangerous for the brain anyway. The local families took her words to heart.

The people on the ferry also believed the lie about needing to pick up their children in Trendelburg. They happily cooperated and agreed to take them along. All they needed was a five-minute sail to the next dock. Trendelburg wasn't located by the river, but about ten miles in from it.

Anne and David climbed onto the ferry. The families cheered and offered them Krombacher, one of German's finest beers.

The one thing neither Anne nor David expected was an elder man wearing an Irish hat offering to fix the Schwimwagen and drive it back.

Anne and David tried to convince him that it wasn't necessary, but Herr Jurgen wouldn't take no for an answer. And neither did the families. Jurgen was a retired mechanic who claimed he could fix any car. It was a matter of pride, after all.

"White or dark Krombacher, Anne?" a friendly local woman asked her as Jurgen hopped into the Schwimwagen so he could fix it right away.

"Either works for me," Anne said while unable to tell Jurgen he had no need to fix it as it wasn't broken. "Either works for me."

"White or dark Krombacher, David?" the woman asked.

"Do I look like white beer guy?" David gritted his teeth, watching Jurgen start the Schwimwagen right up, scratching his head in confusion that it didn't seem broken, and start driving it back to Polle. This meant that soon enough he would tell the police about them.

It was a short ferry ride. A silent one, too, as neither David nor Anne could continue their conversation. They were tired and sleepy, and all David could think about was that women may have written fairytales, not men.

He didn't tell Anne, but it seemed about right to him. Given the themes of the book, and that they'd always been female-centric, why hadn't anyone in the world posed the possibility before? It didn't need a scholar or a detective to investigate the matter. It was like questioning why women would write a book about soccer or baseball. Not that it was impossible or frowned upon, as the two genders equally excelled in every department in past years. But fairytales were written two centuries ago. At a time when a king married several times and was never questioned about the wives that had gone missing.

The ferry dropped them near Trendelburg, right when David was about to ask for another dark beer, which he loved. Then a small transportation carriage led by a bicycle took them to where Anne wanted to go: Hotel Castle Trendelburg.

"Stay here," she told David at the entrance. "I'll be back in a second."

David let her go but didn't let her leave his sight. He watched through the large windows on the first floor as she talked to a woman. The Trendelburg Castle had been turned into some romantic tourist attraction. An attractive hotel with a distinctive restaurant on the main floor. Modern life and old blended nicely. Orange light emanated from inside, lighting up everywhere. Soon Anne returned to him along with the woman.

"This is Helga," Anne introduced her to David.

Helga was in her sixties but stood erect and strong as if she were younger. Her skin was overly wrinkly, and she looked like someone who spent their life farming and working outside. Her hands were gummy and tough, and she had a finger bandaged from a recent injury. Her graying hair still held a golden hue from the past. It was as if her youth wouldn't let her fully age. Her ocean-blue eyes were unmistakably distracting. She wore a traditional German dress called a dirndl, a feminine outfit that originated in the German-speaking areas of the Alps. It was traditionally worn in this region during Christmas and festive times, Anne had pointed out.

"Hello, Helga. I'm David." He stretched out a hand, but Helga hugged him. David felt safe in her arms. It felt irrationally good. He let her touch his face with her rigid hand and inspect it.

"You found yourself a nice man, Anne Anderson," Helga said in relatively good English.

Anne and David had passed the point of trying to explain to people they weren't a couple, so they nodded without commenting.

"Helga owns this hotel," Anne explained to David.

"So did my ancestors since the thirteenth century," Helga said. "You see that Rapunzel Tower? It's more than forty meters in height with walls up to seven meters thick."

"It's impressive, Helga," David said. "I haven't seen anything like it before."

"It used to be a keep in the thirteenth century, in a part of the castle that is no longer here," she explained. "You know what a keep is?"

"A place to keep the residents of a castle safe in times of war, I suppose," David answered. "It's locked from inside and is filled with food and means for living up to a year or so. Only rich families could afford it."

Helga smiled wildly, showing uneven and partially yellowed teeth. She patted David's cheek a little too hard and it came across like a mild slap. "You've found yourself a smart boy, Anne Anderson," she said with pride. "This tower withstood many assaults. Do you know many steps it takes to climb to the top?"

"I don't."

"One hundred thirty steps," she said with more pride. "I see you're a fit man, but can you do it five to seven times a day like I do?"

"I'm not a match to your strength, Helga," David said,

strangely enjoying the conversation with her. "I mean I eat junk food and drink a lot and look at you. You eat from the earth, the healthiest of food."

"You are damn right I do," she said, trying her best to sound American but failing because she sounded too German. "On top of the tower, you can enjoy a view of the fabulous North Hesse countryside. High above the rooftops of old Trendelburg," she said. "Two telescopes up there will help you to see up to even Kassel in the farthest distance."

"Kassel?" David said, exchanging looks with Anne. Neither of them knew how it would come in handy, but it seemed like a curious option.

"Kassel, indeed," Helga said. "Anne told me that you both need a night to spend before you continue your honeymoon trip on the Fairytale Road."

"Honeymoon?" David said, smiling at Anne. "But of course."

Helga, who was much shorter than David, leaned in close and said, "How private would you two like to be?"

"How private do we like to be, honey?" David asked Anne.

Anne didn't play along. Instead, she gently pulled Helga nearby and said, "Could you offer us the Rapunzel room, just for the night?"

"Are you serious?" Helga's eyes widened, leaving David unsure of what was going on. "You know I never open this one up for anyone."

"I know." Anne laced her hands together. "But I'd appreciate it, just for the night."

"Does he know where the Rapunzel room is located?" Helga pointed at David.

"No," Anne said. "I thought I'd surprise him with something very few people in the world know about, Helga," Anne said. "And of course, no one knows we're spending the night inside."

Helga cocked an eyebrow and rubbed her chin. "Were you just in Polle, Anne?"

Anne's face dimmed. "I was."

"Someone's after you, huh?" Helga was quick on the draw. "You found something out about the secrets of the past."

"Yes," Anne said. "Though I'm not sure what it is exactly. Someone wants to stop me from finding it out, I guess—though they also seem to push me to find it."

"Maybe they're pushing you to thinking you will find it, so they can finally prove it doesn't exist," Helga said.

David and Anne both scratched their temples at the same time.

"What do you mean?" Anne asked her.

"You know I hear a lot of stories from travelers in my restaurant," Helga said. "A famous one is that Hitler is still alive—of course, not anymore. What I mean is that he escaped the war. And that he has an offspring that lives in either Brazil or Paraguay. Remember they've never found his body."

"So?"

"Think about it, Anne. To make someone disappear, you can't just say he disappeared. The smarter way is to conduct a worldwide search that everyone can follow and see with their own eyes..."

"And then prove that search led to nothing." David followed her train of thought. "And so you've proven Hitler was dead."

"Was there a huge search for Hitler after the war?" Anne asked. "I don't know about that."

"A global one, darling," Helga said. "News channels, movies, even fortunetellers made so much money out of it. Until one day the people were bored, and Hitler was declared in the collective human conscience dead—and he wasn't; in fact, his offspring still rules a great position of the world under a different name."

David was impressed with Helga. Did she just say "collective conscience"? Maybe he ought to read and educate himself more.

"We'll keep your theory in mind, Helga," Anne said. "How about the Rapunzel room?"

"Let me first understand," Helga said. "Are you telling me there was not a madman who escaped the asylum like they said in the news? They were trying to get to you?"

"Yes," Anne said.

"Does anyone know you're coming here?"

"No," David chimed in, his eyes glaring at Anne.

"Yes," Anne insisted. "We came in a Schwimwagen and a mechanic offered to drive it back to Polle. Soon he will bump into the police."

"He knows you're coming to Trendelburg?" Helga asked.

"Yes," Anne said. "I'm really sorry."

"Don't be," Helga said. "I'd like to see how they're going to find you both when I give you the secret Rapunzel room."

"Thank you so much," Anne said. "It's only a few hours, I promise."

"One last thing," Helga said. "I know you're young and attractive and look like you've only been recently together. Since this secret room is close to my penthouse in the abandoned forest in the back where I sleep, please keep all bed sport as quiet as possible?"

"I'm a shy dude," David said, crossing his heart.

"No, you're not, monkey man." Helga pointed a finger at him. "I come from a generation when three moans were three too many."

# 57

21: 21 (P.M.)

## *Polle, Fairytale Road, Germany*

"So, you know someone who can solve this riddle?" Tom John asked the police officer. Meanwhile, Mr. Wolf knelt beneath the sniper tower inspecting a dead crow, hardly participating in anything. "How is that possible?"

"He is an old local, the most knowledgeable tour guide," the officer said. "He's in his late eighties and has seen and learned things you may never come across."

"I don't think these are the kind of credentials I'm looking for," Tom said, thinking he wanted to call his father and see how he was doing. "This sort of a puzzle, a secret code, or a treasure map. Why is your old man qualified to help?"

"Mr. Otto is no stranger to solving the unsolvable," the officer said. "Did you know he is the one who discovered that Lewis Carroll, the man who wrote *Alice in Wonderland*, was actually Jack the Ripper?"

"No, he wasn't," Tom scoffed, rolling his eyes. "Jack the Ripper was never caught."

"Because he convinced the world he was only a molester of children," another officer added.

"Who, Lewis Carroll? Molester? Are you out of your mind?" Tom said. "Did you forget I'm British?"

"Which means you're the last to know about your history," one officer said. "Don't worry, it happens all the time." He then summoned an old stooping man who was calming his grandchildren after the attack. "Google both facts about Lewis Carroll, by the way. Otto discovered handwriting by Lewis Carroll that was a secret code. An anagram that, if figured out, was a blatant confession of his crimes as Jack the Ripper," the officer said to Tom while Otto approached. "It's not only Hitler who was a nut sack."

The old man with the cane arrived, trudging in the cold. He introduced himself as Otto Lotto, a historian, cryptologist, and game enthusiast.

Tom was on the verge of giving up on this freak show. But he was a stranger in a strange land, left all alone without enough authority to order people around.

"Can you speak English?" Tom said.

"Can you?" Otto waved his cane at the slip of paper Anne and David left behind.

Otto's British accent was surprisingly flawless, formal, and impressive. Tom let him read the puzzle:

> ***Once upon a time, at sixteen-oh-two,***
> ***in the big apple, a river bit through.***
> ***Children used to sing, in streets so mute,***
> ***Deep in abyss mark, two towers tribute.***

"Hmm..." Otto said.

"Hmm..." the police officers echoed.

Finally, Otto spoke. "I will need time to decipher the exact code, but the fundamentals are very clear to me."

"Okay, Einstein," Tom said. "Enlighten me."

"You should be able to figure it out once I explain the misdirection about the words." Otto ran his hand over the written text, showing it to Tom. "Focus on single words. Not the whole sentence."

"Sounds good." Tom saw Otto stop his crooked finger over the words "big apple" and said, "Okay?"

"What does a big apple mean to you?" Otto said.

"I don't know." Tom remembered the pentagram in Westminster Abbey, but he wasn't going to confess anything about it to these strangers. "There are big apples and small apples, right?"

"*Dumm!*" Otto said, which Tom knew meant "dumb" in English. "You know this paper is a mapestry, right?"

"How do you know that?" Tom said.

"I'm a learned man," Otto said. "Anyway, what do mapestries lead to?"

"Another clue, something to help you advance with your search."

"Meaning it could lead to a new time and place to go to next, right?" Otto said. "What is a place you call a Big Apple?"

"New York?" Tom said, hiding that he was fascinated by the interpretation.

"Now, you understand," Otto said, then moving his fingers toward the words "two towers."

Tom's eyes widened. "You don't say."

"Two towers in New York," Otto explained. "Now we know what the subject is about so far. Add the word 'tribute' and you're now on the right track."

"Are you telling me this secret code has something to do with the events of nine-eleven?" Tom liked the explanation, as it fit his sense of paranoia, and would please his superiors.

"Something happened at sixteen O two, which is twenty minutes after four in the afternoon that day," Otto said. "Thus, the hint 'once upon a time.'"

"You're a sick old genius, Otto." Tom pulled the paper from

him. "You think the river mentioned in the puzzle is the Hudson River in New York, then?"

Otto nodded. "'Children used to sing in streets so mute' is probably reflecting on the people who died that day."

"Okay. Okay." Tom felt elated that he could frame Anne and David for eternity. "So what is this 'abyss mark' then?"

"That's the part I need time to solve," Otto said. "But I imagine it's the one thing that will lead you to those you're after."

"I don't need more time," Tom said and took off. He was about to use this information to impress his superiors before he continued his quest after Anne and David. Midway, he stopped and turned to look back at Otto. "So is it true that Lewis Carroll *was* Jack the Ripper, huh?"

"Indeed," Otto said. "A celibate man that photographed young girls, almost naked, British, and was weird enough to write about rabbit holes. Who knows what he meant by that?"

"Do you know how much can be made from something like that?" Tom said, and then left to call his superiors.

# 58

---

## *Trendelburg, Fairytale Road Germany*

David and Anne followed Helga into the ancient castle now turned into this romantic hotel called Burg Trendelburg. From the first moment he had laid eyes on it, he couldn't help but notice the ancient walls, towers, and drawbridge.

Incredible and intricate creativity had been put into converting this wonderful piece of architecture to a modern hotel. Unlike the castle in Polle, which had honestly not impressed him that much, Castle Trendelburg was a place he would escape to. To rent a room in the tower and continue his investigation about his mother's death. Of course, he would also enjoy this place with someone he loved, but he had given up on this idea ever happening. His soul lantern had been out of fire for a long time.

As they climbed the 130-step spiral staircase, Helga explained how the former chapel had been converted into a dining room. Also, that their most rented room was one in the tower where its bathroom was accessible through a wardrobe. A design made centuries ago, and never altered.

They also came across open-beamed ceilings, woodwork, and suits of armor every now and then. Down by the reception and even in this staircase, antique pieces adorned the whitewashed walls inside. The most dominant feature of the tower was that it was windowless. David had little knowledge of the Rapunzel fairytale, and thought a windowless tower fitted just about right. But Rapunzel still needed one window to dangle her hair down, didn't she?

Helga, with her dimly lit, old-fashioned gas lamp, stopped at step 128, where she claimed the secret Rapunzel room was located.

David noticed the recurrence of the number 28 in so many incidents. "The Singing Bone" was tale number 28. The Aarne-Thompson type was 128. And now the Rapunzel room was at step 128.

"I've noticed it, too," Anne said, answering his inquiry. "But I'm unaware of a significance. I'll keep a mental note, though."

"I'm also worried that hiding in a room this high, no matter how safe, is a prison in and of itself," David said. "If they find us, we'll have nowhere to go."

"You can always ask Rapunzel to dangle her hair and climb down, young man," Helga said, leaving David speechless, unsure if she made a joke or hinted at something. "Besides, you're bleeding and will need Anne to take care of you first, so just relax."

"I've been telling him to relax all day," Anne told Helga.

"Men worry all the time, allowing the world to weigh on their shoulders. Look at Atlas, what good did it do him lifting the world on his back?" Helga said. "You, young man, should see what we women go through. Then you'll learn how to relax and laugh and be utterly, incredibly, and unapologetically silly in the darkest of times."

David smiled back at her, and so did Anne. Except Anne's smile was a form of longing for a mother figure, he'd noticed by now. Older women were her all-time weakest point. Unlike her weakness to fairytales, this was a weakness David loved about her. He himself hadn't had this weakness because he saw his mum and remembered her thoroughly. He didn't miss a *mother figure*. He missed *his mother*—and the rest of his family whom he never told Anne about.

Helga then surprised them by running her hand over the tower's inner wall. It looked like she didn't exactly know where the door to the secret Rapunzel room was. David realized that the room was going to be inside the walls. How genius, he thought. Old towers like these, built of stones, needed their walls to be seven meters thick, enough to fit a secret room inside.

"May I?" David knocked on the walls like her and soon came upon a hollow part. "Is this it?"

"See how useful you can be when relaxed?" Helga smiled with her uneven teeth. "Now gently pull back that stone."

David did as he was told, surprised at how heavy a head-sized brick could be. Behind it, he saw the unexpected, a digital keypad. Dusty and probably not all buttons worked.

"Say Open Sesame." Helga nudged him.

David smiled, looking at Anne, who was as enamored with Helga as he was.

"I suppose the code is 128?" David guessed.

"I don't even remember anymore," Helga said, winking to show Anne she was testing him.

Although this wasn't the right time for him to solve a puzzle, he gave it a shot. Closer, he saw that most keys had been deliberately broken and wouldn't work.

"Ah," he considered. "This is easy." He pushed the buttons 7775, which was the numerical translation to GGGE, Beethoven's Fifth.

The door's clockwork chugged open, just like the tunnels back in London.

"That *was* easy," Anne wondered.

"Helga broke all the unnecessary keys and left me with two," David said. "So I gave it a shot."

"Like I said," Helga said, "I forget the numbers, so I made it a no-brainer for me."

"Wouldn't that make it easy for an intruder to get in?" David said.

"If they know this much about the tower, the secret room, and keynotes, nothing will really stop them at this point," Helga said. "Now I'm surprised that none of you worried I used the victory code that also translates to Beethoven's Fifth."

David tensed, wondering if Helga double-crossed them. If the Sisterhood used the victory code in their mapestry, did that mean Helga was one of them?

"V doesn't stand for victory." Helga's face changed, not in features, but she huffed at the gas lamp and summoned the darkness. "But for Viehmann. Dorothea Viehmann."

# 59

### *Saint Peters Basilica's tunnels, the Vatican*

Lily knelt in panic, trying to save Lucia, who'd stumbled to the floor. The poison's effect wasn't as fast, but Lily had slapped her sister violently on the lips. She was forcing her to lose balance and fall next to the Vecchia Melo bottle, crashing against the tunnel's floor.

Lucia screamed in pain, and Lily wasn't sure why. When she knelt, she saw her sister had cut her lower lip on a shard of the broken bottle.

The floor around Lucia's face was stained with the red, poisonous wine. Lily dragged Lucia by her feet away from the smell. She worried the smell would be as effective as the poison itself.

"What are you doing?" Lucia yelled.

"You don't have to die, Lucia," Lily insisted as the nuns tried to pull her away from her sister.

Lily was glad the nuns were older. Although they weren't as short as her, she was resilient and strong enough to free herself from their grip. She picked up a hammer they had used in building the cross and threatened them with it.

"If you come near me or Lucia, I will hang you both on the cross," Lily growled. "Let's see if you really believe in sacrifice."

"Our Queen gave her orders," Lucia still countered. "And you will become a True Sister. Why are you doing this? What happened to you?"

"You're asking me what happened?" Lily yelled back. "Remember the darkness the Six Swans went through? That's what happened. We were never meant to spill blood. We're supposed to stop the blood from spilling."

Suddenly a third nun appeared out of the darkness and knocked Lily down. As she fell to the floor, she heard the nuns calling the Queen on the phone and asking if they should get rid of Lily.

🍎

In the empty basilica above, Father Firelle stood by himself. He was waiting for the Sisterhood's knock on the other side of the tunnel's door. The plan was to open it and allow them entrance through the tunnel, then later let the cleaning men find the girl on the cross. Just like in Westminster Abbey.

If the first sacrifice hadn't shaken the world enough, then the second one should. And if it didn't, there were more sacrifices to come. In a world of short attention spans and distracting social media, it wasn't an easy task waking up the collective conscious of humanity and forcing them to look back. The Queen's plan was brutal, but effective.

Firelle had been a follower of the Sisterhood since long ago. So was his mentor—the one who proposed the second girl on the cross should be killed inside the Vatican. It wasn't a haphazard plan. Both Westminster Abbey and the Vatican had spent years covering the secret about the Singing Bone. Its discovery would crumble their credibility and power—and their intentions.

"Are you ready?" Bloody Mary appeared behind him suddenly.

Father Firelle shivered.

"I'm waiting for them," Firelle said. "But they're late. I'm risking everything for this."

"You're risking everything for Our Queen," Mary said, coming near and offering him a red rose, then acting childishly, swaying her nun's outfit left and right.

"What's this?" Father Firelle looked wearily at the rose. "And why are you acting like that?"

"You don't like me, being a shy nun?" She blinked her doe eyes. She then tilted her head and talked to him sideways. "Or is it you only like boys?"

"How dare you?" He raised a hand at her but then stopped midair. "Why do you like to provoke me, Mary? I'm only looking for redemption."

"I hate that word, Father," she said. "I mean a killer redeems himself by asking for forgiveness and changing into a born-again citizen, blah, blah, blah. Good for him, but how about those he hurt? Do you think it makes a difference if he redeemed himself or not?"

Father Firelle lowered his head, looking sincere and genuine about trying to do the right thing. "Thank you for the rose."

"It's not just any rose, Father," Mary said. "Take a better look at it. It's a five-petal rose."

Father Firelle panicked again and hurled it away in the air.

"Five-petal rose, like a five-pointed apple," Mary chimed happily, then stepped even closer and held his head with both her hands. "The sins of the past, Father, they can be buried six feet under, but the soil of the earth will turn the sin into a seed that will grow a tree from the damp earth, one that is big and angry and unstoppable and will eat everyone around."

"Don't hurt me, please."

"Are you worried if I hurt you, you will lose the prestigious position and the power?" Mary said. "Imagine the pope discovering the secrets you keep."

"Why are you bringing this up now, Mary?" Firelle said in his Sicilian accent.

"No reason in particular." She licked his face like a venomous snake and let go of him. He couldn't do anything about it. "Now get me that dagger you used to cut the apple in half with, please."

"Why?" He grimaced, feeling his legs about to buckle underneath him.

"Lily is resisting orders down there in the tunnels," Mary said. "I think it's time to teach her a lesson on how to become a True Sister."

"I see." Father Firelle nodded and went to get the dagger, too scared to look back at Bloody Mary. She had always made him want to pray for forgiveness in her presence.

When he returned, he was sweating while handing her the dagger.

"Don't worry, Father." She ran the back of her hand on his right temple. "I'm not the devil."

"You're worse," he stuttered. "You're Bloody Mary."

"Shhh," she said, calming him down, yet unnerving him. "I'm like death. I come and people go. There is nothing to be afraid of."

"Sometimes, I don't believe you're an Ovitz." He was drooling now, knowing what she had done and knowing she had killed in the past. "No wonder your sisters call you the scariest of them all."

"But of course I am," she whispered in his ear. "I'm the tallest, after all."

# 60

## *Trendelburg, Fairytale Road Germany*

The light from inside the secret room in the *Rapunzelsturm* castle —as it's called in its native language—shimmered like a distant fire. Helga had immediately turned it on after she puffed out her gas lamp like a big bad wolf.

Anne and David breathed with ease, having suspected foul play just a few minutes earlier. It turned out that Helga was still on their side. She was only educating them about the more specific history of the Sisterhood.

Entering the room was an almost ethereal experience.

Having taken a circular shape of seven meters wide diameter, it turned out to be a whole apartment. One secretly circling the staircase at the 128th step, which was about ten stories up, more or less.

Only one window cut through the outer walls — which David couldn't see earlier since the staircase was built against the inner walls — and it looked over the abandoned forest in the back, which wasn't visible from the front where most people arrived.

Helga also explained that it had been deliberately removed from the blueprints.

Every twenty meters or so, a different piece of furniture was laid at hand. There was a study, a kitchen, a reading space, a bedroom, and a single bathroom that took only three meters of width from the total span of seven.

There were no barriers or curtains separating the spaces. It was meant to be used as one circular apartment. It reminded Anne of a scene in Stanley Kubrick's movie *2001*, in which an astronaut walked a similar circular open space but horizontally without gravity.

Anne left David looking out the windows at the city from above. She had come to get used to his safety precautions by now.

Her eyes took in the ancient-looking interior. The study was made of mahogany wood that still left a scent lingering in the air. The bed and even the exterior of the bathroom were built of the same wood. The wardrobes as well followed the circular design and looked odd in places. So did the two sofas, which were the only modern-looking things in the place. There were no phones, no TV, no electricity sockets even. Helga promised to fill up the single refrigerator with food, and explained that the refrigerator was powered from an outside source.

"Romantic, I must say," Anne told Helga.

"Wasn't always the case," Helga said. "This room was built in 1300 by Konrad the Third. He owned it solely for a whole century. That is the time when Rapunzel's real story happened. It's said that he imprisoned a girl, Rapunzel, or whatever her real name was, in here, and then many others had been trapped here by his descendants."

"Sounds like the Bluebeard story to me," David said.

"They all sound like the Bluebeard story." Helga let out a long breath. "If you ask the locals, they will tell you that Konrad also summoned the devil and killed his wives."

"What's that summoning the devil thing?" Anne asked. "Do you know more about it?"

"All I know is it's not the devil, and that it must a metaphor for summoning the evil from inside all of us," Helga said. "People love to exaggerate and generalize these stories. For example, in the case of Gilles de Rais's story he did summon a demon. It was called Baron." She emphasized its French pronunciation. "Can you imagine? The title Baron has been inspired by a demon that did not exist?"

"It's possible," Anne said. "The origins of words and their etymology is a study that I passed on for the love of fairytales but has always enticed me. For example, I was shocked that the English word 'macabre' originated from *macbara*, meaning 'tomb' in ancient Middle Eastern texts."

"So, who owned this castle after this Konrad guy?" David asked.

"The landgrave of Hesse, Hans von Stoghusen." Helga didn't blink or even struggle to remember these names. "Then the bishop of Paderborn. They both fought over the castle later."

"Why fight over it?" David said. "What was special about a tower where allegedly a girl had been tortured?"

"Like the Brothers Grimm book," Helga said, "those German leaders of the past were looking for the Singing Bone."

"I can't seem to grasp the concept of it yet," David said. "I understand that the Singing Bone is probably more of a metaphor for something. But why does everyone want to sink their teeth into the past? What happened that was important back then?"

"You ask the folklorist about that," Helga said.

"Trust me," Anne told her, "I'm beginning to think I know as little as everyone else."

"I heard stories about soldiers during the Thirty Years' War having captured the castle and the town," Helga said. "They were about to bring the castle down but didn't for some reason."

"Do you happen to think the Singing Bone's mystery is connected to the Thirty Years' War, Helga?" David asked. "It keeps coming up."

"That war was about something bigger than Protestants against Catholics if you ask me," Helga said. "But if you two are going to spend the night here, ask yourself this. Why the American troops and later refugees took lodging at this castle? And why it bothered Hitler the most."

"This happened?" Anne said. "I don't recall something like that."

"That's because you still use the written word, the studies, the prestigious libraries, and god forbid this Google website to find answers," Helga said. "The answers are in people's hearts. Passed on from one generation to another, and to get to it, you will have to make them speak. In this time of technological advancement, the spoken word is the only way to tell the truth. Sleep well, birdies. I will wake you up early in the morning. The door opens with the same code from inside, by the way."

"Speaking of the code"—Anne gently stopped her before she left—"I have to ask you again, Helga, about the V actually referring to Dorothea Viehmann."

Helga took a moment, her eyes moving between Anne and David. "The Sisterhood's Queen used to come here in the nineteenth century, right before they went mad in Kassel."

"The Queen?" Anne said.

"That's the name they gave to Dorothea Viehmann, the leader at the time," Helga said. "They called her My Queen, Our Queen, or something like that. Later, when the leadership was passed through the years, whoever took the title was hailed as Queen."

"Do you know who the Sisterhood's Queen is now?"

"I wouldn't, Anne," Helga said. "I'm not one of them. Never was. Every now and then a so-called True Sister would visit me and ask me for something. Maybe keep someone here for the night. Maybe take care of one of their families who are struggling with money. Simple things, which I do willingly because I don't want anyone to hurt me."

"Hurt you?" Anne said. "I thought the Sisterhood longed for truth and to expose centuries-old secrets. I thought they were the good people."

"There was a time when they were, and probably some of them still are," Helga said. "All until three years ago or so when the new Queen called herself She Who Must Be Obeyed and took a bloody and brutal path in order to uncover the truth. Wait—"

David tensed while Helga cocked her head, thinking she heard something.

"There is someone at the bottom of the stairs," Helga panicked.

"You can hear someone 128 steps below?" David said.

"If you've climbed these stairs up and down for forty years, you can hear every beat of heart, no matter how far," Helga said, hurrying to the door. "I think it's my brother, he always looks for me. He usually drives me wherever I need, so it's good to have him around. But he sometimes thinks he is my bodyguard, too."

"Should we invite him in?" Anne offered and David glared at her.

"No, he is a big man in his forties, my brother," she said. "I better climb down so he doesn't ask questions. Bear in mind, not even he knows about this room, so lock yourself in till morning, birdies."

"And no bed sports or Olympics." David blew her a kiss, trying to be as friendly as possible. "Unless my torch is on fire."

# 61

**BBC News, London**

*Breaking News:*

*Following up today's gruesome murder of a girl on the cross in West-minster Abbey, an anonymous but trusted source have confirmed Anne Anderson and David Tale have left the country to Germany.*

*The German police have confirmed this fact and promised to catch the two fugitives at all costs. While on their trail, Anne and David dropped an important document that hasn't been disclosed yet, but Tom John, who has travelled over for consultation, has announced the following:*

*First of all, my deepest condolences to the family of the victim, Layla Ovitz, who was found dead on the cross this morning. Layla, born to a family of seven sisters, had recently lost her grandmother, too. She was a hard-working student in Queen Mary's University, and was loved by everyone.*

*We promise Layla's family to catch her prime suspect, Anne Anderson.*

*We don't know yet the motive of Professor Anderson, but her finger-prints have been found in the crime scene. Again, we haven't yet talked to her former psychiatrist, but Anne had been on specific medications in the past years that dealt with mental illness. We can't disclose more information about this issue now.*

*However, the most shocking information at this time is that, upon discovering a document she left behind in Germany, we sadly, and unbelievably, have strong evidence to connect her to a most gruesome and unforgivable terrorist attack of the past: The 9/11 attacks in 2001.*

*We will try to be as transparent as possible, but some intricate parts of the case need to stay top secret to help us catch her.*

*Thank you.*

*We'll return soon. Now back to Janine covering the festive Christmas preparations and the dog with three heads at Piccadilly Square.*

# 62

## *Trendelburg, Fairytale Road, Germany*

Anne couldn't sleep, instead watching David snore his highway to heaven. One of the things Rachel hated the most was how Anne snored as kids. Anne had argued so many times that she didn't, until Rachel recorded her while asleep. And boy, did she sound like uninterrupted locomotive breath.

"At least I'm steady and on a beat," Anne argued back before Rachel threw a pillow at her.

Now that Anne had stitched David's wound, she should have used the time to rest as well. Part of it was how embarrassed she was about it, since she wasn't good at stitching and added to his wound. He made a big deal of it and she ended up bandaging his shoulders. The funny part about it was that he didn't notice the extra injury she caused him.

Helga had returned with first aid supplies and told them they were safe for a few hours, and she would alert them if something fishy happened.

A while later, when David fell asleep, Anne told Helga to wait and try to solve the puzzle:

*Once upon a time, at sixteen-oh-two,*
*In a big apple, a river bit through.*
*Children used to sing, in streets so mute,*
*Deep in abyss mark, two towers tribute.*

Helga made some tea and sat with Anne in the kitchen, as far as possible from the snoring detective. Anne had told Helga all about what happened, including the girl on the cross and the mapestry. Helga had always been Anne's most trusted person on the Fairytale Road since she first arrived for her studies. It took Anne a long time to fully trust her with the most intricate details about her research. Helga proved over and over again to be that cheery, easy-living woman who believed in her. So much that Anne had told her too much about her childhood, and about what happened with Rachel.

"Do you have a clue what this poem means?" Anne asked Helga, who sipped her tea almost as loudly as David's snoring.

"I've read so many of these puzzles as a child, Anne," Helga said. "It sounds very familiar."

'What do you mean by that?"

"I can't explain it, but it sounds like something a local would write."

"A Trendelburg local?"

"A Fairytale Road local," Helga said. "You know we're all so dreamy in this region. The backdrop of our folklore history, the architecture, and the lore you see and talk about daily made most of us talk the same."

"This little poem sounds that way, right?" Anne said. "What gave it away?"

"First of all, the part about the 'abyss mark.'"

"What about it?"

"I think in a proper English pronunciation it should be written like 'in an abyss mark' or 'in abyss's mark.' I'm no English expert but you can tell it's told by someone who speaks English as a second language, and doesn't care to be as correct."

"Well, unless abyss mark is more of a noun or a commonly known place, not a description or metaphor, I guess yes."

"Had it been a name of a place, it would have been written in capitals, and I'd have probably heard of it," Helga said. "The point is that the children around here write these kinds of puzzles in our holidays, and they love writing them in English to show them to tourists. Some cities on the Fairytale Road have a Treasure Hunt day which tourists love."

"I know about those, and true, foreigners love them," Anne said. "What else?"

Helga took a long, noisy sip, which accidentally synced with David's symphony, creating a peculiar cacophony around Anne. "From the top of my head it's an invitation."

"Invitation?"

"Since it's a mapestry, it suggests a stupid idea like the Big Apple being New York, and the Two Towers being the World Trade Center—which is utter nonsense, since the mapestry brought you back to the Fairytale Road." Helga wiped her mouth with the tip of her sleeve and put on her glasses.

"Makes perfect sense to me," Anne said. "What do you see, then?"

"'Sixteen O Two' is time, foreshadowed by the word *time* preceding it in 'Once upon a time.'"

"Time of the event I'm invited to?" Anne wasn't sure about Helga's interpretation but didn't mind going along with it.

"Streets so mute is an address," Helga said.

"A characteristic of a certain street, I agree," Anne said. "What about the children?"

"At 16:02 you're going somewhere where the street is mute, but children sing," Helga said. "Hmm..."

"How can children sing on a street so mute?"

"A paradox."

"Could it be that street so mute refers to an abandoned street?"

Anne said. "And the secret to where the event takes place is when you hear children sing nearby?"

"I like that interpretation." Helga flipped the paper on its back but found nothing. "This is fun, actually."

"Since it's almost midnight then it's fair to assume I'm invited to that place tomorrow, four in the afternoon?" Anne said.

"Sounds like it, but where is that street?" Helga said. "Bear in mind you received this clue in Polle."

"So there is a big chance we have to go back." Anne was thinking to herself. "But the mapestry has always progressed into a newer place so far. I doubt that it's an invitation to a place inside Polle."

"I agree," Helga said. "After all, what's there to visit in Polle but the Everstein Castle?"

"And no way they predicted I'd escape in a Schwimwagen to Trendelburg."

"Really?" Helga said. "I mean what was that old vehicle doing there?"

"That's a good point, but no way they knew the events would unfold that way," Anne said. "In Polle, I should have figured out the location of the fortune cookie upon arrival."

"That's also true. I guess I'm being paranoid," Helga said. "Which means that either line two or four in the poem holds the answer to where that mute street exists."

"Line four talks about that abyss mark." Anne read it again. "An abyss is at the bottom of oceans, but could it be a metaphor for something at the bottom of the Weser River?"

"I'd have agreed if it was feasible, diving into the river in this cold," Helga said. "It's such a hard task to do. Why make the solution so unattainable?"

"Besides, there are no streets at the bottom of rivers." Anne's frustration tainted her voice. "What about this 'two towers tribute'?"

"I can't possibly know that part," Helga said. "I mean there are endless towers on the Fairytale Road. There are even endless twin towers. And I don't recall any of these towers having been built as a tribute. Even this tower we're in, it's one, not two."

"Dead end, huh?" Anne remarked. "How about line two?"

"'In a big apple, a river bit through.'" Helga took another noisy sip. "I think I'm pretty sure about the second part of it."

"Really?" Anne grabbed Helga's cup and drank from it so she'd stop her noisy sipping.

"A river that bites through an apple is just a metaphor," Helga said. "It's a relatively common expression here. And since you received this, then the river is definitely the Weser River."

"But the Weser River stops a little before Trendelburg," Anne said, then realized that Helga had helped her figure out half the answer. "This means that the city is up north. We're in the wrong direction." She celebrated by sipping the tea from Helga's cup. "We're looking for a city north that has an apple bitten by a river, whatever that means."

"You're too loud," Helga pointed out. "Try sipping the tea in a softer manner. Aren't you supposed to be a quiet, well-mannered, abiding fairytale girl?"

Anne was shocked at first, then she realized Helga was teasing her in a playful way. "Here, take your tea back," Anne said. "A reward for solving half the puzzle."

"All you need to know is which city on the Fairytale Road produced big apples up north." Helga sipped even louder than before. "That's my take on it."

"The problem is, Helga, that not one city produces apples in the north," Anne said. "The big apple reference is for something else."

The two ladies took a moment to think it over. Helga put down the tea and took off her glasses. They had prided themselves on knowing everything about the Fairytale Road, and they didn't like the fact that they couldn't point out a city up north known for its apples.

Silence was a good way to dig deep into their memories, until David snored again.

"Shut up!" both women said, so loud that David jumped awake in bed.

"Someone arrived?" he said, half awake, one eye open, and half panicking.

"Relax," Helga said. "We've figured out the direction this mapestry leads to."

"You don't say." David stood up and almost tripped barefoot to the kitchen. "Where?"

"A city up north, known for its apples, in an abandoned street, where at a certain house some children will sing," Anne said.

"What?" David's face twitched.

"I know it's vague," Anne said. "But Helga thinks we're invited to an event tomorrow, probably to meet the killer in person."

"Event?" David's eyes flung open. "You mean the one Jacqueline de Rais and Franz Xaver talked about?"

"It crossed my mind," Anne said. "But Kassel is in the south and the poem points north."

"So you ladies haven't figured out anything, and I only slept half an hour." David turned around to go back to bed, pointing at Helga. "Please stop drinking tea, it's annoying and you're too loud."

Before Helga and Anne could comment or laugh, Helga panicked again.

"I hear voices," she said and stood up, running toward the window.

"Relax, Helga," Anne said. "You're always on edge."

"Except this time I'm right." She pointed at the eastern window, downward.

Anne jumped off her chair and went to look, and so did David.

Far, far down below, they saw a police car parked.

"It could be anything," Anne said. "Maybe they're customers. And if not, the police driving is part of their job."

"Not when they're accompanied by this guy." David pointed downward.

Anne looked and saw Hans Jurgen, the elderly man who drove the Schwimwagen back.

# 63

23:29 (P.M.)

**Saint Peters Basilica's tunnels, the Vatican**

On all fours, Lily tried to stand up, realizing she must have been passed out for some time.

"Stop it," Lucia defended her sister, though she didn't approve of Lily's defiance to the Sisterhood. "I'll drink the poison, and then you can hang me on the cross."

The nuns relaxed and Lily began to sob on her knees.

"Take me," Lily said to the nuns. "I do not wish to become a True Sister anymore."

"That's not your call," one of the nuns replied in broken English. "She Who Must Be Obeyed spoke her word. We wish not to break the bond."

Lily saw Lucia reach for another bottle of wine to fulfill her brainwashed destiny. Had the person beside her moved, Lily could've shifted her position and stopped Lucia again. But someone stood right beside her, and she couldn't do it. Lily wondered how many other Sisterhood members occupied the tunnels.

"Don't worry, Lily," Lucia said, gripping the bottle. "I have no place in this world anyway. I'll see you in the Heavens, sister."

Suddenly the lights in the tunnel went out.

"Lucia!" Lily freaked out, not sure what was going on.

And though she wanted to stand up and look for her sister, she couldn't. Fear chained her to the floor, as she heard the nuns drop to their knees one by one. She heard gurgling sounds of betrayal and praying for forgiveness before they left this world.

It all happened fast and without warning. The only upside was when Lily heard her sister call her name back. Both had been spared by whoever had attacked the rest in the dark.

Then the light came back on.

Lily crawled towards her sister and hugged her close.

All around them, three Vatican nuns lay dead on the floor, their throats slit with shards of glass. Before them stood she who once was their sister. The one they, and Lady Ovitz, feared the most as children: Bloody Mary.

"Whooh," she said, holding a shard of glass in her palm and bleeding from it without care. "I thought I'd be poetic and kill them with the glass. Fairytale and all, you know."

"Mary?" Lily was speechless, pulling Lucia behind her.

"Don't worry, sis, I don't need to kill Lucia anymore," Mary said then stood over the bleeding nuns and yelled, "Mirror, mirror on the wall, who is the scariest of them all!"

Lily and Lucia hugged each other closer and crawled back.

"Why did you do that, Mary?" Lily asked.

"I heard you girls whining about the sacrifice. I knew those nuns wouldn't let you go, so I took matters in my own hands," Mary said. "But as always, you never thank me back."

"What will we tell Our Queen now?" Lucia said. "She will be angered I didn't sacrifice myself."

"Don't worry about her." Mary licked blood from her palm. "I talked to her."

"You did?" Lucia said. "And she spared me?"

"She didn't spare you. I spared you," Bloody Mary said. "Now enough with the chitchat and help me hang the sacrifice on the cross."

"You found someone else?" Lily said.

Bloody Mary smirked. "I found an even better volunteer who will shock the world so well, they won't neglect us anymore."

# 64

23:30 (P.M.)

## *Trendelburg, Fairytale Road Germany*

When Tom John arrived the German police were all over the Trendelburg Castle. The police officers blocked all possible escape
routes and one of them was interrogating Helga, the owner.

The conversation was in German, so Tom decided to look
around and wait until the officer told him what Helga said. He
found the man who had driven the Schwimwagen and asked him
why he was sure they must be in the castle.

"They said they left their children in Trendelburg," the German
said in English.

"That doesn't mean they came to this castle of all other places,"
Tom said, disappointed that he may be wasting time. "Anne can't
be that stupid. A folklorist visiting the next landmark on the road.
She must have known we'd come here."

"She actually is that stupid." The German police officer came
back from interrogating Helga. "The owner said they are here."

"Are you sure?" Tom said. "Where are they, then?"

"Up that tower, the owner said." The officer pointed to the

Rapunzel tower. "They asked to rent a room and she gave them one."

"Get all your men up there right now!"

"Let's take it slow and don't rush it," the officer said. "Helga assured me the tower is inescapable. I mean look." The officer showed him a blueprint of the tower showing its thick seven-meter walls.

"That's good news, but why not attack right away?" Tom wondered.

"Two reasons," the officer said. "They rented the last floor and the only way up is a narrow stairway."

"Who cares," Tom said. "I'm sure your men are tough enough."

"She said David, the detective, got drunk," the officer said. "He has a rifle up there with him."

"I see," Tom said.

"When Helga sent room service, he threatened to shoot anyone who came nearby," the officer said. "It's a suicide mission for our men."

"You're right about that," Tom sighed. "David is a sick and troubled man. But hey, no worries, as long as he is stuck up there."

"So you're not in hurry?"

"There are no windows in that tower, right?"

"None," the officer said. "I showed you the blueprint."

"Then I'll be here all night," Tom said. "Go get whatever you need to catch him. Helicopters, negotiators, snipers—I'm not going anywhere." Tom snickered. "You've climbed up to Heaven, David, to realize it's your hell."

🍎

David and Anne were climbing down the other side of the window where the police weren't looking. No one could see the window led them straight into the dark forest in the back. A forest where people got lost. Since the police were sure there were no windows back there, they didn't bother.

Rapunzel's hair, as Helga put it, had been designed years ago to host a show about the known fairytale. Therefore, it was a safety rope with wiring and belts that made it an easier climb down the wall for the performers. The wires had been bolted by the outer walls in the back. These assisted Anne and David whenever they lost balance. Even better, Helga had an architect carve holes for steps on the back wall of the tower to assist the climber while descending. The reason they had chosen the back window by the forest was because they had planned to trim and modernize part of the forest. The idea had proven to be profitable. Then the 2008 recession hit, and Helga no longer had the money to spend on the project.

Anne set foot on the grass and let out a long sigh. One hundred and twenty-eight steps equaled about ten stories. Not an easy task. Even David struggled with it. The best he did was hold tight to her while they both climbed down. After all, she had spent her teenage years climbing a well up and down. It wasn't like she hadn't done it before.

Sometimes, Anne wondered whether Rachel could read the future. She had taught her a lot of things beforehand.

Helga had her driver wait for them in his old Volkswagen Beetle by the edge of the forest, near the main road opposite the river. Anne and David carefully hiked through the thick forest. They were guided by the faint passing lights of vehicles driving by the main road, which was up the hill. A few minutes later, they arrived.

Helga's driver introduced himself as Harry. He spoke English with a weird accent, not quite German but something similar. He rushed them into the car and told them Helga had ordered him to drive them toward any destination they chose. He boasted that his Beetle was black and hard to spot at night.

David sat in the back so he would have enough room to stretch his legs in the cramped car. Anne sat next to Harry, who was also too big for the tiny vehicle.

"Where should we go?" David asked Anne. "North or south?"

"North," Anne said.

"I'm thinking south toward Kassel where Jacqueline de Rais went. We can solve the puzzle on our way."

"No, David," Anne said. "It can't be south. Even if Helga and I misinterpreted the puzzle, it mentioned the Weser River. It ends near Polle and only runs up to the north."

"How many known fairytale cities exist from Polle toward the north?" David said.

"A lot," Anne said. "Bodenwerder, Hamelin, Oldendorf, Nienburg, Buxtehude, Bremen."

"Okay, then." David made an awkward attempt to stretch in the back. "I need twenty-six minutes of sleep to function again."

"Only twenty-six minutes?" Anne said.

"I read in some study that a man can take twenty-six-minute naps and then function for six more hours." David's eyelids slowly gave in. "Of course, the study never mentioned someone who's been running for his life, shot, and being chased for more than twelve hours."

"I wonder if it works for me as well," Anne said and closed her eyes as Harry drove north.

She fell asleep instantly, only to dream of Rachel again.

# 65

## *Midnight, Everywhere...*

Tom John occupied himself with sending messages to his superiors. He was assuring them that soon he would have the Singing Bone in his possession. Martin Wolf, on the other hand, bought himself another pack of gum since he wasn't going home tonight. Helga watched the police officers. She could tell they were unwilling to climb the stairs and risk their mortality. After all, whether they were in on it or not, they'd witnessed a lunatic sniper shoot at people in Polle earlier. It was only two days before Christmas, they said, the worst time of the year to die and upset their families.

Helga drank her tea and watched the officers debate from her reception's glass window, reminiscing about the past. She wondered about the rumors she had heard about Dorothea Viehmann when she visited the Rapunzel room—the main reason why the room's code was the first letter of her name.

Like back in the Marchenhaus in Kassel, people heard chants and singing coming from the Rapunzel room as well. They said

Dorothea Viehmann, like back home in Kassel, played the flute for hours. She spent time arranging certain notes and melodies before she investigated the stories they gathered. Even the Sisterhood didn't know why Dorothea exiled herself in that room for days.

Some said it was the same story over and over. It was as if she was perfecting a lie. That she wanted it to sound as believable and spontaneous as possible. Others said she was memorizing a true story. Why? Which story was it? Why did she experiment with rituals? Why did she play the flute?

Could it be that the legend of the Singing Bone was literally true? That Dorothea, through witchcraft, had found a way to summon the innocent back from the dead and make them tell of their killers?

🍎

A few miles away, Jacqueline de Rais woke up from a long sleep. She and Xaver slept in separate rooms, and each enjoyed a nap until the clock struck midnight.

The event which they were about to attend usually started at dawn. It had been like this for years and occurred twice a year. The attendees liked to start it around four in the morning, as a metaphor for the beginning of a new dawn.

This resonated with their plan. After all, they were changing the world by escaping the dark of dusk and starting a new dawn in history.

Still groggy, she checked her email. The Committee of Memoria were asking for a final list of attendees. Everyone had arrived today thus far. Everyone except Anne Anderson and her companion, David Tale. The email requested deletion of the two absent guests as they hadn't checked in yet.

Jacqueline didn't hesitate to reject the request and announced David and Anne's arrival in a few hours. She even donated a million extra dollars to Memoria to have her reply taken seriously.

🍎

In St. Peter's Basilica, the Vatican cleaners, also known as Sanpetrinos, entered in their specialized uniforms to clean up the place for tomorrow's ceremony. Only twice a year, once in Easter and once before Christmas, did they offer their extraordinary capabilities. Cleaning, polishing, and perfecting the look inside was no easy task. Not only challenging, but it was also risky at times as they had to climb Baldachin, a large Baroque sculpted bronze canopy, and clean it as well.

It was supposed to be a long night before dawn. That is, until they saw a man on the cross hung in the middle of the hall.

Father Firelle hung on the cross with his dagger dug into his chest. His left hand held half an apple, cut horizontally and showing its seeds of a pentagram inside. On the floor underneath him, photos of the girl on the cross from Westminster Abbey were scattered all around.

One large photo of Father Firelle himself had also been added. Probably because the priest, not being a dwarf, was too heavy for the cross, which would sooner or later collapse under his weight.

The final touch was words written in blood at the basilica's entrance:


***Oh, ye shepherd, break my bones, and tell thy story about thy devil's crone...***

# 66

---

1:00 A.M.

### *Fairytale Road Germany*

Anne had been trapped inside a dream for so long. The very dream where she was being chased by her stepfather back in the vineyard in California. She was fifteen years old, and Rachel was nowhere to be found. Even worse, Anne was disoriented, unable to find the well to hide.

In an attempt for diversion, she had run into the vineyard in hopes to hide behind the grapevines. She wore a green dress so she imagined she would blend in without him finding her.

She was right. It worked. Except that she lost her way, confused by the green vines surrounding her. She was now feeling suffocated by the color she loved most.

At dawn, her fear had escalated, and the vineyard was empty. Only her stepfather's wrath echoed. If it wasn't for him being drunk again, he would have found her by now. But that wasn't the scariest thing that happened in the dream. It was her stepfather's friend, the dark figure with no features. He didn't make much noise, as he was sneakier than a snake, and would soon find her.

She wanted to scream Rachel's name but that would give her away.

So Anne ran into every direction, hoping the randomness of her attempts would magically pay off like in fairytales. A deus ex machina that would change the course of her fate, and save her out of nowhere. The way the prince found Snow White, and the shepherd found Fae's bones.

Tired, she tumbled to the ground near the neighbor's winery. The neighbor's grapes were red as blood, and the ground was full of them. As she struggled to stand up again, her legs gave in and she slid sideways, covered with red grapes. Squishy grapes that made ugly sounds and stained her clothes blood red. And her hands. And her face.

That's when she saw him coming. The dark man in the dark dress with the dark hat. He uttered no words and seemed unaffected by the squished grapes at his feet. He was fast and his heavy rain boots helped him trudge his way through the field of grapes.

Anne scrambled and crawled the best she could, but her efforts were in vain.

He was too close, whispering her name just behind her.

And closer.

Closer.

"Come with me," Rachel yelled at her, gripping her by the sleeves and dragging her away from him.

"You're back!" Anne cheered. "Rachel, you're back!"

Rachel, being stronger, sped up and escaped with Anne down the same well they used every time their stepfather got drunk.

Rachel was fast, and the dark man lost them, looming around the well, unsure if they hid inside. Anne was about to speak when Rachel cupped her mouth with her hands.

Rats scurried all around them, and yet neither of them dared react until the man gave up and looked for them elsewhere. As always, they would spend hours in the well. Not leaving before their stepfather and his dark friend drank themselves to sleep. Only then would they climb out again.

To kill time in the well, Rachel told Anne another story. This time it was a story about rats. A story about Hamelin. The city where children like Rachel and Anne escaped a similar dark figure who played a flute to lure them away. A city where the locals, in memory of the kidnapped children, prohibited singing or talking on the very same road the Pied Piper lured them away. A place where children once sang, now, a street so mute.

# 67

---

1:09 A.M.

### *Fairytale Road, Germany*

David bumped his head into the Beetle's ceiling when Anne started whimpering. He had just woken up and saw she was sleeping like a baby in the passenger's seat. She seemed so peaceful, he didn't want to bother her. But now she looked like she had escaped a nightmare and only spoke one word after:

"Hamelin!" Anne almost choked on it. "We're going to Hamelin."

Harry, Helga's driver and brother, stopped the car and pointed behind him. His way of indicating that he had already missed it. Anne told him to turn around and drive back to Hamelin. The very city where the Pied Piper's folktale originated.

"Calm down." David patted her shoulder. "Were you dreaming?"

Anne nodded, catching her breath as Harry drove back. "We didn't pass it by much. It's about twenty minutes back."

"How do you know it's Hamelin now?" David said.

"Hamelin, on the map, had always been a circle," Anne said.

"That's because it had been surrounded by a fortress that protected the city. Until 1602 when it was attacked in war. Which one? I can't recall now."

"'Once upon a time at sixteen o two,'" David recited. "'In a big apple, a river bit through.'"

"The river is Weser and it bit through Hamelin when part of the wall tumbled after the war," Anne said. "The water changed course and cut through the circular city that looked like a whole apple, and made it look like a bitten one now."

"So it never was about growing apples. The city actually looked like a bitten apple on the map," David pondered. He wished he still had a phone to Google it, just out of curiosity. "What about the part about children and the mute streets?"

"That," Anne said, "is something I can only show you when we arrive. I doubt you've ever seen anything like it."

"Okay," David said. "Does the same apply to the fourth line about the abyss mark?"

"No, that part is easy now," Anne said. "Helga was right. It's a play on words. That, like every other mapestry, has two proposed meanings."

"How so?"

"Did you ever hear about Otto von Bismarck?"

"Isn't that like a German designer who built for the Third Reich or something?"

"That's him," Anne said. "There are so many towers in Germany built in his honor. A tribute if you want to put it that way."

"Two towers tribute," David said. "But why two towers?"

"Two of those towers are built right outside of Hamelin," Anne said. "If you climb them and look down, you can see the whole city. It's that small."

"But Anne, I'm still not sure what the abyss mark is." David stopped midway, locking eyes with her. "Abyss mark equals *Bismarck*, from Otto Von Bismarck," he said.

"It fits perfectly. I have a feeling this could be the last puzzle," Anne said.

"Why so?"

"You'll understand when we arrive," she said. "Because there is no turning back from where we're going."

❦

The Advocate left Tom John and his men blaming each other for not climbing the Rapunzel Tower. They still had no luck finding Anne and David. Wondering how they continued to slip out of their grasp, he sat in the backseat of a rented tourist vehicle, a shabby old Audi, resting on his cane.

Driving by himself after Anne and David was going to be a painful journey. His metallic legs underneath his cassock were far from perfect. Not that they hadn't been designed to operate that way, but he hated the feeling of weakness—and being disabled.

In his years of wearing the cassock and killing people, he had almost believed his own lie. That he was invincible. When in fact he was a cripple after what had happened to him in the past. Poisoning the crow had felt so Godlike, but now he had to act like any other human. He had to drive himself after the two people he wished to torture and to kill eventually. Most especially Anne.

And where was his driver? Why did The Advocate have to drive alone? Well, the answer to that question was the dead body in the trunk of his rented Audi.

No, it wasn't his driver's. The Advocate only killed people he had no need for. The body in the trunk belonged to Helga's brother Harry.

# 68

---

2:00 A.M.

## *Hamelin, Fairytale Road, Germany*

Hamelin at 2 a.m. felt like a ghost town.

Anne guided Harry, the driver, to park near the entrance. She showed David the two Bismarck towers imposing themselves upon the narrow streets. The half-timber houses sat only three or four stories high. They were kissed by the orange light from decorative street lamps, giving the town a mysterious aura.

Unlike Trendelburg, the coziness and cluttered houses and intimate streets didn't emanate romance here. They gave David goosebumps, and for the love of his mother he couldn't tell why. Something about Hamelin came across as a horror town at night.

"There is a famous illustration by Errol Le Cain. It depicts children dancing in the streets of Hamelin with the two towers shown in the back," Anne whispered to David. "If you see that painting, you'll understand the darkness that oozes out of this town."

"But I see the towers have different diameters now," David said. "The thinner one looks more recent."

"True. Because over the years, they tumbled down for various reasons. Cheaper and more modern ones were built next to them, just to honor the memory." Anne was still whispering and then looked back at Harry in the car. "Should we let him wait here, or drive back to Helga?"

"I'd say wait here and call Helga. Find out what went on," David said.

"He says he forgot his phone back there when Helga needed him all of a sudden to help us."

"I don't trust him, honestly."

"You say that now, after he saved us?" Anne said. "Don't worry, I trust Helga."

"I trust Luke Skywalker but not his father," David said. "Why are we whispering?"

"Look around," Anne said. "Everyone's asleep. It's a very small town. We don't want to expose ourselves, do we? I bet our photos and descriptions are very popular by now."

She went back and told Harry to wait. She then returned to David with a hand-sized hourglass.

"Make sure it's not tapped or something," David said, unable to scan the narrow street in the semi-darkness. "I don't trust her."

"You didn't even ask why she gave it to me, David."

"It'll be some sticky-sweet tradition or something," David said. "I don't want to know."

"It is a tradition for those who walk the city after midnight," Anne said. "The hourglass lasts for two hours to remind the locals who walk the streets to return home soon."

"And that's because?"

"So the Piper wouldn't take them away. Just like he took the hundred and thirty children from this town over twelve centuries ago," Anne said, rubbing the hourglass with her sleeve.

"Anne." David gritted his teeth and snatched the hourglass from her hand and put it on the ground in front of someone's doorstep. "No more crappy, sappy fairytales. Seriously, I won't go easy on you anymore. This has got to stop. Life is not a fairytale. You can't walk around with such a weakness. You'll get killed."

"You mean you're worried you will get killed?" She crossed her arms.

David realized that, even though he cared about her, something just wasn't right. The sooner he asked her about why she saw a psychologist, the better. "Listen to me, Anne. You must tell me more about Rachel."

"Again?" she hissed, pointing at the streets they were supposed to explore to solve the puzzle at hand. "Why do you keep asking me this?"

"Back in the car, you said you dreamed about Rachel, and that it helped you solve the puzzle," he said. "Is that something that usually happens to you?"

"What kind of question is that, David?"

"Do you always have things revealed to you in your dreams?" he asked. He was aware of the absurdity of the question. "Was this a dream, actually, or a memory?"

Anne's arms were still crossed, but he could see she appreciated him asking. She looked like she wanted to talk about it but never had someone care enough. "It's a bit of both," she said in a fractured voice, trying to keep it as low as possible. "But let me first walk you to the 'street so mute' mentioned in the puzzle. That way, we don't waste time."

"Agreed." He walked beside her, astonished when she grabbed his hand. The city's ancient dread draped over the bright-colored houses on both sides.

"My memories of Rachel aren't always clear," she said, squinting to find her way through the narrow streets. It looked like the locals had just removed the snow today. It wasn't as thick on the ground as in Trendelburg. The sticky and thicker clumps of snow oddly stuck to the porches and front steps of the half-timber houses, making them look like the candy steps from "Hansel and Gretel." "I saw a psychiatrist because when it came to my childhood with Rachel, I couldn't tell dreams from memories. Neither could I differentiate our interactions from daydreaming about the past."

"What happened in the past?" David said. "I'm sorry I have to ask."

"Mother left us when Rachel was three. We never met our real father, so we ended up with her second husband, our stepfather," Anne said.

"Sounds a little convoluted."

"I know, but I was born into the situation, so I never questioned the absurdity of it," Anne said. "We lived in the back of a vineyard where our stepfather worked. He was a troubled soul. Always drunk at night, and he seemed to loath having to take care of us. Although he never left like my mother."

"And you sure your mother left?" David asked. "I mean she didn't die?"

"She died, David, okay?" Anne tensed. "That swan necklace we found in Polle looked like hers. The same one I found at the bottom of the well one day."

"I'm sorry to hear that."

"Th scary thing is, I think Rachel saw her die. Or get killed," Anne said quietly. "But I can't prove that. I'm only sure Rachel didn't tell me all she knew about our mother."

"Until now?"

Anne stopped involuntarily and took a deep breath. Her face looked paler, as if someone had sucked the blood from her. David saw her hands tremble again. She exhaled and continued walking. "No, Rachel keeps her secrets close to her heart. And if you're curious, our stepfather never physically hurt us. He was just so upset, wanting to get rid of us or something."

"Good to know." He squeezed her hands. "So, I guess you stopped seeing your psychiatrist when things got better? I mean when you no longer confused Rachels' memories with your dreams and such?"

"True," Anne said. "Also living continents away helped us both. We've seen darkness in our childhood that I'd rather not talk about. But the confusion, hesitation, and self-doubt returned once I saw the girl on the cross yesterday."

"I can only imagine," he said.

"You want to know something both sentimental and wicked at

the same time?" she asked, walking over a patch of cobblestone bricks sticking out of the snow.

"Uh-huh," he said, following her into a narrower street on the left.

"I was named Anne after my mother," Anne said. "That's what Rachel told me."

"Sentimental," David said. "Why wicked?"

"Because she left—or died—right after," Anne said. "Rumor has it that she named me Anne so that I could take over and replace her. Whatever that means."

# 69

2:11 A.M.

*Hamelin, Fairytale Road, Germany*

David stopped, watching Anne read the sign on the corner.

"*Bungelosenstrasse*," she read, her voice sounding even lower now. It was the name of the street they were about to enter. "'Street without drums' in English."

"Streets so mute." David nodded. "So, it's an actual street that everyone knows about."

"Shhh." She put a finger on his lips. "We're not supposed to talk if we enter it."

"Is that a tradition?" David hissed the lowest he could.

"Indeed," Anne said. "It's the dreariest street in Hamelin. Trust me, you will feel it when you enter."

David cocked his head. He was unimpressed by the narrow streets with cluttered half-timber houses on both sides. True, this street in particular was narrower than the rest. It reminded him of streets in small Mediterranean or South American towns he saw on TV. Ones where balconies form a canopy-like bridge over pedestrians' heads and were close enough you could jump from house to house. But it didn't mesh with Hamelin's mysterious vibe. He even saw a recently built house by the corner that killed the folklore-ish vibe of the city. However, this street was darker as it was barely lit. He wondered if whatever legend it perpetuated kept people away.

"Are you telling me this is the street where the Pied Piper played his flute and let children follow?" David asked.

"It is," Anne said. "Spooky, right?"

"Was his flute a Singing Bone by any chance?"

"Now you are overthinking. Although it could have been."

"I get that this is 'the street so mute' in the mapestry," David said. "But where are the singing children?"

"I guess I'll have to give you a brief history of the Pied Piper of Hamelin story. In the Brothers Grimm book, he was originally known as the Rat Catcher," Anne said. "It's one of the few fairytales that is a fairytale/legend hybrid. And though it comes across as the most believable, it's the most heavily interpreted tale of all. It's neither romantic nor sappy, and had no princes or queens."

"You seem to have forgotten I told you it's my favorite folktale," David said. "A cloaked man in a multicolored—or pied—outfit is summoned, or arrives, at a town infested with rats. He offers to rid the locals of the infestation by guiding the rats out of the town with his magic flute. He delivers on his promise, and when he arrives to collect his fee, he is duped and is left unpaid. Turns out, he is a badass S.O.B, and with the same flute he lures the children out of town and they were never seen again."

"That's the most brutal way I've ever heard anyone tell this story," Anne said. "But you've got it right."

"Facts, not fairytales," David said. "That's what police officers do. I also know about the famous Robert Browning poem that supposedly populated the tale outside of the German culture."

"That is one of the most troubled poems of all time," Anne said. "For one, the rats had barely been mentioned before that poem. Even in the earlier version of the Brothers Grimm tale, the Pied Piper was simply the devil in disguise, kidnapping children from a peaceful town."

"So, the townspeople didn't ask him to help them get rid of rats?"

"No. He was a happy traveler with a flute passing by and he kidnapped the children," Anne said. "A serial killer or kidnapper disguised as a jester."

"I didn't know that," David said. "But it makes much more sense to me. I've always found it confusing that he was presented neither evil nor good. If not a victim in some narrations for not having been paid for the job. The fact that he is pure evil suits me."

"Franz Xaver believed that the Pied Piper is the devil," Anne said. "The same one Gilles de Rais summoned before he killed his wife."

"This is starting to feel like the 'Fairytaleverse,' a universe of its own with interconnected characters." He rubbed his chin. "Do you as a folklorist think of all folklore as one universal story? Is that it?"

"You now understand what folklorists are after," Anne said. "A once and for all definite explanation of all fairytales. As well as what they really mean. Let's find the children that sing in a street so mute, David. Follow me..."

🍎

The Advocate stood looking over the annoying lovebirds walking the dim-lit streets of Hamelin. His binoculars did a crappy job as a feeble fog began to loom over the city.

He remembered the last time he came to Hamelin. It was a few months ago when another client sent him to investigate recent clues about the Singing Bone. He recalled that people complimented him on his disguise.

They said he looked like the Pied Piper. So much so that he ended up playing the part in their annual festival with children all around him. He desperately wanted to give one of them a poisoned apple but didn't need the attention and left.

Even though he couldn't hear what Anne and David talked

about, it was apparent they were bonding. Finally, he saw Anne guiding David into another narrow street and stop. A wide smile formed on his crooked lips.

"Fantastico," he entertained himself, making fun of his native tongue. "The Children of Hamelin have just come home."

# 70

## *Bungelosenstrasse, Hamelin, Fairytale Road, Germany*

Anne led the way, almost tiptoeing and communicating with her eyes. David followed suit. Although, on a scale of one to ten he was at an eleven mode of fight or flight. Advancing forward was what mattered to her when David repeatedly looked behind him. It occurred to her that he hadn't used a gun once in this journey. She made a mental note to ask him why later.

Being mute on this narrow street was an understatement. It felt like someone had sucked the air from their surroundings. She suspected the owner of the houses on both sides stood behind these darkened windows holding their breath.

And watching.

The snow on the ground was thicker than on the other streets. If the locals had cleaned it all over Hamelin earlier, then they'd let it pile here on purpose. Anne wondered whether they neglected the mute street purposely or if it was to help muffle the footsteps of whoever entered it.

She suddenly realized the genius of meeting here. It was the one place no one dared to visit out of superstition.

Truth hiding in plain, yet mute, sight.

David pointed at the houses, and Anne believed he questioned why they were all dark. Someone should have left a light on in a bathroom or patio, but there were none. Sure, the Germans were known for their late-night strict discipline with electricity and energy in general. Rachel had told her that their mother used to read her books until the last strip of sunset sunk into the earth before she turned on the lights. Despite the energy-saving ways, this felt beyond normal. An odd, eerie feeling.

The street lamps on Bungelosenstrasse were too far apart, almost three times the distance of the ones on the outer streets. And they were an older design, honoring older memories—and keeping older secrets.

David suddenly stopped and hissed behind her. She turned around and saw him point at the largest house on the street.

It was about four stories high and enormous in width. So large that it occupied the span of ten houses from before. Its roof was designed to mimic the shape of a triangle. It was built in brick and stone and oozed with the colors of gray that sometimes leaned to a dirty, faint shade of green.

Like most designs on the Fairytale Road, it was half-timbered. Yet its windows were unusually wide and blocked by relatively thin brick columns. This design made them look like part of an ancient prison. The main door was arched with overhead bricks that oddly varied in size. The door itself was made of wood. It somehow gave the feeling of a fortress double door made of steel. Ancient buildings had this authoritative and imposing feel to them sometimes.

"It's the Pied Piper's House," Anne mouthed. "I don't see it being in the spot we're looking for, but you can read the inscription on the wall next to the door."

She followed David, who was approaching it, and then stopped next to him while he read it in silence:

**ANNO 1284 ON THE DAY JOHANNIS ET PAULI, THE**

**JUNE 26TH DORCH WAS A PIPER DECALED WITH
ALL FARVES CXXX CHILDREN ADORED BINNEN
HAMELEN GEBON TO CALVARIE BI DEN KOPPEN
LOST.**

She hadn't the time to explain the language used on the inscription. Instead she pointed at the translation below:

*In the year 1284 on the day of Johannis and Pauli was the 26th of June with all sorts by Pauli 130 children born in Hameln were enticed to lose their calvary at the Koppen.*

"Can we continue our search now?" Anne mouthed, vapor spiraling before her. "This house is nothing but a tourist attraction. There is nothing of importance inside. I know it's big, but it was built in recent centuries to give the tourists a good time, aka the Pied Piper House. It's owned by the government, and empty most of the year."

Instead of mouthing anything back, David pointed at the space in front of the main door. Anne wasn't sure why at first. Why wouldn't David mouth what he wanted to say? Then she realized he did it for impact. David style.

Someone had cleaned up in front of the door with a shovel that left its marks and made space for entry—or departure.

Immediately Anne strolled toward the houses on the opposite side of the street and confirmed it wasn't the case there. No one had dug out the snow in front of any of the smaller buildings. She suddenly realized these haunted houses were empty. People feared living on this street.

"Someone entered?" Anne speculated.

"And left a clue this obvious?"

"What are you thinking?"

"An invitation," David said, pointing at a golden plate on the door. Although it was in German, and he couldn't have understood it, he didn't have to. The number on the door gave it all away: 1602.

---

## 71

### *Bungelosenstrasse, Hamelin, Fairytale Road, Germany*

"'Once upon a time,'" Anne mouthed. "There was a house here in 1602, but it wasn't called the Pied Piper's House."

David cocked his head in a demeanor that said, *Does it matter?*

"So, this is where we've been invited to, huh?" Anne took a few steps back, taking a broader look at the house. It came across as being as dead as the others. Abandoned and left behind. The door didn't look like it would open without an invitation or someone from inside.

"You said this street is silent to honor the lost children of Hamelin?" David mouthed, brainstorming. "Why this street in particular?"

"It's the last street before the highway that leads to the mountain Koppen. From there, it leads to the Weser River." She couldn't point as everything she mentioned was beyond the curb. "Rumor has it that here is where their footsteps were last seen. And sadly, some ripped clothes and blood."

"The Children of Hamelin walked this street," he said, brainstorming on his own.

"What do you have in mind?"

"I'm trying to figure out why we can't hear children sing," David said. "Shouldn't this be the last piece in the jigsaw puzzle? The one that would confirm this Piper House is our desired destination?"

"Did you expect something in particular?"

"I expected to hear someone sing," David said. "I mean, these puzzles are filled with musical notes, codes, and flutes. And since we made it this far, I would have happily followed the sound of a music box, maybe, or someone playing the flute. Something like that."

"Stop." Anne waved a hand and hissed recklessly, not worrying if someone heard her now. The eerie feeling of being watched behind the darkened windows of these houses returned. "Let's go back to you asking about the Children of Hamelin walking these streets."

"Sure," David said.

"We are walking this street now, aren't we?" Anne's eyes widened. "We, in one way or another, are considered the Children of Hamelin at this very moment."

"You mean if this was a play reincarnated, we are the actors?" David asked. "I see what you mean."

"The Singing Bone!" Anne pulled it out and looked at it. "We are the ones who are supposed to sing! Not them singing to us."

"We are the Children of Hamelin, and we're the ones who are supposed to announce our arrival," David agreed. "In a street so mute."

"But which tune should we play?" Anne said.

"I'd say it doesn't matter," David said. "Having come this far, 'Old MacDonald Had a Farm' should work."

Anne played Beethoven's Fifth because it was the shortest and most peculiar. The same melody that Dorothea Viehmann used, supposedly the founder of the Sisterhood.

A short moment passed before someone played the same notes. The music came from inside the Piper House.

ɘ

The Advocate's driver stood atop the smaller house opposite the Piper House, listening to their every word. One thing The Advocate told him was that enthusiastic people always look forward. They forget there is also upward and downward. That was how you tailed someone without them noticing.

Climbing the houses wasn't easy, but killing someone in their sleep was effortless. The driver chose the oldest couple who lived right in front of where Anne and David left the hourglass behind and entered the house. Funny how people in a town that the devil once visited still left their front door unlocked.

A pillow, strength, and psychopathy did the job. The driver suffocated the man and his wife and climbed up to the roof. The houses stood narrow enough to jump from one to another. With snow on top, he was hardly heard or noticed.

"I'll have to call The Advocate's employer and raise my price, too," the driver told himself, now wondering who played the flute from inside the Piper's House.

ɘ

Anne resisted the urge to respond to the melody played from behind the door. Instead, she saw David stand before her to protect her when the door's clockwork began visibly rotating in front of them.

Whoever was behind the door struggled to open it. It looked like it hadn't been used for some time. Did the hosts only shovel the snow to give Anne and David a clue while they entered from elsewhere?

The door sounded rusty and incredibly noisy for a street so mute. Anne wondered if the locals hid behind the windows and kept themselves locked inside or if the street was truly abandoned.

As the door parted, someone's silhouette appeared in front of the darkness draping the house's interior behind them.

Anne craned her neck to look from under David's shoulder. To her surprise, she saw it was a girl in a black cloak.

David nudged Anne to step further back so they could see the woman's face lit by the faint street lamp nearby.

The woman shuffled casually toward them and looked far from threatening.

Anne finally saw her face but didn't recognize her. Neither did David, she could tell. So they must have sent a messenger. But then Anne realized that she didn't know whom to expect in the first place.

"Congratulations, and welcome to the Pied Piper House," she said, shy and hesitant. "You've solved the mapestry."

"And you are?" Anne asked.

"You've met Lisbeth, watched Layla on the cross, and saw Lily escape wearing a red cloak in the footage. However, you probably haven't met Lara, Lucia, or Lilith yet," the girl said. "I'm Lisa Ovitz."

# 72

2:41 A.M.

## *Airport Hotel Room, Florence, Italy*

Lucia watched Bloody Mary twist out the cork from the Champagne bottle and enjoy the fizzle erupt back in her face. They had just arrived in Florence to escape Rome's panic and be closer to their final destination — and sacrifice.

"Whoa!" Mary raised it in the air, dancing barefoot to the song We Will Rock You by Queen.

Lucia, though much shorter, clung to Bloody Mary and imitated her dance moves.

Lilith, aka Bloody Mary, was the wildest of all her sisters. She loved her for that. When it was a fun time, she was fun itself. So what if they were dwarves? So what if they were descendants of a cursed bloodline and had to guard terrible secrets from the past? Who was to tell them what they had to do with their lives?

Sure, Mary, and Lisa, were the tall ones who never understood what it meant to grow up stunted and bullied. But Mary, being taller and once prettiest, was the one the devil chose that night. Of all the Ovitz sisters, he picked her, and she was never the same again. The devil took her when she was still Lilith. When she came back, she was someone else called Bloody Mary. She was still as beautiful but felt as if she were the ugliest on the inside.

"You're short, Lucia!" Mary playfully held her up to dance with her, "But guess what? Life is shorter!"

Lucia cracked up laughing. It was good to see Mary happy. She wasn't happy often.

"We did it!" Mary poured Champagne into Lucia's mouth while pointing at the Italian news covering Father Firelle's murder on the cross. What appeared frightening on the screen, made Mary feel good.

"Looks like a scene from a fairytale," she mimed a camera with her thumb and forefingers. She then tilted her head, looking at the TV screen, "A fucked up one, which is awesome!"

"I can't thank you enough for sparing me," Lucia told her. "Please thank Our Queen for me."

"You will thank her yourself soon," Mary said.

"Social media is going crazy," Lucia said, pointing at her phone. "Top news on Twitter, Instagram, and Facebook — and the BBC, too."

"They can't deny us," Mary wiped champagne off her mouth with the back of her hand. "No one denies the Ovitz's anymore."

"And it's still nighttime," Lucia said. "Tomorrow, the world will be shocked. There are so many speculations, so many theories; so much anger; so many questions and fear online now."

"Let them be angry," Mary said. "Any good theories? I'm curious to see if someone's figured things out?"

"Not much," Lucia said. "Though there is one theory that links the Pentagram to the Five Petal Rose you gave to Father Firelle."

"Oh," Mary's eyes widened. "Did they solve that bit?"

"I wouldn't say 'solve'. The general explanation is that the apple and the rose connect the killer as being the same one in the Vatican and Westminster Abbey."

"That's it?"

"There is also talk about how the apple and the rose both have a five-pointed pentagram inside them."

"And yet they didn't make the connection?" Mary was disappointed.

"No, Mary, they didn't," Lucia said. "We live in a world where no one cares about the past. You thought stuffing the rose into Father Firelle's mouth was a dead giveaway, but most people won't get it. Forget about it. Let's celebrate."

All this time, Lily sat with her hands between her legs. She was hunched over in a chair in the corner of the room. She didn't like what was happening but couldn't do much about it.

"Cheer up, Lily!" Lucia told her. "You're on your way to becoming the youngest True Sister ever."

Lily didn't respond, and Lucia knew what she was thinking. That they were evil, she probably thought about Lady Ovitz and how she wouldn't have allowed such darkness to happen.

Mary's phone chimed with an incoming message.

"It's from Lisa," Lucia read it out loud, *"Anne arrived. Our Queen's plan is flawless"*.

"Anne Anderson is perfect," Mary contemplated. "Had I known she would effortlessly solve the mapestry, I wouldn't have had to hang so many people on the cross."

"The hardest part is yet to come," Lily finally spoke. "We don't know if she is the one."

"If our Queen says she is the one," Mary grunted at Lily. "Then she is the one."

The tension in the room was interrupted by Lara, the youngest, "Lisbeth is saying hi," Lara said. "She called me from the hospital. She is okay."

"Is she wounded?" Lily said with moist eyes.

"Nothing that can't be mended," Lara said. "Though she told me a girl in pink tried to kill her. I'm sure she'll tell us about it when we meet her."

"I think we should be thankful enough and pray for her," Lily said.

That was when Lucia lost her mind and spat out the champagne she was drinking as if to expel her sins, "I haven't prayed today," she panicked. "Who else hasn't prayed?"

"I did," Lily said, raising a proud hand.

"I didn't," Lara gripped her Singing Bone necklace. "I'm sorry."

"Would you help us pray, Lily?" Lara and Lucia pleaded.

Lily agreed and glanced at Mary.

"Don't look at me," Mary scoffed, pointing at the champagne bottle in her hand. "I'm drinking the real holy water here."

# 73

### *The Piper House, Hamelin, Fairytale Road, Germany*

Following the flashlight beam, Lisa ushered David and Anne into the dark hall of the empty Piper House. She had briefly explained that she and Mary were the sixth and seventh sisters. Mary was the rebellious one who orchestrated the murder of the girl on the cross in the Westminster Abbey and Father Firelle in the Vatican.

However, Lisa refused to explain further. Nor did she tell them who gave orders to Mary and Lily or why the mapestry led Anne to the Piper House.

Lisa considered herself a messenger.

"Like Lisbeth in Polle," she said. "I'm here to help."

Anne was curious about the sisters sacrificing their own, but she knew Lisa wouldn't answer her. So she assumed that whoever ordered them to kill had an unbelievably strong influence on them in the absence of Lady Ovitz.

"This isn't about the murder anymore," Lisa said. "This is about you having solved the mapestry that led you to the secret cult of the Sisterhood. You can see what they really do, then I'm gone."

"Aren't you part of the Sisterhood as well?" Anne said.

"My sisters and I used to consider ourselves part of it. Now we've taken matters into our own hands," Lisa said.

"So, it's more of a conflict inside the Sisterhood that's led to this mess," David said.

"The Sisterhood grew corrupt in the past years," Lisa explained. "What was meant to be a noble cause to help women worldwide turned into a multi-national business for the rich. With greed, the cause lost its purpose."

Lisa stopped by a door in the dark and focused the flashlight on both of them. "Neither of you is supposed to be here. I shouldn't even be here," she said. Lisa locked eyes with Anne. "The Sisterhood didn't invite you."

"Then who did?" Anne said.

"The Ovitz invited you. Sort of. And you will be in great danger inside," Lisa said. "The Sisterhood is a criminal organization. What they do is far beyond the strangest conspiracy theory you've ever heard."

"Why not contact the police and tell them about the Sisterhood's meeting place and share whatever your sisters know?" Anne said.

"That's what our mother, Lana Ovitz, did in the past," Lisa said. "She sent evidence and made a plausible case to the authorities. But the Sisterhood is too connected to allow the truth to surface."

"Where is your mother now?" Anne asked.

"Hopefully buried somewhere," Lisa said. "And not left for the crows to eat."

"I'm sorry," Anne said. "I didn't know that."

"The Ovitz are never sorry for our sister's or mother's death," Lisa said. "We die with pride."

" Of course," Anne paid her respects, though she disapproved of the idea of siblings sacrificing one another in the first place. "If you want David and me to expose the Sisterhood, at least that's what I think you said, then why the puzzles and the mapestry? And why me?"

"It has to be you, Anne," Lisa said.

"Because of the book I wrote?"

"Your book is only an extension of who you are," Lisa opened the door behind her that led to a downward spiral staircase. "Like the T.S. Elliot poem about going back to the place for the first time—you will soon return to meet yourself for the first time again."

Speechless, Anne followed Lisa down the stairs into a dark, abandoned basement, David right behind the pair.

"Follow me," Lisa said, down by the last landing. She walked toward a wall further into the basement and ran her hand over it until something beeped. "This is a secret door that will lead you inside."

"What are we supposed to do inside? What should we expect?" Anne asked.

"It's a Sisterhood gathering that only occurs twice a year. Once during Easter, and once before Christmas," she said. "This back-door leads to the bathrooms."

"And?" Anne asked.

"It's the men's bathroom. There are two stalls on your left when you enter. Inside, each of you will find a cloak—black for men, red for women," Lisa explained. "You will also find masquerade masks. Put them on and enter the main hall."

"So, everyone inside acts anonymously?" David wondered. "This does sound like a secret cult."

"You will have to see for yourself," Lisa said. "Once I open the door, you're on your own."

"One last question," Anne stalled. "It's my understanding that only bloodline descendants can join the Sisterhood, right?"

"True," Lisa said.

"Then how are the Ovitz part of the Sisterhood?" Anne said. "I mean the Six Swans were Dorothea Viehman, Lotte Grimm, the Hassenpflug sisters, and Dortchen Wild, and..."

"There you go," Lisa said, seeing Anne had already figured out the answer. "The sixth one was an Ovitz."

"But the Ovitz are Jewish," David said. "And from Romania."

"Never heard about a Romanian Jew who was a peasant and worked in the fields of Kassel in the nineteenth century?" Lisa said. "It was called Wallachia then, by the way. Depending on which history books you believe."

"She was the peasant who first told the story of Gilles de Rais?" Anne asked.

"Yes. Lilliput Ovitz. The dwarf peasant who moved to Germany," Lisa said. "Dorothea Viehman may have created the Sisterhood, but my great grandmother, Lilliput Ovitz, was the catalyst."

A green light chimed underneath Lisa's palm on the wall, prompting the door to slide open. The neon lights from the luxurious bathroom looked like an alien entity welcoming Anne and David into a new world like nothing they had ever seen before.

# 74

## *Bathrooms, The Piper House, Hamelin, Fairytale Road, Germany*

Inside the bathroom stalls, Anne and David donned the cloaks and masks.

"You're sure the Sisterhood isn't a sex cult, right?" David said, watching how ridiculous he and Anne looked in the mirror.

"How should I know?" Anne laughed uncomfortably from under a golden mask with green gemstones. "Inside the stall, I was thinking we should go back and leave all this behind."

"I was thinking the same," David said. "But then I thought about you."

"What about me?"

"Do you want to know something about Rachel?" David's hallowed tone from under the mask gave away his hesitancy.

"I know all I want to know about Rachel, David," Anne said.

"You don't seem to know where she is, yet you seem cool about it. And you haven't tried calling her since London," David said.

"Rachel is an introvert. She disappears often, but she always comes back," Anne said, sounding tense again.

David's silent breathing from under the mask gave away his anxiety, unsure if it was about his mother or Rachel.

Anne reached for the door. "Is it going to be hard to find each other inside if we separate?"

"Not for me," David said. "I'll be able to recognize your eyes through the mask."

"Not funny, David," she quipped, still gripping the handle.

"It's not supposed to be," David said. "It's true."

He enjoyed seeing her baffled and unsure about his underlined implications. Now she gripped the door even harder.

"Are you smiling from under your mask, David?" she asked.

"I can't smile. I twitch, remember?" His light chuckle gave him away. "I think the mask does better at smiling than I do."

Anne let go of the door and approached him, getting closer this time.

David didn't move, so she closed the small gap, the tips of their shoes now touching.

"You should have picked a better time to kiss," he said. "I'm allergic to masks."

"Brown?" She looked into his eyes. "Huh."

"Hazel," David sounded disappointed. "It's a color, you know. It's partially the same flavor of my lips."

"I like strawberry," she said, inhaling his scent.

"Too feminine of a taste for a man's lips," he said.

"Are you afraid to get in touch with your inner feminine again, David?" Anne said.

He had never seen this flirty side of her. He liked it. "I can compromise for you."

"Don't compromise," she said. "I like you the way you are." She tapped him on the chest and stepped away.

David thought she was doing her best not to give in to him. As if she just remembered how ridiculous this moment was, given the circumstances.

He watched her reach for the door again. "You know how I will recognize you inside, David?"

He said nothing, eager for her answer.

"I feel safe around you."

# 75

## Bismarck Tower, Hamelin, Fairytale Road, Germany

On top of the Bismarck tower, the Advocate stood in silence. He had watched Anne and David enter the Piper House while his driver surveilled them from the top of the building.

Although he wished to follow them inside, or send his driver for that matter, the Advocate couldn't fathom what was going on.

Through his binoculars, he saw lines of the most expensive cars in the world parked in the forest behind the Piper House. The exact opposite side from where Anne and David entered.

He wouldn't have seen anything if he hadn't stood in this high spot. Not only did he see cars; he also spied a helicopter upon the crest of what he presumed was Koppen Hill. The same place where the Pied Piper supposedly took many children centuries ago. It was most definitely an escape route in case something happened.

What was going on inside that building? Even to the Advocate, this whole thing was surreal.

It was time he called his employer. He needed to tell him how the plot was thickening and that finding the Singing Bone just got more expensive.

However, he hesitated and postponed calling him for later. Because, given Father Firelle's scandalous murder in St Peters Basilica, the Advocate thought his employer at the Vatican was too busy to make time for him right now.

# 76

## *Main Hall, The Piper House, Hamelin, Fairytale Road, Germany*

Adjusting her eyes, Anne couldn't comprehend the room behind the door. It was a massive hall with a high ceiling, despite being underground. An enormous chandelier with dangling crystals stood overhead in the center of the foyer. Almost immediately, she realized the hall was designed after the interior of Ludwig's II Neuschwanstein Castle in the South.

Next to her, David stood in awe. He watched men and women in black and red cloaks and similar masks drink wine and champagne at different corners of the hall. Their glamorous watches and jewelry glimmered from under their sleeves.

"When does the orgy start?" David said to the butler girl, offering him a drink.

She stopped, her features hidden underneath her mask. She wore a comical white mask, and the male butlers wore the tragic version. The white masks, matching their gloves and shoes, contrasted nicely with their flamboyant black tuxedos.

"Good one, Sir!" She snickered with her hand over her plastic smile while holding the tray with the other. "I'll write that down."

"Please don't," he said. "The last girl who told me so tried to shoot me after."

The girl couldn't stop laughing and gave him a thumbs up.

"Don't drink too much," Anne hissed at him, unable to take her eyes off the paintings on the walls. "And stop being wickedly charming."

The first wall was full of famous authors and folklorists: Lewis Carrol of *Alice in Wonderland*; Charles Perrault, who wrote a favorite version of *Beauty and the Beast*; The Brothers Grimm. Even Hans Christian Andersen, who wrote *The Ugly Duckling* and *The Match Girl*, and whose fairytales had the devil as one of their main protagonists.

On another wall, she saw a large painting of J.R.R. Tolkien, C.S. Lewis, and more modern storytellers whose work was heavily inspired by fairytales.

Then she saw a painting of psychologist Bruno Bettelheim. He was one of the first authors to tackle the psychology behind fairytales in his book, *The Uses of Enchantment*. Next to him, a painting of Sigmund Freud and Carl Jung hung side by side. The two psychologists had proposed the wildest explanations of fairytales and the subconscious.

From the look on David's face, he didn't recognize most of them. He probably wondered why they interested Anne more than the guests in the hall.

"Look." Anne nudged him, pointing at a wall with paintings of six women. "Do you know who these women are?"

"I'm assuming—"

"Dorothea Viehman, the Hassenpflug sisters, Dortchen Wild, Lotte Grimm, and now we know the dwarf is Lilliput Ovitz."

David nodded, pointing to what looked like a list of admission prices underneath the paintings. The price of a ticket to enter this gathering was split into tiers, and the cheapest ticket price was a million dollars.

"How come you and I are here, then?" he asked. "We don't have this kind of money, let alone a ticket."

"But we do," Anne said, pointing out their names at the bottom of the list. They were listed last, a last-minute addition. Their names were jotted down with a blue pen, not printed like everyone else's.

"So, Lisa was telling the truth," David said. "The Ovitz's snuck our names onto the guest list. I hope this doesn't draw attention to us."

"We're behind masks. I'm sure we'll be fine unless someone downright points at us and calls us out," Anne said. "See that small hand-drawn picture of a flute next to our names?"

"Yes, it's a Singing Bone," David said. "Does it imply we'll have to use ours at some point?"

"Maybe the Singing Bone *is* the ticket." Next to the drawing of their flute, it mentioned that it was worth one million dollars.

"Poor us," David pointed at the names with tickets up to twenty million dollars on top of the list. "Look at the top of the list. We are labeled as 'buyers.'"

"Do you think solving the mapestry made this Singing Bone worth that much money?"

"I don't know but ask them if we can cash out," David said.

"Stop joking," Anne said.

"I'm not," he said. "Back in the bathroom, we contemplated whether we should go back or not. With a million dollars, we could be on an island far away, drinking fairyfloss martinis. We could leave this freakshow behind."

"I guess Lisa was right about you being afraid to know what happened to your mother," she said, realizing how brutal it sounded. "Sorry, but I like you because nothing stops you from figuring things out. Just a reminder."

David said nothing, absorbing the blow behind the mask. Anne was about to apologize when he instantly returned to investigation mode. "If we are considered buyers and entered with such an expensive ticket, what are we buying here, Anne?"

Silently, she shared his look at the rumbling room of affluent buyers. Each name with Singing Bone signatures on the list totaled roughly twenty million dollars.

"Lisa was right, I guess," Anne said. "We're not going to be the same again when we leave."

"If we ever leave," David said.

A door opened on the side, and a cloaked man with a mask announced in German-accented English, "The rooms are now open," he said. "Please, make yourself at home."

The crowd cheered and raised their glasses in the air before entering. Anne and David followed them inside. More butlers stood behind a reception bar, and a set of Singing Bones hung like hotel keys on the wall behind them.

# 77

### *Reception, The Piper House, Hamelin, Fairytale Road, Germany*

Numbered and organized, the buyers handed their Singing Bones to the butlers and received new ones from behind the desk. The newer ones looked lavish and modern, with golden inscriptions on the side instead of letters next to the holes.

Reluctantly, Anne handed hers to the butler girl, who took it casually and read, "Deadfae. A rare one. Your number is 4514615."

Anne wanted to remind David about the number being a direct translation to the 'deadfae' melody that eventually became a phone number for a luggage company. From the look on his face, she knew he recalled it vividly.

They watched the butler look for the number on the keys hanging on the wall behind her. Eventually, she found their new Singing Bone. It was on the last row to the far left. This implied that the Ovitzs may have planned this one, too, last minute.

"An exquisite one," the butler set it on the desk. "I've never seen one like it before."

"Excuse me?" Anne asked. She was afraid she would blow their cover if she asked the butler to explain herself.

"With this Singing Bone, you can only get one specific item in exchange. Unlike the rest of the buyers in the House," the butler said.

Anne wanted her to explain further, but the butler girl interrupted her cheerily. "Oh, and the House has increased your buying budget to three point seven million US dollars. Congratulations."

The butler held the bone carefully and offered it to Anne.

"That's one island for you and one for me," David whispered in Anne's ear. "The martinis are on me."

Anne ignored David and smiled back at the butler. She was ready to receive the new Singing Bone. "Thank you."

The butler girl stopped suddenly. "Password, please, ma'am."

"Password?"

"Each new Singing Bone comes with a password, tailored for its buyer," the butler said. "Could you please tell me yours?"

Anne shrugged. With her hands midair, the trembling was a dead giveaway. "Of course, I know mine," she countered. "It's just that I'm uncomfortable sharing it with other buyers around me."

"A plausible concern," the butler said. "But don't worry. This is the last step in the mapestry. In the Piper House, we have no more secrets."

"All the buyers went through a mapestry?" Anne said.

"It must be your first year then. Yes," the butler said. "Each year, the mapestries start on Easter and are expected to be solved by early Christmas. Could you please tell me the password so I can take care of the other buyers?"

Anne found herself on the brink of breaking down. Having solved every puzzle so far, she worried she was about to mess up her final test.

"You forgot the numbers, honey?" David said.

"Hmm..." Anne said, thinking he was stalling. "I had them memorized, but it'll come to me."

"Seven numbers, ma'am," the butler girl said as David

suppressed his twitching so-called smile. He just tricked her into confirming they were numbers. "Please, I'm in a hurry."

"Seven?" David sounded cheeky from under the mask, then said to Anne, "I bet the number 5 isn't one of them."

"1,2,3,4,6,7 and 12," Anne spat it out, unsure she had done the right thing.

"Thank you," the butler girl bowed her head and handed her the Singing Bone. "Sorry for being rude, but we've been warned we may have a couple of imposters here today. It only happened once a few years ago. They stole another buyer's identity and cashed out the money."

"So, we *can* cash out the money, huh?" David mumbled, but Anne heard him.

"Good luck with imposters." Anne faked a confident smile. "I'll make sure to report them if I suspect anyone."

"Thank you," the butler said. "First door to the left leads you to the rooms. Please abide by the House's rules. Your Singing Bone has a peculiar situation, but I'm sure you will be guided inside."

Anne and David left the girl and headed toward the door.

"How did you know it was numbers?" Anne asked David.

"She said the password is tailored to you. You've been adamant about using those numbers forever," David hissed, stopping by the threshold.

A red carpet covered the corridor's floor, and dim lights shone gently from above. The ornate walls were a creamy red, and vintage paintings of fairytale characters hung on both sides. Mysterious, black-padded double doors appeared between the paintings every so often.

"Into the rabbit hole we go," David sighed.

"We're underground, aren't we?" Anne intertwined her arm in his. "Buckle up, Alice."

# 78

### Corridors, The Piper House, Hamelin, Fairytale Road, Germany

The crowd ahead ambled in silence, stopping by the black padded doors to read the inscriptions on the wall beside it. David and Anne played along and casually read the first inscription they came by.

*Room 1740*
*Beauty and The Beast,*
*Aarne-Thompson-Uther tale type 425C.*
*834 versions. 134 translations.*
*12,003 edits.*
*Claimed by the Brothers Grimm, Jacob & William*
*Originally conceived by Suzanne Bardot de Villeneuve.*
*Originally printed in 1740 in The Young American and*
*Marine Tales by Suzanne Bardot de Villeneuve.*

"You know what a 'type tale' is by now," Anne reminded David.

"The number of versions and translations are normal in investigating any original text as a folklorist."

"It says 'claimed' by the Brothers Grimm?" David asked.

"It means 'stolen' or 'forged'—in a more polite way since women wrote fairytales. But we're past that discussion by now," Anne said. "This one was originally collected by Suzanne Bardot de Villeneuve, a renowned French storyteller."

"It was also written before the Sisterhood was formed. Not to mention, Bardot doesn't sound like a name from the bloodline," David said.

"There were storytellers before the Sisterhood, but none of whom united and formed a cult," Anne said. "I'm curious if we're buying an authentic and original fairytale here to own, or if we simply pay to lay eyes upon the text?"

"One million dollars for a peepshow is far too crazy, even for this place," David pointed at the note at the bottom. "And it's not sold, Anne. This is an auction."

Anne took a moment to let it sink in. "The Piper House is an auction house like Sotheby's, but for true original fairytales?"

"Huh. They're auctioning original texts instead of the vintage paintings or Elizabeth Taylor's La Peregrina jewel for the highest price," David said. "This sounds like a lucrative business model."

"So, the Sisterhood started as a noble concept of collecting original folktales, and now it's turned into a billion-dollar cash-grab?"

"Stories as art, who would have thought?" David said. "But why would people bid so much money on these tales?"

Anne continued walking in case their behavior would garner suspicions. Most buyers didn't have prolonged conversations by the doors. They checked whether the story in the room was one they wanted to buy or not and then entered or moved on.

"Jacqueline de Rais had an answer," David said, eyes scanning for security guards walking among them.

"She said that her billions left her with nothing she couldn't buy," Anne contemplated. "So she bought original stories?"

"What makes something valuable more than scarcity?" David

said. "Ultra-rich people worldwide pay crazy money to buy rare paintings, rare coins, and rare swords that once belonged to kings and queens," David said.

"Why not stories, especially if they were true?" Anne said. "Come to think of it. It makes perfect sense."

"The pestering question is: How dark are these stories?" David said, picking up another drink from a butler on the way.

"Dark?" Anne said. "What do you mean?"

"You said the original fairytales were darker. Full of death, rape, and murder," David recalled. "Being the pessimistic, anti-high-class, New-Castle born lad that I am, I know that he who enters an underground dungeon in a masquerade gathering to buy a story buys a dark one. Preferably something illegal, criminal, if not outright sadistic like snuff movies."

"You're being paranoid," Anne said. "But come to think of it, Jacqueline de Rais' original story was a dark one, so your theory is plausible. I mean, the Ovitzs sacrificed their sister. Darkness shrouds this mystery from head to toe."

"Which makes me suddenly understand," David stopped walking and faced her.

"Understand what?"

"Who the girl on the cross really is."

"We know who she is, David. It's Layla Ovitz."

"That's not who she is," David said. "That's who she represents."

"Represents?"

"The same way the priest on the cross in the Vatican is a representation of something, or someone else," David said. "This is why the girl on the cross felt staged. The Ovitz were re-incarnating an old crime."

"Oh, my God," Anne said. "You mean they both represent a darker story that will be sold in the Piper House tonight."

"And the Ovitz family wants us to find it before it's sold to the highest bidder and then forever buried," David said. "Could that be it?"

"If so," Anne started, "then we're searching the auction for a story about a girl on the cross."

Suddenly, two male butlers, looking more like wrestlers, interrupted them. "Excuse me?"

"Yes?" Anne said.

"Our cameras caught you acting a little strange," one of them said.

"Your camera did what?" David said.

"The cameras are fed with an algorithm that is modeled after an intruder's behavior. It can predict burglars and thieves from unusual movements, stops, and walks."

"Holy Philip Dick," David shook his head, staring at the cameras overhead. "You're calling us intruders?"

"I'm afraid so," the butler said. "You will have to come with me."

"Are you serious?" Anne protested. "We're not thieves. We have about four million dollars to spend. We worried that we wouldn't win most of the auctions as they are expensive, so we went on looking for less crowded corridors where we find less desired stories."

"I understand, ma'am," the butler said. "But our manager's rules are strict. Please follow me."

"Your manager?" David asked.

"Of course, Mr. Edmund Xaver."

# 79

3:55 A.M.

## *Bismarck Tower, Hamelin, Fairytale Road, Germany*

Still, on top of the Bismarck Tower, the Advocate watched the driver climbing up the stairs.

"How did you manage to climb this tower, Sir?" the driver asked. "I mean, with the current condition of your legs?"

"It felt like a walk in the park," the Advocate lied.

Truthfully, he had struggled his way up in pain, succumbing to crawling on all fours. However, what drove him to follow Anne was much stronger than the pain from his physical form.

"I assume so, Sir," the driver said. "What is this about? You told me there have been changes."

The Advocate showed his driver the expensive cars in the forest and summarized his theory. "My employer hired me to find the Singing Bone, but I discovered the Sisterhood's headquarters, which is much more than what he asked for. So, I sent him a message, and he is sending backup."

"Backup?" the driver said

"Yes. And guess who, of all people, is joining forces with us?"

"I can't possibly know, Sir."

"Tom John."

"The man whose father you killed?"

"Almost killed," the Advocate said. "Who would have thought that the British royal family would join forces with the Vatican—and the Germans too, by the way."

"Why, Sir?" the driver said. "What does the Sisterhood have on them that shouldn't be revealed to the world?"

"I can speculate, but I don't care," the Advocate said, watching the Piper House through his binoculars.

"What do you care about then, Sir?"

"That it's now Anne and Rachel Anderson against the world."

# 80

***Corridors, The Piper House, Hamelin, Fairytale Road, Germany***

Expecting to meet Edmund Xaver in person was a letdown. The butler politely informed them that he had given a speech in one of the other rooms. It turned out that the algorithm's suspicions were overruled when they learned it was Anne and David's first time in the Piper House.

Newcomers were supposed first to attend Xaver's welcome speech to learn more about the House's rules. The Piper House was the umbrella company that owned his other company, Memoria.

Anne wasn't surprised, as she had told David about it earlier. It was a private company that investigated the elite's ancestry to find valuable information about their past for a hefty price.

Also, they overlooked the fact that Xaver and Jacqueline had lied to them about going to Kassel to attend an event. David supposed this was a safety tactic to protect whatever secret practices they were performing here. A smart move. Kassel was the bigger city that one would expect an organization like the Sister-hood to use as headquarters. But Kassel wasn't the place to keep an eye on; it was the small-town Hamelin with the dark past.

"Why do buyers pay so much for these stories?" David risked it, asking the butler on their way to Xaver.

Anne didn't stop him. They were too deep into this, and she was eager for answers. After all, the butler hadn't figured out they were the intruders, so the question may have come across as genuine, especially since David followed it up with, "My partner and I are fascinated with fairytales and will happily pay millions of dollars, but twenty-million? Come on. A little too much, don't you think?"

"We just sold one for seventy-two million, Sir." The butler stopped outside the room's door. "It was sold to a German tycoon who wished to know where his ancestors hid their gold in WWII."

"So, he was a Nazi German tycoon, you mean?" The answer struck David. "But I get it. The expensive fairytales can be a lucra-tive investment. Do you happen to know which original fairytale offered such information?"

"A contemporary one, not of old," the butler said. "But I'm sure you know that I can't tell you. This conversation may have never happened."

"Since it never happened," David said. "Why don't you tell me more about the kind of buyers who seek these stories."

The butler chuckled from underneath the mask. "To get to the bottom of your inquiry, here is how you might want to think about these stories and their buyers: What if you, the buyer, are a direct descendant of the men and women in the stories?"

"Now that is a conversation that never happened," Anne said. "It makes much more sense to me now. Buying true stories for such high amounts had to have a personal angle to it."

"Agreed," the butler said. "Imagine that your inheritance was left unsettled because of an old signature that could only be traced in one of these stories? What if your inheritance was lost, stolen, or unfairly split, and a story could help you find the truth? Some people want to know how their loved ones died in war centuries ago. What were they like? What were their last words? What words of wisdom did they share last? And what if the buyers felt cursed or unlucky and wanted to know if it was hereditary in some sense?"

"It's fair to say that the Sisterhood ended up collecting more than just fairytales," Anne said.

"Some buyers still believe in the Holy Grail and want the story that leads to its location," the butler said. "The options are endless."

David remembered when he stood in Westminster Abbey, trapped between the girl on the cross and Mary Tudor. What if the girl on the cross gave way to something in the past about Mary Tudor? Or the royal family? And now, possibly the Vatican?

The butler politely showed them into the room, leaving them with one final question, "How much would you pay for a mere folktale from the past if it contained answers about the future?"

# 81

### *Welcome Room, The Piper House, Hamelin, Fairytale Road, Germany*

The folklorist and the detective entered the room and, in David's style, sat in the last row behind about twenty newcomers sitting in front. The buyers wore the same cloaks and masks but oozed posh and prestige and looked like they were enjoying their time.

Seeing Edmund Xaver stand behind the podium on stage, one could sense his unapologetic sense of authority. He put on his thick glasses, wet his thumb with his tongue, and flipped through a book. Anne immediately recognized it as the Brothers Grimm fairytales and wondered if it was the original version.

None of the newcomers dared to make the slightest noise, and silence filled the air with anticipation. Anne could hear the friction of Xaver's unfolding pages from where she sat.

Minutes later, the butlers provided the buyers with new phones, and Anne and David received theirs on a golden tray.

"Our app is installed on this phone," the butler said. "Please enter your username and follow protocol. You're free to use anonymous avatars if you like."

David recognized the app immediately. "It's the one Xaver and Jacqueline used on the jet."

"Bet Time Story," Anne said. "Cool name."

"It's a local network. You can't use it to go online," David said, swiping.

Anne found the app useful. It stated everyone's financial limit and Singing Bone number. It mentioned bonuses and privileges to old-timers and showed a list of the stories being sold in every room. She ran through them but couldn't find one about a girl on a cross.

More time passed. While waiting for Xaver to begin, Anne examined the room around her.

The red walls had a graffiti-like look, a web of intricate images painted on each side. Anne reckoned it was pastel colors, as Rachel used them in her amateur paintings.

On the left wall, she saw a re-imagining of the Six Swans. One part showed them sitting around a table, performing a Seance and summoning spirits. Another depicted them knitting while sipping tea. A third one showed five of them circling Lilliput Ovitz and listening to her stories while she sat on the floor in the middle. Of course, Ovitz, the dwarf, had their undivided attention.

On the right wall, an overhead light spanned the room's length. The light pooled over more paintings of the original True Sisters, revealing more sinister and darkly suggestive scenes.

One part depicted them in a circle with their backs arched backward and their hands up in the air. They looked like witches, chanting, if not communicating with the other side. Lightning cracked in blue and white spirals, forming the ghost of a girl with an apple in her hand. An apple that was cut in half like the one in the Westminster Abbey. Instead of revealing a pentagram, it was a red rose with five petals.

Anne was puzzled by this image but couldn't figure out why. Her best bet was that the rose was too similar to a pentagram. She couldn't make the connection, though she remembered Rachel calling her Rose Red as a child.

*It would help if you toned down this overactive mind, Anne,* Rachel scolded, her voice returning in Anne's mind. *You know that within minutes you will have to face the past. You can feel it. It's on the tip of your tongue, like a bad memory you once buried but is now resurfacing. You won't admit it.*

Anne was about to tell David about the five-petal rose when Xaver knocked on the tiny microphone pinned to his suit to get everyone's attention.

"Ladies and Gentlemen," he began, standing behind the podium with both hands gripping the edges. His reading glasses and his unbuttoned shirt beneath his suit made him look relatable. A wealthy madman who didn't care for looks or money because he had a greater purpose. "It's an honor to have you join us on our quest to expose the world's true history through oral storytelling." He winked at his audience. "And persuade you to buy a few million dollars worth of stories, of course."

Polite laughter resonated among the audience.

"Allow me to introduce myself. I'm folklorist Edmund Xaver," he said. "You may have read my books. I may have lectured in one of the prestigious universities in your cities, especially at the Oral History department of Queen Mary University in London, my favorite of all."

Anne glanced briefly at David to see how he was doing. He seemed as full of anticipation as she was.

"Some of you know me as the owner of the infamous Memoria," Xaver continued. "Where last year we unintentionally uncovered one of the world's richest bloodline mirrored that of Jon Snow's of the Game of Thrones books."

The crowd liked the way he broke the ice with them.

"Forgive me if I reference too many books or act theatrically. I'm a man who still can't get the books he read as a child out of his head," Xaver pointed upward. "As a new dawn awaits outside these walls, we shall all see the truth of our past lives for the first time today."

"Goldfinger has some peculiar charisma," David whispered to Anne. "I can see how he persuades people to buy stories."

"None of this could've been possible without six women nobody talks about, but they bravely saved our history. And by that, I mean her-story." Xaver clapped, pointing at the images on the walls left and right. "Please applaud in honor of the Six Swans, otherwise known as the Sisterhood."

The crowd clapped in response.

"Now, let's get into why you're all here," he announced, interrupting the last few claps, voice dimming. "The history of the Sisterhood: who they were, what they did, and why they did what they did." He gripped the Brothers Grimm book and waved it like a preacher waves the Bible in the air. "Ladies and gentlemen, let me tell you about the true origins of fairytales and what this book was meant to be."

# 82

4:17 A.M.

*Welcome Room, The Piper House, Hamelin, Fairytale Road, Germany*

"In 1801, Dorothea Viehman, a German storyteller who lived in Kassel, wished to collect the German folktales and pass them to the following generations," Xaver said in an articulate voice. He sounded like he had done this a thousand times before. "Joined by Charlotte Grimm, Dortchen Wild, and Jeanine and Amalie Hassenpflug, they created the Märchenhaus, aka the House of Stories Sunday Club in Kassel. If you wonder where your American and British book clubs come from, this was the first one in history."

"Am I going to hear the same story again?" David hissed.

"I assume his version will be more accurate," Anne said. "The devil is in the details."

"The book club met once a week," Xaver said. "They chatted, shared stories, and joked about using the pentagram symbol as their logo. The pentagram represents the Five Elements: spirit, water, air, earth, and fire. And each one of these women felt like one fitted her description best. I'd lie to you if I told you I knew who was who, though."

"He is good," Anne whispered to David. "His voice, his delivery, and his tempo. Rachel used to know how to tell a story like that."

"One day, they were interrupted by a peasant called Lilliput Ovitz," Xaver continued. "A dwarf whose real name was Remi Lafa, short for Reminzka Lafayette."

"I never knew her real name was Remi Lafa. This is why he is the highest-paid folklorist in the world," Anne hissed to David.

"Reminzka Lafayette, a Wallachian Jew, changed her name to Lilliput Ovitz after escaping the Ottoman Empire's wrath in her homeland, which we call Romania today," Xaver stopped, hands still laced behind his back. "In her time, Remi Lafa witnessed the most atrocious crimes. Crimes that had been mostly committed against women and children."

The silence suffocated everyone in the room. Finally, he stopped and stared at his audience with intent.

"You see, it was a man's world back then," Xaver said. "Woman who had been violated would not, in most circumstances, be taken seriously if she spoke her mind." He waved a finger sideways in the air. "Let me carve that picture into your skulls by telling you that in these European regions, some courts of law would not accept a woman's testimony. Women were considered unreliable then."

"What?" David muttered to Anne, who had nothing to say back. She knew about women being oppressed back then but never heard many details on the matter.

"The court would only consider a testimony viable in a murder case if two women separately testified about the same event," Xaver said. "On the other hand, a man's testimony was fully welcomed."

Anne watched Xaver rub his chin. "Of course, there were few women whose word was golden. Above the law, even. In all of history, you could count them on the one hand. They were those women so close to the crown; queens, favorable princesses, aristocrats, and elite friends."

"Isn't this supposed to be about fairytale origins?" David said to Anne. "Where is Goldfinger going with this?"

"I think he is building up a case," Anne said. "It flows nicely, in my opinion."

"So, imagine how much Remi Lafa risked to tell the members of the House of Stories about a true crime she had witnessed herself," Xaver continued. "And by that story, I mean the one about Gilles de Rais, the first known serial killer of women and children in history."

"That's where he is going with it," Anne replied to David.

"When Remi Lafa mentioned that she worked for Gilles de Rais—that she had witnessed his rituals of supposedly summoning demon called 'baron,' and that she had wiped the blood off the floor after he committed his acts—Dorothea Viehman was left perplexed. Remi Lafa handed her an unbearable responsibility she and her housewife friends didn't ask for."

*I can only imagine*, Anne thought to herself. Then, she remembered how hard it was for her to authenticate what she knew so that she could put it in a book without feeling guilty about it.

"These women, who told stories to pass the hours and have a good time, were now exposed to injustice against the elite of the land in a world that only looked down upon storytellers in the first place," Xaver padded the stage slowly. "At the time, society considered storytellers, actors, and circus performers, whatever their genders, to be such imposters that their testimony in court was denied without appeal."

Anxiously, Anne rubbed her hands against her cloak. "I mentioned that in my book. It was why most of my resources were so apathetic and didn't care. No one had believed them in the past."

"Why the French Baron killed these women is a story for another time," Xaver said. "After all, the infamous queen Elizabeth Bathory, also from Hungary, did the same. Years later, she killed young girls and swam in their blood for eternal youth," Xaver stopped and faced the crowd. "What mattered was the injustice done to de Rais' victims, one of many violations committed against women then."

The crowd hummed with inaudible questions.

Xaver knelt by the edge of the stage to confront them. "Imagine you lived back then in those harsh times. Then imagine you saw a crime you could not speak of. What would you have done?"

Anne could feel Xaver's presence touch her soul. He was relentless and confident, though she could not decide whether he was sincere or a damn good salesman.

"Nothing," Xaver whispered to the crowd, imitating the imaginary act of zipping one's mouth. "You do nothing and allow the man with the pen who wrote history to write nothing as well. In fact, the man with the pen will not only bury these past crimes but write them off into his preferred version to pass on. History is written by *he* who documents it first. That's it."

Everyone was on edge, sensing a dark revelation coming from Xaver's mouth.

"That's why the Sisterhood was created," Xaver said. "That was when they decided that these crimes should be collected. They would secretly be passed from generation to generation through an intricate and exclusive system, where word-of-mouth was the one authentic keeper of truth," Xaver stretched his arms sideways. "That is, ladies and gentlemen when Oral History was first conceived, but as a secret and untold art, only practiced by the bloodline of the women of the Sisterhood."

# 83

---

## *Hamelin, Fairytale Road, Germany*

Tom John hadn't met the Advocate before, but his instructions were to co-operate and trust him, having witnessed him succeed in following Anne and David to Hamelin. So now Tom stood next to him, looking through the binoculars and listening to the whole story.

"Do you think they have guns or a militia inside that Piper House?" Tom asked, irked by the Advocate's flamboyant yet repellant look.

"I have no reason to believe that," the Advocate said. "Look at the cars parked in the forest. And that helicopter. There are no guards."

"How come they feel so safe? Gathering without security guards all around?" Tom said.

"The plate numbers of the parked cars belong to the crème de la crème of the rich worldwide," the Advocate said. "They're probably counting on that. They're untouchable if you ask me."

"No one's untouchable," Tom said. "We'll have to raid the place and get that Singing Bone."

"And if not, we need Anne to tell us how to find it," the Advocate suggested. "Problem is how actually to find them inside."

"The German policeman we sent to the Piper House said it was abandoned and that they found no entrances," Tom mentioned. "But you saw them enter it, right?"

"I did."

"I'll take your word for it. We have no choice but to attack from the back of the house, the side by the forest where the cars are parked."

"But it's a solid wall," the Advocate said. "It's like a contained spaceship or something disguised as an ancient fairytale house."

"Technology bought them a house that has no doors. I'll give them that," Tom said. "But it certainly didn't buy them an invisibility cloak."

"Meaning?" the Advocate said.

"If it doesn't have a doorknob," Tom said. "Blow it up."

# 84

*Welcome Room, The Piper House, Hamelin, Fairytale Road, Germany*

"Now that you know about the Sisterhood's plan, you may ask yourself, 'How do you trust people with true stories?' And if you do, how do you ensure that passing them from one generation to another doesn't result in a poorly executed phone game and a different meaning altogether?"

"I can't believe they did that," Anne said to David. "It sounds impossible."

"These paintings make you think they went mad or communed with spirits to help them," Xaver pointed at the walls. "But you're wrong. These images depict them working on a system to help them learn how to memorize the truth. How to have one story-teller guard the story and another keep a piece of it, like two keys needed to unlock one safe."

The silence grew in the room. His words were revealing but hard to fathom.

"They learned how to use what psychologists now call an

'anchor,' which was more of a trigger word or melody that helped them remember. It's had the same effect photographs have on you nowadays. Once you see the picture, it takes you back to that moment and makes you remember more about it," Xaver continued. "The Sisterhood used melodies from flutes, inspired by the true tale of a girl called Fae who was killed centuries ago. By now, I expect you to know it's about a shepherd who used the girl's bones to trace her killer. These bones were carved into flutes and were hung from their necklaces; to each storyteller, her melody; to each storyteller, *her trigger* that will help her remember in detail. That flute/bone would later be known as the Singing Bone. The first story in the Brothers Grimm, but I'll get into that later."

"How did that exactly work?" An audience member asked.

"It's a complex process, but you'll learn about it inside the auctions," Xaver said. "What is important is that when you hear stories about members of the Sisterhood sleepwalking and talking to themselves, you must understand that they weren't possessed or crazy. They were practicing. Honing their system of remembering the exact date, locations, and names of these crimes."

Anne and David exchanged looks of disbelief yet found this the most plausible explanation for many things.

"When you hear stories about Lotte Grimm writing in blood on deerskin and then burning it? That was her experimenting with memory. She used her blood to remind herself that the story she guarded was of a woman or a child's demise that needed justice at some point in the future," Xaver said. "When you hear stories about the Sisterhood burning the books? That was a story that had been engraved in one's soul. It didn't need to exist in the house anymore. If they kept it, the kings and queens would send their men after them."

Anne's breathing faltered, unable to imagine these women's lives.

"On and on, they tried it all," Xaver said. "They didn't sleep, and their mental health began to deteriorate. They discovered that repeatedly reciting a story of children being kidnapped or women being raped and then buried alive messed with their essence. Their soul." Xaver sounded as if he was going to break down and cry. "They became sicker and sicker, and Dorothea realized they needed a better system."

Xaver stood behind the podium again, flipping through pages.

"At some point, Dorothea Viehman locked herself in a secret room in the Rapunzel Tower in Trendelenburg. Without food, and only water, she stayed awake for days, perfecting the system," Xaver said. "And it was there it came to her. She realized that memorizing religious texts and Bible passages came naturally to her. She would remember it any day, any time, just like that," Xaver said, snapping his fingers. "She began to ask herself why."

"Why?" Anne found herself leaning forward, remembering Rachel now.

"Dorothea Viehman was raised to believe these words as a child." Xaver rapped a hand against his chest. "She believed in them as being holy and religious. That upon believing in these words, she would be rewarded a special place in the afterlife. What a reward to make one remember. What an essential belief to make one never forget."

It took some time before the audience gasped, realizing what he was saying.

"To preserve the truth, Dorothea Viehman needed to create a religion," Xaver faced his audience again. "She created a cult of only women bred to pass their stories to their female offspring. These daughters would have these crimes engraved in their minds at a young age and forever live with the purpose and responsibility of guarding the truth and passing it to their grandchildren, unbeknownst to the enemy whose lies are in written words. That is until the time came to unleash the stories to the world."

With the words he spoke, Xaver took everyone's breath away. Even David's heartbeat in his chest with every syllable in a hypnotizing tempo that ended with one final revelation. "Stories that the common reader or listener nowadays thinks are fairytales."

# 85

## *Hotel Room, Rome, Italy*

A little tipsy now, Mary watched her sisters pray in the other room.

She watched them kneel, facing each other, telling the piece of the story they guarded. Then, being the most versed and aspiring to become a True Sister so she could protect a bigger secret all by herself, Lily orchestrated the 'prayer,' which was a term Mary despised.

Lily took Lara and Lucia's Singing Bones and played their anchoring melody. A specific tune that helped them remember the tiniest details in their story.

Lucia's reaction to her melody made her eyes roll back and look like she was possessed. Some girls, the weaker ones, reacted similarly at times, but Mary knew it wasn't as bad as it looked.

There have been stories about the True Sisters who guarded the darker stories. They would violently shudder upon hearing their anchoring melodies, but Mary hadn't seen it herself. The True Sisters repeatedly lived the unforgivable crime they guarded every day and ended up in perpetual trauma.

The session took about thirty minutes. Lara and Lucia guarded a small piece of the Ovitz family's story. Being young and experienced, Lily had always been akin to Lara, having a minor bit of the story.

Mary and Lisa, the tallest and eldest, were given the darker pieces that messed them up early.

Lily hugged Lucia, who was feeling overwhelmed by a detail in her story. It was about a sixteen-year-old girl old from the town of Lohr in Germany who had been killed and buried to keep an important secret from surfacing in 1745.

"I can't believe they did this to her," Lucia cried in Lily's arms. "She was so young and loved those dwarves."

"You'll be all right, Lucia." Lily patted her on the back. "There is darkness in this world, and our purpose is to shed light on it."

"She was killed by that baroness who summoned that demon, 'baron,'" Lucia hiccuped. "So unfair."

"It's okay." Lara, the youngest, hugged her sister from behind.

"How about I play the notes that will cheer you up?" Lily asked and played a long melody from Mozart's 'The Magic Flute.'

Mary saw the girls relax, knowing Lily's melody was an anti-anchor. It took over the story's weight and temporarily allowed them to forget about it. Like ordinary people did in real life, escaping into music or books.

Mary didn't comment but felt for Lucia. Mary also knew she carried the least provoking part of the story about the girl whom Lady Ovitz had split her story among the Sisterhood.

# 86

---

4:49 AM

## *Welcome Room, The Piper House, Hamelin, Fairytale Road, Germany*

Anne watched Xaver take a sip of water behind the podium, allowing everyone to let his words sink in.

"And now, it's time for the big question that should tie every-thing together." He waved the Brothers Grimm book in the air. "What the heck does this have to do with this book, then?"

The audience didn't respond favorably, as if still recovering from The Sisterhood's traumatic story. Anne, like the rest, worried that his final revelation would be as disturbing.

"It's simple. Almost childish and laughable." He said, putting the book down. "Years after the Sisterhood bred to supply their system with young storytellers, and Napoleon threatened to invade Germany. He had invaded a part of Kassel already. The Brothers Grimm, eager to collect fairytales, had the connections and permissions to print and proposed no threat to anyone. After all, they just wanted to write a fantasy book."

Xaver took another sip of water and wiped his mouth with the back of his hand. "On the other hand, the Sisterhood's plan was going to take some time, as their eldest child conceived to create the bloodline was only ten years old. Also, there was the probability that they wouldn't survive Napoleon's attack." Xaver paused. "And here is where their devious yet flawed plan came in handy. A plan that was inspired by a common saying in Germany at the time. It went like this–"

*The greatest trick the devil ever pulled was convincing the world he was someone else,* Anne whispered to herself as Xaver told it to his audience. A saying Rachel recited to her long ago.

"The Sisterhood convinced the two brothers that they could provide all the stories they needed, having gathered them from the peasants who visited them in the House of Stories in Kassel," Xaver moved away from the podium to stand in the center of the stage. "And the Brothers Grimm fell for their plan and ate it up, publishing the book that now lives in the mind and soul of us all. Conceived at childhood, and never forgotten."

Another long silence hit the crowd. Anne could relate. While borderline fantastic but unbelievable, everything that Xaver said resonated with the newcomer's childhood. These stories had been brilliantly etched in the mind of the masses, shaping significant decisions in their lives. So having them now debunked by Xaver hurt in the most puzzling ways.

"A brilliant plan, huh?" Xaver adjusted his loose belt. "Not so much because the Sisterhood couldn't tell the Brothers Grimm the exact dates, names, or locations of these crimes. So, they inserted codes."

"Codes?" one of the women in the audience asked.

"We, the folklorist, like to call it The Fairytale Code," Xaver said.

"A little cliché, don't you think?" The same woman spoke.

"It sounds cheesy, and cliché but so is history itself," Xaver said, still unsatisfied with how his belt pressed on his belly. "I mean, David couldn't have possibly beat Goliath. Yet we brag about it to everyone and still use it as a story of hope, motivation, and strength."

Amidst all this tension, Anne looked at David.

"Are you smiling, Anne?" He leaned forward with a tense jaw.

"He doesn't mean you," she said playfully. "Don't take it seriously."

"Well, he does," David said. "Because he thinks he is Goliath."

"In the end, the Brothers Grimm published the book without knowing anything about the codes inside," Xaver said.

"What kind of codes?" a male member asked skeptically. "Can you give us an example?"

"You understand that telling will only hurt my business, as these codes are what makes the stories we sell," Xaver started. "But here are a few unimportant ones. Other than endless lines that have a different specific meaning when used as an anagram, there is the famous one about why Gilled de Rais was called Bluebeard."

*There is?* Anne whispered to herself.

"De Rais was known to dye his beard blue, the color of the demon he sacrificed women and children for. The color blue was also the dominating color of France a few years before his time, and even when it was changed, many people lived by the older flag." Xaver entirely removed his tie and hurled it away. "Here is why Little Red Riding Hood carried a basket of bread and wine: because it gave away her hometown in Alsfeld, where its locals, devout Christians, were the first in Germany to send wine and bread for the dying. And by dying," he raised his hands in the air like a preacher and recited a phrase from the Bible, "'Pour out your wine and your bread on the grave of the righteous!'" he turned and walked the other direction, eyes on his audience. "Also, the girl, Blanchette Wolf, was violated by her own father, hence the wolf. Blanchette's cloak was yellow, more light brownish, the color of cheap fabrics at the time, which the poor loved to call 'gold' to feel better about themselves. The Sisterhood changed it to red because...." Xaver faced his audience, waiting for their reply. "Does anyone know?"

A woman from the crowd answered, "Because of it being the Sisterhood's outfit."

"Exactly, and there is more," Xaver exhaled. "Only there's not mere codes for incest or murder but of crimes that include well-known kings and public figures."

The crowd stopped asking questions. A minute of silence and contemplation passed to let everyone absorb the information. Whether they believed Xaver or not was up to them.

Finally, two newcomers shook their heads in disbelief and excused themselves, ushered outside by the butlers.

"Now that I've welcomed you and made my case," Xaver said in all calmness. "Let me spell it out in one final sentence, explaining why the world is after the contents of this book and the one Singing Bone that could lead to the original script, aka code." He tapped his finger on the Brothers Grimm book with his knuckles. "The original, handwritten version of this book is a concise documentation of untold crimes against women and children from about ten centuries ago until the nineteenth century."

Anne closed her eyes under the mask, partially disappointed that her quest had ended and partially disappointed she wasn't the one to figure it out. More than anything, she was disappointed that Rachel wasn't here. If anyone deserved to listen to these revelations, she had always suspected, it would be her.

"At this point of my presentation, I'm usually asked to demonstrate how the stories are told to the buyer," Xaver followed up. "So, it's a custom around here to compliment the new buyers with a free demonstration."

"I was thinking the same," David told Anne. "I want to see how this works."

Xaver craned his neck in Anne's direction.

"This year, we're lucky," he said, clearly looking at her, though she still wore her cloak and mask.

Anne felt the room closing in on her.

"Anne Anderson," Xaver waved at her wide smile and an open palm across the room. "Can you please come forward, so we can demonstrate to our buyers how receiving a story works?"

Anne didn't respond, hoping to pressure him to divert his focus and apologize. He couldn't want to play the game with open cards like this.

"Anne Christian Anderson," he insisted. "Please?"

"I think you have me confused with someone," Anne stuttered a little while David was already looking for an escape route.

"I'm not confused, Professor, and I hope you aren't, either," Xaver said, still wearing his plastic smile. "I'm sure you've been told that your Singing Bone is good for one story only. One that has been kept for you here for years. I think it's time for you to face your demons."

# 87

## *Bismarck Tower, Hamelin, Germany*

Tom watched the German police officers spread all over the forest and around the helicopter atop the hill. Down below, the German bombing squad had finished their wiring at the back of the Piper House.

"I don't want to blow up the whole building," Tom instructed the policeman over the radio, who spoke on Martin Wolf's behalf. He didn't care where that inspector was right now.

"Don't worry," the policeman responded. "German explosives are top-notch and would bring this building down in a blink of an eye, so we used British crap."

Tom's face crumbled as he heard the policeman snicker. Behind him, the Advocate advised him to play along and say 'ha-ha.'

Tom rolled his eyes. "Don't blow anything up before I tell you. Again, as a reminder, we're blowing up part of the building to find a way in. Not the whole damn place."

"Aye, aye, Sir," the policeman snickered again, and then there was a pause. "Wait, Sir, just a second."

"What is it?" Tom asked.

"I see two people leaving the building," the policeman whispered. "Posh and high class. Escorted by two funny-looking men."

"Funny looking?"

"They're dressed up in tuxedoes with white gloves and white theatre masks," the policeman said. "Is there anything we should know about what's going on down there, Sir?"

"I'm as oblivious as you," Tom said. "Arrest them!"

"No," the Advocate ordered. "You'll alert everyone inside the building."

Tom found it a sound argument, so he said to the policeman, "Hide, all of you, and watch what happens. Don't do anything until I give you orders."

The Advocate snatched the dispatcher from Tom and spoke into it. "Have the smartest and sleekest of your men figure out how they left the building," he said. "We have an unforced exit on our hands, and we shouldn't lose it."

Tom was disappointed he didn't think of that, but he didn't mind the Advocate's input. "Good collaboration between us."

"Come, see." The Advocate handed Tom a pair of night-vision goggles, revealing the scene of the two newcomers being escorted to their cars in the forest.

They had taken off their cloaks and masks to reveal their evening outfits. They got into their car, but the butlers on both sides knocked on their windows to tell them goodbye. Once they rolled the windows down, the butlers shot them in the head with a silencer.

Tom winced at the heartless execution, but the Advocate showed no emotion.

They watched the butlers loosen the hand-breaks and push the car off the Koppen cliff until it fell off and plunged into the river.

"Why didn't we try to stop them?" a younger policeman protested through dispatch. "We've just allowed a crime to happen."

The Advocate pressed the button to talk to the upset policeman, but his partner shot him in the head with a silencer.

His partner, who was the German policeman snickering at Tom earlier, said, "Did you want to tell me something, Sir?"

"I was going to tell you to shoot him, but talk is cheap, and guns shoot deep," the Advocate smiled. "Now follow the tuxedoed men back to find the way in."

In the back, Tom breathed ruggedly, wondering about these callous men surrounding him. How far would he continue falling into this rabbit hole of ruthlessness?

# 88

4:59 A.M.

## *Welcome Room, The Piper House, Hamelin, Fairytale Road, Germany*

Anne pressed her body against the back of her chair, gripping it tightly. David had no means to comfort her. Endless scenarios swirled in his head, but he couldn't settle on one. Only now did he realize that he liked her. Too soon, he knew, but he hoped he could protect her from what was in store.

Xaver stood by the podium while the naive newcomers urged Anne to accept his invitation on stage. They didn't understand the underlined conflict between her and Xaver. They thought she was here to demonstrate how the stories were told and sold.

Anne stood up and lifted her mask, challenging Xaver's manipulative game. It was hard to tell what he had on his mind, but she approached the stage anyway. After all, she needed to know why the mapestry sent her to this place to become face to face with this man.

David followed suit and took off his mask. When he tried to stop her, she ignored him and faced Xaver.

She stood right in front of him and craned her neck, waiting for him to talk. Rachel had taught her that it was always best to wait and let the enemy speak first in confrontations.

"The masks are wired," Xaver smirked. "That's how I knew you were here—if that's what's on your mind."

"I don't care about how you knew I was here. I want to know why," she said, not caring about the confused audience behind her.

"That's what you and I will figure out together, Professor," he said.

"I find it hard to believe that you don't know what's going on," Anne said. "You and Jacqueline flew us to Polle and must have known we would end up here," Anne said. "Or why would you have lied to us about going to Kassel?"

"You didn't think I'd give away the Sisterhood's meeting location, did you?" Xaver said. "As for the free flight, I wanted to see where Bloody Mary sent you and wished to use you as bait to lead me to her. She is the one who sent me the laptop and planned the whole thing. Although she and I are both in the Sisterhood, we are on opposite sides of the fence. She split the Sisterhood into two factions. Hers is opposing our current business and wants to expose her grandmother's story to the world by using you."

Anne considered this for a moment. It was crucial to understanding this conflict between them, and she couldn't think of another explanation. "Okay, but why me? Why am I involved in this? Why was my name used as an anagram on Mary Tudor's tomb?"

"I'm just as curious to know that," Xaver said. "And trust me, you're not involved because you're a brilliant folklorist or something. We both know I'm the best."

Anne bit her tongue. It was unwise to respond to him while he was pushing her buttons. She couldn't deny her jealousy, knowing she had failed after devoting her life to the quest, and it irked her that she felt that way.

"Now," he stretched out his palm again. "May I please have your Singing Bone, so we know why you're here?"

"Not yet," Anne said. "Not before you explain a detail that is confusing me."

"And that is?"

"Why would Bloody Mary and her sisters create a mapestry for me and send me here? Only to receive a new Singing Bone she left here for me?" Anne asked slyly. "If Bloody Mary left me a Singing Bone that only unlocks a certain thing that I should know about, why hadn't she just told me the story? What's the point of the journey?"

"I'm not sure about the journey," Xaver said. "But you are mistaken about anyone, nonetheless Bloody Mary, knowing the contents of your story."

"How so?"

"Our records show that this Singing Bone was left for you eighteen years ago," Xaver said.

# 89

**Welcome Room, The Piper House, Hamelin, Fairytale Road, Germany**

Xaver climbed down from the stage and excused the rest of the audience, promising a bonus of one million dollars towards their buying powers. The audience took the bait, and David made a subtle comment to Anne about how he never understood people's behavior when offered money.

Only Anne, David, Xaver, and two butlers occupied the room in just a few minutes.

"I'm getting Westminster Abbey vibes all over again," David mumbled, wondering if Xaver had a gun.

He then watched Anne hand Xaver the Singing Bone to examine it.

"Unusual wood," Xaver stated, weighing it on his open palm.

"How unusual?" Anne said.

"Made of human bones," Xaver replied.

"Human bones?" David said.

"Let me see," Anne tried to pull it back, but Xaver gripped it harder and only let her look.

"Just like the first flute made by mankind was made from human bones," Xaver commented.

"Because the first humans hadn't learned to talk yet," David agreed. "They communicated with sound."

"Didn't know you knew that much about evolution, my friend," Xaver momentarily eyed David.

"I'm a Darwin fan. Part detective, part money," David said dismissively, eyes on the bone. "But this bone doesn't look that old. Why would anyone design such a bone for Anne?"

"Two reasons, I believe." Xaver inhaled the bone's odor. "Ah, the smell of the departed. I wonder what story they could have told me."

"Reason number one?" Anne snapped her finger. "Tell me."

"It's an old tradition for one-story-bones to be made of human bones," Xaver said. "To honor the main story of the Singing Bone in the books. After all, all of this is influenced by the idea that the bones of the dead can tell of their past and what happened to them."

"Sounds plausible. Reason number two?" Anne probed.

"It's the bones of someone you know," Xaver said bluntly.

"Can we track back who left me this bone?"

"It's not Rachel if that's what you're asking," Xaver said.

"Because she is not from the Sisterhood," Anne agreed. "Still, can you trace it?"

"No. The Singing Bones are meticulously untraceable for our buyer's privacy," Xaver said.

"Are you sure about that?" Anne said skeptically.

"Single-story-bones are an extremely private matter in here," Xaver said. "It's a complimentary service, which we don't do anymore. A better question you could have asked is this: Who did you know eighteen years ago that was a descendant of the Sisterhood?"

Anne couldn't think of anyone. She hadn't even believed in the Sisterhood until a few hours ago.

"I see that you don't know," Xaver said. "Now, let me ask you the most crucial question about this bone."

"Go ahead."

"Are you capable of unlocking it?"

Anne dropped her head and looked like she did when David asked her about Rachel. He couldn't tell what she was hiding now.

"I would've tried if it had numbers or musical codes next to the holes, like the one before," she said. "But it doesn't."

"Actually, it does have a code."

"No, it doesn't," she insisted, almost tiptoeing with objection. "I'm sure."

Xaver ran his fingers over the flute's surface while rotating it like a Cuban cigar. Nothing was carved on it, and the wood looked clean and untouched.

After a few seconds, Xaver licked his thumb and ran his wet finger over the bone's surface. Four scribbled sentences showed up parallel to the holes. The bone must be rotated in a full circle to read consecutively.

"Revealing ink," Xaver said. "An old trick that only a few people use. It's very unreliable, to be honest, but well-executed here."

"Looks like it doesn't last long, though," David pointed out as the writing began to fade.

"Did you ever use such a technique to hide a message?" Xaver asked Anne.

"I haven't," she said, still sounding defensive. "What makes you think I have?"

"It's a specific technique for sending hidden messages," Xaver said. "This story is yours, and the password to unlock it is tailored for you. I don't think whoever made it for you would leave you with an unfamiliar puzzle you couldn't solve."

"Well, I couldn't, all right?" Anne said, trying to pull it back from him again. "Show me what the writing says."

"Of course," Xaver said. "Just relax."

He brought his thumb to his tongue once more, touching his finger to the flute to reveal the message to Anne:

***I'm so far but always near,***
***I can't blame 'cause you're so dear,***
***to this dwarf that sings her name,***
***in four notes, you'll never hear.***

"Sound like a puzzle you can solve?" Xaver wondered.

"No," Anne said, looking away from the bone. "I have no idea what this means."

"Hmm..." Xaver lowered his gaze. He raised his eyes to meet David's. "How about you advise her to tell the truth, Detective?"

"She isn't lying," David said. "I know her well."

"No, you don't, my friend," Xaver said. "Trust me. You don't."

Anne looked tongue-tied as if she wanted to speak up but was cursed with perpetual silence.

"Anne," Xaver said. "Not only am I sure you know about the secret ink, but I'm also confident that you know whose bones this flute is made of."

## 90

*18 Years Ago*

Rachel felt different today. Anne could tell.

They were hiding at the bottom of the well again, hoping their stepfather's dark friend wouldn't find their secret place. The man in the black cassock had begun to frequently visit them, buying them goodies and even clothes.

Rachel had been answering too many calls these days, leaving the house for more extended hours but making more money. Only a couple of thousand dollars more, and they were out of here, she had told Anne.

But tonight, she seemed tired and worn out. She looked pale, the result of not sleeping enough lately.

Anne suppressed her suspicions and never asked Rachel how she made money, but it was apparent what the most beautiful girl in the vineyard did for money.

"What's wrong, Rachel?" Anne said.

"I'm worried if something happens to me," Rachel said.

"Like what?"

"I don't know, Anne. It's those stories inside my head. They're driving me crazy," Rachel said. "It's like someone is talking inside my mind twenty-four seven."

"Do you need a doctor?"

"No, I'll be fine." She pulled her knees closer to her chest and pressed her back against the round walls. "I want these stories to go away. They become more vivid and intense when I'm exhausted and stressed."

"I'm getting worried now, Rachel," Anne said. "What's going on?"

"You know what also triggers them?" Rachel said. "Music."

"But I thought music makes you feel good? Remember how we danced 'till we dropped last night at the winery?"

"Not that kind of music," Rachel said. "Classical music, or whatever they call it. All this Bach, Mozart, and Beethoven crap. It triggers the stories back—loud, noisy, and epically scary."

"Triggers, you say?"

"It's the best I can think to describe it," Rachel said. "These stories seem to have always been inside me, Anne, and in certain circumstances, they re-surface."

"That's weird, but I hear you," Anne said. "Classical music scares me sometimes. I remember you telling me that mum hated it."

"And lately, there's only one story attacking my senses," Rachel said.

"Just one? What's it about?"

Reluctantly, Rachel looked at Anne and then swallowed hard.

"About what, Rachel?"

"I think it's me," Rachel seemed aware of how insane she sounded. "Imagine a story about a girl who looks like me who had horrible things done to her. She even has my name."

"But you said the stories are centuries-old, Rachel."

"I know, I know." Rachel tucked her head against her knees and whimpered. "I'm going crazy."

"What happens to you in the story?"

"I can't tell you," she said. "You won't believe me."

"Am I there with you?" Anne asked, hugging her cocooned sister.

"I wish you were there, but you're not." Rachel raised her head. "There is a place I saw in a forest. And it doesn't seem to be here in California. So, I found out it's not even in this continent."

"You're not making sense now, Rachel."

"As if I did before!" Rachel yelled. "It's a castle in Germany, I think. What's happening to me?"

"Okay," Anne said. "Tomorrow, we visit a doctor. Maybe you're too exhausted from work."

But Rachel wasn't listening. She picked up one of the bones from the ground and used a boulder's edge to carve something on it. She did it so meticulously and gently that Anne couldn't see what she had written.

"If you wake up one day, and I'm gone," Rachel said, waving the bone in her face.

"Don't say that—"

"Listen to me!" Rachel shook Anne violently. "If anything happens and separates us and I want to make a connection again— or find you, leave you a secret message, or tell you where I am or what these stories are all about. I will find a way to make you come across a similar flute made of human bones."

"You mean a Singing Bone?"

"Call it what you want, as long as it's carved from human bones," Rachel said. "It will be our Singing Bone, telling you how to find me. Because I think other people want what's in my head."

"You're not making any sense, Rachel," Anne could feel the tears forming behind her eyes.

"When you find it, you'll discover it has a secret message for you. One that you'll only be able to read if you drench the bone in water. If it reveals a message, it's me," Rachel said. "Don't ever tell anyone about this, you hear me?"

"But you're not going away, are you?" Anne's voice began to hitch.

"I'm going insane. That's what I know," Rachel said. "And you must know by now that this is why mother left."

"What?"

"She was experiencing similar symptoms," Rachel said. "It started with you in her womb, and then it worsened."

"But I found her necklace in the well, Rachel," Anne said. "Did she fall or something? Was she that insane? Are these her bones?"

Rachel felt a headache, so she quieted Anne and begged her to stop asking many questions. "I don't know what's happening. I know that we're not normal, me, you, and mum. Something about us isn't right. I've always felt it," Rachel admitted. "This man we call our stepfather is here to watch over us. Mother married him a year before she left because I think she knew she was going to leave or die. I'm not sure."

"Watch over us? Why?" Anne said.

"Maybe he wants what's in my head. I have no clue," Rachel said. "And I may have to leave to find out who we are."

"Don't leave me, Rachel," Anne said. "Let me come with you."

"And go crazy like me?" Rachel said. "As far as I know, you do not remember stories. You seem healthy and sane enough. I have the feeling you're different, and I don't want to deny you a better life than mum and I—"

Rachel choked on her words, making Anne feel unsettled. "What is going on?"

"You're the stronger one," Rachel said absently, as if Anne wasn't around her anymore. "You're the one."

Then, without warning, Rachel knocked Anne out with the back of her elbow, leaving her unconscious on the well's ground.

# 91

## *Welcome Room, The Piper House, Hamelin, Fairytale Road, Germany*

Anne's memory was interrupted by David's loud voice. He was accusing Xaver of toying with her with psychology. She must have fainted because she woke up stretched on her back up on stage.

"You speak as if you represent the Sisterhood," David argued with Xaver. "Why do you think you have permission to talk about a cult of only women?"

"My father married into the Sisterhood, marrying a descendant of Lotte Grimm, and thus I'm of bloodline," Xaver said.

"Your father married into your rivals who attacked you for so many years?" David said.

"You know the saying. 'If you can't beat them, join them,'" Xaver said. "I showed them how their noble cause only made them insane and unhappy. And how to make money off these stories. Fair trade. Lucrative, I must add."

"Stop!" Anne screamed, standing erect on stage. She yelled

loud enough to alert the security butlers, prompting them to pull out their guns.

"Repeat that puzzle to me again, Xaver," she demanded, feeling like her memory of Rachel gave her superpowers. "From the first minute I saw the bone in the Westminster Abbey, I wished it was Rachel's. I secretly tested it with a wet thumb and found nothing." She addressed David now. "In fact, this was my real quest, David. I've become a folklorist to find my sister. All this 'origins of fairytales' thing was a lie. Not that I wasn't enamored by the mystery and ended up falling in love with folktales and the beautiful people of the Fairytale Road. But I've always been looking for my sister, David. I'm sorry if I lied to you."

David's pursed his lips to let her know she had betrayed him. She wasn't asking for redemption, but he was the only man she had ever met who stood by her, *just because*. But this was a moment of truth for Anne; as Xaver said, it was time to face her demons.

"This is why I saw a psychologist, David. Well, that wasn't the only reason, but a big part of it." She stepped off the stage, carefully approaching him, worried he would fire back at her. She believed that the thirteen-year-old girl who taught him how to dance had broken David's heart somehow. She couldn't imagine the impact on him now. "That's why I followed the mapestry."

"Why didn't you look for the secret ink when you received the new bone here in the Piper House, then?" David said in a practical voice, doing a great job at hiding his disappointment with her.

Anne blinked, the answer on the tip of her tongue. She reached for the bone in Xaver's hand and snatched it back. This time, she felt strong enough, and he couldn't hold on to it.

"Because I met you."

"Oh, come on," David muttered, waving his hands dismissively.

Xaver scoffed at David. "Romantic."

"I was going to check for the message anyway, but I wanted to delay it. Give it time," Anne said. "Everything we've experienced in such a short time made me realize what kind of imposter I was. Even listening to Xaver here, I realized I could never be the best folklorist in the world. I wasn't good enough, not because I never even tried. I was just a damaged girl looking for my sister. But you made me feel that damaged girls like me have a chance."

"And all this 'I have to call my sister was an act?" David shook his head. "God, Anne. No wonder you needed a psychiatrist. Still need one, by the way." He pointed at the bone in her hand. "Go on, solve this puzzle so we can get moving."

*I'm so far but always near,*
*I can't blame 'cause you're so dear,*
*to this dwarf that sings her name,*
*in four notes, you'll never hear.*

"You have answers now?" Xaver asked.

"I will," Anne wrote it down on the phone within an app before it disappeared again. "Give me a second."

"Okay," Xaver said.

"' I'm so far but always near,' sounds like Rachel," Anne said. "' I don't blame you 'cause you're so dear.' That's her, too, reminding me of what I've done to her."

Anne's eyes reluctantly met David's, knowing he wouldn't want anything to do with her when he found out what happened later.

"What about 'To this dwarf that sings her name'?" Xaver questioned.

"I'm not sure if Rachel wrote that part," Anne said. "But having solved too many of these in the last few hours, the last line gives it away."

Xaver exchanged puzzled looks with David.

"'In four notes you will never hear?" David asked her.

"Sounds most interesting, right?" Anne said. "Who is a dwarf you both know with a name you could never hear?"

"No one has a name you could never hear," David said, raising apologetic hands. "Just saying."

"That's the brilliance of puzzle," Xaver said. "A paradox. A conundrum that, if solved, leads to our password."

"*My* password," Anne insisted. "It's not only you, Xaver, who's good at what he does."

"I never said you're not good. Just not *as* good. If it's a name that I can never hear, how am I supposed to figure it out?"

"Read it, maybe?" David genuinely tried to help.

"It's a poem. We're reading it already," Xaver said to David. "Why don't you stick to dusting fingerprints, my friend?"

"The poem didn't just say a dwarf's name that you could never hear but said four notes you could never hear," Anne explained.

"I was going to the point that out since that's how I first interpreted it," Xaver continued. "But then you hinted at it being a name. Wait!"

"Got smarter, Mr. Goldfinger?" Anne circled him, nodding at David, who denied her a nod back.

"It's a dwarf's name that is written in a musical code," Xaver said. "You're brilliant, Professor."

"A dwarf we know?" David chimed in. "One of the Ovitz?"

"Lara?" Xaver rushed to conclusions.

"The R isn't part of the a-b-c-d-e-f-g musical code," Anne said.

"That's easy then," Xaver said. "If not Lara, then Lily. But Lily isn't a name made from the seven notes. Lisbeth? No. Lisa? No. Layla? No. And not Lucia," he babbled, stopping to stare at Anne. "And Lilith doesn't work, either."

"I don't know, but I feel it's Lady Ovitz," David added.

"It can't be Lady Ovitz, David," Xaver said. "I told you to stick to—"

The three of them exchanged looks as if their eyes were guns in a Mexican Standoff. The security butlers in the back even temporarily forgot about their weapons, curious to know as well.

"Reminzka Lafayette," Anne said. "Lady Ovitz's real name."

"Which was shortened to Remi Lafa." Xaver shook Anne by the shoulder. "I admit it. You're smarter than me!"

David looked back at the two butlers, who shrugged their shoulders, puzzled by Xaver and Anne's claim to have solved the puzzle.

"They love their job," David rolled his eyes at the butler. "A tad too much."

"Can someone explain how Remi Lafa is the dwarf's name you could never hear?" David said.

"Some musicians don't use the traditional seven notes, a-b-c-d-e-f-g," Anne explained.

"They use 'Do, a deer, a female deer; Re, a drop of golden sun," Xaver imitated Julie Andrews' dance in the Sound of Music, stretching his hand sideways. "It's an equivalent system."

"Which is do, re, mi, fa, so, la, ti, do," Anne said. "If you dissect the Remi Lafa name, it's simply re, me, la, fa. A musical code."

"Huh?," the two butlers asked in one breath,

"Re, me, la, fa equals d-e-a-f," Xaver told them enthusiastically.

"Deaf!" Anne said. "Four notes you can never hear!"

"Aha!" David and the butlers bonded over sharing the lowest IQ in the room.

But then Xaver raised his forefinger in the air and growled at them to stop talking. He looked at Anne. "Now we've had our fun. Let's listen to that story that I think is linked to the girl on the cross."

That's when an alarm on one of the butler's phones started going off. Before he could check it, Jacqueline de Rais burst into the room.

"The Piper House has been breached!"

## 92

5:22 A.M.

### *Welcome Room, The Piper House, Hamelin, Fairytale Road, Germany*

"Code Red!" Xaver shouted at his butlers, signaling for Anne and David to follow him. Jacqueline knew already what to do, making Anne wonder if she had been hiding among the masked crowd earlier.

The butlers stood by the door while everyone followed Xaver. He led them to a smaller room backstage with a heavy-duty door resembling a bank's safe.

With a few taps of his phone, Xaver opened the door. Inside, he showed them a panic room with black and white monitors covering the corridors outside.

It was barely the size of a standard living room, but it looked ready for storytelling. Just more private and discreet. A single red chair leaned against the farthest wall, facing about six more on the opposite side of the room. They dashed inside, and Xaver ordered them to sit, waiting for Jacqueline to follow.

"They haven't gone too far into the house," Xaver said,

informed by his app. "They've only entered from the guest's service door by the eastern side near the forest. They tailed two of our men who rushed in before they got caught. The service door is locked into a full concrete door so the intruders won't enter soon."

"Tom John's men," David said. "They fabricated the terrorist attack in Polle to get to us."

"Not you, Detective, but Anne and this Singing Bone," Xaver said, uninterested. "In my time, I've seen presidents, celebrities, and politicians want to kill to stop a story from surfacing. Point is, we have no time."

That was when Jacqueline entered with a young girl, about twenty years old. She had ginger hair and wore a festive German dress like the one Helga from Trendelburg wore. Her freckles made her look a tad too innocent. She looked anxious.

Seeing her reminded Anne of what Lady Ovitz must have looked like when she first met the Sisterhood. She carried a secret that she knew would change everyone's lives, but she could no longer handle it alone, like what Rachel felt in her last days.

"This is Clara," Xaver said, helping her gently sit on the red chair before locking the safe's door behind them. "She guards your story, Anne."

"How do you know that?" Anne asked.

David asked Clara to show Anne her necklace. Like the Ovitz family, this one had a small flute dangling from it. Complete with the letters d-e-a-f carved next to the holes.

"I see," Anne said before kneeling to face Clara. "I'm Anne."

"As I explained to the audience earlier," Xaver said, pointing at both Singing Bones. "Two keys to open one story."

"Are you going to be okay, Clara?" Anne said.

"It's my job," Clara said, sounding brainwashed, "to guard your story, and I'm happy to pass it to you now."

"I appreciate all the suffering you've endured," Anne began, trying her best to show her appreciation. "I think my sister had a story inside her, too."

"Enough with the chit-chat." Jacqueline tapped on her watch.

"Let Clara tell you her story, and then we'll figure out how to deal with the intruders outside."

"Who permitted you to talk?" Anne demanded. "This is *my* story. Can't you see Clara had her youth stolen by this organization? To guard a story as dark as—"

"You know what the story is, don't you?" Jacqueline challenged her back.

Anne looked away from her piercing eyes, wondering why she was suddenly considered the bad one. But Jacqueline was right. Anne had a feeling about the story. However, one question remained: How would Rachel's eighteen-year-old story help her discover why Layla was hung on the cross by her sisters in the Westminster Abbey?

🍎

The team monitoring and guarding the house watched the intruders outside the concrete wall argue and blame each other.

"How did you let them go?" a tall man in a fancy suit shouted at the policemen.

"I don't know," a policeman answered. "It's like they disappeared into the wall, like Ali Baba or something."

"Ali Baba hid in a barrel," the other policeman said.

"Shut up, you two," the man in the suit commanded.

One of the team by the monitors said to the others, "I'm not sure how they missed the men returning, to be honest. Such a bunch of morons."

"They are," the other replied. "But they have a bombing squad with them. And since they are morons, they'll soon use explosives to bring down that wall."

"If they do, we'll be ready, and it'll be a blood bath," the first said. "Also, if they do, shoot that obnoxious man in the fancy suit first."

# 93

*Panic Room, The Piper House, Hamelin, Fairytale Road,*
*Germany*

Xaver shut down the monitors in the panic room and dimmed the
lights. He explained that allowing Clara to tell the story she has
inside her could only be done in a relaxed and meditative
atmosphere.

He informed the group that Clara remembered the main story-
line the same way anyone remembers the synopsis of a book.
However, the flute's triggering notes, aka anchor, make her
remember the details chapter by chapter.

Xaver repeatedly played the 'deaf' notes from Anne's Singing
Bone while Clara played it from hers. Once they managed to play
them in unison, they acted like two keys that unlocked one story.
They played the same note, but the tonality, which differed from
each instrument, is what triggered Clara's mind to remember the
details.

Anne and David winced when Clara's head flipped upward, and

she unconsciously dropped the flute. It only lasted for a few seconds, and then she was back.

She sat straight on her chair, looking in their direction but with eyes that seemed to see nothing. It was as if she had turned into a Clairvoyant or Fortune teller, seeing the story play out in front of her in so much detail that she hardly noticed her real-life surroundings. Her demeanor was calm, and her hands rested peacefully on her lap.

"I am Clara Viehman," she began in a calm voice. "Descendant of the bloodline."

Xaver made sure everyone resorted to complete silence while she told the story.

"I'm not a True Sister. I don't have experience guarding an ancient story as True Sisters do, but I'm happy about having guarded this story for the past four years," Clara said.

Anne was about to say something when Xaver shushed her again. "No talking when she speaks, or she will be distracted."

"How did I guard an eighteen-year-old story, you may ask?" Clara continued, still gazing nowhere. "This story was passed to me from sister Mandy Hassenpflug. She lived in a hospice in London, where I worked three summers ago. It was part of our Sisterhood's 'empathy training' for novices. Mandy was ninety-four and was dying, so she asked the Sisterhood to be relieved of her duties and pass the story to me."

Clara seemed to take a moment to recollect her thoughts.

"About eleven years ago, Mandy was given this story by True Sister Madeline Winston," Clara said. "At the time, Mandy used to live in California. She was trying to locate those who had escaped our bloodline and wished not to serve anymore and try to persuade them otherwise."

Anne closed her eyes, hardly breathing. She knew where this was heading when she heard California.

"Madeline Winston guarded this story for fourteen years before telling it to me," Clara said. "Madeline was a first-generation story-teller, meaning she was the first to be handed the story. It's a rare condition because most stories are centuries-old, and first-generation storytellers are dead by now."

Clara entertained one of her small pauses again.

"Sister Madeline Winston carried this story from the source. Although it wasn't a fairytale, she happily guarded it because it was told by a girl who thought she was a descendant of the bloodline but couldn't tell," Clara said. "At the time, Sister Winston made a living working in a winery. This is where she met eighteen-year-old Rachel Christian Anderson."

Anne gasped.

"Rachel Anderson was haunted by stories in her mind, and a particular story from centuries ago was driving her crazy. Upon hearing this, Sister Winston concluded that somehow Rachel was a descendant of the Sisterhood."

David reached for Anne's hand and squeezed it. He had done it so many times now that she had gotten used to his rough touch. But it meant more now than ever, considering she lied to him.

"Sister Winston had come to this conclusion because Rachel's story resembled a rather important one to the Sisterhood. One that had been lost in the sands of time. " Clara swallowed hard, "an ancient story that was a Keystone story."

"A story that leads to a whole text hidden in the Brothers Grimm book," Xaver whispered as low as possible to Anne. "Hence, a keystone. It opens the doors to many other crimes and secrets."

"The problem was that Rachel didn't trust anyone after seeing her mother go insane and disappear. Even though Winston explained to her who and what the Sisterhood was," Clara said. "Rachel instead decided to tell Winston a story about how her relationship with her sister was shattered to pieces."

Anne began to doubt Clara's version because why would Rachel tell Winston about her conflict with her younger sister instead of the story in her head?

# 94

5:38 A.M.

### *Panic Room, The Piper House, Hamelin, Fairytale Road, Germany*

Clara continued without regard to their whispering and spoke as if no one else was in the room with her.

"Here is the story I guarded that Rachel Anderson told Sister Winston," Clara said as her voice dimmed." The story Anne needed to hear to know what her sister wanted her to do."

The four of them waited as Clara breathed heavily and gripped the sides of her chair. She began to show signs of convulsion and looked like she was choking, but then her neck stiffened, her eyes whitening for a brief second before returning to normal. When she started talking, she fully closed her eyes.

Anne and David finally understood why the Sisterhood had been falsely accused of communing with the spirits. The weight of these stories on their physical and mental health was unbearable.

Anne wondered if Clara would begin with something cliché like 'Once upon a time....'

She didn't.

*I am Rachel Christian Anderson. I'm eighteen years old. Today is a Friday, if my memory still holds. I've been confused for so long. I haven't been able to differentiate reality from the stories in my head, and I'm in a dark place I never thought I'd be.*

*I live near the Navarro Vineyards and Winery with my fifteen-year-old sister, Anne, who I would die for. She is the light of my life. Harris, our stepfather, is always drunk, but other than his fits of anger, he is harmless—if that is the best way to describe him.*

*Anne never met our mother, but I did. I was young, but I still remember her face, and I still remember her going crazy. I always tell Anne that mother left when she was three, but she left when Anne was seven. I watched what happened to my mother unfold when I was old enough to remember.*

*My mother was losing her mind. She lived nearby, lurking in the vineyards. She believed she had a disease and didn't want us to catch it, except that I did.*

*None of what I'm about to tell you happened chronologically. And due to my current mental issues, I can't pinpoint when and how. But I know what happened to me and who we are.*

*The story in me is of a girl who lived two centuries ago. It's dark and bloody, and the typical crowd considers it a fairytale. I wish not to tell because I don't trust this story will fall into the right hands, so I passed it to Anne, my little sister. I'm giving it to her without her permission or knowledge, the same way my mother passed hers to me.*

*This is how I got these stories in my head.*

*My mother, who fell—or was pushed, I don't know—in the well near the house, is now dead and gone. She was a descendant of the Sisterhood; I think that's what they call themselves. A centuries-old cult naively thought they could pass on undocumented crimes against women through stories. I believe they gave up at some point, but I don't want to know what happened. I know that the darkness of holding onto these stories for years traumatized these women and drove them insane.*

*Like me.*

*Like my mother.*

*My mother, originally from Germany, escaped to California and married. She lived with a shell of a man, a drunk loser named Harris, to camouflage a new identity for us. We were now the Andersons. We never met our father because the extremist Sisterhood doesn't believe in fathers, blaming all men in the present life for crimes that powerful and rich men did in the past.*

*My mother had many names: Anne, Harriet, Jacqueline, Mary, and Helga, among others. Her last was Anne. She passed this name to my little sister for some reason, but I only called her mother.*

*When our mother died, I felt like I was responsible for Anne. We were having financial troubles, and Anne was going to leave school. But I made sure she didn't. Instead, I left school and worked in the winery to support her.*

*The boys called me the beautiful one. I never felt beautiful, but I experienced what it meant to be considered that. I had no time for the boys except later when I gave them what they wanted for money.*

*All I wanted was to escape with Anne and start a new life. Sooner or later, the Sisterhood would find us and demand to know the story my mother kept and passed to me.*

*I am the older sister, but I'm still so young. Don't judge my misjudgments. I messed up just like my mother did.*

*I couldn't take it when the stories began to drive me crazy. I decided to find my ancestors, the Sisterhood. To do so, I needed to leave Anne alone with enough money for a while.*

*When I almost had the money we needed, the man in a Romano Capello hat arrived. An Italian man with a tall, strong, and vicious demeanor. He had a disproportioned head like he was a beast from a fairytale. He had made friends with Harris. My snooping around backfired because now someone was interested to know who we were.*

*I had discovered that well by the winery, where Anne and I found bones of dead girls. It was morbid and scary, but we used to climb down it to escape. People thought we left to escape Harris, but Harris was only annoying. We escaped the Italian man in the black cassock, the man who said he owned the Italian winery nearby.*

*The abandoned well was spacious at the bottom, but it was steep.*

I discovered a ladder hung by the edge of the well—a carefully designed and very reliable one to climb down. Looking for a hideaway, I climbed down. I quickly realized that someone had carefully carved steppers into the brick wall. Voids big enough for a foot with a reasonable and frequent distance until the bottom.

That's when the hook rope from above came in handy. While on the steppers on my way up, closer to the top, I had to swing it with all my might and hook it onto the edge of the well. Then, I was able to climb the last few meters up.

Anne and I had always been athletic from being raised in the vineyard, where the only entertainment was to run around all day. My mother once mentioned that all our ancestors were as lightweight, if not lighter, and even shorter.

I never knew who made the well or how mother ended up there. But Anne and I spent our best times together below. I told her about the fairy-tales I read from the books our mother left behind. This was before I knew I had a fairytale carved into my skull without my permission.

When Anne discovered our mother's swan necklace, I lied to her to protect her from the truth and told her that I wasn't sure. But of course, she did, as it resembled her being a descendant of the six swans.

Now that I have summarized our lives, I come to the day my life was changed forever. It wasn't about me going insane or my mother's past.

It was the day the man in the cassock found us in the well and forever traumatized us, suspecting that Anne and I were descendants of the Ovitz family.

And he was right.

Our mother's real name is Linda Ovitz, sister of Lana Ovitz and daughter of Lady Ovitz, whose real name is Reminzka Lafayette.

Lana had seven girls, Lilith, Lisa, Lisbeth, Lily, Layla, Lucia, and Lara. They moved to London.

Linda, my mother, miraculously inherited no symptoms of dwarfism. She moved to California and only had Anne and me, escaping the Sister-hood forever,

🍎

Taking advantage of the somber mood that draped over Anne and David, Xaver reached for his phone. He messaged Jacqueline without them noticing:

*Once Clara finishes the story, shoot her, David, and Anne.*

# 95

---

5:45 A.M.

**Panic Room, The Piper House, Hamelin, Fairytale Road, Germany**

Clara continued.

*Anne and I used the rope with the hook and climbed down the steppers. We are safe at the bottom of the well. We catch our breaths, counting on him getting lost in the winery and not finding the well.*

*Even if he finds it, he can never climb down because...*

Shit.

*It's then I realize what I've done.*

*"Forget something?" he snickers in his Italian accent, waving the rope in his hand from above.*

*I curse with all my might. "I forgot to pull it," I say.*

*I apologize to Anne, and my little sister hugs me and tells me it's not my fault. But when he begins to climb down, I can only blame myself.*

*I lie to Anne and promise her that we will be all right, and she naively believes me. I'm Rachel, after all. I always fix things.*

*I don't know what he wants from us now. Does he know that we are from the Ovitz family? Does he want the story in my head? Or are his intentions much more sinister?*

*What if he, and his people, are repulsed by the Sisterhood?*

*The dark man is coming for us. It seems he has climbed down this well before. Or it's just his robust and athletic build.*

*We throw the dead girls' bones at him, as stupid as it sounds. We scream from the top of our lungs but know no one will come. Why? Because we've done it a thousand times before. That's why the well was our hide-out in the first place.*

*His boots thud on the ground, and I'm too weak against his strength. With the back of one hand, he knocks me down, leaving me semi-unconscious.*

*I can't move, but I can faintly hear him approach Anne.*

Anne's tears rocked her whole body. She was breaking down, and no one around her could save her. Clara's voice frayed. She and Anne couldn't catch their breaths, knowing how the story unfolded. Clara was about to alleviate herself from this burden, but Anne would finally have to confront her guilt.

*I think the dark man looms over Anne because I hear her taking rapid, gasping breaths. I hear Anne's feet screech against the floor, trying to escape him. He doesn't talk, and my words don't have a sound. I think I'm paralyzed or in some temporary coma.*

*I would do anything to save her, and I know she'll do the same.*

*Until I hear her say, "I'm not the one you want!"*

*I'm baffled, and so is the dark man.*

*As if we all misheard her the first time, she repeats herself. "I'm not the one you want. All the boys like Rachel. I'm not the pretty one."*

*It should seem like a trivial detail, but her words break me from the inside. I understand the fear. I understand the need to survive. But if we were going to be hurt and forced to carry this moment on our shoulders for the rest of our lives, I preferred to remember my sister standing up for me. Two sisters who would never part. One like the Rose Red and Snow-White fairytale, where both sisters bond and kill the big bad wolf.*

*It doesn't help when, for whatever reason, the dark man turns to face me. He drags me like a sack, wanting to climb up the well.*

*When confronted by his unsound plan, he slaps Anne unconscious and has his way with me.*

*I don't fight.*

*I don't scream.*

*I'm disheartened by Anne's words. After I was like a mother to her; after I had done all I did to make us money for a better life; after I suffered with all these stories in my head.*

*I tell myself that if the dark man has his way with me, I will still act like a mother to Anne and protect her from him.*

*I know that I'm never going to be the same again.*

*That Anne and I will never be the same again.*

*All I wish is that Anne remembers what I've told her about the shepherd, the bones, and the crone.*

Clara opened her eyes the moment Anne fell to her knees. David knelt beside her, unsure how he could help. But he wanted to be close to her, nonetheless. She was crying without a sound. He could hardly imagine what she was going through.

"You were just a kid, Anne," David hugged her. "It's not your fault."

Behind them, Jacqueline pulled out her gun and aimed it at Clara, but Xaver stopped her immediately. "This story means nothing," Xaver said to her as Anne was still aching on the floor. He turned to Clara. "What is this? Are you sure this all?"

Clara, exhausted but showing signs of relief, nodded.

"What does this story serve?" Xaver growled. "How could it lead to the Singing Bone or the original Brothers Grimm book?"

Clara didn't have the answers.

Suddenly, Anne, lying on her back now, shuddered violently and started reciting a poem.

> *Oh, ye, shepherd, dig my bones,*
> *tell the story about thy devil's crone.*
> *Red the maiden, white the hag,*
> *black is time I can't take back.*

"Oh my God!" Jacqueline knelt next to Anne, gently pushing strands of hair out of her eyes. She held Anne's hands in hers. "You're the one!"

Xaver and David stood in awe. Especially Xaver, who had never seen Jacqueline de Rais emotional. And he knew she didn't like Anne.

"What's going on, Jacqueline?" Xaver asked. "What do you mean by she is the one?"

"Anne knows the keystone story that unlocks the rest. That poem she just told holds the key," Jacqueline explained. "Rachel's story wasn't meant to taunt and blame her sister."

"Then what was the purpose of it?" Xaver asked.

"It was to unlock the story she had inside her," Jacqueline said. "Rachel's story is Anne's trigger to remember. Not a melody from a flute."

A loud siren sounded in the panic room, and one of Xaver's butlers began shouting.

"We're under attack!"

# 96

### *Eastern Wall, the Piper House, Hamelin, Fairytale Road, Germany*

Tom listened to his men on the radio, confirming they'd entered the Piper House.

"We're in," said the usually snickering policeman. "But we're taking it slow."

"Why? What do you see down there?"

"It's like an endless maze, and it's eerily quiet," the policeman whispered. "We're ready to fire and capture our targets, but it's like they know we're here or something. I don't know."

"What do you mean they know you're there?" Tom said. "Of course, they don't. We pulled a great trick on them, acting like morons who don't know what they're doing."

"Maybe they didn't buy the little fight we conjured up in front of their surveillance cameras," the policeman said. "I don't know."

"They couldn't have possibly figured it out," Tom said. "It's a genius plan, the way we got inside."

"Are you standing in front of the camera now?" the policeman said into the crackling radio.

"Of course not," Tom said, knowing the German was only teasing him. He concluded that all the snickering and bullying was to cover how scared they were, but it didn't matter now. They were in. "Keep advancing with your men, and look for any threats. Once you find Anne and David, bring them in."

Tom hung up and turned to shake the Advocate's hand. "Brilliant, Sir," Tom told him. "Making our men wear the butler's outfits and masks to enter the house—just brilliant."

"Of course, it is," the Advocate said, the two original butlers lying dead by his feet.

"They unknowingly showed us the way in. We didn't need explosives or anything," Tom asserted. "And thank you for letting me say it was my idea. It'll help a lot with my superiors."

"Don't worry about it," the Advocate said. "You care about formalities and stepping up in your career, and I only care about Anne Anderson, the one that got away."

Tom didn't understand what the Advocate meant, but the man was an enigma. He didn't want to waste time trying to understand everything he said.

"Good," Tom said with enthusiasm. "I just hope it doesn't turn into a bloodbath inside."

"Oh," the Advocate said. "But it will."

# 97

### *Panic Room, the Piper House, Hamelin, Fairytale Road, Germany*

Jacqueline held Anne close, her body still shuddering from the overwhelming emotional impact the story had on her. None of them, not even Anne, understood the message about the crone and the colors in the puzzle—a message that Anne had buried within the walls of her mind for 18 years.

But it was finally clear that Anne was the storyteller guarding the original keystone story that would lead them to discover who the real girl on the cross was centuries ago.

Meanwhile, David and Xaver were barely tolerating each other.

"The four of us are in this together now," Xaver told David. "It's best that we help each other escape our attackers outside and find the keystone story."

"I don't like you, Xaver." David balled his hands into fists.

"I feel the same!" Xaver exclaimed. "I don't like me, either."

"I thought so," David said. "Tell me you've got an escape plan out of this rabbit hole."

"I've got the Eurocopter 130 nearby," Xaver said while the sirens in the room turned louder with each passing second. "The fastest and quietest helicopters in the world."

"How do we get to it?"

"This is how," Xaver began, showing him a blueprint to the Piper House on his Bet Time Story app. "We have to get to this room first."

"The Amber Room?" David questioned.

"Named after the famous secret room the Soviet Union hid from the Germans behind mundane wallpapers in WWII to protect their precious gold," Xaver said. "I have its true story for sale, by the way."

"I don't like gold," David said nonchalantly, checking their escape route on the blueprint. "I like copper."

"And that's why?" Xaver grimaced at David's dismissal of gold.

"Because I can turn them into bullets and put one in your head after we're done," David shoved the phone into his face. "Are the red dots the intruders?"

"Uh-huh," Xaver said. "The green dots are our buyers."

"Why are your buyers still inside the auction rooms?"

"Because the rooms are sound proof and we haven't alerted them yet," Xaver said. "We have one hundred and seventy-eight people in this basement. You know what kind of massacre will occur if we let them out?"

David was thinking both fast and slow, trying to decide. "I see the red dots are reluctant and carefully slow. Why is that? Why don't they just raid the place?"

"We've evacuated the corridors to intimidate them. The black door to the auction rooms are locked, and they have no way to open them. We also shut down the electricity to the corridors, so they're dark now," Xaver said. "They're treading lightly because they don't know what's going on. Do you have a plan or not?"

"I do," David said, "if you can get us out of this panic room."

"Done." Xaver pressed a few buttons and nodded.

"Done?"

"My two butlers outside are dead, in case we don't trust them,"

Xaver said. "All butler masks have a 0.1 amps electric shock that only I can activate on demand from my app, but they don't know about it. Paycheck is too tempting."

David shrugged, not sure he wanted this to happen. He realized, without a second thought, that Xaver deserved that copper bullet when this was over.

Xaver entered his personal digits into the safe door, and it plunged open again.

David approached Anne and spoke softly to her. "Anne, can you walk?"

"I can," she said, looking stronger now, having dealt with her emotional turmoil. Jacqueline stood ready beside her.

"Clara?" David held out his hand, but she pulled it back, eyes on Xaver.

"He won't let me leave," she said.

"Of course, I won't," Xaver said. "She isn't an asset anymore, and the helicopter isn't that spacious."

"You know, David," Anne said while standing up to Xaver. "I can walk, and I can kick."

Xaver's moan after Anne kicked him in the balls reminded David of a tortoise he saw moaning while having sex on National Geographic once. Even Jacqueline chuckled at his pain.

"Come on, Clara," Anne took her hand to assure her she was safe.

"You may have the chopper," David said to Xaver. "But now you still have the balls?"

David stood by the door, sneaking a glance at the dead butlers on the floor and the empty auction room.

"Do you have a gun?" David asked Xaver, who handed him one from his pocket, still aching from the blow to his manhood. "Good, I'll check the corridors and then let you follow me."

He proceeded carefully, eyes on the main door, standing ajar.

David could see the corridors from here, but the emptiness made them look spooky. Using the app, David watched the reluctant red dots advancing slowly inside the Piper House.

"We're bound to clash face to face with the intruders," David murmured over his shoulder. "But they're far enough. We have to hurry to get to the Amber Room. Come on."

Anne held Clara tight and showed her the way out. Xaver followed David first, and Jacqueline filed in behind Anne and Clara. David had a feeling Jacqueline and Xaver had a sinister plan for them, so he was keeping a sharp eye on them.

Leading with the muzzle of his gun, David slowly advanced through the corridors, not sure whether to speed up or slow down. All that worried him was the red dots getting closer and closer.

As David continued, he heard Anne whisper to Clara. "You should be proud of your great grandmother, Dorothea Viehman. She didn't mean for all this to happen. She was a good woman and took it upon herself to help others."

"Really?" Clara said innocently, sounding like she hadn't made up her mind about her stand in life yet.

David resisted Anne's unintentionally distracting words. He was still disheartened that she lied. But maybe dragging him on this journey without telling him the truth about her looking for Rachel wasn't that bad. After all, he never told her about his own sister. True, he talked freely to Anne about his mother. But he never spoke about his sister, whom he danced with for the last time on her thirteenth birthday.

"They're advancing. Faster now." Xaver pointed at the red dots on the app. "They must have gotten impatient."

"Let's speed up then." David lengthened his stride forward, and the rest followed.

"Take a right," Xaver instructed, reminding him where the Amber Room was located.

The app suddenly beeped.

"What's that?" David asked.

"They're splitting into several corridors," Xaver said. "Not good. They'll confront us sooner this way and from different sides."

"We're trapped," Jacqueline said from the back. "We have to go back."

"Going back is never a good strategy," David said.

"She is right," Xaver said. "Maybe I can bribe them with money."

"Not everything is about money, Xaver!" Anne spat between gritted teeth.

"I have an idea," David said, glancing apologetically at Anne, for it was tainted in grey morality. "Can you open the doors to the auction room?"

"David, no!" Anne said.

"Remember Darwin, Anne," David countered. "He who adapts, survives. And you and Clara, unlike those rich people spending their spare money on stories, have a bigger cause to live for."

Anne stared at him, unsure how to respond.

"Xaver!" David said. "Do you have a code to open all doors at once?"

"Like a master key, you mean? I do," Xaver smirked, hissing into David's ears, "now that we're talking the same language of dog eat dog. See, I'm not that bad. I'm only adapting, my friend."

"Do it," David looked away from him. "Open them all up at once, except the corridor that is the shortest way to the Amber Room."

Instead of using the app, Xaver dialed a regular number. Surprisingly, Jacqueline's phone rang.

"Why are you calling me?" she asked, perplexed.

"Just don't pick up and put it on speaker," Xaver said. "Then press it to the digital pad by the door closely and count to ten."

"You're master code to open all doors is a dial tone?" Anne said.

"Genius, right? Dial tone is a musical note," Xaver said. "Efficient and handy, like a fire escape."

"What if someone put their dial tone on speaker while walking the corridors?" David said.

"It has to be direct and close to the speaker and last for five dial tones," Xaver said, Jacqueline's phone still pressed to the pad. "Three. Two. One."

"They're getting closer," Clara pointed at the red dot in the app.

The black door to the auction room slid open. Surprisingly, no one left the auction room.

"They probably think it's a glitch," David said. "They need some encouragement."

David dashed in with the gun behind his back and yelled at the buyers, "Jesus Christ's origin story is for sale. Three million low entry, though. First door by the entrance!"

He dashed out before the enthusiastic buyers would step over him. In the corridors outside, Anne, Clara, Xaver, and Jacqueline were gone. When he rounded the corner, he saw them exiting different black doors, encouraging the people in the other rooms to do the same.

"Now, this way!" David yelled in the direction of the Amber room.

"I told them Hitler was alive and his true story was by the entrance," Xaver said proudly, out of breath while speeding up.

David shook his head and led the way.

"I told them–" Jacqueline began.

"I don't want to know," David silenced her with his hand. "I'll have nightmares for the rest of my life for what I've just done."

Behind them, the clash of the red dots with green dots had already begun, and none of them wanted to look back.

# 98

### Corridors, The Piper House, Hamelin, Fairytale Road, Germany

Before reaching the Amber Room, Xaver stopped. He pointed at a painting on a wall that looked like the wardrobe from *The Chronicles of Narnia*.

"You've got to be kidding me," David said.

"But you said the Amber room is here," Clara protested, pointing at its location on the app.

"I lied, sue me," Xaver said proudly, pulling down the wallpaper.

Beneath it was another pad with a fingerprint password. Xaver pressed his hand against it, and the wall slid open. "Ladies and Gentlemen," he said with a wink. "Welcome to Narnia."

A policeman caught a glimpse of them and shouted right before aiming his gun. Xaver pushed a button to close the door behind them.

Inside, David pulled Anne and Clara away from the wall as the bullets from the officers' guns jammed into what looked like stainless steel panels.

"We're going to get killed." David looked at Xaver. "What kind of crappy walls are these?"

"Elevator walls," Xaver pulled out an almond from his pocket and munched on it just as the five of them felt the chug upward. "Willy Wonka doesn't own an elevator this cool, by the way."

David closed his eyes. He resisted shooting this rich madman who had never grown up, still living in his own fairytale-infested nightmare.

🍎

Outside, Tom could barely listen to the panic and the gunshots.

"How many people are down there?" he wondered aloud, the Advocate next to him. "I told you they must have a militia inside."

"I don't think so," the Advocate said. "I think your men are about to kill one-tenth of the richest people alive."

"Really?"

The Advocate said nothing. Instead, he pointed at the cars in the forest and then looked at the helicopter atop the hill. "I wonder how you get to that helicopter up there."

"What do you mean?" Tom said. "You get out of the building and get on it."

"And what escape plan would that serve if one had to expose themselves to a threat first before getting on it?" The Advocate said, sounding exceptionally condescending.

Tom's forefinger fiddled with the trigger of the gun on his side, even though the Advocate was right again. Tom wasn't being unreasonable or losing his mind—he just had received newly found footage of his father being poisoned in the British Library. It was clearly the Advocate.

Tom had no means to deal with the conflict at hand. Even though he didn't want to see more blood, he had a feeling he was going to end up shooting the Advocate. But first, he sent a message back to his superiors, asking them who the hell this Advocate was.

Tom knew he was a ruthless assassin and that he was hired by Father Firelle and another named bishop in the Vatican. But who was the Advocate, really? *A scary, dark menace of a human being that clearly possesses no heart,* Tom thought to himself.

"I think the hill is connected to the house," the Advocate pointed out. "Look!"

Tom saw the eager man limp up the hill while pointing his cane at what looked like a door inside the hill's crest.

Now Tom was even more curious about the Advocate. Who did that to his legs?

"You're a genius," Tom praised, playing along as he followed him.

"The last man who called me that is now dead at the top of the tower," the Advocate mumbled. He had fed his driver a poisoned apple before Tom's men had arrived earlier. It wasn't a necessary death, but the Advocate had nothing else to do. Besides, now he didn't have to pay him for his services.

"Don't shoot them when they come out," the Advocate yelled at Tom, who had gathered his men and stood before the elevator door that led to the helicopter, ready to shoot or capture Anne and her friends.

🍎

Far away in the hotel room in Rome, the Ovitz sisters were packing to get on their next flight. Now that Mary had been informed about the incidents at the Piper House, it was clear to her where to go next. Not the exact location, but somewhere in Germany, near a peculiar forest.

"Are you sure about this?" Lily asked Mary.

"Our Queen just told me," Mary said, miffed by Lily's interrogation.

"And how does she know that?"

"She knows everything, Lily," Mary said impatiently. "She has eyes inside."

# 99

---

6:17 A.M.

### *Elevator, the Piper House, Hamelin, Fairytale Road, Germany*

"I think I know where we are going next," Anne said. "Not specifically, but the general area."

"You mean 'going last,'" Xaver said. "This is where the final story about the girl on the cross is revealed. You and I know what the poem about the 'devil's crone' now means, but we'll discuss it once we're safe."

Anne nodded, leaving David, Jacqueline and Clara puzzled.

"I'm sorry for Rachel, if it helps," Xaver said. "She wanted the best for—"

"Don't talk about my sister," Anne said, holding Clara's hands. "You won't understand."

"He won't, I agree," Jacqueline said. "Men can't understand."

David rolled his eyes in silence, still not trusting either her or Xaver and still skeptical of Clara too.

"I admit that I won't, actually," Xaver said. "All I'm saying is that she put a story in your head without your permission, and you...well, you hurt her by being young and naive and...."

"Where is she now?" Clara asked Anne, ever so innocently.

"I don't know," Anne said. "I haven't seen Rachel since that day in the well."

"She is probably dead," Jacqueline said, raising a hand at Anne. "Don't shoot me. I'm just saying the Advocate never leaves anyone alive."

"That's his name?" Anne let go of Clara's hand and stepped up nose-to-nose with Jacqueline. "The man in the dark cassock is called the Advocate? How do you know him?"

"He is supposed to be a myth, but he is real," Jacqueline said. "He's killed so many girls, and he is still alive."

Anne pulled Jacqueline by her hair, shocking everyone with her sudden burst of violence.

"How do you know him, Jacqueline?" Anne said as the elevator came to a stop, the doors remaining closed. Xaver kept the doors shut until the two women stopped fighting.

The veins on Jacqueline's neck stood up as she looked away, but it only encouraged Anne to pull harder.

"Okay, I'll tell you," Jacqueline said. "He is like an assassin or something and works for the highest bidder. He sounds and speaks Italian, but he is of French descent."

"Possibly," Xaver said. "Linguists have found that around 89% of French and Italian words are similar, so they have the same roots."

"Shut up!" Anne warned him.

"I don't know where you can find the Advocate," Jacqueline said. "But did you ever think about who the Sisterhood was really after?"

"Don't change the subject," Anne warned her. "Or I'll pull out these hair extensions and leave you as bald as Xaver."

"I'm not changing the subject," Jacqueline said. "The Advocate is more of an idea than a man, which is why he was considered a myth. Imagine the counter opposite of the Sisterhood. Imagine the men who committed these crimes centuries ago, men who think about themselves as powerful and rich, and narcissistic. Those men believed in the occult, like Hitler, Stalin, and Osama Bin Laden. They all believed they were Gods, that they could shape the world to their liking, and that the 'other' was expandable," Jacqueline raised her voice at Anne so she would listen. "Imagine what their offspring is like, Anne. Or did you think that only good intentions could be passed through a bloodline?"

"Some of them are still the same," David said, understanding Jacqueline's explanation. "At least a percentage of the Nazis' offspring are still Nazis today. Only hiding behind civilized manner and clean clothes, still hanging onto their ancestor's deviant beliefs."

"Exactly," Jacqueline said. "Then imagine what the likes of Bluebeard's descendants are like today. Rich, powerful, and untouchable, like me," she shrugged but sounded sincere, "except that I'm trying my best to be better."

"Spit it out, Jacqueline," David said. "The Advocate's last name is de Rais, right?"

Jacqueline nodded, unable to meet Anne's eyes.

"Time's up," Xaver said. "Though that was entertaining."

And before anyone commented, Xaver pushed the button on his phone, and the elevator door parted.

Tom and his men continued waiting for the elevator to open. Even the Advocate anticipated it. Five minutes passed, and they began thinking they had been fooled.

# 100

## *Bungelosenstrasse, Hamelin, Fairytale Road, Germany*

The parting doors of the elevator let in the freezing air from outside. The five of them were looking at the quiet Bungelosen-strasse in Hamelin where Anne and David first entered. No one dared speak a word.

David squinted against the dark hovering over the white snowy street. "You said you have a helicopter here," David said to Xaver as they stood facing the mute and cold children's street. "I was in the street earlier tonight, and I didn't see one."

"I said nearby," Xaver said. "Now, I would lower my voice if I were you. We don't want to get the police's attention from the other side."

David and Anne looked worried. There was something about the street this time that *sounded* unusual.

"In fact, I did all of you a favor. The attackers are all gathered on the opposite side of the river. They think we're taking the heli-copter on top of the hill," Xaver explained. "Which doesn't work in the first place, so I've always used it as a distraction."

Still, on edge, David listened to Tom John's men attacking the house from behind the forest.

"So, where to now?" David said, lowering his voice.

"I have a vehicle right around the corner," Xaver said. "It will take us to the Eurocopter," Xaver said. "Just tread lightly, or they will find us."

David imagined they were the Children of Hamelin all over again, carefully following Xaver to his vehicle. Taking the same footsteps, the poor kids took after the Pied Piper centuries ago.

"Where are we going?" Clara whispered to Anne.

"Like rats, we're following the Pied Piper, I guess," David mused, coping with resurfacing childhood memories.

David never had an issue taking care of himself, and even Anne could take care of herself most of the time. But having to take care of Clara was harder. What if anything happened to her and Anne? Yes, he still felt strange about Anne's decision not to tell him everything, but it wasn't a matter of liking her now. In his mind, he had to protect the ones he cared about, the people he promised to protect. For whatever reason, Darwin or not, he needed to protect someone from sleeping at night. Especially women, ever since losing his mother and sister.

It didn't help that he hardly trusted Xaver or Jacqueline.

Memories of his thirteen-year-old sister surfaced again, but he wouldn't give in to them. After all, his older sister was the reason his mother became an atheist.

"Don't listen to David about the Pied Piper," Anne said, patting Clara and sending an evil glare in David's direction. "He is always tense and pessimistic. We'll be all right."

"I like him," Clara said. "He has a gun."

"And I can shoot it," David whispered with a furrowed eyebrow. He was pointing his gun at Xaver's back in case he was about to pull a trick on them.

"Yeah," Clara whispered. "You make me feel safe."

Amidst everything, Clara's words hit differently this time. Even better than when Anne told him the same. David did his best not to get emotional as they all marched softly in the thick snow.

"Stop." Xaver waved his hand behind his back, leaning onto an abandoned building on the right side of the street.

"What is it?" David said.

"I feel it," Xaver said. "We're not alone."

David, Anne, Jacqueline, and Clara stopped, snowflakes sticking to their faces and noses.

The light of dawn was shining through the stubborn clouds from above, shyly kissing the half-timbered buildings on both sides.

The intensity of shooting had slowed down by the forest's side, but it still seemed impossible for anyone knowing they were there. Xaver had locked the elevator from the Amber Room and claimed it wouldn't function without his fingerprints.

But the soldiers who shot at them below were going to find a way to get to them sooner or later.

"Could it be someone in the houses?" David craned his head upward at a window. "I think I glimpsed a shadow."

"No, it's not the houses," Xaver said. "Damn it. We need to cross and get to the small alley perpendicular to this street. My vehicle is parked inside a pigpen."

"You keep your escaping vehicle in a pigpen?" David scoffed.

"I like pigs," Xaver said. "They're the most misunderstood creature in the world. The vehicle is there, right before the Christmas Market."

"Christmas market?" David's face twitched. "How is it that we're in Christmas, and the Christmas lights aren't on there."

"And why weren't there any signs when we arrived?" Anne backed him up.

Both David and Anne felt a tug in their hearts.

"Maybe this town isn't really as silent as it wants us to think," David said.

"Stop being paranoid," Xaver said. "I think a couple of policemen are lurking somewhere, waiting for us."

"I'm with David on this one," Anne said, holding Clara closer. "I've always sensed eyes behind these windows, ever since I first arrived. And besides, in the past, this town was vibrating with life and never this mute."

"Are we going to die?" Clara gripped Anne's arm tighter.

"We're all going to die, Clara," Jacqueline mumbled in the back, pointing her gun.

# 101

Lights everywhere flickered on. Through the windows, the locals shot back at the policemen.

"What the hell is going on?" David said, dashing through the pigpen's door.

Xaver proudly stood before a robust, metallic vehicle resembling a Hummer about to go to war. "Do you think you can drive it?"

David scoffed at the question and opened the back door to tug Anne and Clara in.

"I want to play with the pigs," Clara said. "Can we take this one with us? He is cute."

Xaver rolled his eyes. "I hate kids."

"So can we take one with us, Dad?" Anne teased David again.

"Ha," David responded, baffled that she still had the heart to laugh amidst this mini-war in Hamelin.

"No, Clara." David patted her, not sure how to play dad but doing his best. "Just get inside."

"I can't believe she is twenty years old," Jacqueline said, hopping inside.

"She didn't experience childhood." Anne sneered at her, trying her best not to let Clara hear her. "I was like her when I was fifteen. Stunted in my experience with life because some cult decided to feed my teenage brain with the weight of their miseries."

David closed the back door. He rounded the vehicle to open the front door and climbed into the driver's seat. "Tell me what's going on outside, Xaver," he said, pushing the button to ignite the military-grade machine. "Why are the locals protecting us all of a sudden?"

"The beautiful people of Hamelin are here to help," Xaver said, struggling to buckle up in the passenger's seat. "A few million dollars a year in charities makes me own this town. Unofficially, of course, but still."

"They pretended to be asleep all this time until you finished the meeting at the Piper House?"

"They do it only twice a year when we meet," Xaver said. "We timed it with the cleaning of the Vatican's basilica. It's an important event that takes eyes off of us."

Clara clapped her hands. "Amazing. I love German locals."

"See?" Xaver said. "Children love me."

"Yeah, I used to love villains as a kid," David said, putting the vehicle into gear. "Until Heath Ledger died."

The vehicle David was driving looked like a blown-out refrigerator box. It was the size of a Hummer but not as wide and was silver, looking like a rocket on wheels. The bulletproof windows and doors were black and thick, and the interior was a maze of digital electronics sticking out of padded ceilings and doors.

Had David seen this thing as a child, he'd have thought it was the lead-lined refrigerator Harrison Ford hid inside to survive a nuclear detonation in Indiana Jones and the Crystal Skull.

"What are you waiting for?" Xavier asked, looking at David. "Don't worry about the pigs. They'll make room for you to get out." Xaver said,

The city outside had turned into a battleground between the locals and Tom John's men."

"I need to make sure we're not going to be shot at," David said.

"It's bulletproof, my friend," Xaver said. "I was also told rocket-proof, but I'm not close enough friends with Elon Musk to test it."

"How bulletproof is 'bulletproof'?" David gripped the wheel.

"Just follow this GPS to the road outside. It will get us to my helicopter," Xaver said, pointing at the dashboard screen. "Trust me."

David sighed and pushed the pedal ahead. He broke out of the warehouse, still unsure about the vehicle's ability to withstand the onslaught ahead. "Everybody duck down!"

The machine's momentum was like nothing David had ever experienced, the power and speed momentarily scaring him. But it felt solid and grounded.

In the mirror, he saw the Hamelin people terrorizing Tom John's men, causing them to scatter left and right. And though it was strange that Clara clapped with enthusiasm, it made him feel better. Something about her presence made him want to work harder.

"There," Xaver said. "To the left. Take the slope off the main road and down into the forest."

David hadn't the slightest doubt that this beast of a vehicle could make it. They couldn't even hear the bullets shot at them.

"Where did you get this thing? How many are even available?" David took the slope down, gripping the wheel harder now that they were off the well-traveled road. The dark forest loomed ahead.

"There is only one," Xaver said. "Took it from Bin Laden's son. Custom made."

"Who?" David grimaced at Xaver.

"I sold him a story," Xaver tucked an unlit cigar into his mouth. "And he was willing to pay anything for it."

"No. You didn't," David sneered, unable to decide whether this was funny or outrageous.

Xaver looked at Clara and then back to David. He leaned closer and said in his ear, "It was a story about his mother," Xaver said. "She pulled a Jon Snow on him."

# 102

"We both know the first two lines are taken from the main Singing Bone story in the Brothers Grimm book," he began. "It's lines two and four where the juice is. I mean, the message Rachel put in your head should lead you to figure out what story the Ovitz family has guarded for centuries."

Jacqueline interrupted. "How does it feel to find out you're an Ovitz, by the way?"

"I don't know how I feel," Anne said. In her heart, she didn't know who she was anymore. It was hard admitting she faked calling her sister for all those years because she could never cope with what happened. Keeping an imaginary version of Rachel by her side gave her hope that they would meet again and that she'd be able to apologize. It also made her realize she needed help. Seeing her psychiatrist didn't sound like a bad idea anymore. "I don't want to discuss that now."

"That's a shame because it's always a pleasure to meet a fellow descendant of the bloodline." Xaver bit on his cigar and winked.

"We're not of the same bloodline, and we'll never be," Anne said. "I still can't wrap my head around being one myself. I'll only do this to make Rachel happy and hope to God, whether she is alive or dead, she'll forgive me."

"Bloodline or not," David said, "I'll put a bullet in your skull when this is over."

"Here," Xaver pulled out a golden gun from his compartment. "Use this when you do." His smile at David scared everyone. "I'm Franz Xaver. When I die, I want a golden bullet between my eyes."

Anne was about to shield Clara's ears with her hands, but she was too late. Even David, reluctantly taking the gun, looked intimidated by Xaver's death wish.

"Now that we're all set," Xaver chimed happily, "let's start with the three colors mentioned in lines three and four of the poem."

"Red, White, and Black," Anne said. "Three colors tied to apples, hags, and time." She hesitated for a moment and then continued. "Red, white, and black in folklore have always been reserved for one specific fairytale."

"Snow White?" Clara chimed in.

"Yes." Anne smiled feebly.

"Lips red as blood, skin pale as snow, and hair black as night."

"Well, that's what Disney wants us to think." Xaver rubbed his thumb against his forefinger and middle finger, making the universal sign for money. "The truth is that Snow White had blonde hair and was a real person in history."

"True," Anne agreed as David focused on the GPS. "In Germany, black hair was a most desirable attribute in girls back then. It was rare."

"But Snow White was average looking and not as desirable as the story makes her out to be," Xaver said. "Sorry, Clara."

"Don't talk to her," David said, eyes focused on the road.

"So, she wasn't a poor, beautiful girl from the valley?" Clara pouted. It broke Anne and David's hearts that she still sounded like this naive twelve-year-old who never grew up.

"She came from a relatively rich family, but that's beside the point," Anne said. David hit another bump in the road, stopping at the base of a helipad in the middle of the forest, Xaver's helicopter parked in the center. "The point is that the three colors are one of the most discussed Fairytale Codes."

David watched the helicopter in awe. The landing pad had a large letter X on it, a reference to Xaver Enterprises.

"X marks the spot," Xaver said, pointing at himself. "It's fun to be rich."

They all hopped out and faced two men wearing army uniforms with the X insignia on the back. A pilot waited in the cockpit, ready to take off.

The Eurocopter 130 itself was eye candy. Clara let out a cheery 'Wow' with both arms raised in the air, relieved to be far from the conflict in the streets of Hamelin. The sun was beginning to shine brighter through the thick clouds. It was a new day.

"Now that we're set to fly, please continue, Anne," Xaver said. "Tell them about one of the greatest Fairytale Codes of all time. The one that helped sell your book to the masses."

"It's an unusual explanation, but the three colors—red, white, and black—refer to what fairytales, in their essence, had always been about," Anne said. "The three colors represented the three stages of womanhood."

# 103

## *Lufthansa Airplane, Europe*

The four Ovitz sisters sat first class, trying to call Lisa and Lisbeth to instruct them to meet at the final destination.

Having booked this flight with forged passports provided by the Queen, they pretended they were bratty and rich youngsters from the Swiss Bradfeld family: The same family famous for hiding millions of dollars for wealthy Americans, Arabs, and Nazi clients.

Since the Bradfelds had been kept out of the public eye for many years, impersonating them wasn't hard, especially when they were known to have what they called a 'genetic setback' of occasional dwarfism in their family.

Since the Queen had booked most of First Class, the sisters turned it into a mess. Champagne on ice and a party on fire.

Lara, the youngest, didn't drink but couldn't remember the last time she had laughed so much. Lucia had to stop drinking once her visits to the bathroom hit three an hour. Even Lily gave in, allowing the liquor to take her edge off. After all, this would end soon, but whether the outcome would be good or bad was beyond her.

The wildest, of course, was Bloody Mary. She not only drank but attempted to seduce the hostess, a cute French girl her age. Mary found it hard to explain to her that she wasn't going to kill her. After all, Mary had sex with all genders but only killed men—and she never could resist performing the Bloody Mary trick in the mirror.

"No Disney movies!" Lucia shouted at the stewardess, who suggested she put on Beauty and Beast as an attempt to slow down the first-class party.

"Oh, I'm sorry," the stewardess said. "I guess I should put on Snow White and the Seven Dwarves?"

The music stopped in first class, and the four sisters sobered up. Though the stewardess didn't intend for it to be mean, her ignorance towards those born different in this world bothered them.

"Oh," the stewardess said. "I'm sorry, again."

The Ovitz sisters glared at her.

"I guess we have to chop this one up, huh?" Mary told her sisters, licking a plastic knife. "In half? Making two dwarves out of her? What do you think, girls?"

"No, please, I'm sorry," the stewardess begged, panicking.

"Don't worry." Mary waved a hand in the air, and the four sisters laughed hysterically. "Do we look like we would harm anyone?"

"Of course not," the stewardess said. "You're all so...cute."

"Put on Pan's Labyrinth," Lily said, finally loosening up. "It's my favorite real fairytale movie."

"I say put on Ginger Snaps," Mary said. "That's the real fairy-tale I prefer."

"I love that movie!" Lucia said, wanting to watch Mary's recommendation about the girl who turns into a werewolf on her period days.

Later, when they finally put a movie on, and everyone felt exhausted, Mary tried to seduce another girl from first-class and failed again. A little tired, she slumped down the chair in the back and reminded herself of how far she had come from being Lilith Ovitz to badass Bloody Mary.

While promises of tears formed behind her eyes, she remembered a few years back to the night when she became Bloody Mary. The night when coming home from her Oral History class at Queen Mary University in London, she met the Advocate for the first time.

# 104

7:25 A.M.

## *Eurocopter 130, Midair, Germany*

"Womanhood?" Jacqueline asked Anne.

They had all strapped up and taken their seats in the helicopter, which uncannily was very low in noise.

"Stages of womanhood," Anne explained. "It's an interesting idea, repeatedly discussed in Paganism and reflected in other beliefs from the past."

"It's an idea that Dorothea Viehman was taught as a child, too," Xaver added. "That's the part Anne doesn't know because guess what? She used to not believe in the Sisterhood. Why won't you summarize the concept to them, Professor?"

"It goes like this," Anne told them. "A girl was believed to be a maiden until her first period, hence the red color, which also is used as a metaphor for ripe apples. The first stage of womanhood."

Anne noticed that words hit Clara differently. It was as if she suddenly realized she was missing something. The expression 'from girl to woman' made her look a little lost.

"Go on," Jacqueline said.

"A girl who was ripe and got her period—now considered 'red' in her tribe—must grow up and become a mother: The second stage of womanhood," Anne explained. "Motherhood lasts only until her period finally ends, signifying the shift from red to black. Aging has a 'black' tint to it, so *'time she can't bring back'* is considered 'black,' as mentioned in the poem."

"In some texts, it's a macabre insinuation to being close to the grave, too," Xaver said. "Which is usually made of black soil in a certain region in Germany."

"Let's not jump to conclusions," Anne said, knowing which city Xaver suggested.

"But it's true," Xaver insisted. "You and I know it's the only place in the Fairytale Road that represents these three colors perfectly."

"Point made, but we'll get back to it," Anne nodded, addressing the others again. "There is another more sinister reason, and it rather fits why the second stage of womanhood was considered black in color," she said. "It's because women of that age not only couldn't get time back but were jealous of the younger, red maidens."

"Snow White vibes already?" Xaver said.

"Later in life, the maiden who was once a mother now becomes a grandmother—an elderly, a hag."

"Or a witch." Xaver couldn't stop himself. "Tell them the real description of the old hag-witch-grandmother, Anne. Tell them."

Anne felt embarrassed to call an elderly by that description, but she had to say it. "A crone."

"A devil's crone," Xaver said, wiggling his eyebrows at Jacqueline, who didn't find it funny in the least.

Anne and David's eyes met, not even needing to spell it out for each other. They both realized that the three stages of womanhood were coincidently present in the helicopter.

Clara, Anne, and Jacqueline. Maiden, woman, and hag.

"Why call her the devil's crone?" Clara asked.

"Witchcraft was a thing back then," Anne said. "Women who

rebelled spoke out, or showed uncommon behaviors were labeled witches without remorse."

"And burned at stake," Xaver pointed his unlit cigar at David.

"Like the girl on the cross, you mean?" David said.

"I'm just saying," Xaver said, shaking his shoulders.

"Again, it's too soon to jump to conclusions," Anne insisted. "Now that it's clear that Rachel's story, which is the same story the Ovitz family guarded for centuries, is actually the origin story of Snow White, we need to decide where to go for the final revelation."

"Doesn't that make Rachel's story a mapestry, too?" David remarked. "Except that it's a precise one, about one story—Snow White. One storyteller, Rachel, and one clue, the girl on the cross?"

"It's a reasonable way to describe it, yes," Anne said. "But I still can't see how Snow White is considered a girl on a cross. The only girls on crosses mentioned so far are the wives of Gilles de Rais."

"And even that is refutable," Jacqueline said.

"May I remind you that Tom John, if not the whole world, is after us?" Xaver said.

"He's got a point," David said. "But it's your story, Anne, your sister, and your bloodline, and it's up to you where to go next."

"Okay, then. Let's go to the place where the apples are ripe, the soil is black, and the general demographic is one of the oldest in the world. Where elders are called hags for having white hair," Xaver said, tilting his head at Anne.

"I guess you're right," Anne said. "Lohr in the Fairytale Road is the only place I can think of where Snow White was buried."

"Lohr?" Clara asked.

"It used to be called Folk-Lohr in the past. The locals think it's the only city that exposes the *folklore* background of Maria Sophia von Erthal's story. People believe it's where she was buried."

"Is that her name?" Clara asked. "The real Snow White?"

"Yes," Anne nodded but then addressed Xaver. "But we're not going because of the color suggestions you made. In fact, you're very wrong about your assumption."

"Says the folklorist who *isn't* the best in the world," Xaver huffed.

"Actually, I'm the best this time," Anne said. "Because the three colors aren't only representing womanhood. They also symbolize the one and only mirror of its kind, which was also mentioned in the fairytale."

"What are you talking about?" Xaver said.

"I'm talking about the real-life, one and only mirror, mirror on the wall."

# 105

### *X Landing Pad, Main Forest, Hamelin, Fairytale Road, Germany*

Tom preferred to sit in the Jeep while the Advocate and his men inspected Xaver's helicopter pad in the middle of the forest. He wore protective shades, considering the irony of shrouding himself with so much darkness that he couldn't look the daylight in the eyes anymore.

He persuaded himself that he was just tired and didn't want everyone commenting on his eyebags.

He had just hung up with his father, Jonathan Gray. He confirmed the Advocate's identity and advised him to stay true to Her Majesty's office. That although the Vatican, the British, and the German elite were working hand in hand now, it was all temporary until the Fairytale Code was revealed.

Tom wanted to ask how this whole thing worked. How was it possible official authorities that were supposed to protect people were so blunt about faking the news and killing innocent bystanders?

News outlets reported the attack on Hamelin, saying the Germans were still searching for the associates of the mad assassin in Polle. The footage was even forged to show Hamelin's locals helping the police find the terrorist.

In the age of cellphone cameras, what you saw on TV or the Internet was heavily influenced by the words that described it: Not the pen that documented history first but by the mouth that attacked the innocent first.

His father didn't answer that part, though. All he said was that the authorities realized Bloody Mary's plan: that she wanted to blow up the Anne and David story and was trotting the globe, chasing centuries-old secrets about a girl on a cross.

Mary thought committing crimes like the one in the Vatican would get the world's attention. Instead, Father Firelle's death hadn't been yet explained to the public, and the whole Anne and David and Bloody Mary story were being gaslighted by the season finale of some popular show—ironically about fairytales.

"Just keep an eye on the Advocate," his father advised. "And come home in one piece, son."

Tom wasn't used to having a passionate father, but he knew it wouldn't last, knowing it was only the aftermath of a near-death experience. "I'm watching the Advocate from inside the Jeep now. We're trying to figure out how to trace the helicopter Anne and David used to escape," Tom said. "How about you? Are you feeling better?"

"I am," his father coughed. "All except these ancient stories I was unaware were inside of my head. They're driving me crazy and giving me headaches. It's been like this since that Bloody Mary played her flute after giving me the antidote to my poisoning."

# 106

---

8:02 A.M.

*Eurocopter 130, Midair, Fairytale Road, Germany*

"Before we tell them about the real magic mirror in Lohr," Xaver said, "why don't you tell them more about the real Snow White?"

"It's all in the book," Anne said. "And I think you know more."

"They haven't read your book, Anne," Xaver said. "Entertain us. It's a two and half hour flight to where Snow White once lived, south of the Fairytale Road."

"Tell us, Anne," Clara backed him up.

"Well, the locals of Lohr call her Maria Sophia Von Erthal," Anne began, trying her best to be as good of a storyteller to Clara as Rachel was to her as a child. "They even have a monument of her and the seven dwarves near the Snow White museum."

"Are we going to see it when we arrive?" Clara said.

"I don't think we have the time, Clara. We're more interested in the mirror inside the museum," Anne said. "Anyway, once upon a time, this kind-hearted young woman suffered under the authority of her harsh stepmother—"

"When Anne says, 'once upon a time,'" Xaver interjected, winking at Clara, "she means 'this really happened.'"

"What did I say?" David pointed at the golden gun Xaver had given him. "Don't talk to her."

"The Von Erthal family owned a good portion of the coal mines in the Spessart forest near Lohr," Anne continued. "They lived in a castle where an exquisite mirror hung on the wall. A mirror that was sent as a gift by the Spessart Glass Company, the best at the time."

"Why is it called Spessart?" Clara asked.

"After the largest, and one of the darkest, German forests in the Spessart area," Anne said. "It's also named after woodpeckers, a prominent species in the region. Maria was said to have escaped the henchman in these forests, but I'll get to that later."

"Was it a magic mirror in her castle?" Clara asked.

"A talking mirror, that was the rumor," Anne said. "You see, a man called Lustus Von Libeling first invented the type of mirrors as we know them today. Earlier mirrors had black surfaces and were made of different materials. Long story short, the glass company in the Spessart forest belonged to Libeling's offspring, who perfected mirrors by making them concave, and more importantly white, not black."

"What is a concave mirror?" Clara said.

"Don't worry about that," Anne replied. "What mattered was that Maria's family owned one of the very few transparent mirrors in the world at the time."

"They described 'transparent' as 'white' back then?" Clara questioned, making a mental note.

"Exactly," Anne said. "The castle, which is now a museum in Lohr, was built near the Spessart Glass company. The miners were said to have been friends with the young Maria, but they hated her stepmother."

"Why?"

"Stories vary," Anne explained. "Some said that miners were mostly dwarves who'd inherited their stunted heights from their ancestors contracting diseases of working in mines in the past. The mines *were* far from healthy. Plus, the coal made it harder to breathe properly—"

"And most of all," Xaver interrupted, talking to David instead of Clara. "The miners worked in the tunnels, which forced them to stoop, and it is said this turned their offspring into dwarves."

"That doesn't make sense," David said.

"Says the man interested in evolution," Xaver raised an eyebrow. "He who adapts survives. Isn't that what Darwin said?"

"The point is the miners were short, and Maria had always been kind to them," Anne said. "So, they developed a friendship that in its time was frowned upon because—"

"Maria was rich, and they were poor," Clara predicted.

"Yes," Anne said. "Also, because most of the miners were older men, and Maria was a sixteen-year-old girl."

"But they were funny men, right?"

"Funny men, indeed," Anne played along, thinking Rachel would have done the same had Anne suggested it when they were in the well. "Now Maria was one of baron Philipp Christoph von Erthal's many daughters."

"Baron?" Jacqueline questioned.

"It was just a title all over Europe," Anne said, knowing what Jacqueline had in mind. "I know Gilles de Rais invented the title, inspired by a demon's name, but it just stuck, and people forgot about its origins."

"We'll see about that." Jacqueline didn't look convinced.

"There are also records of Maria having caught smallpox as a child," Anne continued. "Which may have made her see only in black and white and red."

"I can understand black and white," David asked. "But why red?"

"It's the myth, David, but if you insist." Anne briefly glanced at Clara. "It was said that the color of blood was so strong it was seen by even the partially blind."

David nodded, realizing that he got so immersed in the story that he was starting to ask questions like annoying children who constantly ask, "Why this?" and "Why that?"

"Maria's mother, Philipp's wife, died at a young age. He later married Claudia Elisabeth von Reichenstein."

"Such a villainous name," Xaver pointed out. "Reichenstein."

"Then, in Phillip's absence, just like in the Snow White fairytale, Maria was left in a perpetual conflict with Claudia, her stepmother, about the miners. Claudia treated them as servants, and Maria loved them as friends. Phillip had left the mirror for Maria to use, but Claudia, being the woman of the house, confiscated it."

"So far, it still sounds like a fairytale," David said.

"You're right, David," Anne said. "That's why I'm not sure about going to Lohr because I can't imagine this story hiding a secret code this important."

"We'll figure it out," Xaver insisted. "The devil is in the details. Tell us how Phillip died."

"It's said that Claudia killed Maria in her father's absence," Anne said. "She sent a henchman after her into the forest, and the miners failed to save her. There are vague mentions of another Spanish prince falling in love with her, but Maria died in the end."

"You forgot to mention why the stepmother killed Maria," Xaver raised a finger to emphasize his point. "To get her hand on these mines where a powerful item was hidden."

"I don't buy any of this, Xaver. It really does sound like a folklore story now," Anne challenged before looking at David. "The only part that seems relevant here is the Talking Mirror."

"Why is that?" David said.

"It disappeared after Maria's death," Anne said. "Guess why?"

David shrugged his shoulders.

"The mirror was haunted and witnessed Maria's death," Xaver said. "So, it technically was also a Singing Bone."

"Finding the mirror would expose Claudia as the killer," Anne said. "That's where the whole 'mirror, mirror on the wall' came from."

"And it's not just about proving Claudia von Reichenstein was the killer,' Xaver continued. "It's about knowing who she represented when she killed her and why."

# 107

## *Lufthansa Airplane, Outside of Frankfurt, Germany*

Though her plane was about to land, Bloody Mary acted drunk and excused herself to the airplane's bathroom. Inside, she stared at her image in the mirror and kept turning the light button on and off.

"Bloody Mary," she said in the dark, hands gripping the sides of the sink.

She turned the light on, realizing she was about to cry.

Light off.

"Bloody Mary," she said in the dark.

Light on.

This time, her moist eyes were going to fully expose her pain. She didn't want to cry and wasn't going to. She needed to maintain her strong image. No one would see her ever shed a tear.

Light off.

"Bloody Mary," she said for the third time, taking a deep breath before flipping the light on again.

This time, he was there.

In her mind, she knew.

A memory so real it manifested itself behind her as a man in a black cassock.

Mary broke into tears and turned the light off, remembering what had happened four years ago. Two days after her eighteenth birthday, at a time when she was still naive enough to believe in her grandmother's pure ideologies.

Ambling out of Queen Mary University after finishing her favorite Oral History class, she was on her way to pick up Lily from a cafe nearby. Lily, like her sister, loved Oral History.

This class, art or science or both, had been the brainchild of Dorothea Viehman, who had been inspired by their great grandmother Lilliput Ovitz. It was an honor to learn more about it.

Nothing made the young Mary, called Lilith then, prouder.

She had planned to meet with Lily and gossip about all they had learned today. Later, they would pray and exchange the parts of the story given to each of them. That evening, the seven sisters were going to meet in the cramped apartment in London above the library and pray together while reminding each other about all the parts of the story.

Snow White's story.

Sixteen-year-old Maria Sophia Von Erthal and her evil stepmother.

Mary had recently learned about the other side of the Ovitz family in California. Lady Ovitz called them the ones who got away. Only then did they learn that Mary and her sisters didn't have the whole story. That is a genius move on Lady Ovitz's part; she split the story even wider without any of them knowing the major part. A portion of the story she called the Keystone tale.

The part that had been given to Rachel from her mother in California.

Mary was only a few blocks from the cafe where Lily studied and decided to take a shortcut through an alley to make up some time.

That's when he snatched her and pressed a needle into her neck.

It happened fast, and she was taken off guard. She lost consciousness and woke up in a basement.

Nobody cared what happened to anyone in this city. Mary could have been anywhere, except that water was dripping nearby, and a hanging lamp swayed against a mirror ahead in the semi-darkness.

Her hands were tied behind her back, knotted around the back of a rusty chair. Facing her sat the Advocate, a name she would soon learn. He was pouring red wine into a glass, telling her that he may have to force her to drink it all if she wouldn't cooperate.

The Advocate wanted to know where the Singing Bone was.

"The final one, the real one, the one with the Fairytale Code. Not any of the others," he explained. "The one that looks like a small telescope."

Mary knew nothing. An item like that was beyond her scope of knowledge. She was barely a young girl in the Sisterhood: Only True Sisters beheld such crucial secrets about the details.

But the Advocate tortured her.

In unspeakable ways, she was forced to cover herself with too many tattoos later. Down in the basement in London, Mary thought she would die.

She was willing to die for the cause, but when the pain became unbearable and the Advocate messed with her head, she began to wonder if keeping a centuries-old secret was worth the humiliation and trauma.

"Don't lie to me, Lilith," the Advocate hit her. "Or I will do to you what I did to your relatives in California." His stinky breath neared her cheeks as he whispered. "Do you know what I did to Rachel Christian Anderson?"

All Mary saw was the cracked version of herself in the mirror while the lamp swayed from above. It was as if the universe was giving her permission to transform—to grow up, and become someone else. Someone as distorted as the reflection in the mirror.

"You know the myth about Bloody Mary?" the Advocate said. "You say her name in the mirror three times, and she comes back and slits your throat?"

"I'm the male version of her," the Advocate reached for the lamp overheard and clicked it off.

"Bloody Mary," he whispered in her ears.

Lilith panicked, thinking he would kill her in the dark.

Light on.

She saw him standing behind, looking into that humid mirror.

Lights off.

She anticipated his words this time but still shivered when he spoke. "Bloody Mary."

Light on.

Her reflection of her fidgeting, trying to free herself, made her think she had died from a heart attack.

Light off.

"This is your last, Lilith. The third calling." He spoke so softly she was wondering if she imagined it. "If I turn the light on one more time...Oh, the things I will do to you."

Light on!

Mary, no longer Lilith, shrieked as the lights hit her eyes for the third time.

Except that this time, a woman showed up behind the Advocate. Someone was here to save Mary.

Someone who was here for revenge, whom Mary would forever love and cherish.

# 108

## The Piper House, Hamelin, Fairytale Road, Germany

The German police prepared for an intensive investigation, confiscating all the evidence in the Piper House. They found the security tapes and guest log, riddled with elite names from celebrities and bankers to money launderers and professional art thieves. The names were endless, and the counties of origins were many.

"Look," one policeman pointed at a computer screen full of paid stories. "I know who Bin Laden's wife slept with."

"Wait until you hear what really happened on 9/11," another said.

"I have a real one," the third said. "I know who manufactured the Black Death plague."

"None of you could imagine what I have," another said, joining in on the fun. "Here is a list of Kings who were pimps, Queen who were whores, Princesses who married their bastard-child brother to keep the crown in the family. It goes all the way back to the Tudors and even further back to King Henry VII."

"Nothing about Hitler?" one of them joked. "I mean, I'd like to know who advised him to keep that mustache?"

"If I had billions of dollars like these maniacs here," the shorter policeman said, "I'd pay a couple of million to know that."

A loud crackle suddenly came from the walls, as if someone was living inside.

"What the hell is that?" the young one blurted out, placing his hand on his gun.

"Didn't we disarm Tom John's explosives?"

"I'm sure we did," the snickering policeman said, pointing at a hole at the bottom of the wall. "It's just rats."

"We're in Hamelin, after all."

"Should we follow the rats to keep them from messing with crucial evidence?" one suggested.

"I'd shoot some rodents for fun," another one said before following the leader.

"I miss this British guy, Tom," the snickering policeman said. "It was so much fun making fun of him."

The number of rats increased, multiplying in quantity and growing in size, scurrying in the direction of the policemen. Large rodents, appearing as if they'd been through some military lab experiment.

"What the..."

Some of the police officers backed off.

"Can you hear something ticking?" Another said.

"Are these rats carrying...?"

And that was that.

The Piper House exploded. With all the evidence.

Once and for all.

While in the helicopter, Xaver received a confirmation message.

*The Piper House is gone, as you asked after we pulled that silly rodent joke of yours.*

Xaver smiled broadly and typed back a response.

*Anonymously call the BBC, and show them footage of Tom John's men wiring the house with explosives, then announce that The Piper House accidentally exploded by the German police's explosives, which were irresponsibly planted without a warrant.*

The messenger replied quickly.

*Are you sure you want to play this game with the press? Why not leave them to draw their own conclusions?*

Xaver wrote back.

*It's not a game. Tomorrow it's going to be called history, and like I taught you, history is created by he who documented it first.*

🍎

Tom John sat in the backseat, eyes on the Advocate, who was sitting next to the German pilot in uniform. The helicopter they took was one of the three, all on a mission to locate Anne and David. Tom kept thinking about his father's words about his headaches and the stories, remembering that Mary had told him something like this would happen. Maybe he was suffering from some sort of aftershock.

The pilot spoke up, "We've received information about a helipad being cleared for landing in one of Xaver's companies in the town of Lohr."

# 109

***Lohr, the Snow White Town, Fairytale Road, Germany***

Anne woke to Jacqueline's gentle patting.

"We've arrived," Jacqueline said. "The Airbus will land in Lohr in a few. You should wake them up."

Anne, realizing she had dozed off for a couple of hours, saw that Jacqueline was pointing at Clara, who had fallen asleep hugging David.

"Had he been older," Jacqueline said. "They would have made a good father and daughter. You, too, slept on his shoulder."

"Oh," Anne said. She didn't mind, but Clara's trust in David tugged at her heart. She reminded herself that Clara said she trusted David earlier because he was the man with the gun. After all, there was little Anne knew about Clara's parents or what had happened to her in the Sisterhood.

"Older brother and little sister, I guess," Anne said to Jacqueline.

"Makes sense," Jacqueline said. "David lost his sister, after all."

"He had a sister?" Anne rubbed her eyes. "I thought it was his mother who—"

"His older sister had some sickness, a deformity or something, that got her relentlessly bullied in school," Jacqueline said. "An autoimmune disease that, for some reason, irritated the bullies everywhere. Every now and then, David had to fight one of these bigger bullies to protect her. It was how he learned to fist-fight and rarely ever resorts to guns now. That's also where the phrase 'I'm not God, I'm David' came from."

"Meaning?" Anne inquired.

"The bullies, twice his size, joked that they were Goliath and that he was just David, the young and weak kid who wished to protect his weird sister. They told him he acted as if God was on his side when he had no chance defending her all alone."

"I see," Anne said, watching Clara snoring in David's arms. "If he thought he was God, why does he always say he is not God now?"

"His sister ran away in the end and was never seen again," Jacqueline said. "Either escaped or died or was killed, who knows? But she had hinted to him that she wanted to escape this world and one day return and avenge herself when she became stronger. Hence, David realized he was just David, not God, unable to protect his sister from Goliath."

"Hence him being an atheist?" Anne asked.

"His mother became an atheist first," Jacqueline said. "The idea that she gave birth to a quote, 'weak link,' aka his sister, made her read too much into evolution. She realized and accepted this world was a dog-eat-dog world. It just all depended on what kind of dog you were, which was an evolutionary thing that you had no chance of choosing and chasing. A bulldog was born a bulldog, and a chihuahua was born a chihuahua."

"I'm sorry she felt that way," Anne said.

"It's said that her studying evolution made her discover something of universal interest to certain powerful people. It got her killed," Jacqueline said. "But that's all I know."

"Speaking of what you know," Anne said. "How come you know so much about him?"

"Through me," Xaver said from the front seat. "It took me an hour to research his past. I have connections, and I needed to know more about the people I was transporting for the final countdown."

"You don't trust David?" Anne scoffed.

"I don't trust you either, Anne," Xaver said. "I mean, you have stories in your head you don't even know about. What's there to trust?"

A few minutes later, the helicopter landed on a private patch of land located on the grounds of a manufacturing company.

"Welcome to the Spessart Glass Company," Xaver said, the sun shining unusually brighter today. "Tell them about it, Anne."

"It's the oldest glass manufacturing company in Germany," Anne said to David, holding Clara's hand. "But I didn't know Xaver bought it."

"I bought a lot of things on the Fairytale Road. It's a story of mine, after all," he said, pointing in the direction of two of his Hummer-like, bullet-proof vehicles arriving to pick them up. "Come on, tell them what this historical company did in the past: The company that was created by the descendant of Justus von Liebig, the man who invented mirrors as we know them today."

Anne sighed, opening the door for Clara to sit in the back of one of the vehicles. "This manufacturing company designed the Snow White mirror."

"Come again?" David hopped in the driver's seat again, Xaver taking the front passenger seat.

"Anne means the 'mirror, mirror, on the wall,' my friends," Xaver said, checking out pimples on his face in the compartment mirror.

"That was a real thing?" David was ready to drive, watching a similar vehicle driven by another chauffeur ahead.

"It is still a real thing," Anne told him. "That's why Rachel's poem sent us here."

"We're going to see the Evil Queen's real mirror?" Clara said, not sleepy anymore.

Anne brushed her through her hair. "Yeah, we're going to the Snow White Museum in Lohr, where they keep all of the artifacts, including the evil Queen's mirror that has a red frame, black mahogany body, and a centuries-old mirror."

"So, it's a full circle," Jacqueline said, looking intrigued. "Three special colors, womanhood, and a mirror hundreds of years old."

"My chauffeur is going to show the way, David," Xaver said. "Let's go."

"Why two vehicles?" David asked skeptically.

"One for us," Xaver said. "And one to make it look like it is us inside. Trust me. I know how to deal with this, Tom John."

"Not bad." David knew some of Xaver's tactics had saved them so far. "But I thought you said Osama Bin Laden's son owned only one of these?"

Xaver laughed so hard that his weight shook the vehicle. "Do I look like a man you should believe, David? Come on, drive."

# 110

10:23 A.M.

## *Lohr, Fairytale Road, Germany*

Lohr reminded David of Polle, a small picturesque town of 15,000 people that looked like it had been cut out of the pages of a children's fairytale book. The faint morning sun took off the edge of the brisk, snowy environment, and the pooling rays of sunshine surrounding them made him think of rainbows from the Wizard of Oz.

David's sister's favorite character was Dorothy Gale. She used to call her bullies the Wicked Bitches of the West since they were raised in west New Castle. Abigail Tale not only had a strong name, but she also possessed an impressive potty mouth at a young age.

Following the chauffeur in the vehicle ahead deeper into the city, David thought about modern-day moviemakers of Hollywood, who probably used Lohr as their muse when creating period pieces depicting the Middle Ages and Renaissance Europe.

He was driving through a town of fairytale castles with tall, foreboding towers and stunning churches for the devout Catholic, once protestant, in the countryside of Bavaria. Half-timbered buildings, originally built in previous centuries, filled the town's center. The squares were decorated with sandstone fountains, with small shops and bistros sprinkled all around.

Xaver, acting like a tour guide amidst their predicament, told him about what he solely understood about this town—and the whole Fairytale Road in general.

"You know what makes this region feel magical and enchanting?" Xaver said. "It's full of poor towns with dark histories hiding underneath the rich's delicate but deceiving rainbow-tinted paint."

"I'm not sure I understand," David said.

"Really look at all the half-timbered houses, forests, mines, and down-to-earth locals in these small towns. What do you see?" Xaver said. "I'll tell you what you see: poor towns where most of us were raised. Even the castles around here: Look at how small and modest they are. They're not the grandeur castles we see in movies."

"What's your point?" David said, making conversation, nothing else.

"It's my most valuable secret," Xaver lowered his voice. "This land once belonged to the Protestant rebels who were more or less poor and valued relationships, not money. Who prioritized art and family, not propaganda and the power of an overbearing church. That's where the meditative and cozy feel comes from. Then when the Catholics came—who valued the crown, royalty, grandeur, and power through the church—they said, 'Oh, this looks so poor and cozy. Why don't we paint it in bright colors and write epic histories about it and make it sound like blood was never shed here? And that the Thirty Year War that killed their sons, daughter, mothers, and fathers never happened?'"

David wasn't sure why Xaver was telling him this, though it sounded like something to consider. The intriguing conversation came to a halt when David finally saw Schloss, the Snow White museum, on his right side.

Unlike what David had imagined, it was too small of a castle, but he waited until they got closer for more detailed observation.

Xaver pointed up to the left toward a tall, ancient but reno-vated tower, "That's the Bayer Watchtower," Xaver said. "The last remaining tower of the city's walls since World War II."

Now David listened, remembering the assassin in Polle hiding in a smiler one.

"The tower was named after the former guardian family, Bayer, led by Napoleon, when France conquered most of the German south," Xaver continued. "It's the highest tower in Bavaria, and Lilliput Ovitz used it for solitude. Just like Dorothea Viehman used the Rapunzel tower to design the melodic triggers, finding ways to split her story among her offspring, forever guarding them."

"Why here?" David said before a thought struck him. "Oh, wait. I assume because of this," he stated, pointing at the Snow White museum across the street.

"We've got a new folklorist on our hands, Anne." Xaver was now smoking a pipe, a change from his usual cigar, nodding at her in the front mirror.

"He'd make a fine one," Anne said. "Why are your men up there, Xaver?"

Xaver chuckled. "And you make a good detective, Anne."

"I agree," David added, squinting against the sun pooling through the tower's arches at the top. "I failed to spot them myself." He noticed several men pretending to do renovations. "How do you know they are Xaver's men?"

"For one, they don't know anything about renovations, so it's an act," Anne said. "Two, we would have already been shot at had they not been on our side."

"Folklorist David Tale, meet detective Anne Anderson," Xaver said. "Why don't you take a right, so we enter the museum from its secret backdoor now, David."

Seeing the chauffeur in the advancing vehicle parking at the front door of the museum across the tower on the other side of the street, David did as he was told. Xaver's plan wasn't bad. If Tom John's men arrived and recognized Xaver's vehicle parked in front, they would arrest the chauffeur, alerting them to escape from the back.

If this plan didn't work out for some reason, Xaver's men in the tower would attack and stall Tom's men.

The only problem was that local families were entering the museum. Not many, as it was a small town, but David didn't want to endanger civilian life. Again.

They parked next to garbage cans at the back of the museum, their vehicle overlooking the forest. It seemed like a recurring pattern for buildings in Germany to have a front on the main street and a backside overlooking a forest.

"I know the curator," Xaver said. "An old man who still thinks fairytales are children's books. I'll pretend you are my family: My cousin Anne and her husband, David; his younger sister Clara; and my wife, Jacqueline. Not in real life, but you know what I mean."

They entered the museum. David walked off and took his time to scan the place. It wasn't the best of ideas to separate from the group, but he wanted to get a feel of it. After all, he didn't quite understand what clues they would be looking for.

That was Anne and Xaver's job: looking for that magic mirror that supposedly belonged to the Evil Queen (whoever she really was), and explaining the red, black, and white color references.

He casually walked around and heard a local woman educating some children about the museum. He eavesdropped that the museum was originally a castle from the eighteenth century and that it had many names, some calling it 'The Schloss,' which was a direct translation to 'The Castle' in English.

David heard the woman explain that it wasn't any castle. It was always called The Castle, as in *the one and only*, though she never understood why. David thought he might know why. If this was the place to find the final part of the story that the Ovitz guarded, then it definitely was The One and Only Castle.

In her relatively broken English, the guide also confirmed that this was one of Germany's smaller and most neglected museums and tourist attractions, the whole castle being about the size of Lady Chapel's hall in the Westminster Abbey.

The museum was small and poorly designed. There were small rooms, making it hard to navigate, and columns that stopped the flow. It felt like an annoying maze.

David left to look for Anne after the guide told the children that the locals truly believed this was where Snow White, Maria Sophia Von Erthal, once lived.

Right behind one of the annoying columns, David found Anne, Clara, Xaver, and Jacqueline staring at something, back to the column.

Had he not seen what they were looking at, he would have thought they'd been hypnotized. Their eyes were fixated on a nostalgic idea about mirrors on the wall that had been etched into every child's skull.

David didn't quite understand what to feel when he stared at the actual mirror that Snow White's psychologically deranged stepmother talked to.

Red frame, black wood, and almost-white glass.

Right above it, a sign said, *The Talking Mirror*.

# 111

## *Frankfurt, the Fairytale Road, Germany*

Mary sat in the backseat of their rented compact Ford Focus headed to Lohr. Lisbeth and Lisa had joined them on the thirty-minute drive. The Queen's orders were plain and simple: Carefully watch Anne follow Rachel's instructions until it leads to the third and final Singing Bone.

Lisbeth, Lara, Lucia, and Lily watched in silence as Mary and Lisa, the taller ones, handled their machine guns. Only the taller sisters knew how to shoot; the shorter ones would help deceive and distract.

Mary, knowing Tom John was going to be there, wondered if she could use him on her side again. And then kill him once she got what she wanted. Surely he must have figured out that she had lied about his father's antidote, but Tom was weak and would always fall for her tricks.

She dialed his phone number.

"I can give you what you want, Tommy," Mary teased him.

"I know where they went," Tom said. "I don't need you. What

did you do to my father, by the way? He remembers stories you put in his head!"

"It's just one story, and it will come in handy soon. I'll explain later," Mary said. "How about we join forces now against Xaver?"

"I said I don't need you," Tom quipped, sounding aggressive. She reckoned the journey had thickened his skin. "And I'll come for you after I finish my work. You're an outlaw, Mary."

"Take off that mask, Tommy. It doesn't suit you," she said. "And even if you know Anne and David are going to Lohr, do you know where? Do you know what they're looking for? Are you going to risk them escaping Lohr like they escaped Hamelin?"

"How do you know all of this?"

"How many times do I have to tell you–"

"You're Bloody Mary, I know," he said. "You know everything. What do you want then?"

"Just back me up when you attack Anne and her friends and don't harm my sisters. They're the dwarf cuties, by the way."

"Deal," Tom said. "If you promise to wait until Anne finds the final bone."

"Seems like we're on the same page," Mary said, feeling her heart skip a beat for some reason. She didn't quite understand why, but it had never happened to her before.

"Mary?" Tom said. "You still there?"

Mary said nothing, feeling her heart flutter again.

"Mary!" Lily screamed. "What's happening to you?"

The world spun around her, and she was unable to talk. Had she been poisoned? Did she accidentally drink from the Vecchio Melo in the hotel room?

"Mary!"

Her sister stopped the car. Mary could no longer feel her arms or legs. She couldn't feel her lips. She stopped feeling altogether, and she was desperate to know why.

*Did one of my sisters poison me?* she thought, her vision becoming more blurry by the second.

*Lily?*

Of course. It had to be her.

But then it hit her. It wasn't Lily.

"Mary," Tom said again.

That's when it hit her. She had heard *his* voice in the background. The Advocate. He was coming to Lohr with Tom.

She had no idea that Tom was working with the man she'd wanted to kill for so many years.

🍎

On the other side of the phone, the Advocate asked Tom about the phone call. When he told him it was his contact agent and that she called herself Bloody Mary.

The Advocate brushed it off. The last time he had seen her, she was still the innocent Lilith and hadn't known what she called herself now.

# 112

## *The Schloss, Lohr, Fairytale Road, Germany*

Anne stood amidst the group but alone in her head.

Xaver and Jacqueline seemed excited about the mirror. To them, it made all the sense in the world to end up here, standing in front of it, waiting for the final clue.

Clue for what? She didn't know. Was this about finding out who Snow White really was? How could that story be a threat to the royal family and the Vatican?

And if not, was this about finding Rachel? Did she design an intricate labyrinth to make Anne pay for what she had done to her? Was Anne supposed to prove her love and show her repentance by jumping through hoops on this journey?

Regardless, the mirror did feel like the final piece of the puzzle —something about wanting to stand in front of it and ask the iconic question of all time.

'*Mirror, mirror on the wall....*'

It was so enticing and nostalgically fascinating that it surpassed all logic and convoluted plots.

Anne doubted there was anyone who didn't know what this iconic sentence meant.

"We have to hurry, Anne," David said, standing by the column, watching the small crowd in the museum.

"We're safe, Detective; just relax," Jacqueline said. "Xaver's men by the tower will take care of any surprise attacks, and we can always escape from the back."

"I'm worried about the children in here," David said. "This isn't like in Hamelin, where everyone is in on the secret. These look like normal civilians enjoying a museum a few days before Christmas. I worry for them."

"Why would you worry for Germans?" Xaver said, biting on his pipe.

"What?" David shot a look at Xaver.

"Why worry about those you don't know?" Xaver said. "What is a few more sacrifices to expose the men who sacrificed thousands of women and children in the past?"

David felt the golden gun tucked in the back of his trousers. Xaver definitely deserved that bullet sooner or later.

"Look at the words on the frame," Clara interrupted, breaking the tension. "Is this French?"

"Yes," Anne said. "It reads, 'Pour la recompense et pour la peine,' meaning 'for reward and punishment.'"

"Why does it say that?" Clara asked.

"Probably because the myth is real," Jacqueline. "The mirror witnessed Maria's murder, aka Snow White, thus the metaphor."

Clara's remark inspired Anne to also scan the frame. It was about five feet tall and mostly red. The wood portions that should've been black looked silver now, but Anne knew this was due to restorations. It was an artistic choice by the renovators to paint it silver instead of keeping the raw black wood from the iconic Spessart forest.

The mirror's wooden frame was said to be 'pecked' by a supernatural spirit that took the shape of a Woodpecker. As the story goes, his voice would guide people lost in the forest.

The mirror's concave surface was in rough shape. It was no

wonder people described it as 'white,' as it was almost impossible to see a steady reflection.

"So...what is it, Anne?" Xaver said. "Why did Rachel send us here?"

"I'm still not sure," Anne said. "I told you I've never believed that Snow White lived in Lohr. It's too much of a feel-good story compared to the darkness in most folklore origins."

"May I suggest something?" Xaver said.

"Like what?"

"Let's take this mirror with us back to my factory."

"What?" Anne answered, stunned Xaver would suggest such a thing. "This is a historical piece of art. The pride of this town. You aren't taking anything back with you."

"I can buy it," Xaver said. "And don't give me that crap about 'money can't buy me love,' because the Beatles sang it while filthy rich."

Something caught Anne's attention in the mirror, drawing her away from the ludicrous debate.

"Is it me, or does the reflection in the mirror get clearer when I step back?" she asked the group.

"I noticed that," David said as he stood with an angle next to the column behind Anne's back. He turned towards Xaver. "Is that common in older mirrors to get clearer with distance?"

"Concave mirrors hardly do," Xaver said. "Unless it was designed like that on purpose."

"The problem is that this column behind me prevents me from going back further, even if I wanted to see a clearer reflection," Anne said with her back to the wall, looking sideways at David.

"I'm not going to blow up the wall if that's what you're asking," David responded flatly.

Anne resisted smiling. She still couldn't tell if he was stoically making jokes or being dead serious.

"Maybe move away from the wall?" Clara suggested.

"And then what?" Anne tilted her head. "How would I be able to see myself clearer?"

"Stand sideways like David," Clara suggested, pointing at

David. "His reflection is only partially showing, but it's clearer from that angle."

Anne didn't think it was a sound idea, but she was willing to try anything.

And it worked.

Standing opposite David on the other side of the column, she could see her angled image clearer now, but it looked awkward.

"I wonder if this column was built here on purpose," Anne wondered aloud. "But isn't it too close to the mirror..."

That's when Anne realized the brilliance of her sister's puzzle.

Anne pointed at the wall itself now, directly facing the mirror.

"Holy duck," David said, resisting his urge to swear in front of Clara. "The trick is to move away from the wall so that you can read the words carved in the column and reflected backward in the mirror."

"Exactly," Anne tilted her head, even more, trying to read the words she found carved on the wall behind through the mirror. "The puzzle carved on the wall is written backward, so you'd only be able to read it by looking through a mirror—"

"And at such a hard angle, so it's not accessible to just anyone," David said.

"I'll take a photo of the mirror with the reflected puzzle." Xaver stood behind Anne and awkwardly did his best to take a photo of the mirror, but he struggled with the difficult angle.

Anne borrowed a pen and newspaper from an older woman in the crowd. On the margin of the German newspaper, she wrote the puzzle she read from the wall.

"It's from Rachel," Anne said.

"How do you know?" David asked.

"It has my name in the beginning," Anne's heart raced. "In fact, most of it is straightforward, not like puzzles before. I know what most of it means at first glance. Here," Anne said, handing it over to the other, "take a look for yourselves."

The group gathered around and read the message.

*Annie, Annie on the wall,*
*I'm in a castle where hills can roll*
*Deep in the forest where woods are pecked.*
*in a tower on Northern walls*
*All the folks who live in Lore,*
*mistaken truth for their folk-lore*
*Thirty years, survived this war,*
*my final bones, come sing, explore.*

A little lower in a larger font, it read:

*It's a con,*
*plus a cave,*
*in a frame,*
*that'll fall.*
*If you break,*
*you can take,*
*bones that sing,*
*my final song.*

# 113

### *Outside the Schloss, Lohr, Fairytale Road, Germany*

Sitting in the back of the German police car, Tom John donned his bulletproof vest.

This time, he was going to join his men. He was fed up chasing Anne and wanted to have his own say in the matter, never mind his shooting inexperience.

Mary's text about her search for the Advocate alerted him. Tom knew he had poisoned his father, but he wondered what he had done to her. And since he hadn't the courage to confront him, he made a deal with her.

*Hand me the Advocate, and I'll give you Anne, the Singing Bone, and a worldwide list of the Sisterhood's descendants who won't come out because they're afraid to speak what they know.*

Tom's car entered Lohr, unaware of the Xaver's men in the tower.

Once Mary caught her breath, Lara asked her what had happened. She and Lucia were concerned and wished to help, but Mary brushed them off as if she hadn't had an episode in the first place.

The final clash was coming, and they knew Mary hardly cared what had happened to her.

Still sweating and looking as pale as a ghost, Mary messaged the Queen's agent in the Snow White museum:

*Did she find Rachel's Singing Bone yet?*

The Queen's agent responded within a minute:

*She found a message about a place that points to the final destination. I'm waiting for Anne to spell it out and then kill all of them.*

# 114

### *The Schloss, Lohr, Fairytale Road, Germany*

David's sense of sniffing danger was intensifying. His eyes scanned the families around them while Anne re-read Rachel's puzzle:

> *Annie, Annie on the wall,*
> *I'm in a castle where hills can roll*
> *Deep in the forest where woods are pecked.*
> *in a tower on Northern walls*
> *All the folks who live in Lore,*
> *mistaken truth for their folk-lore*
> *Thirty years, survived this war,*
> *my final bones, come sing, explore.*

"The puzzle is clear to me," Anne said. "And I know where she is."

"You know where *who* is?" Clara said.

"Either Rachel or the real Snow White's body," Anne said. "But it's so clear to me."

"Where should we go, then?" Jacqueline looked as intense as David. "Tell us."

"First, you should know Maria Sophia Von Erthal isn't Snow White," Anne said.

"Nonsense," Xaver said. "It must be her. I'm not going to waste more money on another interpretation. I want to stick with what we have."

"Didn't you read Rachel's puzzle?" Anne pointed at the slice of paper in her hand. "She says it loud and clear in the third line—"

"'All the folks who live in Lore, mistaken truth for their folk-lore,'" Jacqueline read aloud. "Anne is right. It sounds like Rachel specifically explains that the locals in Lohr, sometimes spelled Lore, made up this story of Snow White and stuck with the 'lore' for centuries but are 'mistaken.'"

"Nice play on words, too," Clara said. "Lohr, and lore."

"It's nothing new," Xaver sounded irritated. "Lohr was called Folklore in the past. I told you this before, but it seems like no one is listening."

"Then you should've researched this town more than," David said, barely participating in the conversation, still looking for the looming threat. "It's a dead giveaway if you ask me."

"Okay, Maria isn't Snow White," Xaver said. "Who is the real Snow White, then?"

"Whoever she is, I know where her bones are," Anne said. "I know where hills roll, the forest where woods are pecked, and the castle with northern walls. It's all too easy for me," Anne said. "All I need is to find the final Singing Bone when I arrive."

"When *we* arrive," Xaver said.

"Anne," Jacqueline said. "How far is this castle from here?"

"Thirty minutes by car," Anne said. "Then a ten-minute walk. You can't reach it by transportation from a certain point."

"A good forty minutes," Jacqueline glanced sideways at Xaver, who pretended he didn't see her. He began typing a message on his phone. "That doesn't sound too long."

"But what are the last two sentences about?" Clara chimed in. "Lines five and six?"

Anne looked reluctant but said, "They don't make sense to me. What's a 'con plus a cave and a frame that will fall'?"

"Maybe that is the final puzzle in the castle we are headed to," Clara said.

"I hope so." Anne patted her on the shoulder. "Trust me. I'm so exhausted. I really hope so."

Shots from the Bayer Tower outside echoed off the walls, making everyone in the museum duck on the floor.

🍎

Outside, Tom hardly found anything to hang onto as his Jeep flipped two times in the middle of the street in front of the museum. It was a shocking attack, and he couldn't find his bearings to see where the shots were coming from. All he knew was that someone had aimed at the tires and that his body was aching terribly in the backseat.

Realizing he was sprawled against the ceiling of the upside-down Jeep now, he heard the screaming outside. Civilians in this scarcely populated town had probably never seen anything like this before.

He couldn't find his gun. Tom craned his neck and saw the driver's face smashed against the glass windshield, dripping with blood.

"Another one bites the dust," a gruff voice mumbled next to him.

"You're alive," Tom said to the Advocate, who was unrecognizable, having lost his Romano Cappello. His disproportionate and disfigured face made Tom wonder what had happened to this man in his past.

"I'm alive, Tom," the Advocate said apathetically. "Trust me, I've tried to die so many times, but the universe wants me here to fulfill my quest."

Another shot hit the side of the car, and Tom quickly realized he didn't care about anyone else. He needed to man up and crawl out of this Jeep before it was the end of him.

David's heart throbbed in his ears, feeling as though he was fighting in a war. The screaming children reminded him of his sister Abigail. *Shit*, he thought. He wasn't going to let that happen again.

"Anne," he shouted. "Take Clara and go with Xaver to the castle. Now!"

"What about you?"

David's eyes told it all. He wasn't going with her. This was it. The end of their fast-paced journey. She had seen the same look on Rachel. The look that said, *I don't give a fuck. I have to do it.*

The shots outside were creating panic inside the museum. And if Anne had learned anything, it was that panic was a catalyst for bad decisions.

"Go!" David said, not sure if she was safe enough with Xaver. But she had a quest to finish, and he knew she could take care of herself.

"All right!" she yelled over the noise. "If you want to save the children, there is a storage room by the large wooden table with artifacts. The door looks like a wall from outside; it was a fun trick the museum provided for the children to play."

"Good," David said, the shooting escalating outside. "Now go!"

"Bye, David." Clara insisted on waving at him while Anne pulled her away. David looked away, not wanting his emotions to take over.

"You!" He pointed at one of the mothers in the crowd. "Come with me and bring the children along."

Xaver had just finished messaging Jacqueline when Anne told him to guide her to his car outside. He wrote:

. . .

*Don't shoot Anne and Clara until we're in that castle, and only after we get our hands on those letters.*


Jacqueline read it as she took Anne's hand and discreetly nodded in agreement.

But that's when Anne stopped and changed her mind.

"No," Anne said, pulling Clara back. "I'm not leaving the museum, not yet."

# 115

---

12:23 (P.M.)

***Outside the Schloss, Lohr, Fairytale Road, Germany***

Mary involuntarily ducked into the backseat as their rented vehicle succumbed to a shower of bullets near the museum.

Lisa gripped the wheel tighter, trying her hardest to maintain control. Mary advised her to detour toward the tower.

"It doesn't matter if we crash," Mary shouted. "They are shooting at us from up there. The closer we are, the harder it will be for them to shoot us."

Lisbeth steered the wheel to the right, away from the museum and toward the Bayer Tower. The spin disoriented all of them, but Mary couldn't get the Advocate's silhouette from behind the swaying lamp out of her head.

Lisbeth lost control of the wheel, crashing the rental into a German police car in front of the tower.

Mary took a deep breath, aiming her machine gun, and her sisters began to cry. Mary plowed against the back door and rolled out on her back on the cobblestone, taking a couple of shots at the tower. She didn't hit Xaver's men, but she was able to hold them off from shooting for a few seconds.

"Come on!" she shouted at her sisters. "Bring Lisa over and hide right under the tower."

The tower had a protruding balcony at the top, making it easier for them to hide and impossible for the assassins to shoot them.

With her back against the wall, and her sisters dragging Lisa over the concrete street, Mary's eyes looked for the Advocate. Two German police vehicles had been turned over near the museum's front entrance.

The other two cars were closer to her, being used as a shield by the policemen against the raining bullets from above. *Where is the Advocate?* She thought.

Mary knew innocent people were going to die today, but the one she didn't expect first was Lisa. She fell to her knees beside Mary, drenched in blood, her limp head falling right into Mary's arms.

The second Ovitz sister to die in the past thirty-six hours.

❧

Tom crawled his way outside, feeling blessed that he was still alive. He may have been wounded, but he couldn't care less. He cowardly pretended he was dead whenever someone with a gun ran nearby and then would crawl toward the museum when he had a chance.

He was bleeding from one leg and didn't want to risk walking in case it was broken. But he would find a way to get what he wanted.

Behind him, the Advocate was gone.

# 116

## *The Spessart Museum, Lohr, Fairytale Road, Germany*

Xaver tried to stop Anne from going back to the mirror, but she kicked him in the balls. Jacqueline stood alert behind Anne, curious why Anne wanted to return to the mirror.

The museum itself hadn't been attacked from the inside yet. Anne heard David taking care of the children in the neighboring room, collaborating with the museum's security guards to stop anyone from entering. David told the guards that once they kept the museum safe, he had to go outside and save as many families as possible.

"Why are we back inside?" Clara asked Anne as she stood before the mirror again.

Xaver was still moaning at the backdoor, but Jacqueline followed Anne like a shadow.

Anne answered Clara by reciting the fifth and sixth lines in the puzzle: "'It's a con, plus a cave, in a frame, that'll fall. If you break, you can take, bones that sing, final songs.'"

"Didn't you say we were going to use it once we reached the castle?" Clara said.

"I did, but then I was wrong." Anne was thinking out loud, not sure her instincts of returning to the mirror were sound. "This line brought me back: 'It's a con, plus a cave.'"

"Doesn't con mean a trick?" Clara said.

"That's what I was thinking, but then I wondered, Why did she say, 'a con *plus* a cave.' Why not 'con and a cave'?"

"When you say it fast, it sounds like concave." Jacqueline was getting better at these puzzles.

"True," Anne said, still staring at the mirror. "A concave mirror, which is what the Talking Mirror is."

"'In a frame that will fall!'" Clara said with excitement. "Does this mean we have to take the mirror?"

"I think it means we have to separate the frame from the mirror," Jacqueline suggested.

"I thought so, but no," Anne said. "Because in the line after, she explains it 'if I break,'" Anne said, snatching Jacqueline's phone from her. "'Then I can take.'" She used to break the centuries-old mirror. "'Bones that sing.'"

Anne shielded Clara with her back against the splintering shard of glass.

She heard Jacqueline gasp, loud enough to give away that what she saw inside the mirror's hollow box was something she had been tirelessly searching for.

Anne turned and looked at it before completing the puzzle. "'Final songs.' Rachel, *your* final song."

She reached for the final Singing Bone inside the box and picked it up. It was bigger than the rest, the size of a small telescope.

"Well, I'm not upset that you kicked me in my balls, then," Xaver said from behind, urging them to go.

With Xaver in front and Jacqueline in the back, Anne and Clara hurried outside and hopped into his military-grade vehicle, ready to go to the castle Rachel described.

Though Anne knew exactly where this abandoned and beautiful castle was, she wouldn't tell any of them until they were close enough. Clara saw Anne suppressing her smile and clasped her hand in hers.

In between Anne's hands, Clara saw a swan necklace, which Anne had found next to the bone.

A similar necklace like that which belonged to her mother.

# 117

13:05 (P.M.)

## *Outside the Schloss, Lohr, Fairytale Road, Germany*

Mary left Lisa behind, urging her devastated sisters to climb up the tower.

"Go distract those men up there!" she ordered them. "Are you listening to me?"

"How can you be so cruel!" Lily cried, Lucia, Lara, and Lisbeth backing her up.

Mary didn't need to reply. A bullet struck close to their group, bringing the sisters back to reality. They needed to keep moving.

"Go up and distract those men. Avenge your sister," Mary said.

Mary should have been advancing toward the museum, but she couldn't stop looking for the Advocate.

Her phone chimed, and she struggled to pick it up. She looked around the curb for shelter. The message came from her contact named The Queen's Eyes Inside.

We found it. The Singing Bone. I mean the final one. We're heading to some castle now.

Mary wrote back immediately.

*Good, send me a live location, and kill whoever you think needs killing once you feel like you don't need them anymore.*

After she hit send, she looked up and saw the Advocate crawling out of the upside-down Jeep near the museum. When she was preparing to take the shot, her arm went numb, and past memories surfaced again—the worst time to have one of these panic attacks.

What if the Advocate saw her and shot her while she was drowning unconsciously in this memory? But Mary knew memories were like wounds; once they surfaced, they never left, and they could only be healed by the blessings of time.

Mary saw herself in that basement in London, her hands tied behind the rusty chair. She still wasn't sure what the Advocate had wanted from her. All she understood was that they were enemies: one wished to spread the true stories to the world, and the other wanted to find the source of the Fairytale Code and destroy it.

When he played that sadistic game with her, turning the lights on and off, she thought she was going to die, whether from him torturing her or from the sheer traumatic experience.

But then *she* rose behind him.

The girl who changed Mary's life.

The one who taught her that people like them were destined to an ill fate, regardless of their good intentions. She taught her that the only way out was to give in to that darkness and to do whatever she thought was right, even if it was wrong. To ensure justice by being unjust.

A woman with black hair, blue eyes, and pale skin appeared behind the Advocate. She was beautiful but ruthless. And much older.

When she hit the Advocate in the face with an inverted water pipe, she left him forever disfigured. She wanted to make him unrecognizable but keep him alive.

Without a word, Mary saw her tying the Advocate to a chair. In a brutal act of revenge, Mary watched the girl circle him before breaking one of his legs with the broken pipe.

"That's for climbing down the well after me," she whispered in his ears.

Then she hit him again.

"That's for having legs to stand upon after what you did to me." She was enjoying this.

"You know how long I've been looking for you?" She circled him while the lamp above her swayed, shedding light on her for a second and then draping her in darkness.

"I kept looking for you for so many years." She hit his knees with the pipe, screams escaping him in pitches Mary didn't think he could possibly reach. "Only to realize you escaped to a different continent. Not city, not country, but a continent."

Mary idolized her and instinctually knew they must have had something in common.

"I know you're looking for the final Singing Bone, the one that looks like a telescope." She broke his other leg. "How about I make you sing to the breaking of your own bones!"

And he did. A dark song. One that sounded like a devil's cry.

And though the room was wet, it echoed with his screams.

Mary watched Rachel finish him with one last hit.

"And this is for coming between my sister and I, never allowing me to forgive her for telling you to come for me instead of her."

# 118

13:21 (P.M.)

## *The Schloss, Lohr, Fairytale Road, Germany*

David locked the children inside the hidden room and advised their mothers not to call the police. He didn't trust them. He suggested they call their brothers, sisters, mothers, fathers, and spouses to pick them up from the backdoor.

The security guards had helped him lock the museum from inside while they watched the mini-war outside take place. It had toned down, but when the *real* German police arrived, it escalated again—same uniform, different agenda, all shooting at each other.

"There is no way you could have saved the families outside," the security guard said, pointing out that they were either dead or had escaped already.

David saw Tom outside the museum, but he didn't care about him. Behind Tom, a severely injured man was crawling after him.

In his peripheral vision, he saw Xaver's spare bullet-proof vehicle parked with its doors closed. He couldn't see the driver behind the black windows and didn't know whether he was still inside or not. If he could only get him to drive back and pick up the children. Three families were too many, but he was sure he could squeeze them in under the circumstance.

"Open the door for me," David instructed the security guard. "Make the children wait in the back. I'll be there with a ride in five minutes."

"That's suicidal, Sir," the security guard said.

"Open the door!"

The security guard gave in. "But I won't let you in again."

"Deal," David said, loading Xaver's golden gun.

"You're not God, you know!" the security guard yelled from behind.

David stepped out with a mere six bullets.

"Watch me."

🍎

Xaver drove his bullet-proof vehicle, guided by the GPS Anne gave him.

Knowing she and Clara were in danger, Anne gave coordinates to a random destination in the Spessart forest, leaving Xaver and Jacqueline both guessing where they were going.

Anne rubbed Clara's shoulder, smiling at how smart Rachel was. This forgotten castle of all famous ones in Germany was a genius choice. It wasn't accessible by regular transportation since it was located in the middle of a lake.

And even though it would be vacant now, its ancient German owners still lived quietly in its southern tower. The same owners who once owned the Navarro Winery in California.

🍎

Back in London, Jonathan Gray didn't have the energy to think about what was happening to his son right now. Although he was sick from his recent poisoning, he found himself going back to The British Library, where this "Bloody Mary" had performed some voodoo melodies on his brain.

He sat on the couch in his office, trying to interpret the memories in his head. Did she implant them? Was that even possible? And if it was, why him?

If there was one thing he had learned from what he considered a near-death experience, it was that none of this really mattered: the luxury, the fame, the power. Not even his stance in the academic society mattered. Death left a bitter taste on his soul.

"Well, it sure tasted like a poisoned apple," he mumbled aloud, rubbing his hand against his trousers.

The story in his head felt so real, but he couldn't tell how he knew it, or why. He decided to flip through a German history book he picked up from the museum's library, attempting to make sense of everything buried in his mind.

It was a translated version of disputed events occurring in sixteenth-century Germany. Most translations of this era had been a subject of dismissal. This century, fresh off what historians liked to call the end of the Dark Ages—from 500 AD to 1500AD—was stained with lies, inconsistencies, and residual dark practices from the past, especially in Europe.

Had he not been recently kissed by death, he would have never given it a second thought. He remembered his mother always telling him that it was either old age or a brush with death that would slow him down and appreciate the raw beauty of life.

The story in Jonathan's head was from this dark era. Although he found it implausible, he reminded himself that he once considered poisoned apples to be a far-fetched notion.

Jonathan Gray flipped through the pages, searching for the name Margaretha von Waldeck, who was poisoned at the age of twenty-one from a cyanide-infested apple.

The same ingredients killed Alan Turing, the English Mathematician, centuries later.

# 119

## BBC News

*In an utterly insane thirty-six hours of unexplained murders in London and the Vatican, including cold-blooded assassinations and an ongoing shootout in Germany, the world is left with no comprehensible explanations for what is going on.*

*Our sources are conflicted, and theories are preposterous. Though news channels never like to admit it, we don't have any answers at the moment.*

*In such a strange time in our modern history, where we paradoxically have information available at the swipe of a finger yet can't really know what's true or false, we hesitate to pass on unconfirmed explanations.*

*And though we still won't speak our mind right now, we would like the viewers to share their thoughts with us:*

*Do you think that history as we know it is an authentic account of the past or otherwise?*

*Also, would you say that what's happened in history has affected your decisions and how you judge other people?*

*We understand it's an unusual poll to take, but we're doing our best to*

*gather perspective before authorities announce extremely sensitive informa-*
*tion tonight.*

*To our knowledge, and only two nights away from Christmas, this*
*sensitive declaration and apology will take place exactly forty-eight hours*
*after the Girl on the Cross was discovered, which was around midnight*
*yesterday.*

*The event will be hosted by the pope himself in St. Peters Plaza tonight.*
*It will shatter many people's perspectives about their childhood, historical*
*events, and the future.*

# 120

13:36 (P.M.)

*Outside the Schloss, Lohr, Fairytale Road, Germany*

David ducked his way toward the bullet-proof vehicle, and Xaver's driver reluctantly opened the door for him. He considered him more than lucky, having easily made it into the car amidst the shooting surrounding him.

"Drive us to the backdoor," David said. "We're picking up children."

"My orders are to only pick you up so you can follow them to where Professor Anne is sending them," the driver said.

"That's okay with me," David said. "We pick up the children, drive them somewhere safe, and then follow the others. Come on, go!"

"I can't pick up the children, Sir," the driver insisted. "I have orders."

Though David didn't have the patience for this absurd conversation, he asked the man, "Do you have children?"

"What, Sir?"

"Stop calling me 'Sir.' Talk to me, man to man." David rested his gun on the dashboard. "Do you have children?"

"I do, Sir."

"I told you don't call me Sir," David said. "So, what if one of your children was inside?"

The driver looked conflicted, unable to answer him, his eyes escaping David's as he fiddled with a necklace he wore. One that had the picture of his two children dangling from it.

"Good," David gripped the gun and waved it at him. "Then drive ahead."

The driver nodded, ashamed of himself, and put the vehicle into gear. As he made a U-turn, it seemed surreal to be this safe inside a car, watching the world fall apart outside.

"Stop!" David said all of a sudden. "Drive up to her."

"Who?" the driver asked.

"The girl with the tattoos and the machine gun," David said.

There, Mary was lying on the floor by the foot of the tower.

۞

Down by the tower's entrance, the Ovitz sisters watched the silver vehicle approach. They hadn't climbed up the tower like Mary had told them to and instead hid at the bottom of the stairs. Seeing Mary about to faint, Lucia and Lara wanted to help her but were stopped by Lily and Lisbeth, who believed that Lisa and Layla were now dead because of Mary.

"Why is David coming back for Mary after what she did to him?" Lara said.

"He is a good man," Lisbeth told them, who had met David in Polle. "I think he wants to help. Maybe we should ask him for a ride in his untouchable vehicle."

۞

Risking his life, David got out of the car, only to end up shocked when

Mary pointed the machine gun at him in the middle of the chaos. Well, he wasn't *that* shocked—it was Bloody Mary, after all. But he did wish she would treat him differently because he'd always cared for her.

"I won't kill you," Mary said, "if you don't come closer."

"Let me take you with me," he pointed at the driver behind him. "We'll keep you alive and talk everything over later."

"Take my sisters," Mary pleaded, nodding sideways with her head.

David saw her sisters unapologetically run toward the car. They knocked on the lower part of the door, and David signaled to the driver to let them in. Lara and Lily wanted to take Lisa's corpse with them, but David yelled at them to hop in before they got shot. He turned back to face Mary.

She was gone.

"Mary!" he yelled, bringing too much attention to himself.

A bullet passed within an inch of his head. David ducked behind a car and shot back, not even considering who he was aiming at. He crawled on all fours to look for Mary and saw her walking fearlessly in the middle of the street. She was calling out for the Advocate, whoever that was.

David took a deep breath and ran toward her, ordering the driver to open the door once he gave the go-ahead. He kicked Mary in the knees from behind with all his might, forcing her to the ground. She dropped the machine gun. He fiercely wrapped her left elbow around his neck and pulled her behind him, both dragging and choking her.

"Sorry," he mumbled. "I know there is no other way to get you in this car."

When the driver reached out to help bring her in, a bullet hit him right in the head. David didn't need to check to see if he was still alive.

He pulled the driver out of the car, tucking Mary into the passenger seat. He climbed over her, closed the door behind him, and sat in the driver's seat. Making sure she was breathing, he ignited the war vehicle and locked the doors.

He had to elbow Mary again in the face while he took the U-turn to calm her down. At least he bought himself a couple of minutes before she woke up.

Once David arrived at the backdoor, he called the security guard to bring the children out.

"Only the children. I have no room for their parents," David said. "They can meet us at the nearest church or something."

David closed the door and instantly felt the cold sensation of Mary's handgun on his temple.

"You shouldn't have saved me, David!" she shouted between bloody lips. "Why do you always want to save people?"

"It's a bad habit, I admit," he said, noticing her sisters tucked silently in the backseat, unable to deal with the tension. She aimed the gun at the middle of his forehead.

"I wanted to find him and kill him, and you prevented that from happening," Mary said.

"I don't know who you're talking about," David said. "But I doubt he is as important as the mess you put us all in."

His words struck her like a pebble in a face, and she seemed to remember what was really at stake. "Has Anne found the final bone yet?"

"She is on her way. I can take you there," David said, not sure this was the right thing to do. He needed to find a way to reach for his gun tucked between his back and the padded seat.

"I know where she is going," Mary pulled out her phone and showed him a live location of the Queen inside, who was riding in Xaver's other vehicle.

"The Queen's Eyes Inside?" David read the location sender's name. "One of them is working with you?"

"Could be Xaver. Could be Jacqueline," she teased him, fiddling with the gun. "Could be Clara, for all I know."

"Don't bring her into this," he said.

"You don't even know her," Mary said. "In fact, do you know Anne, David? Like really know her?"

Even with the gun pointed between his eyes, the question hit hard. No, he didn't know Anne, not after lying and pretending she called her possibly-dead sister on the phone.

"Maybe we should call her psychiatrist," Mary said.

"You have her number?"

"Oh, you care about her," Mary said with a slight smirk. "I saw the way you looked at her."

Suddenly, the security guard from the museum knocked on the door, coincidentally from Mary's side.

David pulled out his gun while she looked out her window and pointed it at her skull.

He could hear the sisters in the backseat gasp. Now David and Mary each had a gun pointed at their foreheads, both standing their ground.

As the tension saturated the air, the back door opened. Seven children climbed up into the large backseat next to the Ovitz sisters.

"Cool!" one of the kids with colored hair said. "Guns!"

David cocked an eyebrow at her, trying to silently communicate that neither of them would shoot with the children around.

"Why don't you kids play with your new friends?" David slowly pulled his gun back. The kids introduced themselves to the sisters, thinking they were just larger children.

The sisters effortlessly played along. They talked to the children about David being a superhero who saved them from the shooting outside the museum.

Eyes still on Mary, David wiggled his brows toward the digital clock at the dashboard and said, "Mary, Mary on the wall, tick that tock, or we die all."

Mary finally lowered her gun, saying, "That is the worst made-up poem I've ever heard."

"Strange," David hit the pedal. "I was going for the Pulitzer Prize."

# 121

## *The Spessart Forest, Near Mespelbrunn, Bavaria, Fairytale Road, Germany*

Xaver drove through the bumpy forest, repeatedly asking if Anne really knew where they were heading.

"I told you, I know this place by heart, Xaver," Anne said. "Drive on."

"It's just that I could have taken the main road instead of this hassle," he protested.

"We could be easily followed on the main road," Anne told him, sitting in the back next to Clara with Jacqueline in the passenger seat. Anne had learned from David always to sit in the last row and watch.

"I'm a folklorist, Anne," Xaver said. "I know these forests well. Soon enough, I will know where we're heading. Just tell me."

"Besides, we're all in this together," Jacqueline said, gripping the dashboard.

"I trust none of you," Anne said. "In fact, you should consider it a privilege I brought you along. This is between my sister and me."

She watched Jacqueline and Xaver exchange a fast glance, one they seemed to think went unnoticed.

# 122

---

### *The Spessart Forest, Bavaria, Fairytale Road, Germany*

"You're sure about your source?" David said, driving with Mary next to him. "I mean the GPS from the Queen's Eyes Inside, do you trust it?"

They had dropped off the children at the nearest church, where Mary insisted her sisters stay.

"I just want to live like a normal person," Lily had said to Mary, getting Lara, Lisbeth, and Lucia out of the car. Lisbeth, the feisty one from Polle whose arms were still bandaged, had asked David to say goodbye to Anne for her as she left the car.

"I don't blame them," David said. "This is no life to live, especially with the burden of these horrific stories on your shoulders."

"You can't escape who you are, David," Mary had replied. "Look at Anne's mother. She tried her best to escape to a different continent with a different name. Despite her efforts, her children were still forced to return and face the Sisterhood."

Now that they were following the GPS that supposedly led

them to Anne, Mary said, "Those who work for the Queen are most loyal, David. So yes, I trust the agent inside."

"You can say it," he said, struggling with driving in the snow. "It's Jacqueline. She works for the Queen, too. She probably helped fund the murder, the plane tickets, and everything else. Is she going to be a threat to Anne and Clara?"

"You don't know who the Queen is," Mary said, looking at the road ahead.

"That wasn't my question. Is she going to be a threat to Anne?" David shouted.

"Don't worry," Mary said. "Jacqueline is only after the letters. Once she gets them, you can have Anne and Clara all for yourself."

"What letters?" David resisted his impulse to stop the car and choke the answers out of Mary's slow tongue.

"What do you think this all about in the end, David? More mapestry puzzles?" Mary said. "The final bone, which I had no access to, leads to the authenticated five-centuries old letters."

"I've never heard anything about them. What about Anne and Xaver?"

"Anne and Xaver don't know what they're chasing. They're driven by their emotional impulses and need to heal their pasts," Mary said. "I've been after the letters since the beginning. They were written in June 1554."

David gripped the wheel tighter against a stubborn bank in the snow. "Let me guess. Those letters confirm the story the Ovitz family protected is real."

"Yes, David," Mary said. "The story that will not only open a flood of historical disputes all over the world but will bring the Vatican and British family to their knees."

"What's in the letters, Mary?"

"A confession."

"Elaborate, or I will...."

"Will what, David?" She pointed the gun at his head while he was driving. "Kill me?"

"No, Mary. But I'm fed up with the breadcrumbs you keep

feeding us," he said, steering the vehicle recklessly to the far left. "So I'll just kill us both!"

"David!"

But David wasn't in the car anymore. Not really. His mental darkness had caught the best of him, and although he cared about Anne and Clara and wanted answers, he took his hands off the wheel.

"Stop it!" Mary jolted in her seat.

His actions had no rhyme or logical reason behind them. He had been keeping it together for so long, but he was far from stable on the inside. In fact, he realized he probably needed a psychiatrist, too. Anne and Clara had ignited something in him he had never understood before, and he had no way to protect them now.

He wanted the universe to tell him that he wasn't alone—for once. So, he gave it complete control of the wheel.

"Snow White wrote the letters," Mary screamed. "They tell what happened to her, how she suspected someone slowly poisoned her, and how she investigated it before her death, in detail."

"That's not enough!"

David watched the vehicle swerve to the steep slope. They would either crash into the tree ahead, or the vehicle would flip on its side by the abandoned ranch on the right.

"Snow White isn't Maria von Erthal," Mary said. "She never was. It's a cleverly fabricated trick by those who want to bury the truth. They made up the story, made up the museum, and made up the mirror."

"Then who was she?"

The crash into the tree was imminent, and David couldn't stop it now, even if he tried.

"Her name is Margarette von Waldeck," Mary yelled. "She lived in Bad Wildungen not Lohr."

Right before the vehicle crashed into the tree, a hedge in the snow forced the wheels to redirect their path, tipping the vehicle sideways. They were now gliding into the horses' ranch.

"But it's not important who Margarette was. It's the Evil Queen whom this is about," Mary continued.

# 123

---

**British Embassy Transportation, Bavaria, Fairytale Road, Germany**

The men from the embassy positioned Tom in the back of the car, wounded and limping. He stopped and looked at the terrible aftermath of the shootout behind him. People will be baffled when they look back on the bloodshed from today.

"Her Majesty's orders are to get me back to London?" Tom asked the embassy's representative.

"Her Majesty?" an older man asked. He called himself Oswald Barnaby. He was a gruff man and wore an expensive suit Tom knew was worth thousands. "You know Her Majesty?"

"I'm Tom John, Protection Command," he said from the backseat. "I work for her."

"Never heard of you, my friend," Oswald said. "But we'll bring you back home, as long as you don't remember anything."

"What?" Tom was furious. "I do remember everything."

Oswald's punch into Tom's face was so swift that his head bounced against the back seat. He caught Tom's head before he lost consciousness and slapped him lightly on his cheek. "Do you still remember?"

Tom said nothing.

He had seen his fellow secret agents do the same to others in his time, so resisting was futile. Things had gotten out of hand, and now they wanted him out of the picture. It made him remember Mary once telling him that he didn't know who he was working for.

"Am I allowed to remember someone called the Advocate?" Tom asked, shielding his face with his hand.

"You never met him, and if you did, you were dreaming," Oswald said, leaning forward. He tucked a card into Tom's hand. "Email me if you know where we can find him, though."

"Sure," Tom acknowledged, tucking the card into the back of his trousers. "Can I ask why I'm being brought back to London?"

"Your father wants to see you." Oswald leaned back. "He is dying, yes?"

"What makes you think that?"

"He talks to himself and looks weary," Oswald said. "Anyway, I'll provide you with a phone once we get you back on that plane. We'll have to fix you up, though," he chuckled. "A makeup artist can cover up these wounds pretty easily. As for the new limp, tell them you stumbled over reality while chasing a dream."

Oswald laughed at his joke, winking at the stoic driver in front.

Tom wanted to see his father. He realized that he shouldn't have been so hard on him after his mother passed.

He watched Oswald swipe at some social media app on his phone, humming the following words:

*"Yesterday, upon the stair,*
*I met a man who wasn't there*
*He wasn't there again today*
*I wish I wish he'd go away...."*

🍎

The story in Jonathan Gray's head matched most of the documents he found, except that no one had ever believed these documents.

But here it was, the story in his head about Margarette von Waldeck, traveling abroad and falling in love with Prince Philip II of Spain. Margarette had the same attributes as Maria Sophia von Erthal—so much so that a familiar painting of Margarette was often mistaken for Maria.

They both came from wealthy Bavarian families. Margaretta lived in Bad Wildungen, which wasn't far from Lohr. He realized now it was deliberately named Folklore by some Barons in the time of Napoleon to provide distraction and misdirection from the real Snow White.

Jonathan remembered the old forgotten German saying: *The greatest trick the devil ever pulled was convincing the world he was someone else.*

The documents in the library backed up the story stuck in his head. The story played like a movie on repeat, except his recollection stopped when the story got darker. The part of the story the world needed to know to discover what really happened to Margarette and, most importantly, who did it to her. The so-called Evil Queen.

Jonathan couldn't wait to see Tom and tell him everything he'd uncovered.

# 124

### *The Spessart Forest, Near Mespelbrunn, Bavaria, Fairytale Road, Germany*

Xaver's eyes were glued to the mirror when Clara interrupted them, claiming she heard a crash nearby.

"I didn't hear anything, Clara," Jacqueline said. "Let Anne tell us about the castle."

"But I'm sure I heard something back there," Clara said.

"Then I better speed up," Xaver said, pressing his foot on the gas.

Anne patted Clara gently, thinking she was only anxious and confused.

"Let's start with this line: '*Annie, Annie, on the wall, I'm in a castle where hills can roll*,'" Anne said. "Annie is me, which goes without saying. The *castle is where hills can roll,* which means it's near 'rolling hills.' This translates to the German expression for the vast green hills surrounding this forest."

"Oh," Xaver said, smiling a little. "And it then says, "' *deep in the forest where woods are pecked,*' which I guess means the forest we're driving through, correct?"

"The Spessart forest is named after Woodpeckers that are famous in this area." Anne nodded. "Hence the *woods are pecked*."

"But that describes the whole Spessart forest," Xaver said. "It doesn't say we're in the right spot. And I don't see a *tower on northern walls* nearby."

"That tower is inside the castle we're heading to," Anne said. "But it's also a hint because only the northern wall is abandoned in that tower, and it has been rumored to conceal ancient secrets."

"I don't know of such a place," Xaver said. "Unless the '*Thirty Years War'* means something...Oh, damn it."

"You know where we're going?" Jacqueline asked eagerly.

"The Thirty Years War was the war between the Catholics and Protestants, "Xaver said. "And in the poem, Rachel says the *castle survived*, which is nearly impossible because the Catholics raided it and intentionally wiped out all Protestant buildings."

"Not bad for being the second-best folklorist in the world," Anne said from the back.

"Not funny," Xaver quipped. "I'm the best."

"Then why don't you know which castle it is?"

"Because it can't exist in this area," he said.

"Are you sure?" Anne tested him.

"I am! Because it's geographically impossible." Xaver rechecked his GPS and pointed at his phone. "Nothing survived here once the Catholics raided the area. There are newly erected places, like the horse ranch we passed by, but no ancient castles. It's impossible."

"So, is she playing games with us?" Jacqueline asked, pointing at Anne.

Xaver stopped the car in the middle of the snow. "Anne, don't make me force it out of you."

"I'm glad I am seeing your true colors, Xaver," she said. "But the problem is that only *I* know where the castle is, and force won't make me speak."

"What do you want, then?" Xaver asked, both he and Jacqueline turning in their seats to face Anne in the backseat.

"Nothing from you," she said. "I am just enjoying the game. Rachel is such a genius," Anne said, nodding her head at something behind Xaver and Jacqueline.

When they turned around, they saw what they had missed—a beautiful, ancient castle, barely visible behind the thick forest. If anything in the Fairytale Road looked like it was borderline fantasy, it was this castle with its exquisite turrets.

"The Mespelbrunn Castle," Anne said, getting out of the car. "Protected by the lake. It ended up being the only castle surviving the Catholic and Protestant wars."

"How did I forget about this beauty?" Xaver followed her out. "The family that owns it blew up the bridges from the forest to stay safe during the war."

"It also helps that the forest's thick trees come up to the lake's edges and that the last ten miles of forest before the lake could only be accessed by a super vehicle like yours. Or horses."

"That explains the ranch we passed by," Clara said as Jacquline joined them walking toward it past the trees. "It's beautiful."

When they arrived, the four shared the view of the moated castle on the territory of what was an island but was called the town of Mespelbrunn.

A fortified castle with towers, walls, and a moat was built in 1427. It was what every Disney fairytale depicted as fantasy in movies, but they all fell short compared to this real-life piece of heaven on earth.

"And there it is," Jacqueline pointed at the round tower. "The Northern tower. Are we going to need to solve more puzzles to locate the final piece in that tower?"

"Nope," Xaver said, pointing at the final bone in Anne's hands —the one she took from the Talking Mirror. "Why do you think it's a telescope?"

Anne knew what the telescope was for, but she didn't expect Xaver to have figured it out. It was supposed to be her last free card to get her and Clara safely to the tower. Now, she realized she didn't have any leverage.

Xaver smirked. "I may have missed the castle, but I've seen a lot of Singing Bones in my life. May I?"

"No, you may not." Anne pulled Clara behind her and stepped back, a little too close to the lake's edge.

"What's the telescope about?" Jacqueline asked.

"It's like an 'X marks the spot,'" Xaver explained. "There are small round marks running down from the top of the tower. But you can only see them with a telescope. The telescope's round lens fits one of them perfectly if you stand in the correct spot somewhere in the forest while the lake separates you from the castle. It reveals the exact floor of the castle that contains what we are looking for."

"And that's where I can find the box of letters?" Jacqueline said.

"Box of letters?" Anne said.

"The letters Margarette von Waldeck wrote, documenting exactly what had happened to her and how she was poisoned," Jaqueline said, pulling out her gun.

"How did she document it while dead?" Anne asked.

"Oh," Xaver said. "You seem to think that the Girl on the Cross was poisoned right away," Xaver explained. "Don't you get it yet, Anne?"

"Get what?" Anne said. "What are you talking about?"

"That apple seeds have little cyanide in them and can't kill you," Xaver said. "But if I feed you these small amounts of the seeds, in whichever way possible, be it wine or food, for a long period, you get slowly sick, never knowing why, and then finally die."

Anne stood speechless. Xaver answered a question that had been on her mind earlier: *why not just poison the girl on the cross with cyanide instead of using apple seeds?*

"You must have thought that apple seed poisoning was some allegory or metaphor to insinuate that fairytales were connected to the murders," Jacquline added. "When it bluntly hinted to how Snow White's killer got away with the perfect crime."

"Given that no one must have known about the apple seeds back then, let alone the effect of cyanide," Anne said absently. "it *was* a perfect crime. I doubt they had the means of performing an autopsy, so the victim was thought to have died naturally."

"That's why in some versions of Snow White's fairytales, the henchman is said to have ripped out her heart and liver to give them to the Evil queen so she can eat them," Jacquline said. "Why do you think that is, professor Anderson? Do you get the allegory?"

"Because cyanide destroys one's heart and liver," Anne said, looking at Xaver, who seemed surprised Jacqueline knew that much. "So the Sisterhood's code was to hint at its effect by also eluding the common person to think that the Evil Queen was a cannibal."

"Good girl. Since we're a few steps away from those letters now," Jacquline sighed, exchanging glances with Xaver again. "Thank you, and your sister, for the trouble you took to get us here. But, unfortunately, your job is very much over now, Anne."

# 125

---

## *Horse Ranch, the Spessart Forest, Germany*

Mary's eyes popped open when she heard the sounds of horses. After surviving so much in one day, she began to believe divine intervention was helping her complete her mission.

Upside down, she saw the blurry visions of horses still locked in the ranch's stable, the snow blocking parts of her view. A splotch of blood fell on her cheek, but she couldn't tell where it came from. Xaver's super machine survived without a broken window, but she did notice something odd. The driver's side door was open.

"David!" she shrieked, crawling out of the vehicle on all fours.

The wind pushed her so hard she struggled to stand up, but then she saw David's bloody footsteps leading back to the house. She assumed he was injured, but she hardly cared. She needed to know how to get to Anne and whether David was still alive.

Her phone beeped nearby, so she crawled back into the car to look for it. Picking it up, she read the message from the Queen's Eyes Inside:

. . .

*Where are you? I know where the letters are. Should I take the shot?*

Mary typed while she trudged through the snow:

*Just take it. I'm fed up with waiting. You've found the castle, so I'm sure we'll find the letters.*

The reply came fast.

*I will take the shot, Queen Mary. It's been a pleasure serving you.*

🍎

David swayed left and right inside the house, kicking furniture out of his way and opening all kinds of cupboards. The accident exasperated his gunshot wound from Polle, and now the cut sliced along the length of his arm, making it harder not to scream.

"I'm the one-armed man now," he mumbled in pain. "One arm is a useless arm, and the other is the arm with the gun," he wrapped some kitchen towel around the wound, "I shoulda been a poet, I guess, sitting on my ass and writing puzzles all day."

He then put his arm on the counter, looking for something to numb the pain.

"Here you are, my friend," he said, pulling out a Bavarian whiskey bottle that said 'whiskey' on the yellow label. "Straight to the point," he said. He uncorked the top with his teeth and began gulping like a maniac.

His need for the drink had surpassed any logic. He chugged half of the bottle down in one long shot, and the pain in his left hand numbed a little.

Mission accomplished.

"Are you kidding me?" Mary burst into the room. "You're drinking again?"

"Nah," David said. "It's mouthwash, whiskey flavor."

Without warning, he hurled the whiskey bottle away, gripped the gun with his good hand, and shot Mary in the shoulder.

Mary dropped to her knees, moaning in pain and shocked at his behavior. He was fast and vicious; she regretted he wasn't on her side.

David strolled around as if he were an unfunny Jack Sparrow. "German whisky," he said. "So good."

He went out to the stable and picked out a horse. "Okay, my friend," he drunkenly said to the horse as he climbed on its back. "Let's go save some good people."

# 126

15:41 (P.M.)

## *The Spessart Forest, Near Mespelbrunn, Bavaria, Fairytale Road, Germany*

Anne needed to think fast.

Jumping into the river and swimming to the castle was her best option. Given that she doubted Xaver or Jacquline would jump into the water after her and that the nearest bridge to the castle was far enough they would take forever to chase her, swimming would have given her a good head start to reach the tower.

But she feared Clara wouldn't be able to react fast enough and jump in with her.

"I have the bone," she said. "I'll throw it in the water before you shoot me."

"I never miss," Jacqueline said. "But I'm ready for some amusement. Show me what you've got. Any last words?"

"You don't know all you need to know about Margarette von Waldeck," Anne bluffed.

"You don't know anything about her either. Or you would have mentioned her in your book," Xaver said.

"I wanted to," Anne said. "but I couldn't find enough evidence to support her being Snow White. How come you two seem to know all about her?"

"I do," Jacqueline said. "Xaver doesn't know as much as me."

"What do you know, then?"

"I know she fell in love with Prince Philip II of Spain," Jacqueline said. "It's documented everywhere. And that she was poisoned with cyanide from an apple before she could marry him, which is what should be documented in her letters to him before she died."

"Who poisoned her?" Anne asked.

"The Evil Queen," Jacqueline said sarcastically but meant it.

"Her stepmother?" Anne was genuinely curious. "What was her name? And why did she do it?"

"That's why you don't realize how important this is to everyone," Jacqueline said. "You just don't know!"

"Then tell me, damn it!" Anne demanded. "I'm going to die anyway, right?"

"The Evil Queen isn't her stepmother," Jacqueline said. "She is an important historical figure, and she killed her for a pretty messed up reason."

"Stop being so vague," Anne said. "I need to know what plagued Rachel's mind all these years. Who was the Evil Queen, and why would she kill Margarette? I don't see the historical importance here."

"Well, for one, this story is a Keystone story. It will open up *all* the hidden stories of the past," Jacqueline said. "Imagine if all these stories come out and history undergoes a serious re-writing. Think how these revelations will change our perception of the world."

"I would worry about that later," Anne said. "Right now, I care about the story itself. Who is the Evil Queen, and why—"

"Shoot her, Jacqueline," Xaver said impatiently. "She talks too much and will waste our time. You know how much I can sell this story for if it's true?"

"I guess I have to take the shot," Jacqueline said. "After all, the Queen gave me the green light."

"The Queen?" Xaver squinted.

"Not the Evil Queen," Jacqueline said. "But, my Queen. The one I work for."

"Who do you work for?" Anne asked, puzzled.

"She Who Must Be Obeyed," Jacqueline said, raising the gun in the air. The loud crack of the gun echoed off the trees.

Like Bloody Mary had instructed, she put a bullet between Xaver's eyes.

# 127

### *Horse Ranch, the Spessart Forest, Germany*

David was about to ride out in the snow when Mary shot at him from behind. The wind had picked up, making it harder to see through the white-out conditions.

He was glad that he still had a grip on the horse. He rode away from the stable to save the horses from Mary's stray bullets.

"Stop it, Mary!" he shouted against the wind. "Ugh, I should've killed you."

"That's why I chose you, David!" she yelled from behind the veil of white everywhere. "You're angry and aggressive, but you have a sweet spot. I've known about your mother and sister all along. You were the perfect partner to help me play my nerdy game and sneak under the radar."

David decided to leave. Playing games with her wasn't going anywhere, and he still had to overcome the impossible task of riding this horse to where Anne and Clara went. Without GPS and sufficient visibility, he had to use his instincts.

As he rode away, he heard Mary scream behind him.

"Don't go there, David," she pleaded. "You're interfering between two sisters. Just let them sort their differences."

🍎

Tucked in economy class, Tom found himself unusually relaxed on his way back to London. The people around him were the kind of people he grew up with as a kid; not poor, but not rich. He was raised by a father who was once a devoted librarian. Until he discovered how much money could be made from selling art and how big of a business it was.

"Can I help you, ma'am?" Tom asked the single mom with three kids, failing to shove her thick bag into the compartment above.

The woman thanked him.

When he sat back, he realized how good it felt.

Being here in the middle of everyone else made sense to him. He wondered if his children would believe what he had seen in the last forty-eight hours or if he would have to tell it as a dark fairytale.

All in all, he was eager to see his father. Tom turned on his phone to find an unread message from his father a few hours ago.

*They killed her because she was a Protestant.*

# 128

---

**The Spessart Forest, near Mespelbrunn, Bavaria, Fairytale Road, Germany**

Again, Anne failed to cover Clara's eyes as Xaver's blood splattered on them before he fell backward into the lake. The look on his face made her wonder what he was thinking in that split second before Jacqueline pulled the trigger. Did he see this coming?

"What have you done?" Anne screamed at Jaqueline. "Why?"

"These letters are mine, Anne," Jaqueline said. "And you're going to give them to me."

Anne shrugged, unsure how to deal with Clara, who was sobbing. Anne pulled her close and whispered in her ear. "She will shoot you, so calm down and let me deal with it. Okay?"

"Who is she?" Clara sobbed. "The Evil Queen?"

Jacqueline roared with laughter. Her demeanor had changed since she took the shot. Even her accent, which had always been tainted in French, suddenly seemed very American.

Anne also noticed her makeup was quite strange. Sure, she was an older, athletic woman with at least ten cosmetic surgeries, but

Anne noticed something was off about her. Maybe it was because she never really stared at her sagging flesh out of respect for the elderly.

"Who are you?" Anne asked.

"Clara said it best," Jacqueline said. "Consider me an Evil Queen." Jacqueline laughed again. "Now pull out that telescope and find the spot on that tower."

"As long as you don't lay a finger on her," Anne warned, pointing at Clara.

"Don't worry, Anne," Jacqueline said. "I don't want her dead. After all, she is young with little to no past sins, unlike you."

Anne wasn't sure what Jacqueline meant by that but raised the telescope and scanned the tower. It didn't change focus or zoom in or out. Instead, Anne had to walk around and use trial and error until her distance matched the circular frame of the telescope's visor and met one of the round dots painted on the tower's outer surface.

"I found it," Anne said. "Last floor."

"That's the worst puzzle I've ever seen," Jacqueline mused, aiming the gun at her. "Now move to the bridge and show me the way."

# 129

15:29 (P.M.)

## *Horse Ranch, the Spessart Forest, Germany*

David pulled the reins back to stop his horse.

Mary's words had pierced through his ears, and he froze. Turning around and calling her name, he said, "This isn't one of your games, is it?"

"If it was, you can't risk it, can you?" Mary stood right before him without a gun but challenged him anyway.

"What did you mean by sisters?" David said, his drunken heartbeat soaring through his ears.

"Years ago, I met Rachel," Mary said. "She had run off to London to look for us, the Ovitz. She wanted to know more about who she was. She saved my life."

"Talk slower, and I will blow your head off," David said flatly, urging her to get to the point.

"I was naive then, but Rachel had grown into a leader. She still believed in the Sisterhood's cause but despised them for what her mother and Anne did to her," Mary said. "Rachel had given her all to their family. Dealing with the mad stories in her head put there by her mom without her permission, and Anne giving up on her in the well after Rachel had been having sex with strangers to help her escape."

"I mean it," David said. "Get to the point...."

"When I met her, she told me she had put the story in Anne's head because she was going insane but then regretted it months later when she realized it was a Keystone story that, if told, would let her find all the hiding sisters in the world. Rachel wanted to free them from the pain and burden of being keepers of the truth, as she knew how it messed up her life. She wanted to use it to find other sisters around the world and revolt against the Sisterhood," Mary said. "She was full of rage. When she met me, she realized she wasn't alone, furious that her bloodline forced her to put the weight of the world on her shoulders. So, we went and looked for others like us. And we swore to use everyone, the Sisterhood, the Vatican, the Royal Family, as we saw them all as enemies, destroying the lives of storyteller girls worldwide."

"Elaborate on this part?"

"Easy," Mary said. "You know how many True Sisters worldwide live isolated, alone, waking up and reciting these dark stories to themselves daily and then passing them to their offspring?" Mary said. "Did you know that most of them live in hiding because, for two centuries, none of these stories came out? Their cause became meaningless, yet they held onto their dark inheritance."

"Don't tell me Rachel's plan was to sell them out." David closed his eyes.

"That was her plan," Mary said proudly. "To rid the poor girls from a made-up religion disguised as a cult—a cult backed by high morals that were unattainable and unappreciated by most of the world."

David was in a hurry, but he saw Mary begin to break down. "What did it matter if women, not men, wrote fairytales? What did matter if men killed poor women for years? What did it matter when Snow White was a Protestant girl killed by the Catholic Church to stop her from marrying the Catholic Prince of Spain and disrupt the power of money and religion altogether?"

David's horse let out a moan.

"The problem was that Rachel needed to entice those girls to come forward," Mary explained.

" And to do so, she had to get the world's attention," David guessed, "pushing you to stage the girl on the cross and get Anne involved to find the last bones, which would lead to the box of letters left by Margarette von Waldeck exposing her Catholic killer. A five-centuries old crime. I can't believe this."

"Anne was the key," Mary said.

"Because Rachel had put the story's clues in her head," David nodded. "And she was the only one who could find the final bone, but to do that we had, Rachel had to test her loyalty first."

"Loyalty? To whom?"

"To her goddamn sister, David," Mary said. "Don't you get it? Rachel needed to see Anne repent and know if she could trust her after what happened in the well. That was what the mapestry was for...."

"A prolonged test for Anne to prove her resilience to go after the truth and also show her capabilities for the final test," David continued on Mary's behalf.

"And to use her journey to help us garner the world's undivided attention," Mary said. "Murders, mayhem, and explosions, all connected to Anne. It worked, and the world finally took notice."

"And you let all these people get killed?" David wondered if he had to shoot her now.

"I know you think I'm crazy, but—"

"I'm the last person to judge anyone," David cut her off. "Just tell me if Rachel is the Queen's Eyes Inside."

"Yes," Mary admitted, sinking to her knees.

"Does that make you the Queen, Mary?" David said. "Did you take the reins from Rachel? But, wait, maybe all you just told me were lies. Maybe the truth is that Rachel was angry, and you convinced her to do all of this."

"I loved her," Mary said. "Like really loved her. And I know she loved me because we could no longer love a man. Whoever was the Queen, it didn't matter. Sometimes I called her the Queen, and other times she called me the Queen. We may be two girls, but we're one soul."

"Okay," David said. "Hop on the horse behind me."

"Really?" Mary craned her neck up.

"I'm counting on you not stabbing me in the back even though I feel you will eventually do it," David said. "But for once, we have a common interest. I want to save Anne before Jacqueline kills her, and you need to save Jacqueline before she does something stupid."

Hesitantly, Mary took David's hand and climbed up behind him. He closed his whisky-weighted eyelids, expecting her to stab him, but she didn't. *Maybe there's hope after all*, he told himself.

Before he took off, Mary said, "When you mentioned Jacqueline, you understand that she is Rachel, right?"

"I was hoping not," David said. "But now you've spelled it out."

"Her anger drove her to make billions," Mary said. "She used the money to find the poor girls who still believe in the Sisterhood worldwide. She was never a de Rais descendant. She liked the idea, which motivated her to feel like a powerful villain."

"I understand." David pulled the reins to go find Anne. "I guess she will go down in history as the only thirty-something-year-old girl who fooled the world by faking the identity of an older rich woman in her late fifties."

## 130

*Papal Office of the Holy See, the Vatican City, Italy*

Pope Nicholas VIII sat with laced hands and rested his elbows on his desk, listening to Father Firelle's atrocities. Bishop Cabrielli had gathered most of the available evidence and explained it to the pope. It took them four hours to debate what to do next.

"I can't say I will pray for Father Firelle," Pope Nicholas said. "Neither can I promise that I will pray for many past popes."

Bishop Cabrielli bowed his head, expressing his sympathies and understanding.

"The image of Father Firelle hanging on the cross will be carved into the pages of history for centuries to come," Pope Nicholas said. "I regret it happened in my time, as the church will not be forgiven for it."

"An extremist cult killed him," Bishop Cabrielli noted. "It's not our fault. It's a violation that we could stand victim to and gain our people's sympathy for."

"Listen to yourself!" Pope Nicholas rapped a palm against the desk, his Sicilian-tinted Italian making him sound like a gangster. "Trying to make excuses for us."

Pope Nicholas stood up, fighting the tears welling behind his eyes, "Father Firelle was killed by a cult of women who exist because of our past sins."

"It was a war," Bishop Cabrielli argued. "And it's long past due. Who hasn't made mistakes? We've repented and apologized so many times. What else can we do?"

"We tell the truth," Pope Nicholas said. "Justice in and of itself is more or less of a fairytale. We may catch sinners, but we can't bring people back. We can't fix their offspring, raised without mothers and fathers. We can't bring them back. All we can do is apologize and move forward."

"What are you going to tell the people?" Bishop Cabrielli scoffed. "That we killed Snow White? Do you know how ridiculous that sounds?"

"It sounds ridiculous because that's not her real name," Pope Nicholas said. "Her name was Margarette von Waldeck. A simple girl who died at the age of twenty-one. She may be just one girl, but she represents thousands of othere like her in her time. Margarette was poisoned by—"

"You're not going to say the Evil Queen, are you?" Bishop Cabrielli challenged him.

"She may have been evil, or not. God only knows," Pope Nicholas said. "But she was troubled, nonetheless. I'll call her by her name when I speak to the people today."

Bishop Cabrielli sighed and bowed his head again. "I suppose most people know who she is by now," he said, pointing at the picture of Father Firelle hanging on the cross, a red rose with five petals stuffed in his mouth. "But she was troubled, nonetheless. I'll call her by her name when I speak to the people today."

Bishop Cabrielli sighed and bowed his head again. "I suppose most people know who she is by now," he said, pointing at the picture of Father Firelle hanging on the cross, a red rose with five petals stuffed in his mouth.

## 131

16:00 (P.M.)

### The Mespelbrunn Castle, Bavaria, Fairytale Road, Germany

Anne cautiously crossed the small bridge to the abandoned tower, hoping the owners were secretly watching them from inside the castle. She didn't know if they would remember her, though, or if they would help her against Jacqueline.

It was hard to trust anyone anymore.

They walked past an expansive space overlooking the lake, with the castle behind them. In Anne's mind, the tower stood prominent and unmistakable, stained invisible with blood from the past.

Even Clara, who had been crying minutes ago, stopped, taken by the enchantment of the place.

"Climb up," Jacqueline said from behind her.

"Under one condition," Anne said, turning around and facing her. "Clara's journey ends here."

"No way," Jacqueline said.

"Then shoot me." Anne took a step forward. "Because guess what? There is one last puzzle left to open the box of letters above."

"You're bluffing."

"When I used the telescope to locate the painted circles on the tower's walls, I saw a puzzle from where I stood in the forest."

"You're bluffing," Jacqueline said hesitatingly, fiddling with the trigger.

"Why do you think the final bone was a telescope then?" Anne said with a poker face. "Just to point to a circle? I read the puzzle and memorized it. If you want to read it for yourself, then here," she urged, handing Jacqueline the telescope. "Go back and read it from afar."

"You little bitch," Jacqueline grunted.

"Let Clara go. She won't go far, or she will get lost. I just want her safe while we're up there."

Jacqueline reluctantly agreed.

Clara kissed Anne on the cheek. "I'll go find David."

"No, you won't," Jacqueline threatened. "Because Bloody Mary will kill him."

A few miles back, David had to force Mary to talk to him, scared that she would faint from bleeding. He wasn't sure if he regretted shooting her. David knew how he was going to find Anne—it was simple and very doable. But he didn't tell Mary his plan.

While riding, David found an engraved collar wrapped around the horse's neck.

*Property of Counts of Ingelheim, Mespelbrunn Castle, Anastasia Ingelheim.*

It not only gave away the castle's name—and possibly the owner's—but his gut told him these horses were trained to know their way back and forth in case someone got lost in the forest or around the lake. The Russians used this strategy in the past, and he hoped he was right about it.

## 132

### *Northern Tower, Mespelbrunn Castle, Germany*

Anne climbed up the tower, seriously doubting the owners were anywhere nearby. The Ingelheim family had owned this place for centuries. Still, years ago, they were forced by the German government to live in only part of the castle so the rest could become a highly profitable tourist attraction. They ended up choosing to live in the southern corner, but as rich as they were, they didn't spend much time there, either. It was a long shot thinking they were here now.

Due to the castle's obscure location and the snowy weather conditions, there didn't seem to be many tourists. Like Jacqueline once told Anne, the Germans didn't know how to monetize their precious folklore. Had the likes of Disney owned the Fairytale Road? Oh boy.

"What did the puzzle on the outside say?" Jacqueline said, still aiming her gun at Anne, who was now standing on top of the tower.

"There was no message," Anne said.

Jacqueline gritted her teeth and closed her eyes. "You've always been like that," she spat. "Such a liar."

"But you don't know me, Jacqueline, do you?" Anne said, still trying to figure out who she really was. "While climbing the stairs up, you said something about being used to climbing down wells. You didn't know Rachel, did you?"

"Don't distract me and just find me the box, Anne," Jacqueline demanded, "and I may let you live."

"I don't see a box, but I see this." Anne pointed at the writing on the wall.

A long sentence in unintelligible handwriting was carved in a horizontal, straight line across the round inner wall at eye level. Anne had to turn a full circle to finish reading it, ending where she had started.

"How did you see this?" Jacqueline said.

"I'm so used to puzzles by now. It seems I can spot them anywhere," Anne said. "Pull out your phone and record a video of the writing on the wall while you do a full circle. That way, we can invert it and read it."

"Good idea." Jacqueline handed her the phone. "You do it."

Anne did as she was told, although she wished Jacqueline would have taken the bait. She hoped Jacqueline would start to feel dizzy while taking the video—or at least vulnerable. Just enough so Anne could snatch her gun, even though she didn't know how to shoot a gun.

"Here." Anne held the phone out to Jacqueline, showing her the video of the carving on the wall:

*Mirror, Mirror on the wall,*
*who's the ruthless of them all?*
*Luther's girl down by the floor,*
*died in one and five and five and four.*

*Mirror, Mirror on the wall,*
*roses rise when apples fall.*

***Five, my petals, never four,***
***Cross not Crucifix I'm hung tall.***

"So, it *is* Margarette von Waldeck," Jacqueline said upon reading. "I thought I was chasing a phantom."

"You don't strike me as an amateur story chaser anymore," Anne said. "Who are you, Jacqueline?"

"Look," Jacqueline said, not even registering Anne's words. "The fourth line says, '***Luther's girl down by the floor.***' Luther means Lutheran, one of the five branches of the Protestant religion. Margarette von Waldeck was Protestant."

Anne was impressed and began to suspect who Jacqueline was.

"'***Died in one and five and five and four***' is puzzling, though," Jacqueline wondered. "Do you know what it means, Anne?"

"I don't."

"Could be like a ritual, as in The Evil Queen poisoned Margarette in counts of one, five, five, and four," Jacqueline suggested, unable to control her excitement. "Another Fairytale Code?"

"What about the other lines?" Anne said, trying to figure out if Jacqueline's plastic surgeries were fake or if this was, in fact, her real face.

"'***Mirror, mirror on the wall, who is the ruthless of them all,***'" Jacqueline repeated. "That doesn't give away much. Of course, the Evil Queen was the most ruthless of them all."

"Why? Maybe she was a victim."

Anne was testing her, wanting Jacqueline to speak more. Something about her was off.

"Because if Margarette was a Protestant about to marry the charming Catholic Prince Philip of Spain, then whoever killed her was Catholic," Jacqueline said. "It's a ruthless act. Don't you get why the Vatican doesn't want this to be revealed to the world? What if this opens a can of worms for all churches, shedding light on the crimes they have done to others in the past?"

"Aren't we done with the past?" Anne stalled, allowing her to learn more about Jacqueline.

"We would be done with the past if the history we were left with was true," Jacqueline said flatly. "But if it's not true, and we have the evidence to prove it, then monarchies, governments, and total beliefs will fall apart. It will be a new world."

"Okay," Anne said, playing along. "So maybe Prince Philip killed Margarette, not the so-called Evil Queen. Who said he had to be Prince Charming? That would still make him ruthless."

"Possible," Jacqueline didn't argue. "But we need to look harder at other sentences. You must know what they mean, Anne. Please, you're the brilliant one!"

"Am I?" Anne re-read the first and second lines, wondering what had happened to Jacqueline de Rais' personality. As each minute passed, she was starting to act more like a child. "This part is interesting, '*Roses rise when apples fall*.'"

"It's interesting, right?" Jacqueline said.

"But what does it mean?" Anne asked. "I mean, we've seen pentagram apples and poisoned apples, which could be a metaphor–"

"A metaphor for what? Apples fall? Gravity?" Jacqueline theorized. "You think this has something to do with Sir Isaac Newton?"

"I don't see what he has to do with folklore," Anne admitted. "What about the phrase, '*roses rise*'? It has a little ring to it and starts with the same letters."

"The only way I can think of it is that roses and apples are enemies," Jacqueline said. "Is there any such story in fairytales where one faction was represented by roses and another by apples?"

"Not in fairytales, but according to the story, you're speculating about Margarette being a Protestant, then–"

"Then what?"

"Oh my God, David was right."

Anne panicked, unable to collect her thoughts. It was so wrong and so right at the same time. David had almost solved the whole case the first moment he saw the girl on the cross.

"David?" Jacqueline said.

Anne continued reading the poem, "***Five my petals and never four***," she gasped. "***Cross not crucifix I'm hung tall.***"

Jacqueline gasped. "***Cross and crucifix***," she said. "The cross is used by Protestants and the crucifix by the Catholics. A cross is just a T-shaped symbol, whereas a crucifix is a cross with the sacred body of Jesus depicted over it. It was a major difference at the time of the war."

"I guess by '***hall***' it means Chapel Hall in Westminster Abbey," Anne said. "The girl was on a ***cross, not a crucifix***. "

"Not that it was possible to hang her on a crucifix, but we get the point," Jacqueline said. "But go on."

"The point is that the girl on the cross was a metaphor for Margaret von Waldeck, the real Snow White," Anne said. "Yes, she wasn't put on a cross in the fairytale, and she probably didn't die on a cross in real life. But she was a protestant. The cross wasn't used in Westminster Abbey to tell us **how** she was killed but ***who*** killed her."

"The story's darker secret is not about Snow White, but the Evil Queen. Go on, Anne," Jacqueline urged. "You're so close to figuring this out."

"Margarette was a Protestant girl killed by a Catholic," Anne said. "And she had a five-pointed apple in her hand."

"Apple, not rose?"

Anne could hardly breathe. "What's the difference? They're both the same. They have been for centuries."

Jacqueline's eyes dimmed, finally understanding. Her finger fiddled with the trigger.

"Goodbye, sister," Jacqueline said. "You've made up for all your past sins."

# 133

16:31 (P.M.)

## *London*

Tom dashed out of the airport, running as he spoke on his headset.

"Father," he said. "I'm on my way to the BBC. Tell me all you know."

"I don't know if you should trust them," Jonathan said. "Who knows which side they are on."

"I'll bet on them this time. I think they're on the side of 'Breaking News.'" Tom jumped into a taxi and told him where to go. "This is not breaking news. This is breaking our perception of reality as we know it. Also, the pope is supposed to be on air in a few. Tell me what you know."

"Roses and apples, Tom."

"You said they're the same, the girl on the cross in Westminster Abbey and Father Firelle in the Vatican," Tom said eagerly. "Explain it to me."

"When cut horizontally, an apple's seeds form a pentagram," his father said, though Tom had heard it many times already. "So does a five-petaled rose."

"Fuck me!" Tom blurted out.

"Excuse me, sir?" the Indian driver said, glancing in his review mirror at Tom.

"Just coughing," Tom said. "Please continue, father."

"If you connect the lines between the main points of a five-petal rose, you get the same pentagram," Jonathan said. "And given both are red, they are the same."

"I get it. They express the same message. But what the bloody hell does it mean?"

"It's the most famous red rose of all time, son," Jonathan said. "A rose that was created from nonexistence to mean something royal and larger than life, if not downright holy, to us Brits."

"Holy shit," Tom leaned back in his seat, not paying attention to the unsettled driver. "It's the Tudor Rose, isn't it?"

# 134

### *Northern Tower, Mespelbrunn Castle, Germany*

"You're not my sister," Anne argued in the face of this woman's gun, whoever she really was.

"Denial, Anne," Jacquline said. "Always denial, the same way you denied what happened to me by pretending I called you on the phone. You know how sick this makes you."

"You're not Rachel!" Anne said, not sure anymore. Like Xaver had told her before, and Jacquline reminded her now, how was she to trust herself if she pretended she was calling her sister while she was gone?

Could it be that Anne was insane like every other sister with stories in her head?

"So be it if you'll never acknowledge me or what you did to me," Jacquline said, the flesh of her forefinger visibly pressing against the trigger. "But let me tell you how what I did changed everything before I kill you, sister."

Anne was still in a haze, unable to do much but listen to her.

"My plan changes everything," Jacquline said. "Imagine figuring out that every character in fairytales is someone well-known and historically significant, like The Evil Queen," Jacqueline said. "'*Five my petals and never four, Cross not Crucifix oh stand tall,*'" she swallowed as she talked faster. "'*Roses rise,*' aka Tudor Roses, and '*Apples fall.*' Margaretta was poisoned by the apple seeds by the Tudors."

And suddenly, Bloody Mary entered to add fire to the burning coal.

"The Evil Queen met Prince Philip II and was going to marry him," Mary said, looking wounded, while David pointed a gun at her back. "Marriage was political power back then because it merged nations' forces against their enemies. Countries with powerful armies would have their Queen marry a King from a country with infinite food resources, and so on."

"In her case, it was Britain and Spain," Jacquline completed Mary's thought. "More than anything, Catholic power over the revolting protestants in Europe."

Mary coughed, and though her injuries should have stopped her from talking, she followed up, "Poor women had no say in their marriages, and neither did queens. It was a man's world then. The British Queen had to fulfill her country's needs and marry a Spanish prince."

"She never found love, although she wanted to," Jacqueline added. Anne could tell Jacqueline and Mary not only knew each other, but they liked each other. "And no one wanted to marry her, either. She was a queen, too powerful for men."

"Maybe she was just ugly," Mary said to Jacqueline. The two talked to each other as if Anne and David were no longer in the room. "So, she empowered herself by becoming the most ruthless of them all.."

"By burning the protestants on the stake," Jacqueline took Mary's hands in hers, and they raised their chins like arrogant monarchies.

"And then came that beautiful girl," Mary continued. "Young, ripe, and desired."

Jacqueline and Mary held each other's hands, and Jacqueline

lowered her gun. Anne and David exchanged looks as they listened.

"Margarette-von-fucking-Waldeck," Mary said. "Prince Philip couldn't resist her. A German beauty from Bavaria versus the devil's crone from Greenwich, Britain."

"Black hair, blue eyes, red lips, and youthful, white skin," Jacquline said.

"The Queen couldn't help it, and she had to do something," Mary said. "She would be in the same room with Margaretta, and no one would pay attention to her. She would eavesdrop on the maids who would joke that she looked so jealous she made the evilest stepmother."

"So, the Queen had to kill Margarette." Mary and Jacqueline looked at Anne. "But she was known to kill Protestants at the stake already. And if she burned Margaretta, she would be exposed."

"So, she played the greatest trick the devil's crone had ever planned," Mary smiled back at Jacqueline, touching her face. "She poisoned her."

Mary stuck out her tongue and wiggled it like a snake at Anne. "Slowly."

"Apples," Anne said. "Right?"

"But Margarette didn't like apples," Mary said, flailing her hands sideways in a dramatic display, almost as if she were acting in a Broadway play of Pride and Prejudice.

"But she drank wine," Jacqueline backed her up, placing hands over her mouth. "Oh, no!"

"What a righteous, virgin bitch!" Mary snickered at Jacqueline.

"So she, Her Majesty, The One Who Must be Obeyed—that's what they called her then—sent someone to poison Margaretta's wine with a version of Vecchio Melo, or so they said, and slowly Margaretta got sick, which she mentioned in the letters she sent to her father and her beloved Prince Philip II," Jacqueline concluded.

Anne could tell David found this part interesting.

"And slowly," Jacqueline said, "she was dying. Withering away, without anyone noticing."

"And another one bites the dust," Mary said. "Another one to go down in history's tomb of the forgotten."

"And only Lilliput Ovitz, after exposing the Gilles de Rais story, would find this out from a British peasant who worked for the Queen," Jacqueline said. "In favor of the one and only–"

"Mary Tudor," David said.

"Mary Tudor, the first Queen of England, is the Evil Queen from the fairytale," Anne said, knowing she would have never gotten close to this conclusion without their help.

"That's why the girl on the cross was looking at her tomb. So you let all the people die for this?" David questioned, showing Mary and Jacqueline the box of letters Clara had given him at the bottom of the stairs.

Anne had found them from the first moment she looked through the telescope. It was never the last floor in the tower but the fifth. The one with five rose petals, painted inside the circle.

Clara had waited until Jacqueline and Anne went up the tower. She entered the fifth floor and found the box in a glass chamber, treated like some useless old antique from the past that no one bothered to open or look into.

"Give it to me!" Jacqueline pointed her gun at David, but Anne was faster. In one move, she pulled Jacqueline by her hair while David elbowed Mary in her sore shoulders and pulled the gun from Jacqueline.

Then Anne, while Jacqueline fought her, did the unexpected.

Forced to defend herself, Anne threw Jacqueline off the tower.

"No!" Mary wailed. "You've just killed your sister, Rachel...*again!*"

# 135

22:00 (P.M.)

## *The Vatican & London*

In the Vatican, Pope Nicholas spoke out to the people almost precisely forty-eight hours after the murder of the girl on the cross in Westminster Abbey. This time of year, his speech would have customarily been tame and ordinary, adorned with the best Christmas wishes, like every other year. But recent events changed things.

Bloody Mary's evil and dark plan worked. She had succeeded in making the world care, and now the Pope would have to face the truth.

He told them about the most shocking discovery of his lifetime. He backed up his words with authenticated copies of Margarette Von Waldeck's poisoned letters sent to Prince Philip II of Spain and her father, Philip IV, Count of Waldeck-Wildungen. Seven letters made her sick for months, as Mary Tudor poisoned her.

Anne Anderson, the same folklorist who refused to authenticate a fake version of the Brothers Grimm fairytales forty-eight hours ago, had authenticated and sent over the letters.

The letters detailed her decline, and pinned to them was the confession of the person who was assigned to poison her red wine. Once Margarette discovered that she was dying at such a young and healthy age, she began investigating and slowly realized Mary Tudor's plan. She literally called her 'The Evil Queen of England,' which remained in fairytales forever.

The Pope then described the endless puzzles and stories told by storytellers, who guarded pieces of the story all over the world. And though he was hesitant, he mentioned the one detail that he found most convincing, reading from the final puzzle on the inner walls of the Northern tower in Mespelbrunn Castle:

**Luther's girl down by the floor, died in one and five and five and four.**

Margarette Von Waldeck died in May 1554, and Queen Mary I of England married Prince Philip II in June of that same year. It was well-documented that Mary had been trying to convince the prince of Spain to marry her for two years. However, they split up just one year after they wed, further hinting that it was a forced and shady marriage, beginning with the murder of an innocent girl.

There were also papers signed by local doctors proving that Margarette was poisoned.

Historians have not denied the relationships between Prince Philip II, Mary Tudor, and Margaretta von Waldeck. However, they were split on believing the rest of the story. More so, they couldn't see how fairytales were written by women in the first place — because history in general, according to them, had always been written by men.

Pope Nicholas ended his speech on two notes.

The first was his acceptance of the Sisterhood's existence. He admitted he had always been aware of them, whether he approved of their methods or not. He also welcomed other stories exposing the Vatican's crimes and promised to reveal them to the world if they were proven sound and trustworthy.

His second note was the most shocking. He declared that the following morning, the Vatican would perform a funeral for Margarette von Waldeck. They would honor her and all Protestants and other factions or religions falsely annihilated by the Catholic Church.

In his final words, he urged all-powerful institutions of spiritual beliefs to look back on their own sins and admit prior violations. He prayed that the world could move on, as we all were still learning how to be better human beings day by day.

🍎

Against Her Majesty's warnings, Tom John confessed all the incidents that occurred in detail on live TV. He confessed his mistakes and the violations in the past forty-eight hours.

Tom's speech stirred more emotions than the Pope's, backing his claims with facts and occurrences he witnessed.

On his way out of the studio, Oswald told him that he would burn for what he had done and that Her Majesty's office would deny they had anything to do with it.

Tom didn't care about Oswald. He only cared about his father telling him he was proud of him.

## 136

*Afternoon, The Day After, London*

Anne stood behind bars separating her from David, wondering why he'd asked her to come to bail him out.

"You're here because of a speeding ticket?" Anne cupped her mouth with her hands.

"I wanted to be home so much once we returned. I drove fast," David said before pointing at a young gentleman in uniform standing on the opposite side of the room. "And that police officer stopped me."

"And, of course, not having identification is what actually put you behind bars," Anne said, gripping the bars with her hands.

"I also had blood all over me, so that didn't help," David added.

"I assume the blood was why the officer arrested you," Anne said.

"I told him to watch the news and that I knew the girl who exposed the church," David said. "But he was in favor of the church, so again, not helpful."

"You could've told him who you were, David," Anne said. "You're a police officer."

"I was worried he was one of Bloody Mary's secret henchmen and would shoot me dead. I guess I have severe trust issues now," David confessed. "Besides, these cells are super comfy." He rapped his fingers on the bench he sat on while winking at a fellow prisoner.

"Don't test me, David," the big man said. "I'm playing nice because I want you to look good in front of your girl."

Anne laughed harder.

"Don't worry," David said. "Harriet will bail me out."

"So you don't want me to bail you out?" Anne asked.

"I have Olympic plans for you," he raised an eyebrow. "So I don't want the money to get between us."

"David!" she snapped, hitting the bars. "Behave, or I'll call Helga."

"Okay, okay, I'll behave." He raised a guilty hand in the air.

They both let their laughs slow down, settling back into reality.

"Did you see the funeral the Vatican hosted this morning?" she said. "Snow White's funeral. Can you believe it?"

"I like to watch summaries and recaps. It's easier for me that way," he said. "Let's talk about you."

"What about me?" she said, pointing at her outfit. "I got my trench coat back."

"Good, because that's what matters, right?" His words slowed down a little. "How do you feel about throwing your sister from that tower?"

"She wasn't Rachel. You know that," Anne said.

"You told me, but I couldn't tell either way."

"She was Jacqueline de Rais in the flesh."

"How did you know?"

"I pulled at her skin," Anne said. "It was real. Besides, I'd recognize Rachel anywhere."

"I'm sure you will," David said. "So, Jacqueline de Rais fooled poor Lilith Ovitz to believe she was Rachel?" David said.

"Yes, so she could convince her she was her relative and that they were close and had a common enemy. She pulled this hoax on everyone, too," Anne said. "She was rich and bored, with sadistic needs, so she designed her own billion-dollar adventure."

"By messing up the young girl's life," David said, alluding to Bloody Mary. "Jacqueline de Rais had it in her bloodline, I guess."

"The descendant of a vicious serial killer who summoned demons," Anne said. "I guess the bloodline is real, but who are we to judge?"

"Well, she is dead, thank goodness," David said, relieved. "It's Bloody Mary I'm worried about. The German police have her, and they're trying to send her back to England."

"I will pray for her," Anne said.

"I wish I could do that," David said. "But who do I pray to?"

"I understand," Anne said.

"I mean, who says religions aren't fairytales, too?"

"I don't think so, but it's a plausible argument," Anne said. "But fairytale or not, I'll pray you to find your mother's killer and your sister."

"I will do the same about you and Rachel. Maybe you will find her one day," David said, standing up and approaching the bars. "I don't mean I will pray, though. But I will investigate. Hard evidence. Facts. No fuckin' fairytales, huh?"

Their eyes met, bodies still separated by the bars. David reached out and put his hands over hers before bowing down and kissing her. It was a quick kiss, but one that made his point.

When she opened her eyes, she saw his eyes were still closed. So she waited until he opened them, gripping the bars harder, and said, "I picked the worst time to kiss you, though."

"Why?" Anne said.

"I'm allergic to bars," he said. "I want it all."

She turned around and left him eager for more, hoping she would see him soon. She turned around once more. "Was that all you wanted to tell me?"

"Smart woman," he said with a smirk. "Remember when I told you I was never convinced with your role in all of this?"

"I think I do," she said. "Being an Ovitz and a folklorist didn't seem good enough reason for me to get involved. Your words."

"And I was right." He pulled her hand to his and placed the swan necklace she found by the final bone in her palms. "The lab analyzed it and found a fingerprint on it."

"A single fingerprint?" Anne's heart raced.

"Yes," David said. "I traced her, and she is waiting for you in the British Library now."

"Who?"

"You'll find out," David said. "She told me to remind you of the T. S. . Elliot poem about—"

"Going back and experiencing the place for the first time."

Anne pecked him on the lips and ran out.

---

## 137

### *The British Library, Main Hall*

Anne met Jonathan Gray, who welcomed her with open arms, looking and behaving like a different human being. He ushered her to the main hall, explaining that he had evacuated it so she could have all privacy she needed.

Anne stepped inside and saw Annabelle, the white-haired woman, looking serene and content while sitting in her wheelchair.

"Why is my daughter always late?" Annabelle said, smiling.

"Mom!" Anne ran into her arms, kneeling to match the height. She gripped her hand and held it tight. This was all she wanted from the beginning.

"What took you so long?" Anne said. "Do you know where Rachel is?"

"I'm sorry, dear." Annabelle lifted Anne's head to look at her. "I'm truly sorry. I don't know what happened to her or where she is. All you need to know is that this journey was for and because of you."

"What do you mean?"

"I'm sure Bloody Mary told you about all the sisters in hiding because they've given up on the cause of exposing past stories," Annabelle said.

"Yes, they told me."

"The few of us good ones left. We needed to find the good souls in the bloodline. You were on top of the list, but you had to be tested," Annabelle said. "There are only a few like me left. When I witnessed the corruption within the Sisterhood, I thought of rebuilding it the right way."

"And?"

"As I said, we're very few. Though I left so no one would trace you and Rachel, I saw what you did," Annabelle shrugged. "And we, the new Sisterhood, considered it a test."

"Test? For what?"

"Only someone who fought for the right things until the very end could become a True Sister," Annabelle pulled out a phone and showed her the world map. "Please look."

Anne watched Annabelle's map show pinned locations worldwide, each pin labeled as a sister. "They couldn't have done it without you," Annabelle said. "They saw what you did, forcing the pope and British to admit the unbelievable, and you gave them the courage to come out now."

"All of these are sisters?" Anne asked incredulously.

"All of these are stories left untold," Annabelle said and hugged her close. "Crimes left unsolved."

"That's why this story was considered a Keystone story because it would unlock the rest," Anne said. "of all reluctant sisters who escaped like you all over the world."

"You are a True Sister now," Annabelle said. "The first to truly expose the origins of a crime disguised as a fairytale."

## 138

*The Château de Tiffauges, France*

German Inspector Martin Wolf was as silent as ever. He felt intimated, waiting in the luxurious room that once belonged to Gilles de Rais. The thought of this castle being a burial ground for the women and children the Baron killed, sent shivers down his spine. It reminded him of the story his grandmother told him as a child, the one about the dark man with a flute who came to Hamelin and took its children away.

People were under the impression that Martin's vow of silence had been in memory of his family, that had been killed in a terrorist attack years ago. Little did they know, his silence was in memory of something deeply sinister, and much older.

Martin was summoned to serve de Rais' last true descendant. They planned to bring back the days when the barons ruled the world under the guidance of the so-called devil they believed they summoned.

Martin wasn't there for the devil. He was here to collect a hefty paycheck. Shaken by the Pope's confession today, the idea of solving older crimes of the past enticed him more than ever.

"The Last Baron will see you now," A beautiful, young blonde girl dressed in an ancient French dress bowed next to him. She wore a long high-waisted gown with conservative, long sleeves. She wore it over a kirtle with a linen chemise and looked like she had stepped through time.

Martin stood up and followed her, wondering if The Last Baron would have her for dinner tonight.

"Don't worry, Mr. Wolf," the girl said in a German-Italian accent. "I know you're not big on talking, so nod yes or no when talking to The Baron. He understands."

With hands behind his back, Martin Wolf nodded and let her show him the way.

"Also, please excuse my accent," the girl said. "As you know, the Italians and French have more common words and heritage than most European countries. The Baron's accent is more Italian, though. He will see you now."

Martin Wolf entered the Baron's room with an interior design cut out of an ancient, wicked fairytale, except for a large screen showing the world map on the far wall. It was filled with red dots. Each dot was labeled 'storyteller.'

In the middle of the room, he saw two nurses and a doctor operating on someone. He hesitated to advance, but one of the nurses called for him.

His shoes echoed on the fancy marble floor while Beethoven's Fifth Symphony played somewhere nearby. When he arrived, he found himself looking over a man with no lower half, lying on the operating bed. His upper half was not a pretty sight, and his face was covered with a skincare mask.

"Sorry, you've caught me in my beauty sleep," The Baron said sarcastically.

Martin said nothing, utterly intimidated by The Baron.

"Did you know that Beethoven was deaf and couldn't write music for a pence?" The Baron asked Martin, pointing at the source of the loud music from a room nearby. "I was told he stole his melodies from the Pied Piper of Hamelin, but I'm yet to find that original story somewhere."

Martin Wolf said nothing, wondering why The Baron mentioned the ancient legend of Hamlin, as it meant a lot to him.

"I know why you're silent, Mr. Wolf," The Baron said. "People think your silence is in memory of your wife and child killed by that terrorist. But you and I know that's not the case."

Now Martin laced his hands forward, challenging the Baron with his eyes. He couldn't possibly have known the reason behind Martin's silence.

"You honor the Children of Hamelin, Martin," The Baron said. "because you descend from the one who escaped."

If there was ever a time for Martin to break his vow and speak, then it was now. He didn't expect The Baron to know who he was. Now his forehead broke into beads of sweat.

"I'll let you find the Pied Piper if you help me find them," The Baron pointed at the screen with the red dots.

Martin understood. Now that the reluctant storytellers naively exposed themselves after Anne uncovered the Keystone story, it was a fair trade.

The French girl offered Martin a hefty cheque on a golden plate. Martin made sure it was in his name and pocketed it.

"I think it's time we stop dealing with all these Fairytale Codes," The Baron said. "And focus on the coming Fairytale Plague."

Martin's mind raced, not sure what he meant. Yet, he had a vague idea.

"Start with finding this girl," The Baron handed him a piece of paper with a name on it: Abigail Tale.

Martin Wolf saluted The Baron in agreement.

But before he left, The Last Baron pulled at him with his gloved hand and said, "Please, call me The Advocate."

**THE END**

Thank You for reading The Fairytale Code. If you have time, I'd
appreciate a review (even a few words helps others find this book)
—Cameron Jace

## The Fairytale Plague
### (Anne Anderson book 2)

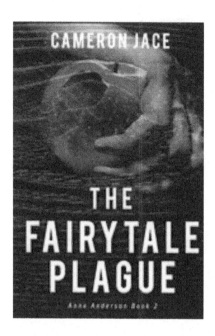

*In The Fairytale Code, the stories led to uncover past historical crimes, in the Fairytale Plague, the stakes are the future of Mankind...*

# AUTHOR'S NOTE

Thanks for reading.

The Fairytale Code is my first book in this genre. I spent two years in Europe researching and writing it. It was a labor of love — and obsession — above all. It's utterly humbling and exciting to see many readers enjoy this book.

I learn — and still do — a lot about writing and publishing since I've started this journey. And I've benefited immensely from your heartfelt feedback that was also your labor of love.

I encourage you to write me directly on cam@fairytale-code.com (I use this email exclusively for the Anne Anderson series) The wisdom, generosity, and kind words I've received have absolutely helped my writing career — and helped me understanding why you read book, and the things that matter from the things that don't.

If you have time to write a review, know that I will read and take it seriously, whether it's positive or negative, I consider all reviews positive. Because remember that every review is important as it increases other readers discover the book, and will influence what I will write in the future.

# ACKNOWLEDGMENTS

I need a whole book to enlist the people who made this happen. From close family and friends ( leaving me be and giving me space and tolerating not knowing where I'm in the world right now, lol) to every beta reader and fan whose enthusiasm and love for the story topped my own.

And since my readers know I answer almost every message and email, I'm sure you know who you are and that you won't complain about not seeing your name here, as it will never take from your input in my writing.

For professional purposes, I will thank Nicole Elise Bennett, Amanda Noonan, & Christine LaPorte. Greetje Wis—and the Storykiller Team, all 93 of you, you know who you are—for dealing with my hectic schedules, scattered brain, and giving it all their best to make it shine.

# ABOUT THE AUTHOR

Cameron Jace spent years studying architecture before retiring to pursue his two true passions: writing fiction and folklore.

He had an early success with the Insanity bestselling fantasy series, spanning nine books, and based on facts about Lewis Carroll of Alice in Wonderland.

And though it's been a most rewarding experience, he wanted to transfer his years-long — and still ongoing — research about fairytales to non-fantasy thriller fiction readers. Because folklore is real and based upon true-life crimes — or so he claims :)

Cameron was born in Germany, but spent most of his youth in California, and now lives somewhere in Europe — it depends on the tale he is chasing.

Made in the USA
Monee, IL
27 August 2022

12653257R00292